Susan E. Smith

JUGGERNAUT

The juggernaut is huge: as long as a football pitch, it weighs 550 tons. Its task – to transport a transformer through Nyala, an oil-rich West African state.

Neil Mannix leads the Anglo-American convoy on its dangerous journey. Mannix is a troubleshooter and his London-based boss has sensed that trouble is what Mannix will find. And he does: Nyala erupts in civil war.

The juggernaut becomes a mobile hospital – for civilians and soldiers. A means of escape, a symbol of hope for the thousands of refugees who pour out of their villages to travel alongside.

In *Juggernaut*, a story of daring and death, of ambush and threat, Desmond Bagley is in masterful form: fast-paced, intriguing and triumphant.

Desmond Bagley

JUGGERNAUT

COLLINS
8 Grafton Street, London W1
1985

William Collins Sons & Co. Ltd
London · Glasgow · Sydney · Auckland
Toronto · Johannesburg

First published 1985
© Brockhurst Publications Ltd 1985

BRITISH LIBRARY CATALOGUING IN PUBLICATION DATA

Bagley, Desmond
Juggernaut.
I. Title
823'.914[F]   PR6052.A315

ISBN 0-00-222890-4

Photoset in Linotron Times by
Rowland Phototypesetting Ltd
Bury St Edmunds, Suffolk
Made and printed in Great Britain by
William Collins Sons & Co. Ltd, Glasgow

1

The telephone call came when I was down by the big circular pool chatting up the two frauleins I had cut out of the herd. I didn't rate my chances too highly. They were of an age which regards any man of over thirty-five as falling apart at the seams; but what the hell, it was improving my German.

I looked up at the brown face of the waiter and said incredulously, 'A phone call for me?'

'Yes, sir. From London.' He seemed impressed.

I sighed and grabbed my beach robe. 'I'll be back,' I promised, and followed the waiter up the steps towards the hotel. At the top I paused. 'I'll take it in my room,' I said, and cut across the front of the hotel towards the cabana I rented.

Inside it was cool, almost cold, and the air conditioning unit uttered a muted roar. I took a can of beer from the refrigerator, opened it, and picked up the telephone. As I suspected, it was Geddes. 'What are you doing in Kenya?' he asked. The line was good; he could have been in the next room.

I drank some beer. 'What do you care where I take my vacations?'

'You're on the right continent. It's a pity you have to come back to London. What's the weather like there?'

'It's hot. What would you expect on the equator?'

'It's raining here,' he said, 'and a bit cold.'

I'd got used to the British by now. As with the Arabs there is always an exchange of small talk before the serious issues arise but the British always talk about the weather. I sometimes find it hard to take. 'You didn't ring me for a weather report. What's this about London?'

5

'Playtime is over, I'm afraid. We have a job for you. I'd like to see you in my office the day after tomorrow.'

I figured it out. Half an hour to check out, another hour to Mombasa to turn in the rented car. The afternoon flight to Nairobi and then the midnight flight to London. And the rest of that day to recover. 'I might just make it,' I conceded, 'But I'd like to know why.'

'Too complicated now. See you in London.'

'Okay,' I said grouchily. 'How did you know I was here, by the way?'

Geddes laughed lightly. 'We have our methods, Watson, we have our methods.' There was a click and the line went dead.

I replaced the handset in disgust. That was another thing about the British – they were always flinging quotations at you, especially from *Sherlock Holmes* and *Alice in Wonderland*. Or *Winnie the Pooh*, for God's sake!

I went outside the cabana and stood on the balcony while I finished the beer. The Indian Ocean was calm and palm fronds fluttered in a light breeze. The girls were splashing in the pool, having a mock fight, and their shrill laughter cut through the heated air. Two young men were watching them with interest. Goodbyes were unnecessary, I thought, so I finished the beer and went inside to pack.

A word about the company I work for. British Electric is about as British as Shell Oil is Dutch – it's gone multi-national, which is why I was one of the many Americans in its employ. You can't buy a two kilowatt electric heater from British Electric, nor yet a five cubic foot refrigerator, but if you want the giant-sized economy pack which produces current measured in megawatts then we're your boys. We're at the heavy end of the industry.

Nominally I'm an engineer but it must have been ten years since I actually built or designed anything. The higher a man rises in a corporation like ours the less he is concerned with purely technical problems. Of course, the jargon of modern management makes everything *sound* technical and the sub-committee rooms resound with phrases drawn from critical path analysis, operations research and industrial dynamics, but all that flim-flam is discarded at the big boardroom table, where the serious decisions are made by men who know there is a lot more to management than the mechanics of technique.

There are lots of names for people like me. In some companies I'm called an expeditor, in others a troubleshooter. I operate in the foggy area bounded on the north by technical problems, on the east by finance, on the west by politics, and on the south by the sheer quirkiness of humankind. If I had to put a name to my trade I'd call myself a political engineer.

Geddes was right about London; it was cold and wet. There was a strong wind blowing which drove the rain against the windows of his office with a pattering sound. After Africa it was bleak.

He stood up as I entered. 'You have a nice tan,' he said appreciatively.

'It would have been better if I could have finished my vacation. What's the problem?'

'You Yanks are always in such a hurry,' complained Geddes. That was good for a couple of laughs. You don't run an outfit like British Electric by resting on your butt and Geddes, like many other Britishers in a top ranking job, seemed deceptively slow but somehow seemed to come out ahead. The classic definition of a Hungarian as a guy who comes behind you in a revolving door and steps out ahead could very well apply to Geddes.

The second laugh was that I could never break them of the habit of calling me a Yank. I tried calling Geddes a Scouse once, and then tried to show him that Liverpool is closer to London than Wyoming to New England, but it never sank in.

'This way,' he said. 'I've a team laid on in the boardroom.'

I knew most of the men there, and when Geddes said, 'You all know Neil Mannix,' there was a murmur of assent. There

7

was one new boy whom I didn't know, and whom Geddes introduced. 'This is John Sutherland – our man on the spot.'

'Which spot?'

'I said you were on the right continent. It's just that you were on the wrong side.' Geddes pulled back a curtain covering a notice board to reveal a map. 'Nyala.'

I said, 'We've got a power station contract there.'

'That's right.' Geddes picked up a pointer and tapped the map. 'Just about there – up in the north. A place called Bir Oassa.'

Someone had stuck a needle into the skin of the earth and the earth bled copiously. Thus encouraged, another hypodermic went into the earth's hide and the oil came up driven by the pressure of natural gas. The gas, although not altogether un-expected, was a bonus. The oil strike led to much rejoicing and merriment among those who held on to the levers of power in a turbulent political society. In modern times big oil means politi-cal power on a world scale, and this was a chance for Nyala to make its presence felt in the comity of nations, something it had hitherto conspicuously failed to do. Oil also meant money – lots of it.

'It's good oil,' Geddes was saying. 'Low sulphur content and just the right viscosity to make it bunker grade without refining. The Nyalans have just completed a pipeline from Bir Oassa to Port Luard, here on the coast. That's about eight hundred miles. They reckon they can offer cheap oil to ships on the round-Africa run to Asia. They hope to get a bit of South American business too. But all that's in the future.'

The pointer returned to Bir Oassa. 'There remains the natural gas. There was talk of running a gas line paralleling the oil line, building a liquifying plant at Port Luard, and shipping the gas to Europe. The North Sea business has made that an uneconomical proposition.'

Geddes shifted the pointer further north, holding it at arm's length. 'Up there between the true desert and the rain forests is where Nyala plans to build a power station.'

Everyone present had already heard about this, but still there were murmurs and an uneasy shifting. It would take more than one set of fingers to enumerate the obvious problems. I picked one of them at random.

'What about cooling water? There's a drought in the Sahara.'

McCahill stirred. 'No problem. We put down boreholes and tapped plenty of water at six thousand feet.' He grimaced. 'Coming up from that depth it's pretty warm, but extra cooling towers will take care of that.' McCahill was on the design staff.

'And as a spin-off we can spare enough for local irrigation and consumption, and that will help to put us across to the inhabitants.' This from Public Relations, of course.

'The drought in the Sahara is going to continue for a long time yet,' Geddes said. 'If the Nyalans can use their gas to fuel a power station then there'll be the more electricity for pumping whatever water there is and for irrigating. They can sell their surplus gas to neighbour states too. Niger is interested in that already.'

It made sense of a kind, but before they could start making their fortunes out of oil and gas they had to obtain the stuff. I went over to the map and studied it.

'You'll have trouble with transport. There's the big stuff like the boilers and the transformers. They can't be assembled on site. How many transformers?'

'Five,' McCahill said. 'At five hundred megawatts each. Four for running and one spare.'

'And at three hundred tons each,' I said.

'I think Mister Milner has sorted that out,' said Geddes.

Milner was our head logistics man. He had to make sure that everything was in the right place at the right time, and his department managed to keep our computers tied up rather considerably. He came forward and joined me at the map. 'Easy,' he said. 'There are some good roads.'

I was sceptical. 'Out there – in Nyala?'

He nodded thoughtfully. 'Of course, you haven't been there

9

yourself, have you, Neil? Wait until you read the full specs. But I'll outline it for you and the others. After they got colonial rule their first president was Maro Ofanwe. Remember him?'

Someone made a throat-slitting gesture and there was a brief uneasy laugh. Nobody at the top likes to be reminded of coups of any sort.

'He had the usual delusions of grandeur. One of the first things he did was to build a modern super-highway right along the coast from Port Luard to Hazi. Halfway along it, here at Lasulu, a branch goes north to Bir Oassa and even beyond – to nowhere. We shouldn't have any trouble in that department.'

'I'll believe that road when I see it.'

Milner was annoyed and showed it. 'I surveyed it myself with the boss of the transport company. Look at these photographs.'

He hovered at my elbow as I examined the pictures, glossy black-and-white aerial shots. Sure enough, there it was, looking as though it had been lifted bodily from Los Angeles and dumped in the middle of a scrubby nowhere.

'Who uses it?'

'The coast road gets quite a bit of use. The spur into the interior is under-used and under-maintained. The rain forest is encroaching in the south and in the north there will be trouble with sand drifts. The usual potholes are appearing. Edges are a bit worn in spots.' This was common to most African tarmac and hardly surprised me. He went on, 'There are some bridges which may be a bit dicey, but it's nothing we can't cope with.'

'Is your transport contractor happy with it?'

'Perfectly.'

I doubted that. A happy contractor is like a happy farmer – more or less nonexistent. But it was I who listened to the beefs, not the hirers and firers. I turned my attention back to Geddes, after mending fences with Milner by admiring his photographs.

'I think Mister Shelford might have something to say,' Geddes prompted.

Shelford was a political liaison man. He came from that

department which was the nearest thing British Electric had to the State Department or the British Foreign Office. He cocked an eye at Geddes. 'I take it Mr Mannix would like a rundown on the political situation?'

'What else?' asked Geddes a little acidly.

I didn't like Shelford much. He was one of the striped pants crowd that infests Whitehall and Washington. Those guys like to think of themselves as decision makers and world shakers but they're a long way from the top of the tree and they know it. From the sound of his voice, Geddes wasn't too taken with Shelford either.

Shelford was obviously used to this irritable reaction to himself and ignored it. He spread his hands on the table and spoke precisely. 'I regard Nyala as being one of the few countries in Africa which shows any political stability at the present time. That, of course, was not always so. Upon the overthrow of Maro Ofanwe there was considerable civil unrest and the army was forced to take over, a not atypical action in an African state. What was atypical, however, was that the army voluntarily handed back the reins of power to a properly constituted and elected civil government, which so far seems to be keeping the country on an even keel.'

Some of the others were growing restive under his lecturing, and Geddes cut in on what looked like the opening of a long speech. 'That's good so far,' he said. 'At least we won't have to cope with the inflexibility of military minds.'

I grinned. 'Just the deviousness of the political ones.'

Shelford showed signs of carrying on with his lecture and this time I cut in on him. 'Have you been out there lately, Mister Shelford?'

'No, I haven't.'

'Have you been there at all?'

'No,' he said stiffly. I saw a few stifled smiles.

'I see,' I said, and switched my attention to Sutherland. 'I suggest we hear from the man on the spot. How did you find things, John?'

11

Sutherland glanced at Geddes for a nod of approval before speaking.

'Well, broadly speaking, I should say that Mister Shelford seems correct. The country shows remarkable stability; within limits, naturally. They are having to cope with a cash shortage, a water shortage, border skirmishes – the usual African troubles. But I didn't come across much conflict at the top when we were out there.'

Shelford actually smirked. Geddes said, 'Do you think the guarantees of the Nyalan Government will stand up under stress, should it come?'

Sutherland was being pressed and he courageously didn't waver too much. 'I should think so, provided the discretionary fund isn't skimped.'

By that he meant that the palms held out to be greased should be liberally daubed, a not uncommon situation. I said, 'You were speaking broadly, John. What would you say if you had to speak narrowly?'

Now he looked a little uncomfortable and his glance went from Geddes to Shelford before he replied. 'It's said that there's some tribal unrest.'

This brought another murmur to the room. To the average European, while international and even intercounty and inter-city rivalries are understandable factors, the demands of tribal loyalties seem often beyond all reason; in my time I have tried to liken the situation to that of warring football clubs and their more aggressive fans, but non-tribal peoples seemed to me to have the greatest difficulties in appreciating the pressures involved. I even saw eyebrows raised, a gesture of righteous intolerance which none at that table could afford. Shelford tried to bluster.

'Nonsense,' he said. 'Nyala's a unified state if ever I saw one. Tribal conflict has been vanquished.'

I decided to prick his balloon. 'Apparently you haven't seen it, though, Mister Shelford. Conflict of this sort is never finished with. Remember Nigeria – it happened there, and that's almost next door. It exists in Kenya. It exists throughout Africa. And we know that it's hard to disentangle fact from fiction, but we can't afford to ignore either. John, who are the top dogs in Nyala, the majority tribe?'

'The Kinguru.'

'The President and most of the Cabinet will be Kinguru, then? The Civil Service? Leading merchants and businessmen?' He nodded at each category. 'The Army?'

Here he shook his head. 'Surprisingly enough, apparently not. The Kinguru don't seem to make good fighters. The Wabi people run the military, but they have some sort of tribal affiliation with the Kinguru anyway. You'll need a sociologist's report if you want to go into details.'

'If the Kinguru aren't fighters they may damn well have to learn,' I said, 'Like the Ibo in Nigeria and the Kikuyu in Kenya.'

Someone said, 'You're presupposing conflict, Neil.'

Geddes backed me. 'It's not unwise. And we do have some comments in the dossier, Neil – your homework.' He tapped the bulky file on the table and adroitly lightened the atmosphere. 'I think we can leave the political issues for the moment. How do we stand on progress to date, Bob?'

'We're exactly on schedule,' said Milner with satisfaction. He would have been pained to be behind schedule, but almost equally pained to have been ahead of it. That would show that his computers weren't giving an absolutely optimum arrangement, which would be unthinkable. But then he leaned forward and the pleased look vanished. 'We might be running into a small problem, though.'

There were no small problems in jobs like this. They were all big ones, no matter how small they started.

Milner said, 'Construction is well advanced and we're about ready to take up the big loads. The analysis calls for the first big haul to be one of the boilers but the government is insisting that it be a transformer. That means that the boiler fitters are going to be sitting around on their butts doing nothing while a transformer just lies around because the electrical engineers

13

aren't yet ready to install it.' He sounded aggrieved and I could well understand why. This was big money being messed around.

'Why would they want to do that?' I asked.

'It's some sort of public relations exercise they're laying on. A transformer is the biggest thing we're going to carry, and they want to make a thing of it before the populace gets used to seeing the big flat-bed trundling around their country.'

Geddes smiled. 'They're paying for it. I think we can let them have that much.'

'It'll cost us money,' warned Milner.

'The project is costing them a hundred and fifty million pounds,' said Geddes. 'I'm sure this schedule change can be absorbed: and if it's all they want changed I'll be very pleased. I'm sure you can reprogramme to compensate.' His voice was as smooth as cream, and it had the desired effect on Milner, who looked a lot happier. He had made his point, and I was sure that he had some slack tucked away in his programme to take care of such emergencies.

The meeting carried on well into the morning. The finance boys came in with stuff about progress payments in relationship to cash flow, and there was a discussion about tendering for the electrical network which was to spread after the completion of the power plant. At last Geddes called a halt, leaned over towards me and said quietly, 'Lunch with me, Neil.'

It wasn't an invitation; it was an order. 'Be glad to,' I said. There was more to come, obviously.

On the way out I caught up with Milner. 'There's a point that wasn't brought up. Why unship cargo at Port Luard? Why not at Lasulu? That's at the junction of the spur road leading upcountry.'

He shook his head. 'Port Luard is the only deep water anchorage with proper quays. At Lasulu cargo is unshipped in to some pretty antique lighters. Would you like to transship a three hundred ton transformer into a lighter in a heavy swell?'

'Not me,' I said, and that was that.

I expected to lunch with Geddes in the directors' dining room

14

but instead he took me out to a restaurant. We had a drink at the bar while we chatted lightly about affairs in Africa, the state of the money market, the upcoming by-elections. It was only after we were at table and into our meal that he came back to the main topic.

'We want you to go out there, Neil.'

This was very unsurprising, except that so far there didn't seem to be a reason. I said, 'Right now I should be out at Leopard Rock south of Mombasa, chatting up the girls. I suppose the sun's just as hot on the west coast. Don't know about the birds though.'

Geddes said, not altogether inconsequentially, 'You should be married.'

'I have been.'

We got on with the meal. I had nothing to say and let him make the running. 'So you don't mind solving the problem,' he said eventually.

'What problem? Milner's got things running better than a Swiss watch.'

'I don't know what problem,' Geddes said simply. 'But I know there is one, and I want you to find it.' He held up a hand to stop me interrupting. 'It's not as easy as it sounds, and things are, as you guessed, far from serene in Nyala under the surface. Sir Tom has had a whisper down the line from some of the old hands out there.'

Geddes was referring to our Chairman, Owner and Managing Director, a trinity called Sir Thomas Buckler. Feet firmly on the earth, head in Olympus, and with ears as big as a jack rabbit's for any hint or form of peril to his beloved company. It was always wise to take notice of advice from that quarter, and my interest sharpened at once. So far there had been nothing to tempt me. Now there was the merest breath of warning that all might not be well, and that was the stuff I thrived on. As we ate and chatted on I felt a lot less cheesed off at having lost my Kenya vacation.

'It may be nothing. But you have a nose for trouble, Neil,

15

and I'm depending on you to sniff it out,' Geddes said as we rose from the table. 'By the way, do you know what the old colonial name for Port Luard used to be?'

'Can't say that I do.'

He smiled gently. 'The Frying Pan.'

2

___

I left for Nyala five days later, the intervening time being spent in getting a run down on the country. I read the relevant sections of *Keesing*'s *Archives* but the company's own files, prepared by our Confidential Information Unit, proved more valuable, mainly because our boys weren't as deterred by thoughts of libel as the compilers of *Keesing*.

It seemed to be a fairly standard African story. Nyala was a British colony until the British divested themselves of their Empire, and the first President under the new constitution was Maro Ofanwe. He had one of the usual qualifications for becoming the leader of an ex-British colony; he had served time in a British jail. Colonial jails were the forcing beds of national leaders, the Eton and Harrow of the dark continent.

Ofanwe started off soberly enough but when seated firmly in the saddle he started showing signs of megalomania and damn near made himself the state religion. And like all megalomaniacs he had architectural ambitions, pulling down the old colonial centre of Port Luard to build Independence Square, a vast acreage of nothing surrounded by new government offices in the style known as Totalitarian Massive.

Ofanwe was a keen student of the politics of Mussolini, so the new Palace of Justice had a specially designed balcony where he was accustomed to display himself to the stormy cheers of his adoring people. The cheers were equally stormy when his people hauled up his body by the heels and strung it from one of the very modern lampposts in Independence Square. Maro Ofanwe emulated Mussolini as much in death as in life.

17

After his death there were three years of chaos. Ofanwe had left the Treasury drained, there was strife among competing politicians, and the country rapidly became ungoverned and ungovernable. At last the army stepped in and established a military junta led by Colonel Abram Kigonde.

Surprisingly, Kigonde proved to be a political moderate. He crushed the extremists of both wings ruthlessly, laid heavy taxes on the business community which had been getting away with what it liked, and used the money to revitalize the cash crop plantations which had become neglected and run down. He was lucky too, because just as the cocoa plantations were brought back to some efficiency the price of cocoa went up, and for a couple of years the money rolled in until the cocoa price cycle went into another downswing.

Relative prosperity in Nyala led to political stability. The people had food in their bellies and weren't inclined to listen to anyone who wanted a change. This security led outside investors to study the country and now Kigonde was able to secure sizeable loans which went into more agricultural improvements and a degree of industrialization. You couldn't blame Kigonde for devoting a fair part of these loans to re-equipping his army.

Then he surprised everybody again. He revamped the Constitution and announced that elections would be held and a civil government was to take over the running of the country once again. After five years of military rule he stepped down to become Major General Kigonde, Commander in Chief of the Armed Forces. Since then the government had settled down, its hand greatly strengthened by the discovery of oil in the north. There was the usual amount of graft and corruption but no more so, apparently, than in any other African country, and all seemed set fair for the future of Nyala.

But there were rumours.

I read papers, studied maps and figures, and on the surface this was a textbook operation. I crammed in a lot of appointments, trying to have at least a few words with anybody who was directly concerned with the Nyala business. For the most part these were easy, the people I wanted to see being all bunched up close together in the City; but there was one exception, and an important one. I talked to Geddes about it first.

'The heavy haulage company you're using, Wyvern Haulage Ltd. They're new to me. Why them?'

Geddes explained. British Electric had part ownership of one haulage company, a firm with considerable overseas experience and well under the thumb of the Board, but they were fully occupied with other work. There were few other British firms in the same field, and Geddes had tendered the job to a Dutch and an American company, but in the end the contract had gone to someone who appeared to be almost a newcomer in the business. I asked if there was any nepotism involved.

'None that I know of,' Geddes said. 'This crowd has good credentials, a good track record, and their price is damned competitive. There are too few heavy hauliers about who can do what we want them to do, and their prices are getting out of hand – even our own. I'm willing to encourage anyone if it will increase competition.'

'Their price may be right for us, but is it right for them?' I asked. 'I can't see them making much of a profit.'

It was vital that no firm who worked for us should come out badly. British Electric had to be a crowd whom others were anxious to be alongside. And I was far from happy with the figures that Wyvern were quoting, attractive though they might be to Milner and Geddes.

'Who are they?'

'They know their job, all right. It's a splinter group from Sheffield Hauliers and we think the best of that bunch went to Wyvern when it was set up. The boss is a youngish chap, Geoffrey Wingstead, and he took Basil Kemp with him for starters.'

I knew both the names, Wingstead only as a noise but Kemp and I had met before on a similar job. The difference was that the transformer then being moved was from the British industrial midlands up to Scotland; no easy matter but a cake-walk compared with doing any similar job in Africa. I wondered if Wyvern had any overseas experience, and decided to find out for myself.

To meet Wingstead I drove up to Leeds, and was mildly startled at what I found when I got there. I was all in favour of a new company ploughing its finances into the heart of the business rather than setting up fancy offices and shop front prestige, but to find Geoff Wingstead running his show from a prefab shed right in amongst the workshops and garaging was disturbing. It was a string-and-brown-paper setup of which Wingstead seemed to be proud.

But I was impressed by him and his paperwork, and could not fault either. I had wanted to meet Kemp again, only to be told that he was already in Nyala with his load boss and crew, waiting for the arrival of the rig by sea. Wingstead himself intended to fly out when the rig was ready for its first run, a prospect which clearly excited him: he hadn't been in Africa before. I tried to steer a course midway between terrifying him with examples of how different his job would be out there from anything he had experienced in Europe, and overboosting his confidence with too much enthusiasm. I still had doubts, but I left Leeds and later Heathrow with a far greater optimism than I'd have thought possible.

On paper, everything was splendid. But I've never known events to be transferred from paper to reality without something being lost in the translation.

Port Luard was hot and sweaty. The temperature was climbing up to the hundred mark and the humidity was struggling to join it. John Sutherland met me at the airport which was one of Ofanwe's white elephants: runways big enough to take jumbos and a concourse three times the size of Penn Station. It was large enough to serve a city the size of, say, Rome.

A chauffeur driven car awaited outside the arrivals building.

I got in with Sutherland and felt the sweat break out under my armpits, and my wet shirt already sticking to my back. I unbuttoned the top of my shirt and took off my jacket and tie. I had suffered from cold at Heathrow and was overdressed here – a typical traveller's dilemma. In my case was a superfine lightweight tropical suit by Huntsman – that was for hobnobbing with Cabinet ministers and suchlike – and a couple of safari suits. For the rest I'd buy local gear and probably dump it when I left. Cheap cotton shirts and shorts were always easy to get hold of.

I sat back and watched the country flow by. I hadn't been to Nyala before but it wasn't much different from Nigeria or any other West African landscape. Personally I preferred the less lush bits of Africa, the scrub and semi-desert areas, and I knew I'd be seeing plenty of that later on. The advertisements for Brooke Bond Tea and Raleigh Bicycles still proclaimed Nyala's British colonial origins, although those for Coca-Cola were universal.

It was early morning and I had slept on the flight. I felt wide awake and ready to go, which was more than I could say for Sutherland. He looked exhausted, and I wondered how tough it was getting for him.

'Do we have a company plane?' I asked him.

'Yes, and a good pilot, a Rhodesian.' He was silent for a while and then said cautiously, 'Funny meeting we had last week. I was pulled back to London at twelve hours' notice and all that happened was that we sat around telling each other things we already knew.'

He was fishing and I knew it.

'I didn't know most of it. It was a briefing for me.'

'Yes, I rather guessed as much.'

I asked, 'How long have you been with the company?'

'Seven years.'

I'd never met him before, or heard of him, but that wasn't unusual. It's a big outfit and I met new faces regularly. But Sutherland would have heard of me, because my name was

21

trouble; I was the hatchet man, the expeditor, sometimes the executioner. As soon as I pitched up on anyone's territory there would be that tightening feeling in the gut as the local boss man wondered what the hell had gone wrong.

I said, to put him at his ease, 'Relax, John. It's just that Geddes has got ants in his pants. Trouble is they're invisible ants. I'm just here on an interrupted vacation.'

'Oh quite,' Sutherland said, not believing a word of it. 'What do you plan to do first?'

'I think I'd like to go up to the site at Bir Oassa for a couple of days, use the plane and overfly this road of theirs. After that I might want to see someone in the Government. Who would you suggest?'

Sutherland stroked his jaw. He knew that I'd read up on all of them and that it was quite likely I knew more about the local scene than he did. 'There's Hamah Ousemane – he's Minister for the Interior, and there's the Finance Minister, John Chizamba. Either would be a good starting point. And I suppose Daondo will want to put his oar in.'

'He's the local Goebbels, isn't he?'

'Yes, Minister for Misinformation.'

I grinned and Sutherland relaxed a little more. 'Who has the itchiest palm? Or by some miracle are none of them on the take?'

'No miracles here. As for which is the greediest, that I couldn't say. But you should be able to buy a few items of information from almost anyone.'

We were as venal as the men we were dealing with. There was room for a certain amount of honesty in my profession but there was also room for the art of wheeling and dealing, and frankly I rather enjoyed that. It was fun, and I didn't ever see why making one's living had to be a joyless occupation.

I said, 'Right. Now, don't tell me you haven't any problems. You wouldn't be human if you didn't. What's the biggest headache on your list right now?'

'The heavy transport.'

22

'Wyvern? What exactly is wrong?'

'The first load is scheduled to leave a week from today but the ship carrying the rig hasn't arrived yet. She's on board a special freighter, not on a regular run, and she's been held up somewhere with customs problems. Wyvern's road boss is here and he's fairly sweating. He's been going up and down the road checking gradients and tolerances and he's not too happy with some of the things he's seen. He's back in town now, ready to supervise the unloading of the rig.'

'The cargo?'

'Oh, the transformers and boilers are all OK. It's just that they're a bit too big to carry up on a Land Rover. Do you want to meet him right away?'

'No, I'll see him when I come back from Bir Oassa. No point in our talking until there's something to talk about. And the non-arrival of the rig isn't a topic.'

I was telling him that I wasn't going to interfere in his job and it made him happier to know it. We had been travelling up a wide boulevard and now emerged into a huge dusty square, complete with a vast statue of a gentleman whom I knew to be Maro Ofanwe sitting on a plinth in the middle. Why they hadn't toppled his statue along with the original I couldn't imagine. The car wove through the haphazard traffic and stopped at one of the last remaining bits of colonial architecture in sight, complete with peeling paint and sagging wooden balconies. It was, needless to say, my hotel.

'Had a bit of a job getting you a room,' Sutherland said, thus letting me know that he was not without the odd string to pull.

'What's the attraction? It's hardly a tourist's mecca.'

'By God, it isn't! The attraction is the oil. You'll find Luard full of oil men – Americans, French, Russians, the lot. The Government has been eclectic in its franchises.'

As the car pulled up he went on, 'Anything I can do for you right now?'

'Nothing for today, thanks, John. I'll book in and get

23

changed and cleaned up, do some shopping, take a stroll. Tomorrow I'd like a car here at seven-thirty to take me to the airport. Are you free this evening?'

Sutherland had been anticipating that question, and indicated that he was indeed available. We arranged to meet for a drink and a light meal. Any of the things I'd observed or thought about during the day I could then try out on him. Local knowledge should never be neglected.

By nine the next morning I was flying along the coast following the first 200 miles of road to Lasulu where we were to land for refuelling before going on upcountry. There was more traffic on the road than I would have expected, but far less than a road of that class was designed to carry. I took out the small pair of binoculars I carried and studied it.

There were a few saloons and four-wheel drive vehicles, Suzukis and Land Rovers, and a fair number of junky old trucks. What was more surprising were the number of big trucks; thirty- and forty-tonners. I saw that one of them was carrying a load of drilling pipe. The next was a tanker, then another carrying, from the trail it left, drilling mud. This traffic was oil-generated and was taking supplies from Port Luard to the oilfields in the north.

I said to the pilot, a cheerful young man called Max Otterman, 'Can you fly to the other side of Lasulu, please? Not far, say twenty miles. I want to look at the road over there.'

'It peters out a mile or so beyond the town. But I'll go on a way,' he said.

Sure enough the road vanished into the miniature build-up around Lasulu, reemerging inland from the coast. On the continuation of the coastal stretch another road carried on northwards, less impressive than the earlier section but apparently perfectly usable. The small harbour did not look busy, but there were two or three fair-sized craft riding at anchor. Not easy to tell from the air, but it didn't seem as though there was a building in Lasulu higher than three storeys. The endless

24

frail smoke of shantytown cooking fires wreathed all about it.

Refuelling was done quickly at the airstrip, and then we turned inland. From Lasulu to Bir Oassa was about 800 miles and we flew over the broad strip of concrete thrusting incongruously through mangrove swamp, rain forest, savannah and the scrubby fringes of desert country. It had been built by Italian engineers, Japanese surveyors and a mixture of road crews with Russian money and had cost twice as much as it should, the surplus being siphoned off into a hundred unauthorized pockets and numbered accounts in Swiss banks – a truly international venture.

The Russians were not perturbed by the way their money was used. They were not penny-pinchers and, in fact, had worked hard to see that some of the surplus money went into the right pockets. It was a cheap way of buying friends in a country that was poised uncertainly and ready to topple East or West in any breeze. It was another piece laid on the chess-board of international diplomacy to fend off an identical move by another power.

The road drove through thick forest and then heaved itself up towards the sky, climbing the hills which edged the central plateau. Then it crossed the sea of grass and bush to the dry region of the desert and came to Bir Oassa where the towers of oil rigs made a newer, metal forest.

I spent two days in Bir Oassa talking to the men and the bosses, scouting about the workings, and cocking an ear for any sort of unrest or uneasiness. I found very little worthy of note and nothing untoward. I did have a complaint from Dick Slater, the chief steam engineer, who had been sent word of the change of schedule and didn't like it.

'I'll have thirty steam fitters playing pontoon when they should be working,' he said abrasively to me. 'Why the bloody hell do they have to send the transformers first?'

It had all been explained to him but he was being wilful. I said, 'Take it easy. It's all been authorized by Geddes from London.'

25

'London! What do they know about it? This Geddes doesn't understand the first damn thing about it,' he said. Slater wasn't the man to be mealy-mouthed. I calmed him down – well, maybe halfway down – and went in search of other problems. It worried me when I couldn't find any.

On the second day I had a phone call from Sutherland. On a crackling line full of static and clashing crossed wires his voice said faintly, '. . . Having a meeting with Ousemane and Daondo. Do you want . . . ?'

'Yes, I do want to sit in on it. You and who else?' I was shouting.

'. . . Kemp from Wyvern. Tomorrow morning . . .'

'Has the rig come?'

'. . . Unloading . . . came yesterday . . .'

'I'll be there.'

The meeting was held in a cool room in the Palace of Justice. The most important government man there was the Minister of the Interior, Hamah Ousemane, who presided over the meeting with a bland smile. He did not say much but left the talking to a short, slim man who was introduced as Zinsou Daondo. I couldn't figure whether Ousemane didn't understand what was going on, or understood and didn't care: he displayed a splendid indifference.

Very surprising for a meeting of this kind was the presence of Major General Abram Kigonde, the army boss. Although he was not a member of the government he was a living reminder of Mao's dictum that power grows out of the muzzle of a gun. No Nyalan government could survive without his nod of approval. At first I couldn't see where he fitted in to this discussion on the moving of a big piece of power plant.

On our side there were myself, Sutherland, and Basil Kemp, who was a lean Englishman with a thin brown face stamped with tiredness and worry marks. He greeted me pleasantly enough, remembering our last encounter some few years before and appearing unperturbed by my presence. He probably had

26

too much else on his plate already. I let Sutherland make the running and he addressed his remarks to the Minister while Daondo did the answering. It looked remarkably like a ventriloquist's act but I found it hard to figure out who was the dummy. Kigonde kept a stiff silence.

After some amiable chitchat (not the weather, thank God) we got down to business and Sutherland outlined some routine matters before drawing Kemp into the discussion. 'Could we have a map, please, Mister Kemp?'

Kemp placed a map on the big table and pointed out his bottlenecks.

'We have to get out of Port Luard and through Lasulu. Both are big towns and to take a load like this through presents difficulties. It has been my experience in Europe that operations like this draw the crowds and I can't see that it will be different here. We should appreciate a police escort.'

Daondo nodded. 'It will certainly draw the crowds.' He seemed pleased.

Kemp said, 'In Europe we usually arrange to take these things through at extreme off-peak times. The small hours of the night are often best.'

This remark drew a frown from Daondo and I thought I detected the slightest of headshakes from the Minister. I became more alert.

Kigonde stirred and spoke for the first time, in a deep and beautifully modulated voice. 'You will certainly have an escort, Mister Kemp – but not the police. I am putting an army detachment at your service.' He leaned forward and pressed a button, the door of the room opened, and a smartly dressed officer strode towards the table. 'This is Captain Ismail Sadiq who will command the escort.'

Captain Sadiq clicked to attention, bowing curtly, and then at a nod from Kigonde stood at ease at the foot of the table.

Daondo said, 'The army will accompany you all the way.'

'The whole journey?' Sutherland asked.

'On all journeys.'

27

I sensed that Sutherland was about to say something wrong, and forestalled him. 'We are more than honoured, Major General. This is extremely thoughtful of you and we appreciate it. It is more of an honour than such work as this usually entails.'

'Our police force is not large, and already has too much work. We regard the safekeeping of such expeditions as these of the greatest importance, Mister Mannix. The army stands ready to be of any service.' He was very smooth, and I reckoned that we'd come out of that little encounter about equal. I prepared to enjoy myself.

'Please explain the size of your command, Captain,' Daondo said.

Sadiq had a soft voice at odds with his appearance. 'For work on the road I have four infantry troop carriers with six men to each carrier, two trucks for logistics purposes, and my own command car, plus outriders. Eight vehicles, six motor-cycles and thirty-six men including myself. In the towns I am empowered to call on local army units for crowd control.'

This was bringing up the big guns with a vengeance. I had never heard of a rig which needed that kind of escort, whether for crowd control or for any other form of safety regulations, except in conditions of war. My curiosity was aroused by now, but I said nothing and let Sutherland carry on. Taking his cue from me he expressed only his gratitude and none of his perturbation. He'd expected a grudging handful of ill-trained local coppers at best.

Kigonde was saying, 'In the Nyalan army the rank of captain is relatively high, gentlemen. You need not fear being held up in any way.'

'I am sure not,' said Kemp politely. 'It will be a pleasure having your help, Captain. But now there are other matters as well. I am sorry to tell you that the road has deteriorated slightly in some places, and my loads may be too heavy for them.'

That was an understatement, but Kemp was working hard at diplomacy. Obviously he was wondering if Sadiq had any

28

idea of the demands made by heavy transport, and if army escort duty also meant army assistance. Daondo picked him up and said easily, 'Captain Sadiq will be authorized to negotiate with the civil bodies in each area in which you may find difficulty. I am certain that an adequate labour force will be found for you. And, of course, the necessary materials.'

It all seemed too good to be true. Kemp went on to the next problem.

'Crowd control in towns is only one aspect, of course, gentlemen. There is the sheer difficulty of pushing a big vehicle through a town. Here on the map I have outlined a proposed route through Port Luard, from the docks to the outskirts. I estimate that it will take eight or nine hours to get through. The red line marks the easiest, in fact the only route, and the figures in circles are the estimated times at each stage. That should help your traffic control, although we shouldn't have too much trouble there, moving through the central city area mostly during the night.'

The Minister made a sudden movement, wagging one finger sideways. Daondo glanced at him before saying, 'It will not be necessary to move through Port Luard at night, Mister Kemp. We prefer you to make the move in daylight.'

'It will disrupt your traffic flow considerably,' said Kemp in some surprise.

'That is of little consequence. We can handle it.' Daondo bent over the map. 'I see your route lies through Independence Square.'

'It's really the only way,' said Kemp defensively. 'It would be quite impossible to move through this tangle of narrow streets on either side without a great deal of damage to buildings.'

'I quite agree,' said Daondo. 'In fact, had you not suggested it we would have asked you to go through the Square ourselves.'

This appeared to come as a wholly novel idea to Kemp. I could see he was thinking of the squalls of alarm from the London Metropolitan Police had he suggested pushing a 300-

29

ton load through Trafalgar Square in the middle of the rush hour. Wherever he'd worked in Europe, he had been bullied, harassed and crowded into corners and sent on his way with the stealth of a burglar.

He paused to take this in with one finger still on the map. 'There's another very real difficulty here, though. This big plinth in the middle of the avenue leading into the Square. It's sited at a very bad angle from our point of view – we're going to have a great deal of difficulty getting around it. I would like to suggest –'

The Minister interrupted him with an unexpected deep-bellied, rumbling chuckle but his face remained bland. Daondo was also smiling and in his case too the smile never reached his eyes. 'Yes, Mister Kemp, we see what you mean. I don't think you need trouble about the plinth. We will have it removed. It will improve the traffic flow into Victory Avenue considerably in any case.'

Kemp and Sutherland exchanged quick glances. 'I . . . I think it may take time,' said Sutherland. 'It's a big piece of masonry.'

'It is a task for the army,' said Kigonde and turned to Sadiq. 'See to it, Captain.'

Sadiq nodded and made quick notes. The discussion continued, the exit from Port Luard was detailed and the progress through Lasulu dismissed, for all its obvious difficulties to us, as a mere nothing by the Nyalans. About an hour later, after some genteel refreshment, we were finally free to go our way. We all went up to my hotel room and could hardly wait to get there before indulging in a thorough postmortem of that extraordinary meeting. It was generally agreed that no job had ever been received by the local officials with greater cooperation, any problem melting like snowflakes in the steamy Port Luard sunshine. Paradoxically it was this very ease of arrangement that made us all most uneasy, especially Basil Kemp.

'I can't believe it,' he said, not for the first time. 'They just love us, don't they?'

'I think you've put your finger on it, Basil,' I said. 'They really need us and they are going all out to show it. And they're pretty used to riding roughshod over the needs and wishes of their populace, assuming it has any. They're going to shove us right down the middle in broad daylight, and the hell with any little obstacles.'

'Such as the plinth,' said Sutherland and we both laughed.

Kemp said, 'I think I missed something there. A definite undercurrent. I must say I haven't looked at this thing too closely myself – what is it anyway – some local bigwig?'

Sutherland chuckled. 'I thought old Ousemane would split his breeches. There's a statue of Maro Ofanwe still on that plinth: thirty feet high in bronze, very heroic. Up to now they've been busy ignoring it, as it was a little too hefty to blow up or knock down, but now they've got just the excuse they want. It'll help to serve notice that they don't want any more strong men about, in a none too subtle sort of way. Ofanwe was an unmitigated disaster and not to be repeated.'

3

During the next few days I got on with my job, which mainly consisted of trying to find out what my job was. I talked with various members of the Government and had a special meeting with the Minister of Finance which left us both happy. I also talked to journalists in the bars, one or two businessmen and several other expatriates from Britain who were still clinging on to their old positions, most of them only too ready to bewail the lost days of glory. I gleaned a lot, mostly of misinformation, but slowly I was able to put together a picture which didn't precisely coincide with that painted by Shelford back in London.

I was also made an honorary member of the Luard Club which, in colonial days, had strictly white membership but in these times had become multi-racial. There were still a number of old Africa hands there as well, and from a couple of them I got another whiff of what might be going bad in Nyala.

In the meantime Kemp and Sutherland were getting on with their business, to more immediate ends. On the morning the first big load was to roll I was up bright and early, if not bushy tailed. The sun had just risen and the temperature already in the eighties when I drove to the docks to see the loaded rig. I hadn't had much chance to talk to Kemp and while I doubted that this was the moment, I had to pin him down to some time and place.

I found him and Sutherland in the middle of a small slice of chaos, both looking harassed as dozens of men milled around shouting questions and orders. They'd been at it for a long time already and things were almost ready to go into action. I stared in fascination at what I saw.

The huge rig wasn't unfamiliar to me but it was still a breathtaking sight. The massive towing trucks, really tractors with full cab bodies, stood at each end of the flat-bed trailer onto which the transformer had been lowered, inch by painful inch, over the previous few hours. Around it scurried small dockside vehicles, fork-lift trucks and scooters, like worker ants scrambling about their huge motionless queen. But what fascinated and amused me was the sight of a small platoon of Nyalan dock hands clambering about the actual rig itself, as agile and noisy as a troop of monkeys, busy stringing yards of festive bunting between any two protruding places to which they could be tied. The green and yellow colours of the Nyalan flag predominated, and one of them was being hauled up a jackstaff which was bound to the front tractor bumpers. No wonder that Kemp looked thunderstruck and more than a little grim.

I hurried over to him, and my arrival coincided with that of Mr Daondo, who was just getting out of a black limousine. Daondo stood with hands on hips and gazed the length of the enormous rig with great satisfaction, then turned to us and said in a hearty voice, 'Well, good morning, gentlemen. I see everything is going very well indeed.'

Kemp said, 'Good morning, Mister Daondo – Neil. May I ask what –'

'Hello, Basil. Great day for it, haven't we? Mister Daondo, would you excuse us for just one moment? I've got your figures here, Basil . . .'

Talking fast, waving a notebook, and giving him no time to speak, I managed to draw Kemp away from Daondo's side, leaving the politician to be entertained for a moment by John Sutherland.

'Just what the hell do they think they're doing?' Kemp was outraged.

'Ease off. Calm down. Can't you see? They're going to put on a show for the people – that's what this daylight procession has been about all along. The power plant is one of the biggest things that's ever happened to Nyala and the Government wants to do a bit of bragging. And I don't see why not.'

'But how?' Kemp, normally a man of broad enough intelligence, was on a very narrow wave length where his precious rig was concerned.

'Hasn't the penny dropped yet? You're to be the centrepiece of a triumphal parade through the town, right through Independence Square. The way the Ruskies trundle their rockets through Red Square on May Day. You'll be on show, the band will play, the lot.'

'Are you serious?' said Kemp in disgust.

'Quite. The Government must not only govern but be seen to govern. They're entitled to bang their drum.'

Kemp subsided, muttering.

'Don't worry. As soon as you're clear of the town you can take the ribbons out of her hair and get down to work properly. Have a word with your drivers. I'd like to meet them, but not right away. And tell them to enjoy themselves. It's a gala occasion.'

'All right, I suppose we must. But it's damn inconvenient. It's hard enough work moving these things without having to cope with cheering mobs and flag-waving.'

'You don't have to cope, that's his job.' I indicated Daondo with a jerk of my thumb. 'Your guys just drive it away as usual. I think we'd better go join him.'

We walked back to where Daondo, leaning negligently against the hood of his Mercedes, was holding forth to a small circle of underlings. Sutherland was in the thick of it, together with a short, stocky man with a weathered face. Sutherland introduced him to me.

'Neil, this is Ben Hammond, my head driver. Ben, Mister Mannix of British Electric. I think Ben's what you'd call my ranch foreman.'

I grinned. 'Nice herd of cattle you've got there, Ben. I'd like to meet the crew later. What's the schedule?'

'I've just told Mister Daondo that I think they're ready

34

to roll any time now. But of course it's Mister Kemp's show really.'

'Thank you, Mister Sutherland. I'll have a word with Daondo and then we can get going,' Kemp said.

I marvelled at the way my British companions still managed to cling to surnames and honorifics. I wondered if they'd all be dressing for dinner, out there in the bush wherever the rig stopped for the night. I gave my attention to Daondo to find that he was being converged upon by a band of journalists, video and still cameras busy, notebooks poised, but with none of the free-for-all shoving that might have taken place anywhere in Europe. The presence of several armed soldiers nearby may have had a bearing on that.

'Ah, Mister Mannix,' Daondo said, 'I am about to hold a short press conference. Would you join me, please?'

'An honour, Minister. But it's not really my story – it's Mister Kemp's.'

Kemp gave me a brief dirty look as I passed the buck neatly to him. 'May I bring Mister Hammond in on this?' he asked, drawing Ben Hammond along by the arm. 'He designed this rig; it's very much his baby.'

I looked at the stocky man in some surprise. This was something I hadn't known and it set me thinking. Wyvern Haulage might be new as an outfit, but they seemed to have gathered a great deal of talent around them, and my respect for Geoff Wingstead grew fractionally greater.

The press conference was under way, to a soft barrage of clicks as people were posed in front of the rig. Video cameramen did their trick of walking backwards with a buddy's hand on their shoulder to guide them, and the writer boys ducked and dodged around the clutter of ropes, chain, pulleys and hawsers that littered the ground. Some of the inevitable questions were coming up and I listened carefully, as this was a chance for me to learn a few of the technicalities.

'Just how big is this vehicle?'

Kemp indicated Ben Hammond forward. Ben, grinning like

35

a toothpaste advertisement, was enjoying his moment in the limelight as microphones were thrust at him. 'As the transporter is set up now it's a bit over a hundred feet long. We can add sections up to another eighteen feet but we won't need them on this trip.'

'Does that include the engines?'

'The tractors? No, those are counted separately. We'll be adding on four tractors to get over hilly ground and then the total length will be a shade over two hundred and forty feet.'

Another voice said, 'Our readers may not be able to visualize that. Can you give us anything to measure it by?'

Hammond groped for an analogy, and then said, 'I notice that you people here play a lot of soccer – football.'

'Indeed we do,' Daondo interjected. 'I myself am an enthusiast.' He smiled modestly as he put in his personal plug. 'I was present at the Cup Final at Wembley last year, when I was Ambassador to the United Kingdom.'

Hammond said, 'Well, imagine this. If you drove this rig onto the field at Wembley, or any other standard soccer pitch, it would fill the full length of the pitch with a foot hanging over each side. Is that good enough?'

There was a chorus of appreciative remarks, and Kemp said in a low voice, 'Well done, Ben. Carry on.'

'How heavy is the vehicle?' someone asked.

'The transporter weighs ninety tons, and the load, that big transformer, is three hundred tons. Add forty tons for each tractor and it brings the whole lot to five hundred and fifty tons on the hoof.'

Everybody scribbled while the cameras ground on. Hammond added, airing some knowledge he had only picked up in the last few days, 'Elephants weigh about six tons each; so this is worth nearly a hundred elephants.'

The analogy was received with much amusement.

'Those tractors don't look big enough to weigh forty tons,' he was prompted.

'They carry ballast. Steel plates embedded in concrete. We have to have some counterbalance for the weight of the load or the transporter will overrun the tractors – especially on the hills. Negotiating hill country is very tricky.'

'How fast will you go?'

Kemp took over now. 'On the flat with all tractors hooked up I dare say we could push along to almost twenty miles an hour, even more going downhill. But we won't. Five hundred and fifty tons going at twenty miles an hour takes a lot of stopping, and we don't take risks. I don't think we'll do much more than ten miles an hour during any part of the journey, and usually much less. Our aim is to average five miles an hour during a ten hour day; twenty days from Port Luard to Bir Oassa.'

This drew whistles of disbelief and astonishment. In this age of fast transport, it was interesting that extreme slowness could exert the same fascination as extreme speed. It also interested me to notice that Nyala had not yet converted its thinking to the metric unit as far as distances were concerned.

'How many wheels does it have?'

Hammond said, 'Ninety-six on the ground and eight spares.'

'How many punctures do you expect?'

'None – we hope.' This drew a laugh.

'What's the other big truck?'

'That's the vehicle which carries the airlift equipment and the machinery for powering it,' said Kemp. 'We use it to spread the load when crossing bridges, and it works on the hovercraft principle. It's powered by four two hundred and forty-hp Rolls Royce engines – and that vehicle itself weighs eight tons.'

'And the others?'

'Spares, a workshop for maintenance, food and personal supplies, fuel. We have to take everything with us, you see.'

There was a stir as an aide came forward to whisper something into Daondo's ear. He raised his hand and his voice. 'Gentlemen, that will be all for now, thank you. I invite you all to gather round this great and marvellous machine for its dedication by His Excellency, the Minister of the Interior, the Right Honourable Hamah Ousemane, OBE.' He touched me on the arm. 'This way, please.'

As we followed him I heard Hammond saying to Kemp, 'What's he going to do? Crack a bottle of champagne over it?'

I grinned back at him. 'Did you really design this thing?'

'I designed some modifications to a standard rig, yes.'

Kemp said, 'Ben built a lot of it, too.'

I was impressed. 'For a little guy you sure play with big toys.'

Hammond stiffened and looked at me with hot eyes. Clearly I had hit on a sore nerve. 'I'm five feet two and a half inches tall,' he said curtly. 'And that's the exact height of Napoleon.'

'No offence meant,' I said quickly, and then we all came to a sudden stop at the rig to listen to Ousemane's speech. He spoke first in English and then in Nyalan for a long time in a rolling, sonorous voice while the sun became hotter and everybody wilted. Then came some ribbon cutting and hand-shakes all round, some repeated for the benefit of the press, and finally he took himself off in his Mercedes. Kemp mopped his brow thankfully. 'Do you think we can get on with it now?' he asked nobody in particular.

Daondo was bustling back to us. In the background a surprising amount of military deployment was taking place, and there was an air of expectancy building up. 'Excellent, Mister Kemp! We are all ready to go now,' Daondo said. 'You will couple up all the tractors, won't you?'

Kemp turned to me and said in a harassed undertone, 'What for? We won't be doing more than five miles an hour on the flat and even one tractor's enough for that.'

I was getting a bit tired of Kemp and his invincible ignorance and I didn't want Daondo to hear him and blow a gasket. I smiled past Kemp and said, 'Of course. Everything will be done as you wish it, Minister.'

38

'Good,' he said. 'I must get to Independence Square before you arrive. I leave Captain Sadiq in command of the arrangements.' He hurried away to his car.

I said to Kemp, putting an edge on my voice, 'We're expected to put on a display and we'll do it. Use everything you've got. Line 'em up, even the chow wagon. Until we leave town it's a parade every step of the way.'

'Who starts this parade?'

'You do – just tell your drivers to pull off in line whenever they're ready. The others will damn well have to fall in around you. I'll ride with you in the Land Rover.'

Kemp shrugged. 'Bunch of clowns,' he said and went off to give his drivers their instructions. For the moment I actually had nothing to do and I wandered over to have another look at the rig. It's a funny thing, but whenever a guy looks at a vehicle he automatically kicks a tyre. Ask any second-hand auto salesman. So that's what I did. It had about as much effect as kicking a building and was fairly painful. The tyres were all new, with deep tread earthmovers on the tractors. The whole rig looked brand new, as if it had never been used before, and I couldn't decide if this was a good or a bad thing. I squinted up at it as it towered over me, remembering the one time I had towed a caravan and had it jackknife on me, and silently tipped my hat to the drivers of this outfit. They were going to need skill and luck in equal proportions on this trip.

Kemp drew up beside me in the Land Rover with a driver and I swung in the back. There was a lot of crosstalk going on with walkie-talkies, and a great deal of bustle and activity all around us.

'All right, let's get rolling,' Kemp said into the speaker. 'Take station on me, Ben: about three mph and don't come breathing down my neck.' He then said much the same thing into his car radio as drivers climbed into cabs and the vast humming roar of many engines began throbbing. Captain Sadiq rolled up alongside us in the back of an open staff car and saluted smartly.

'I will lead the way, Mister Kemp. Please to follow me,' he said.

'Please keep your speed to mine, Captain,' Kemp said.

'Of course, sir. But please watch me carefully too. I may have to stop at some point. You are all ready?'

Kemp nodded and Sadiq pulled away. Kemp was running down a roster of drivers, getting checks from each of them, and then at last signalled his own driver to move ahead in Sadiq's wake. I would have preferred to be behind the rig, but had to content myself with twisting in the rear seat of the car to watch behind me. To my astonishment something was joining in the parade that I hadn't seen before, filtering in between Kemp and the rig, and at my sharp exclamation he turned to see for himself and swore.

The army was coming in no half measures. Two recoilless guns, two mortars and two heavy machine guns mounted on appropriate vehicles came forward, followed by a tank and at least two troop carriers. 'Good God,' said Kemp in horror, and gave hasty orders to his own driver, who swung us out of the parade and doubled back along the line of military newcomers. Kemp was speaking urgently to Sadiq on the radio.

'I'll rejoin after the army vehicles, Captain. I must stay with the rig!'

I grinned at him as he cut the Captain off in mid-sentence.

'They're armed to the teeth,' he said irritably. 'Why the hell didn't he warn me about all this?'

'Maybe the crowds here are rougher than in England,' I said, looking with fascination at the greatly enhanced parade streaming past us.

'They're using us as an excuse to show what they've got. They damn well know it's all going out on telly to the world,' Kemp said.

'Enjoy the publicity, Basil. It says *Wyvern* up there in nice big letters. A pity I didn't think of a flag with *British Electric* on it as well.'

In fact this show of military prowess was making me a little uneasy, but it would never do for me to let Kemp see that. He was jittery enough as it was. He gave orders as the tanks swept past, commanders standing up in the turrets, and we swung in behind the last of the army vehicles and just in front of the rig, now massively coupled to all its tractors. Ben Hammond waved down to us from his driving cab and the rig started rolling behind us. Kemp concentrated on its progress, leaving the other Wyvern vehicles to come along in the rear, the very last car being the second Land Rover with John Sutherland on board.

Kemp was watching the rig, checking back regularly and trying to ignore the shouting, waving crowds who were gathering as we went along, travelling so slowly that agile small boys could dodge back and forward across the road in between the various components of the parade. There was much blowing of police whistles to add to the general noise. We heard louder cheering as we came out onto the coastal boulevard leading to the town centre. The scattering of people thickened as we approached.

Kemp paid particular attention as the rig turned behind us into Victory Avenue; turning a 240-foot vehicle is no easy job and he would rather have done it without the extra towing tractors. But the rig itself was steerable from both ends and a crew member was spinning a ship-sized steering wheel right at the rear, synchronizing with Ben Hammond in the front cab. Motorcycle escorts took up flanking positions as the rig straightened out into the broad avenue and the crowd was going crazy.

Kemp said, 'Someone must have declared a holiday.'

'Rent-a-crowd,' I grinned. Kemp sat a little straighter and seemed to relax slightly. I thought that he was beginning to enjoy his moment of glory, after all. The Land Rover bumped over a roughly cobbled area and I realized with a start that we were driving over the place where Ofanwe's plinth had been only a few days before.

We entered the Square to a sea of black faces and colourful robes, gesticulating arms and waves of sound that surged and

41

echoed from the big buildings all around. The flags hung limply in the still air but all the rest was movement under the hard tropical sun.

'Jesus!' Kemp said in awe. 'It's like a Roman triumph. I feel I ought to have a slave behind me whispering sweet nothings in my ear.' He quoted, '*Memento mori* – remember thou must die.'

I grunted. I was used to the British habit of flinging off quotations at odd moments but I hadn't expected it of Kemp. He went on, 'Just look at that lot.'

The balcony of the Palace of Justice was full of figures. The President, the Prime Minister, members of the Government, Army staff, some in modern dress or in uniforms but some, like Daondo, changed into local costume: a flowing colourful robe and a tasselled hat. It was barbaric and, in spite of my professed cynicism, a touch magnificent.

The tanks and guns had passed and it was our turn. Kemp said to me, 'Do we bow or anything?'

'Just sit tight. Pay attention to your rig. Show them it's still business first.' Off to one side of the parade, Sadiq's staff car was drawn up with the Captain standing rigidly at the salute in the back seat. 'Sadiq is doing the necessary for all of us.'

The vast bulk of the rig crept slowly across Independence Square and the troops and police fought valiantly to keep the good-humoured crowd back. As soon as our car was through the Square we stopped and waited too for the rig to come up behind us, and then set off again following Sadiq, who had regained his place in the lead. The tanks and guns rumbled off in a different direction, and the convoy with its escort of soldiers crept on through narrower streets and among fewer and fewer people.

The town began to thin out until we were clear of all but a few shanties and into the beginning of the croplands, and here the procession came to a halt, with only an audience of goats and herd boys to watch us.

Sadiq's car came back. He got out and spoke to Kemp, who

had the grace to thank him and to congratulate him on the efficiency of his arrangements. Clearly both were relieved that all had gone so well, and equally anxious to get on with the job in hand. Within minutes Kemp had his men removing the bunting and flags; he was driving them hard while the euphoria of the parade was still with them.

'This is all arsey-versey,' I heard him saying. 'You've had your celebration – now do something to earn it.'

'I suppose they'll do their celebrating tonight,' I remarked to him.

Kemp shook his head.

'We have a company rule. There's no hard liquor on the journeys: just beer, and I control that. And they've got a hell of a few days ahead of them.'

'I guess they have,' I said.

'A lot of trips,' Kemp said. 'Months of work. Right now it's a pretty daunting prospect.'

'You only have this one rig?'

I still felt I didn't know as much about Wyvern as I ought to. Having seen a tiny slice of their job out here, I was in a fever to talk to Geddes back at home, and to get together with Wingstead too. Reminded of him, I asked Kemp when he was due to come out.

'Next week, I believe,' Kemp said. 'He'll fly up and join us during the mid-section of the first trip. As for the rig, there's a second one in the making and it should be ready towards the end of the job. It'll help, but not enough. And the rains start in a couple of months too: we've a lot of planning to do yet.'

'Can you keep going through the wet season?'

'If the road holds out we can. And I must say it's fairly good most of the way. If it hadn't existed we'd never have tendered for the job.'

I said, 'I'm frankly surprised in a way that you did tender. It's a hell of a job for a new firm – wouldn't the standard European runs have suited you better to begin with?'

43

'We decided on the big gamble. Nothing like a whacking big success to start off with.'

I thought that it was Wingstead, rather than the innately conservative Kemp, who had decided on that gamble, and wondered how he had managed to convince my own masters that he was the man for the job.

'Right, Basil, this is where I leave you,' I said, climbing down from the Land Rover to stand on the hard heat-baked tarmac. 'I'll stay in touch, and I'll be out to see how you're getting on. Meanwhile I've got a few irons of my own in the fire – back there in the Frying Pan.'

We shook hands and I hopped into John Sutherland's car for the drive back to Port Luard, leaving Kemp to organize the beginning of the rig's first expedition.

4

We got back to the office hot, sweaty and tired. The streets were still seething and we had to fight our way through. Sutherland was fast on the draw with a couple of gin and tonics, and within four minutes of our arrival I was sitting back over a drink in which the ice clinked pleasantly. I washed the dust out of my mouth and watched the bubbles rise.

'Well, they got away all right,' Sutherland said after his own first swallow. 'They should be completely clear by nightfall.'

I took another mouthful and let it fizz before swallowing. 'Just as well you brought up the business of the plinth,' I said. 'Otherwise the rig would never have got into the Square.'

He laughed. 'Do you know, I forgot all about it in the excitement.'

'Sadiq damn nearly removed Independence Square. He blew the goddamn thing up at midnight. He may have broken every window in the hotel: I woke up picking bits of plate glass out of my bed. I don't know who his explosives experts are but I reckon they used a mite too much. You said it wouldn't be too subtle a hint – well, it was about as subtle as a kick in the balls.'

Sutherland replenished our glasses. 'What's next on the programme?'

'I'm going back to London on the first possible flight. See to it, will you? And keep my hotel room on for me – I'll be back.'

'What's it all about? What problems do you see?'

I said flatly, 'If you haven't already seen them then you aren't doing your job.' The chill in my voice got through to him

45

and he visibly remembered that I was the troubleshooter. I went on, 'I want to see your contingency plans for pulling out in case the shit hits the fan.'

He winced, and I could clearly interpret the expressions that chased over his face. I wasn't at all the cheery, easy-to-get-along-with guy he had first thought: I was just another ill-bred, crude American, after all, and he was both hurt and shocked. Well, I wasn't there to cater to his finer sensibilities, but to administer shock treatment where necessary.

I put a snap in my voice. 'Well, have you got any?'

He said tautly, 'It's not my policy to go into a job thinking I might have to pull out. That's defeatism.'

'John, you're a damned fool. The word I used was contingency. Your job is to have plans ready for any eventuality, come what may. Didn't they teach you that from the start?'

I stood up. 'When I get back I want to see those plans laid out, covering a quick evacuation of all personnel and as much valuable equipment as possible. It may never happen, but the plans must be there. Get some guidance from Barry Meredith in the Zambian offices. He's had the experience. Do I make myself clear?'

'You do,' he said, clipped and defensive, hating my guts.

I finished my drink. 'Thanks for the life-saver. Send the air tickets to the hotel, and expect me when you see me. And keep your ears open, John.'

He couldn't quite bring himself to ask me what he was supposed to listen for, and I wasn't yet ready to tell him. I left him a sadder and a none the wiser man.

I got back to London, spent a night in my own apartment, which God knows saw little enough of me, and was in to see Geddes the next morning. It was as though time had stood still; he sat behind his desk, wearing the same suit, and the same rain pattered against the windows. Even the conversation was predictable. 'You're looking very brown,' he said. 'Good weather out there?'

'No, I've picked up a new suntan lamp. You ought to try it some time. How's your prickly feeling?'

'It's still there. I hope you've brought some embrocation.'

'I haven't.' I crossed the room, opened the discreet executive bar and poured out a neat Scotch.

'You've picked up some bad habits,' Geddes said. 'Early morning drinking wasn't your line.'

'It's almost noon, and this isn't for me, it's for you – you'll need it. But since you invite me I'll join you.' I poured another, took the drinks to the desk and sat down.

Geddes looked from the glass to me. 'Bad news?'

'Not good. At the same time, not certain. It's one of those iffy situations. I've looked over the Nyala operation, and there's nothing wrong with our end of it. It's running like a well-oiled machine, and I'm mildly impressed by Wyvern, with reservations. But I put my ear to the ground, talked some and listened more, and I didn't like what I was hearing. Do you want it now or should I save it for a board meeting?'

'I'll have it now, please. I like to be ahead of any committee.'

'OK. A few years ago, after Ofanwe, there was military rule and Abram Kigonde was top dog. When he pulled out and allowed elections there were two basic parties formed, one rather grandly called the Peoples' Agrarian Party and one with the more prosaic name of the Nationalist Peoples' Party. The Agrarians won the first election and set out to reform everything in sight, but in a rather middle-of-the-road fashion; they were not particularly revolutionary in their thinking.'

I sipped some whisky. 'Times change. Because of the political stability, quite a lot of investment money came in, and then with the oil strikes there was still more. After a while the moderates were squeezed out and the Nationalists took over at the next elections. They are a lot more industry orientated. And of course by now Nyala had become self-financing and there were a lot of pickings to be had. And that's the nub – had by whom?'

47

'We know a lot of pockets have been lined, Neil. That's fairly common. Damn it, we've done it ourselves.'

'As common as breathing. But I think too much of it has gone into the wrong pockets – or wrong from one point of view anyway.'

'Whose point of view?'

'Major General Abram Kigonde.'

Geddes pursed his lips and nodded thoughtfully. 'What's he got to do with all this?'

'Everything. He's having trouble keeping the army in line. When he handed over power to the civil authority there were grumbles from some of his officers. A few senior types thought the army should hang on; they'd had a taste of power and liked it. But then nothing much happened, because there wasn't much power, or much loot, to divide. Then came industrialization and finally, to top it all, the oil strikes. Now there's a hell of a lot of loot and the army is split down the middle. They know the Government lads are creaming it off the top and some of those senior officers are licking their lips. Of course what they're saying is that the country which they saved from the evils of Maro Ofanwe is now being sold down the river by other equally evil politicians, but that's just for public consumption.'

'Yes, it sounds highly likely. Who's the main troublemaker?'

'A Colonel Sagundisi is at the bottom of it, the word says. He hasn't put a foot wrong, his popularity with the younger officers is increasing, and he's preaching redemption. If Kigonde lets him he'll go right out on a limb and call for army reforms again. '

'With what results?'

'Could be a *coup d'état.*'

'Um,' said Geddes. 'And the timetable? The likelihood?'

'That's hard to guess, naturally. It depends partly on the Air Force.'

Geddes nodded tiredly. 'The usual complications. They're playing both ends against the middle, right?'

'Right now the army is split in two; half for Kigonde and

48

the *status quo*, half for Sagundisi and the quick takeover. Word
is that they're level pegging with Sagundisi making points and
Kigonde losing them. The influence of their so-called Navy
is negligible. But the Air Force is different. If it comes to
open conflict then the side that has air power is going to
win.'

'A poker game.'

'You're so damned right. The Air Force Commander is a
wily old fox called Semangala and he's playing it cool, letting
each side of the army raise the ante alternately. The Government is also bidding for support in all this, naturally, tending
to Kigonde's angle but I wouldn't be surprised if they jumped
whichever way would get them into the cream pot.'

'It seems to come down to Semangala, the way you see it.
When he makes his mind up you expect a crack down one way
or the other.'

'There are other factors, of course. Student unrest is on the
increase. The pro-Reds are looking for a chance to put their
oar in; and in the north – where the oil is – the country is largely
Moslem and tends to look towards the Arab states for support
and example. Oh yes, and when all else fails there's always the
old tribal game: all of the lesser tribes are ready to gang up on
the too successful Kinguru, including their cousins the Wabi,
who make up the army backbone. Take your pick.'

Geddes picked up his glass and seemed surprised to find
that he'd drained it. 'All right, Neil. When do you think it will
blow open?'

'The rains will come in nearly two months if they're on
schedule which they may not be. They've been erratic the last
few years. But if they do come they will effectively put a damper
on any attempted *coup* –'

Geddes smiled without mirth at my unintended pun.

'Anyway, no army commander will take that chance. I'd
say that if it happens, it will be within the month or not for
another six months.'

'And if you had to bet?'

I tapped the table with my forefinger. 'Now.'

'And us with a three year contract,' mused Geddes wryly. 'What the hell's happened to Shelford and his department? He should know about all this?'

'How could he when he doesn't take the trouble to go and find out? I'd kick him out on his ass if I had my way.'

'We don't do things that way,' said Geddes stiffly.

I grinned. No, Geddes would shaft Shelford in the well-bred British fashion. There'd be a report in the *Financial Times* that Mr Shelford was going from strength to strength in the hierarchy of British Electric and his picture would smile toothily from the page. But from then on he'd be the walking dead, with his desk getting emptier and his phone more silent, and eventually he'd get the message and quit to grow roses. And wonder what the hell had hit him. A stiletto under the third rib would be more merciful.

'But Sutherland should have known,' Geddes was saying. 'He should have told us.'

Although I had put the frighteners into John Sutherland myself I did not think he ought to share Shelford's imagined fate – he had much to learn but a great deal of company potential and I wanted him kept on the job. So I let him down lightly.

'He tried, back in that boardroom, but Shelford shouted him down. He's a good man and learning fast. It's just that he works too hard.'

'Oh yes?' Geddes was acidly polite. 'Is that possible?'

'It surely is. He should take out more time for his social life. He should get around more, do some drinking: drinking and listening. How the hell do you think I got all the dope I've just given you? I got it by damn near contracting cirrhosis of the liver drinking with a lot of boozy old colonial types who know more about what makes Nyala tick than the President himself. They're disillusioned, those men. Some have lived in Nyala all their lives but they know they'll always be on the outside because their skins are white. They're there by grace

50

and favour now, discounted by the country's new masters, but they look and listen. And they *know*.'

'That's a précis of a Somerset Maugham story,' said Geddes sardonically. 'Does Sutherland know all this? Has he got the picture now?'

I shook my head. 'I thought I'd have a word with you first. Meantime I wouldn't be too surprised if he doesn't put some of it together for himself, while I'm away. I jumped on him a bit to frighten him but I don't think he's the man to panic.'

Geddes pondered this and clearly approved. Presently he said, 'Is there anything else I ought to know?'

'Kigonde's used half the army to help the rig along its first journey. I'll tell you more about that later; it's off to a good start. And I believe he's moved an infantry brigade up to Bir Oassa.'

'Quite natural to guard an oilfield. Does he expect sabotage?'

'The Government is leaning heavily on our operation for propagation purposes, as you'll see in my full report. There was the damnedest celebration you ever did see when the first transformer left Port Luard. If it should *not* get to Bir Oassa, or if anything happened to it up there, the Government would be discredited after all the hoopla they've made. Which makes it a prime target for the opposition.'

'Christ!' Geddes was fully alert for the first time. 'Have you told Kemp all about this?'

'No, I haven't. The guy is under a lot of strain. I had a feeling that if any more piled up on him he might fall apart. The man to tell, the man who can take it, I think, is Geoffrey Wingstead.'

'He'll be down here tomorrow, to hear your report to the board, Neil. Then he's flying out to Nyala.'

'Good. I want time with him. In fact, I'd like to fix it so that we can go out together. Why the hell did you pick this shoestring operation in the first place?'

Geddes said, 'They could do very well. Geoff has a good

51

head on his shoulders, and a first-rate team. And their figures tally: they've cut it to the bone, admittedly, but there's still a lot in it for them. They're building more rigs, did you know that?'

'One more rig. I met the guy who developed their prototype. He seems fast enough on the ball, but what happens if something goes wrong with Number One? Collapse of the entire operation, for God's sake.'

'Wingstead has a second rig on lease from a Dutch company which he's planning to send out there. He and Kemp and Hammond have been pushing big loads all their lives. They won't let us down.'

He thought for a moment, then said, 'I'll arrange things so that you go back out with Wingstead, certainly. In fact, I'll give both of you the company jet. It's at Stansted right now, and you can get away tomorrow, after the briefing.'

It was the speed of his arrangements that made me realize that the prickle at the back of his mind had turned into a case of raging hives.

5

Port Luard was cooler when we got back – about one degree cooler – but the temperature went down sharply when I walked into John Sutherland's office. It was evident that he'd been hoping I'd disappear into the wide blue yonder never to return, and when he saw me you could have packaged him and used him as a refrigeration plant.

I held up a hand placatingly and said, 'Not my idea to turn around so fast – blame Mister Geddes. For my money you could have this damn place to yourself.'

'You're welcome, of course,' he said insincerely.

'Let's not kid each other,' I said as I took a can of beer from his office refrigerator. 'I'm as welcome as acne on a guy's first date. What's new?'

My friendly approach bothered him. He hadn't known when to expect me and he'd been braced for trouble when he did. 'Nothing, really. Everything has been going along smoothly.' His tone still implied that it would cease to do so forthwith.

It was time to sweet-talk him. 'Geddes is very pleased about the way you're handling things here, by the way.'

For a moment he looked almost alarmed. The idea of Geddes being pleased about anything was odd enough to frighten anybody. Praise from him was so rare as to be nonexistent, and I didn't let Sutherland know that it had originated with me. 'When you left you implied that all was far from well,' Sutherland said. 'You never said what the trouble was.'

'You should know. You started it at the meeting in London.'

'I did?' I saw him chasing around in his mind for exactly what he'd said at that meeting.

'About the rumours of tribal unrest,' I said helpfully. 'Got a glass? I like to see my beer when I'm drinking it.'

'Of course.' He found one for me.

'You were right on the mark there. Of course we know you can't run the Bir Oassa job and chase down things like that at the same time. That was Shelford's job, and he let us all down. So someone had to look into it and Geddes picked me – and you proved right all down the line.' I didn't give him time to think too deeply about that one. I leaned forward and said as winningly as I knew how, 'I'm sorry if I was a little abrupt just before I left. That goddamn phoney victory parade left me a bit frazzled, and I'm not used to coping with this lot the way you are. If I said anything out of line I apologize.'

He was disarmed, as he was intended to be. 'That's quite all right. As a matter of fact I've been thinking about what you said – about the need for contingency plans. I've been working on a scheme.'

'Great,' I said expansively. 'Like to have a look at it sometime. Right now I have a lot else to do. I brought someone out with me that I'd like you to meet. Geoff Wingstead, the owner of Wyvern Haulage. Can you join us for dinner?'

'You should have told me. He'll need accommodation.'

'It's fixed, John. He's at the hotel.' I gently let him know that he wasn't the only one who could pull strings. 'He's going to go up and join the rig in a day or so, but I'll be around town for a bit longer before I pay them a visit. I'd like a full briefing from you. I'm willing to bet you've got a whole lot to tell me.'

'Yes, I have. Some of it is quite hot stuff, Neil.'

Sutherland was all buddies again, and bursting to tell me what I already knew, which is just what I'd been hoping for. I didn't think I'd told him too many lies. The truth is only one way of looking at a situation; there are many others.

For the next few days I nursed Sutherland along. His contingency plan was good, if lacking in imagination, but it improved as we went along. That was his main trouble, a lack of imagination, the inability to ask, 'What if . . .?' I am not knocking him particularly; he was good at his job but incapable of expanding the job around him, and without that knack he wasn't going to go much further. I have a theory about men like Sutherland: they're like silly putty. If you take silly putty and hit it with a hammer it will shatter, but handle it gently and it can be moulded into any shape. The trouble is that if you then leave it it will slump and flow back into its original shape. That's why the manipulators, like me, get three times Sutherland's pay.

Not that I regarded myself as the Great Svengali, because I've been manipulated myself in my time by men like Geddes, the arch manipulator, so God knows what he's worth before taxes.

Anyway I gentled Sutherland along. I took him to the Luard Club (he had never thought about joining) and let him loose among the old sweaty types who were primed to drop him nuggets of information. Sure enough, he'd come back and tell me something else that I already knew. 'Gee, is that so?' I'd say. 'That could put a crimp in your contingency plans, couldn't it?'

He would smile confidently. 'It's nothing I can't fix,' he would say, and he'd be right. He wasn't a bad fixer. At the end of ten days he was all squared away, convinced that it was all his own idea, and much clearer in his head about the politics around him. He also had another conviction – that this chap Mannix wasn't so bad, after all, for an American that is. I didn't disillusion him.

What slightly disconcerted me was Geoff Wingstead. He stayed in Port Luard for a few days, doing his own homework before flying up to join the rig, and in that short time he also put two and two together, on his own, and remarkably accurately. What's more, I swear that he saw clear through my little ploy with Sutherland and to my chagrin I got the impression that he approved. I didn't like people to be that bright. He impressed me more all the time and I found that he got the same sense of enjoyment out of the business that I did, and that's a rare and precious trait. He was young, smart and

55

energetic, and I wasn't sorry that he was in another company to my own: he'd make damned tough opposition. And I liked him too much for rivalry.

Getting news back from the rig was difficult. Local telephone lines were often out of action and our own cab radios had a limited range. One morning, though, John Sutherland had managed a long call and had news for me as soon as I came into the office.

'They're on schedule. I've put it on the map. Look here. They're halfway in time but less than halfway in distance. And they'll slow up more now because they have to climb to the plateau. Oh, and Geoff Wingstead is flying back here today. He has to arrange to send a water bowser up there. Seems the local water is often too contaminated to use for drinking.'

I could have told Geoff that before he started and was a little surprised that he had only just found out. I decided that I wanted to go and see the rig for myself, in case there was any other little detail he didn't know about. I was about due to go back to London soon, and rather wanted one more fling upcountry before doing so.

I studied the map. 'This town – Kodowa – just ahead of them. It's got an airstrip. Any chance of renting a car there?'

He grimaced. 'I shouldn't think so. It's only a small place, about five thousand population. And if you could get a car there it would be pretty well clapped out. The airstrip is privately owned; it belongs to a planters' cooperative.'

I measured distances. 'Maybe we should have a company car stationed there, and arrange for use of the airstrip. It would help if anyone has to get up there in a hurry. See to it, would you, John? As it is I'll have to fly to Lasulu and then drive nearly three hundred miles. I'll arrange to take one of Wyvern's spare chaps up with me to spell me driving.' I knew better than to set out on my own in that bleak territory.

I saw Wingstead on his return and we had a long talk. He was reasonably happy about his company's progress and the logistics seemed to be working out well, but he was as wary as a cat about the whole political situation. As I said, he was remarkably acute in his judgements. I asked if he was going back to England.

'Not yet, at any rate,' he told me. 'I have some work to do here, then I'll rejoin the rig for a bit. I like to keep a finger on the pulse. Listen, Neil . . .'

'You want something?' I prompted.

'I want you to put Basil Kemp completely in the picture. He doesn't know the score and he may not take it from me. Why should he? We're both new to Africa, new to this country, and he'll brush off my fears, but he'll accept your opinion. He needs to know more about the political situation.'

'I wouldn't call Kemp exactly complacent myself,' I said.

'That's the trouble. He's got so many worries of his own that he hasn't room for mine – unless he can be convinced they're real. You're going up there, I'm told. Lay it on the line for him, please.'

I agreed, not without a sense of relief. It was high time that Kemp knew the wider issues involved, and nothing I had heard lately had made me any less uneasy about the possible future of Nyala. The next morning I picked up Ritchie Thorpe, one of the spare Wyvern men, and Max Otterman flew us up to Lasulu. From there we drove inland along that fantastic road that thrust into the heart of the country. After Ofanwe had it built it had been underused and neglected. The thick rain forest had encroached and the huge trees had thrust their roots under it to burst the concrete. Then came the oil strike and now it was undergoing a fair amount of punishment, eroding from above to meet the erosion from below. Not that the traffic was heavy in the sense of being dense, but some damn big loads were being taken north. Our transformer was merely the biggest so far.

The traffic varied from bullock carts with nerve-wracking squeaking wheels plodding stolidly along at two miles an hour to sixty-tonners and even larger vehicles. Once we came across a real giant parked by the roadside while the crew ate a meal.

57

It carried an oil drilling tower lying on its side, whole and entire, and must have weighed upwards of a hundred tons.

I pulled in and had a chat with the head driver. He was a Russian and very proud of his rig. We talked in a mixture of bad English and worse French, and he demonstrated what it would do, a function new to me but not to Ritchie. Apparently it was designed to move in soft sand and he could inflate and deflate all the tyres by pushing buttons while in the cab. When travelling over soft sand the tyres would be deflated to spread the load. He told me that in these conditions the fully loaded rig would put less pressure on the ground per square inch than the foot of a camel. I was properly appreciative and we parted amicably.

It was a long drive and we were both tired and dusty when we finally came across Wyvern Transport. By now we had passed through the rainforest belt and were entering scrubland, the trees giving way to harsh thorny bush and the ground strewn with withering gourd-carrying vines. Dust was everywhere, and the road edges were almost totally rotted away; we slalomed endlessly to avoid the potholes. We found the rig parked by the roadside and the hydraulics had been let down so that the load rested on the ground instead of being taken up on the bogie springs. They had obviously stopped for the night, which surprised us – night driving at their speed was quite feasible and much cooler and normally less of a strain than daywork.

I pulled up and looked around. Of the men I could see I knew only one by name: McGrath, the big Irishman who had driven the lead tractor in the parade through Port Luard. Ritchie got out of the car, thanked me for the ride up and went off to join his mates. I called McGrath over.

'Hi there. Mister Kemp around?' I asked.

McGrath pointed up the road. 'There's a bridge about a mile along. He's having a look at it.'

'Thanks.' I drove along slowly and thought the convoy looked like an oversized gypsy camp. The commissary wagon was opened up and a couple of men were cooking. A little further along were the other trucks, including the big one with the airlift gear, and then the camp of Sadiq and his men, very neat and military. Sadiq got to his feet as I drove up but with the light fading I indicated that I would see him on my return from the bridge, and went on past. I saw and approved of the fact that the fuel truck was parked on its own, well away from all the others, but made a mental note to check that it was guarded.

The road had been blasted through a low ridge here and beyond the ridge was a river. I pulled off the road short of the bridge and parked next to Kemp's Land Rover. I could see him in the distance, walking halfway across the bridge, accompanied by Hammond. I waved and they quickened their pace.

When they came up to me I thought that Kemp looked better than he had done in Port Luard. The lines of his face fell in more placid folds and he wasn't so tired. Obviously he was happier actually doing a job than arranging for it to be done. Ben Hammond, by his side, hadn't changed at all. He still had his gamecock strut and his air of defensive wariness. Some little men feel that they have a lot to be wary about.

'Hello there,' I said. 'I just thought I'd drop by for a coffee.'

Kemp grinned and shook my hand, but Hammond said, 'Checking up on us, are you? Mr Wingstead's just been up here, you know.'

Clearly he was saying that where Geoff had gone, no man need go after. His voice told me that he thought a lot of his boss, which pleased me. I sometimes wondered if I was as transparent to other people as they appeared to me.

I jerked my thumb back up the road. 'Sure I'm checking. Do you know what that transporter is worth? Landed at Port Luard it was declared at one million, forty-two thousand, nine hundred and eighty-six pounds and five pence.' I grinned to take the sting out of it. 'I still haven't figured out what the five pence is for. If it was yours, wouldn't you want to know if it was in safe hands?'

Hammond looked startled. Kemp said, 'Take it easy, Ben,'

59

which I thought was a nice reversal of roles. 'Mister Mannix is quite entitled to come up here, and he's welcome any time. Sorry if Ben's a bit edgy – we have problems.'

I wasn't a bit surprised to hear it, but dutifully asked what they were. Kemp held out a lump of concrete. 'I kicked that out with the toe of my boot. I didn't have to kick hard, either.'

I took the lump and rubbed it with my thumb. It was friable and bits dropped off. 'I'd say that someone used a mite too much sand in the mix.' I pointed to the bridge. 'Milner said the bridges would prove dicey. Is this the worst?'

Kemp shook his head. 'Oh no. This isn't too bad at all. The really tricky one is way up there, miles ahead yet. This one is run-of-the-mill. Just a little shaky, that's all.' He and Hammond exchanged rueful smiles. 'It's too risky to move in the dark and there's only half an hour of daylight left. We'll take her across at first light. Anyway it will be our first full night stop for nearly a week, good for the lads.'

I said, 'I came just in time to see the fun. Mind if I stick around? I brought Ritchie Thorpe up with me.'

'Good show. We can use him. We'll rig a couple of extra bunks after we've eaten,' Kemp said, climbing into his car. Hammond joined him and I followed them back to camp, but stopped to say a few polite and appreciative things to Sadiq on the way. He assured me that any labour necessary for strengthening the bridge would be found very quickly, and I left him, marvelling at the self-assurance that a uniform lends a man.

My mind was in top gear as I thought about the bridge. Someone had made a bit of extra profit on the contract when it was built, and it was going to be interesting to watch the passage of the rig the next day. From a safe vantage point, of course. But if this bridge was run of the mill, what the hell was the tricky one going to be like?

I laid my plate on one side. 'Good chow.'

There was humour in Kemp's voice. 'Not *haute cuisine*, but we survive.'

Two of the tractors were parked side by side and we sat under an awning rigged between them. Kemp was certainly more relaxed and I wondered how best to take advantage of the fact. We weren't alone – several of the others had joined us. Obviously Kemp didn't believe in putting a distance between himself and the men, but I wanted to get him alone for a chat. I leaned over and dropped my voice. 'If you can find a couple of glasses, how about a Scotch?'

He too spoke quietly. 'No thanks. I prefer to stick to the camp rules, if you don't mind. We could settle for another beer, though.' As he said this he got up and disappeared into the night, returning in a moment with a four-pack of beer. I rose and took his arm, steering him away from the makeshift dining room. 'A word with you, Basil,' I said. 'Where can we go?'

Presently we were settled in a quiet corner with our backs up against two huge tyres, the blessedly cool night wind on our faces, and an ice cold can of beer apiece.

'You've got it made,' I said, savouring the quietness. 'How do you keep this cold?'

He laughed. 'There's a diesel generator on the rig for the lights. If you're already carrying three hundred tons a ten cubic foot refrigerator isn't much more of a burden. We have a twenty cubic foot deepfreeze, too. The cook says we're having lobster tails tomorrow night.'

'I forget the scale of this thing.'

'You wouldn't if you were pushing it around.'

I drank some beer. It was cold and pleasantly bitter. A little casual conversation was in order first. 'You married?'

'Oh yes. I have a wife and two kids in England: six and four, both boys. How about you?'

'I tried, but it didn't take. A man in my job doesn't spend enough time at home to hang his hat up, and women don't like that as a rule.'

'Yes, indeed.' His voice showed that he felt the same way.

'How long since you were home?'

'About two months. I've been surveying this damned road.

61

I reckon it'll be a while before I'm home again.'

I said, 'Up at Bir Oassa the government is just finishing a big concrete airstrip, big enough for heavy transports. It's just about to go into operation, we've been told, though we're not sure what "just about" means.'

Kemp said, 'No parades up there though, with no-one to see them.'

'Right. Well, when it's ready we'll be flying in the expensive bits that aren't too heavy, like the turbine shafts. There'll be quite a lot of coming and going and it wouldn't surprise me if there wasn't room for a guy to take a trip back to England once in a while. That applies to your crew as well, of course.'

'That's splendid – we'd all appreciate it. I'll have to make up a roster.' He was already perking up at the thought, and I marvelled all over again at what domesticity does for some men.

'How did you get into heavy haulage?' I asked him.

'It wasn't so much getting into it as being born into it. My old man was always on the heavy side – he pushed around tank transporters in the war – and I'm a chip off the old block.'

'Ever handled anything as big as this before?'

'Oh yes. I've done one a bit bigger than this for the Central Electricity Generating Board at home. Of course, conditions weren't exactly the same, but just as difficult, in their way. There are more buildings to knock corners off in Britain, and a whole lot more bureaucracy to get around too.'

'Was that with Wyvern?'

'No, before its time.' He knew I was pumping him gently and didn't seem to mind. 'I was with one of the big outfits then.'

I drank the last of my beer. 'You really *are* Wyvern Transport, aren't you?'

'Yes. Together with Ben and Geoff Wingstead. We'd all been in the business before, and when we got together it seemed like a good idea. Sometimes I'm not so sure.' I saw him wave his hand, a dim gesture in the darkness, and heard the slight bitter touch in his voice. I already knew that financially this was a knife edge operation and I didn't want to spoil Kemp's mood by raking up any economic dirt, but I felt I could get a few more answers out of him without pressing too hard.

He carried on without my prompting him. 'We each came into a little money, one way or another – mine was an inheritance. Ben had ideas for modifying current rigs and Geoff and Ben had worked together before. Geoff's our real ideas man: not only the financial end, he's into every angle. But if we hadn't landed this contract I don't think we'd have got off the ground.'

I had had my own doubts about giving this enormously expensive and difficult job to a firm new to the market but I didn't want to express them to Kemp. He went on, though, filling me in with details; the costly airlift gear, which they only realized was necessary after their tender had been accepted, was rented from the CEGB. Two of the tractors were second-hand, the others bought on the never-never and as yet not fully paid for. The tender, already as low as possible to enable them to land the job, was now seen to be quite unrealistic and they did not expect to make anything out of the Nyalan operation: but they had every hope that a successful completion would bring other contracts to their doorstep. It was midsummer madness, and it might work.

I realized that it was late, and that I hadn't yet broached the subject of security or danger. Too late in fact to go into the whole thing now, but I could at least pave the way; Kemp's practical problems had rendered him oblivious to possible out-side interference, and in any case he was used to working in countries where political problems were solved over the negotiation table, and not by armies.

'How are you getting on with Captain Sadiq?' I asked.

'No trouble. In fact he's quite helpful. I'll make him into a good road boss yet.'

'Had any problems so far? Apart from the road itself, that is.'

'Just the usual thing of crowd control through the villages. Sadiq's very good at that. He's overefficient really; puts out a guard every time we stop, scouts ahead, very busy playing soldiers generally.' He gestured into the night. 'If you walk down there you'll stand a chance of getting a bullet in you unless you speak up loud and clear. I've had to warn my chaps about it. Road transport in the UK was never like this.'

'He's not really here just as a traffic cop,' I said. 'He is guarding you, or, more to the point, he's guarding the rig and the convoy. There's always a possibility that someone might try a bit of sabotage. So you keep your eyes open too, and pass that word down the line to your men, Basil.'

I knew he was staring at me. 'Who'd want to sabotage us? No-one else wanted this job.'

He was still thinking in terms of commercial rivalry and I was mildly alarmed at his political naïvety. 'Look, Basil, I'd like to put you in the picture, and I think Ben Hammond too. But it's late and you've a major job to do in the morning. It's nothing urgent, nothing to fret about. Next time we stop for a break I'll get you both up to date, OK?'

'Right you are, if you say so.' I sensed his mind slipping away; mention of the next day's task had set him thinking about it, and I knew I should leave him alone to marshall his ideas.

'I'll say good night,' I said. 'I guess you'll want to think about your next obstacle course.'

He stood up. 'We'll cross that bridge when we come to it,' he said sardonically. 'Sleep well. Your bunk is rigged over there, by the way. I sleep on top of one of the tractors: less risk of snakes that way.'

'I know how you feel,' I grinned. 'But with me it's scorpions. Good night.'

I strolled in the night air over to the rig and stood looking up at the great slab of the transformer. Over one million pounds' worth of material was being trundled precariously through Africa by a company on the verge of going bankrupt, with a civil war possibly about to erupt in its path, and what the hell was I going to do about it?

I decided to sleep on it.

6

Everybody was up early in the dim light before dawn. I breakfasted with the crew, standing in line at the chuck wagon. The food was washed down with hot, strong, sweet, milky tea which tasted coppery and which they called 'gunfire'.

'Why gunfire?' I queried.

'That's what they call it in the British Army. The Army fights on this stuff,' I was told.

I grinned. 'If they could stomach this they'd be ready to face anything.'

'It's better than bloody Coca-Cola,' someone said, and everybody laughed.

After breakfast there was a great deal of activity. I went in search of Captain Sadiq, and found him sitting in his command car wearing earphones. He saw me approaching and held up his hand in warning as he scribbled on a notepad he held on his knee. Then he called to a sergeant who came trotting over. Sadiq took off the earphones and handed them to the sergeant. Only then did he come around the car to meet me. 'Good morning, Mister Mannix.'

'Good morning, Captain. Sorry I was in a hurry last night. Any problems? Mister Kemp says he is very gratified by all your help.'

He smiled at that. 'No problems at all, sir,' he said, but it was a brushoff. He looked deeply concerned and abstracted.

The sun was just rising as I heard an engine start up. It had a deep roar and sounded like one of the big tractors. A small crowd of curious onlookers had materialized from nowhere and were being pushed back by Sadiq's men. Small boys skylarked about and evaded the soldiers with ease.

I indicated the crowd. 'These people are up early. Do you have much of this kind of thing?'

'The people, they are always with us.' I wondered for a moment whether that was an intended parody of a biblical quotation. He pointed. 'These come from a small village about a mile over there. They are nothing.'

One of the military trucks fired up its engine and I watched it pull out. Mounted on the back was a recoilless gun. The range of those things wasn't particularly great but they packed a hell of a wallop and could be fired from a light vehicle. One thing you had to remember was not to stand behind when they fired. 'Nice piece of artillery,' I said. 'I haven't seen one of those since Korea.'

Sadiq smiled noncommittally. I sensed that he was itching for me to be off.

'Is there anything I can do for you, Captain?' I wanted to see how far he'd let me go before he pulled rank on me, or tried to. But outside influences had their say instead.

'Nothing at all, Mister Man . . .'

His words were drowned as three jets streaked overhead, making us both start. They were flying low, and disappeared to the south. I turned to Sadiq and raised my eyebrows. 'We are quite close to a military airfield,' he said. His attempt at a nonchalant attitude fooled neither of us.

I thanked him and walked away, then turned my head to see him already putting on the earphones again. Maybe he liked hi-fi.

I wanted to relieve myself so I pushed a little way into the bushes by the side of the road. It was quite thick but I came across a sort of channel in the undergrowth and was able to push along quite easily. What bothered me was that it was quite straight. Then I damn near fell down a hole, teetered for a moment on the edge and recovered by catching hold of a branch and running a thorn into my hand. I cursed, then looked at the hole with interest. It had been newly dug and at the bottom

66

there were marks in the soil. The spoil from the hole had been piled up round it and then covered with scrub. If you had to have a hole at all this was one of the more interesting types, one I hadn't seen since I was in the army.

I dropped into it and looked back the way I had come. The channel I had come along was clearly defined right up to the road edge, where it was screened by the lightest of cover, easy to see through from the shady side. Captain Sadiq was clearly on the ball, a real professional. This was a concealed machine gun pit with a prepared field of fire which commanded a half mile length of road. Out of curiosity I drummed up what I had been taught when Uncle Sam tried to make me into a soldier, and figured out where Sadiq would have put his mortars. After a few minutes of plunging about in the scrub I came across the emplacement and stared at it thoughtfully. I didn't know if it was such a good idea because it made out Sadiq to be a textbook soldier, working to the rules. That's all right providing the guys on the other side haven't read the same book.

When I got back to the rig Kemp hailed me with some impatience, shading into curiosity. I was dusty and scratched, and already sweating.

'We're ready to move,' he said. 'Ride along with anyone you like.' Except me, his tone added, and I could hardly blame him. He'd have enough to do without answering questions from visiting firemen.

'Just a minute,' I said. 'Captain Sadiq appears to be cemented to his radio. How long has that been going on?'

Kemp shrugged. 'I don't know – all morning. He does his job and I do mine.'

'Don't you sense that he's uneasy?' I asked with concern. I'd seldom met a man so oblivious to outside events as Kemp. 'By the way, what did you make of those planes?'

'They say there's an airfield somewhere about. Maybe they were just curious about the convoy. Look, Neil, I have to get on. I'll talk to you later.' He waved to Hammond, who drove up in the Land Rover, and they were off in a small cloud of dust. During my absence the rig and most of the rest of the convoy including my car had moved off, so I swung myself on to the chuck wagon and hitched a lift down to where the others were grouped around the approach to the bridge.

The scene was fascinating. Kemp was using only one tractor to take the rig across the bridge and it was already in place. Another tractor had crossed and waited on the far side. The rig was fitted with its airlift skirts and looked rather funny; they seemed to take away the brute masculinity of the thing and gave it the incongruous air of one of those beskirted Greek soldiers you see on guard in Athens. Though no doubt Kemp, who had been outraged by the bunting in Port Luard, saw nothing odd about it. Behind it was the airlift truck to which it was connected by a flexible umbilicus. Through this the air was rammed by four big engines.

If Kemp was nervous he didn't show it. He was telling the crew what they were to do and how they were to do it. He was sparing of words but most of this team had worked with him before and needed little instruction. He put the Irishman, McGrath, in the tractor and Ben Hammond and himself on the rig.

'No-one else on the bridge until we're clear across,' he said. 'And keep that air moving. We don't want to fall down on our bums halfway across.' It brought a slight ripple of amusement.

McGrath revved the tractor engine and there came a roar from the airlift truck as one after another the engines started up. A cloud of dust erupted from beneath the rig as the loose debris was blown aside by the air blast. I knew enough not to expect the rig to become airborne, but it did seem to rise very slightly on its springs as the weight was taken up from the axles and spread evenly.

The noise was tremendous and I saw Kemp with a microphone close to his lips. The tractor moved, at first infinitesimally, so that one wasn't sure that it had moved at all, then a very little faster. McGrath was a superb driver: I doubt that many people could have judged so nicely the exact pressure to put on an accelerator in order to shift a four hundred and thirty-ton load so smoothly.

The front wheels of the tractor crossed the bitumen expansion joint which marked the beginning of the bridge proper. Kemp moved quickly from one side of the control cab to the other, looking forwards and backwards to check that the rig and the tractor were in perfect alignment. Behind the rig the air umbilicus lengthened as it was paid out.

I estimated that the rig was moving at most a quarter of a mile an hour; it took about six minutes before the whole length of the combine was entirely supported by the bridge. If you were nervous now was the time to hold your breath. I held mine.

Then above the uproar of the airlift engines and the rush of air I heard a faint yell, and someone tugged at my arm. I turned and saw Sadiq's sergeant, his face distorted as he shouted something at me. At my lack of comprehension he pulled my arm again and pointed back along the road leading up to the bridge. I turned and saw a column of vehicles coming up: jeeps and motorcycles at the front and the looming, ugly snouted silhouettes of tanks behind them.

I ran towards them with the sergeant alongside me. As soon as the volume of noise dropped enough to speak and be heard I pulled up and snapped, 'Where's Captain Sadiq?'

The sergeant threw out his hand towards the river. 'On the other side.'

'Christ! Go and get him – fast!'

The sergeant looked dismayed. 'How do I do that?'

'On your feet. Run! There's room for you to pass. Wait. If Mister Kemp, if the road boss sees you he may stop. You signal him to carry on. Like this.' I windmilled my arm, pointing forwards, and saw that the sergeant understood what to do. 'Now go!'

He turned and ran back towards the bridge and I carried on towards the armoured column, my heartbeat noticeably quicker. It's not given to many men to stop an army single-handed, but I'd been given so little time to think out the implications that I acted without much reflection. A leading command car braked to a stop, enveloping me in a cloud of dust, and an angry voice shouted something in Kinguru, or so I supposed. I waved the dust away and shouted, 'I'm sorry, I don't understand. Do you speak English, please?'

An officer stood up in the passenger seat of the open command car, leaning over the windscreen and looking down at the bridge with unbelieving eyes. When he turned his gaze on me his eyes were like flint and his voice gravelly. 'Yes, I speak English. What is going on there?'

'We're taking that load across the bridge. It's going up to the new power plant at Bir Oassa.'

'Get it off there!' he shouted.

'That's what we're doing,' I said equably.

'I mean move it faster,' he shouted again, convulsed with anger. 'We have no time to waste.'

'It's moving as fast as is safe.'

'Safe!' He looked back at his column, then again at me. 'You don't know what that word means, Mister Englishman.' He shouted a string of orders to a motorcyclist who wheeled his bike around and went roaring back up the road. I watched it stop at the leading tank and saw the tank commander lean down from the turret to listen. The tank cut out of the column and ground to a rattling halt alongside the command car. The officer shouted a command and I saw the turret swivel and the barrel of the gun drop slightly.

I was sweating harder now, and drier in the mouth, and I wished to God Sadiq would show up. I looked round hopefully, but of Sadiq or any of his military crowd there was no sign.

'Hey, Captain,' I shouted, giving him as flattering a rank as possible without knowing for sure. 'What are you doing? There are four hundred and thirty tons on that bridge.'

His face cracked into a sarcastic smile. 'I will get it to go faster.'

I sized him up. He was obviously immune to reason, so I would have to counter his threat with a bigger one. I said,

'Captain, if you put a shell even near that rig you'll be likely to lose it and the whole bridge with it. It's worth a few million pounds to your government and Major General Kigonde is personally handling its wellbeing. And I don't think he'd like you to wreck the bridge either.'

He looked baffled and then came back with a countermove of his own. 'I will not fire on the bridge. I will fire into the trucks and the men on the river bank if that thing does not go faster. You tell them.'

His arm was upraised and I knew that if he dropped it fast the tank would fire. I said, 'You mean the airlift truck? That would make things much worse.'

'Airlift? What is that?'

'A kind of hovercraft.' Would he understand that? No matter: at least I could try to blind him with science. 'It is run by the truck just off the bridge and it's the only way of getting the rig across the bridge. You damage it, or do anything to stop our operation and you'll be stuck here permanently instead of only for the next half-hour. Unless you've brought your own bridge with you.'

His arm wavered uncertainly and I pressed on. 'I think you had better consult your superior about this. If you lose the bridge you won't be popular.'

He glared at me and then at last his arm came down, slowly. He dropped into his seat and grabbed the microphone in front of him. The little hairs on the back of my neck lay down as I turned to see what was happening at the bridge.

Sadiq's troops had materialized behind our men and trucks, but in a loose and nonbelligerent order. They were after all not supposed to protect us from their own side, assuming these troops were still their own side. Beyond them the rig still inched its way painfully along as Kemp stuck to the job in hand. Sadiq was standing on the running board of one of his own trucks and it roared up the road towards us, smothering me in yet another dust bath on its arrival. Before it had stopped Sadiq had jumped down and made straight for the officer in the command car.

71

Captain Whoosit was spoiling for a fight and Sadiq didn't outrank him, but before a row could develop another command car arrived and from it stepped a man who could only have been the battalion commander, complete with Sam Browne belt in the British tradition.

He looked bleakly around him, studied the bridge through binoculars, and then conferred with Sadiq, who was standing rigidly to attention. At one point Mr Big asked a question and jabbed a finger towards me. I approached uninvited as Sadiq was beginning to explain my presence. 'I can speak for myself, Captain. Good morning, Colonel. I'm Neil Mannix, representing British Electric. That's our transformer down there.'

He asked no further questions. I thought that he already knew all about us, as any good commander should. 'You must get it out of our way quickly,' he said.

'It's moving all the time,' I said reasonably.

The Colonel asked, 'Does the driver have a radio?'

'Yes, sir,' said Sadiq. A pity; I might have said the opposite.

'Talk to him. Tell him to move faster. Use my radio.' He indicated his own command car, but as Sadiq moved to comply I said, 'Let me talk to him, Colonel. He will accept my instructions easier.'

'Very well, Mister Mannix. I will listen.'

I waited while Sadiq got on net with Kemp and then took the mike. 'Basil, this is Neil Mannix here. Do you read me? Over.'

'Yes, Neil. What's going on back there? Over.'

'Listen and don't speak. There is an army detachment here which needs to use the bridge urgently. I assume you are moving at designated speed? It will be necessary for you to increase to the –'

The Colonel interrupted me. 'What is this designated speed?'

'Hold it. Over. It works out about a mile an hour, Colonel.' I ignored his stricken face and went on into the mike, 'Basil? Increase if necessary. How long do you estimate as of now? Over.'

'Fifteen minutes, perhaps twenty. Over.'

Taking his cue, Kemp was giving answers only. He could

pick up clues pretty smartly. There was no such thing as a designated speed and Kemp knew this. I went on, 'Get it down to no more than fifteen, ten if possible. Over.'

I was praying for an interruption and for once I got lucky. Sadiq's military unit had got restless and several vehicles, including those carrying the guns, started down the road towards us. The commander turned alertly to see what was going on. In that moment, with nobody listening except the Colonel's driver, I said hastily, 'Basil, if you don't get the hell off that bridge we'll have shells coming up our ass. These guys are trigger-happy. Go man go. Acknowledge formally. Over.'

It was all I had time for, but it was enough. The Colonel was back, looking more irritated than ever, just in time to hear Kemp's voice saying, 'Message understood, Neil, and will be acted upon. Going faster. Out.'

I handed the microphone back to the driver and said, 'That's it, Colonel. He'll do the best he can. You should be on your way in a quarter of an hour. I'll arrange to hold all the rest of our stuff until you're through.'

The muscles round his jaw bunched up and he nodded stiffly, casting a quick glance skywards, and then began snapping orders to his Captain who got busy on the radio. All down the line there was a stir of activity, and with interest and some alarm I noted that machine guns were sprouting from turret tops, all pointing skywards. I remembered the jets that had gone over and wondered what Air Chief Marshal Semangala, or whatever his title might be, was doing just at that moment. Away in the distance I saw the four barrels of a 20-millimetre AA quickfirer rotating.

I said, 'Has a war broken out, Colonel?'

'Exercises,' he said briefly. 'You may go now.'

It was a curt dismissal but I wasn't sorry to get it. I joined Sadiq and we drove back to our lines. I passed the word for everyone to remain clear of the bridge and to let the army through, once the rig was safely on the other side and uncoupled from its umbilicus. Everyone was bursting with curiosity and

73

the tension caused by the rig's river passage had noticeably increased, which wasn't surprising. But I had little to tell them and presently everyone fell silent, just watching and waiting.

Seventeen minutes later the rig was clear of the bridge and safe on firm land again. Things are comparative, and after the bridge even the most friable and potholed road would seem like a doddle, at least for a time. The airlift truck was uncoupled, its hoses stowed, and it was moved back from the bridge approach. The Colonel came towards us in his staff car.

'Thank you,' he said abruptly. Graciousness was not a quality often found out here and this was the nearest we'd get to it. He spoke into the mike and his leading motorcycles roared off across the bridge.

I said, 'Mind a bit of advice, Colonel?'

He speared me with dark eyes. 'Well?'

'That bridge really isn't too safe: it's been cheaply made. I'd space out my tanks crossing it, if I were you.'

He nodded shortly. 'Thank you, Mister Mannix.'

'My pleasure.'

He peered at me uncertainly and then signed to his driver to go ahead. As he drove off already talking into his microphone, I sighed for the days of the mythical bush telegraph. The battalion that followed was mostly armour, tanks and a battery of self-propelling guns, with a few truckloads of infantry for close defence work. Even as small a unit as a battalion takes up an awful lot of road space and it was twenty dusty minutes before the rearguard had crossed. I watched them climb the hill on the other side of the river and then said, 'Right, you guys. Let's go and join Mister Kemp, shall we?'

As the convoy started I turned to Sadiq. 'And then, Captain, perhaps you'll be good enough to find out from your driver, and then tell me, what the hell is going on. I know you'll have had him radio-eavesdropping right from the beginning.'

And then for some reason we both glanced quickly skywards.

7

Both Kemp and Hammond looked shaken. I couldn't blame them; nobody likes being at the wrong end of a big gun. Hammond, as could be expected, was belligerent about it. 'This wasn't allowed for in any contract, Mannix. What are you going to do about it?'

'It's hardly Neil's fault,' said Kemp.

'I am going to do something about it,' I said. 'Something I should have done before this. I'm going to put you two properly in the picture.'

'Was that what you said you wanted to talk about?' Kemp asked, giving me a chance to cover myself. I nodded. 'Overdue,' I said. 'But first I want another word with Captain Sadiq. Want to come along?'

Kemp and Hammond conferred briefly, then Kemp said, 'Yes. Everyone's a bit jittery still. We shouldn't move on until we know the situation. I wish to God Geoff was here.'

'We'll try to contact him,' I said. I didn't see what he could do but if his presence was enough to calm his partners' fears it would be a big bonus. We found Sadiq, as expected, glued to his earphones in his car, and according to the usual ritual he handed them to his sergeant before joining us. I said, 'All right, Captain. What's the story?'

His voice was neutral. 'You heard Colonel Hussein. The Army is holding manoeuvres.'

I stared at him. 'Don't give us that crap. No army captain is going to threaten to shell a civilian vehicle during war games. He'd be scrubbing latrines next. And that was damn nearly more than a threat.'

Kemp said, 'You'll have to do better than that, Captain.'

I jerked my thumb towards the sergeant. 'You've been monitoring the wavebands pretty constantly. What have you heard?'

Sadiq shrugged. 'It's difficult to tell. There's a lot of traffic, mostly in code. There seems to be much troop movement. Also a lot of aircraft activity.'

'Like those jets this morning.' I had plenty of ideas about that but I wanted his version. 'What do you *think* is happening?'

'I don't know. I wish I did,' he said.

'What does Radio Nyala have to say?'

'Nothing unusual. Much music.' Kemp and I glanced at one another. 'There was a little about us, news of the new power plant at Bir Oassa. And other talk as well . . .'

He was getting closer to the real thing. His voice had become very careful. I said nothing but waited, out-silencing him. He went on at last, 'There was other news from Bir Oassa. The new airfield was opened today, with a ceremony.'

I gaped at him. 'But it isn't meant to be ready for a couple of months at least. Who opened it?'

'The Air Chief Marshall.'

My first irrelevant thought was that I'd guessed his title right after all. Then I said, 'Semangala. Right?'

'Yes, sir.'

Kemp said, 'Isn't he the chap who was in France when we left Port Luard? The only military bigwig who couldn't attend?'

'Yes,' I said grimly. 'And what's more, he's meant to be in Switzerland right now. He left two days ago with his family. I saw him at the airport when I left for Lasulu. He got all the usual military sendoff, except that he was in civvies. Are you *sure*, Sadiq?'

'Yes, sir.' His eyes were sad now. 'He made a speech.'

'Who exactly is Semangala?' asked Hammond. 'Is he that important?'

'He's the Air Force boss and right now he's the most important man in Nyala. Wouldn't you say so, Sadiq?'

76

I was pushing him and he hated it. 'I don't know what you mean, sir.'

'Oh yes, you do. You're not stupid, Sadiq, and remember, neither am I. I know the score as well as you or anyone else in your army. Listen, you two; I'm going to have to make this short and sharp. This country is on the verge of civil breakdown and military takeover, and if you didn't guess that it's only because you're new here and you've had your hands full with that giant of yours. The Army is split; half supports the Government and half wants a military junta to take over. It's complex but don't worry about the reasons for now. Both sides need the Air Force to give them a victory, and up to now Semangala has been playing one side against the other. Am I right so far, Sadiq?'

'I am not a politician,' he said.

I smiled. 'Just a simple soldier, eh? That's an old chestnut, my friend. Now, Semangala has been in France, probably buying planes or missiles. He comes back and decides he needs a holiday: a funny time to choose but he's his own boss. He flies out openly with his wife and kids, but he's back the next day. He probably had a plane on standby in Zurich. My guess is that he's made up his mind and has parked his family out of the way. Now he's bulldozed through the opening of the Bir Oassa airfield, which means that it's squarely in his hands instead of being run by the civil aviation authority. The only question that needs answering is, which side did he come down on?'

Hammond and Kemp were listening carefully. Hammond said, 'I'll be damned. Usually I just read about this stuff in the press.'

Kemp asked, 'Just how much does it matter to us which side he's on? Either way they'll still want the power plant.'

'Don't be naïve. Of course they do, but that doesn't mean we can go on trundling through the country with a shield of invincibility around us. This is going to be a shooting war.'

Sadiq nodded. 'Very bad for you. I do not know how to protect you.'

He meant that he didn't know which side to protect us from.

77

I said, 'If there's a war, whoever wins will want us. But they have to win first. Meantime we're going to be up to our necks in it, and accidents happen all the time. If the Air Force is against the Government they might decide to take us out, simply to help topple the economy. And what the hell could we do about it?'

'But you're talking about civil war!' Kemp said.

'What else? Captain Sadiq, which side will you be on?'

He looked aghast. 'I do not know. I told you I know nothing of these affairs. I must obey my orders from Major General Kigonde.'

'And if you get no orders? Confucius he say that man who walks down middle of road gets run over. You'll have to make up your own mind sometime. Now that Colonel Hussein – who's side is he on, do you think?'

'He is Kigonde's man.'

'Where's he heading for, and why?'

Sadiq showed a flash of irritation. 'He didn't tell me. Colonels don't make a habit of telling captains their orders.'

Kemp asked, 'What did he tell you concerning us?'

'To stay with you. To protect you. To watch out for sabotage.'

'And you'll do that – even if your own army buddies start shooting at you?'

He didn't answer and I couldn't blame him. For the moment my mind had ground to a halt, and I felt that without a great deal more data to work on I couldn't begin to make any decisions regarding our mission. Then to my surprise and my considerable relief the matter was taken firmly out of my hands. Basil Kemp had become inattentive during the last few exchanges, and was drawing patterns in the dust with his toe. I was starting to think that he was in the grip of the same uncertainty as held me, when he suddenly straightened up and spoke with decision.

'We've work to do. I think we're wasting time, Neil. We have to get on the road at once. We can discuss things as we go.'

78

'Go where?' I asked.

'To Bir Oassa. While you've been jabbering I've been thinking. The war hasn't started yet and we don't know that it ever will. All this is speculation so far. If there is no war we're still in business. But if there is I would like to be a good deal closer to Bir Oassa than we are now. Sadiq has told us that the new airfield is open, so there's one escape route for us at least. Here there's nothing – we're like sitting ducks. And we can't go back. If there is a war the two main towns will be worst hit and the docks a shambles.'

His words made sense and his voice was firm.

Ben Hammond was almost jubilant. 'Right, let's get on with it. We've got pretty good fuel reserves, water too. We were supposed to be restocked with food but we're not short yet.' His mind was into top gear, sorting out the priorities and he was obviously glad to have something positive to do.

Kemp went on, 'Captain Sadiq thinks there may be shooting. We must talk this over with the men. Ben, call them all together for me, please. I still wish to God Geoff was with us. He's better at this sort of thing.'

'You're doing fine,' I said. 'Better than me. I agree that we can't just sit here, and there's another good reason for pressing on.' My mind was working again.

'And what's that?'

'Tell you in a moment. You go on ahead; I want another word with the Captain first.' I stared hard at him, and as before, he picked up my cue and said at once, 'Right. See you soon.' He went off, taking Ben with him. I turned to Sadiq.

'This is a hell of a mess, Captain. I'm glad you intend to stick with us. I've been admiring your foresight. The gun emplacements, for example.'

He expanded. 'You noticed that? I was told to be aware of possible danger.'

'What do you really think is going on?'

He took off his cap and scratched his head, and the smart soldier became an ordinary, slightly baffled man. 'Colonel

79

Hussein is going to meet the Seventh Brigade, which is stationed at Bir Oassa. Then they will all come south. Back here, unfortunately.'

'Won't they stay there to protect the oilfields?'

'No-one will attack the oilfields. Both sides will need them. But here at Kodowa . . .' He took out a map. Kodowa was about thirty miles north of us, sprawled across the great road, and the only sizeable town in the vicinity. We had reckoned on using it as a major restocking depot.

'From Kodowa a road also goes east and west,' Sadiq was saying. 'So it is a crossroad. Also the heart of Kinguru country. If it was taken by rebels there would be little Kinguru resistance left. So the Seventh Brigade must come down here to protect it, to hold this bridge as well. Hussein will meet them somewhere north of Kodowa.'

'Christ! We're right in the thick of it, then. What about the air force base near here?'

'It is just outside Kodowa. It makes it very difficult to take the town, if the Air Force has really gone with the rebels. That is why Hussein will not stop there.'

'And do you think the Air Force has gone over – or will?'

He shrugged. 'Very hard to say, Mister Mannix. But I think . . .'

'Yes. So do I.' We were silent for a moment, and then I went on. 'I thank you for your frankness. It is very necessary that we keep each other aware of all that we know, Captain. I think I must go and join Mister Kemp now.'

I had a hundred questions still. For one thing, I would very much like to have asked his personal convictions. As a Moslem he might well be against the Kinguru rule; he already had one Moslem superior and the head of the Seventh Brigade might be another. But there was a limit to what I could ask him, and for the moment I had to rely on the fact that our convoy might be felt worthy of protection by both sides, so that Sadiq's loyalty would not affect his usefulness to us. But it was one hell of a nasty situation.

80

I joined Kemp just as his meeting broke up. There was much talk as the crew went about its business, and Kemp turned to me with relief. 'They're all a bit shocked, naturally, but they're willing to bash on,' he said. 'There's been some talk of danger money, though.'

'Good God! There's not a shot been fired yet – and may never be.'

'It's just one man. A trade union smart boy.'

'You'd better remind him he's in darkest Africa, not home in dear old England. The guy who comes at him with a rifle won't ask if he believes in the brotherhood of man, or look at his union card. Who is he?'

'Look, he hasn't –'

'Basil, I must know *all* the factors. Who is he? I'm not going to say or do anything, just keep an eye open.'

'His name's Burke, Johnny Burke. He's a damned hard worker and a good crewman. For God's sake don't make much of this.'

'Okay, I promise. But if he starts making waves I have to know. Now, I want to fill you in.' I quickly told him of my conversation with Sadiq and some of my own speculations. He said, 'You wanted to tell me something else, presumably out of Sadiq's hearing.'

'Yes. I think the less Sadiq hears of our plans or discussions the better. You've got a map of Nyala? Let's have it.'

We both bent over the map. From Kodowa our road continued in a more or less northerly fashion, through increasingly sparse scrubland and into the semi-desert regions where Bir Oassa's oil derricks were pumping out the country's newly discovered lifeblood. The river we had just crossed, like two others before it and one more to come, were all fairly major tributaries of the huge Katali, which ran up from the coast north of Lasulu to form the boundary with Manzu, Nyala's neighbouring state. And from Kodowa another road, not as massive as the one we were travelling on, ran right across the country from the east to the western boundary, towards the

81

Katali river. Here there was no bridge, but a ferry carried goods and people over the river from one country to the other, doing desultory trade and forming a second route to the oilfields.

I pointed to this road. 'Do you know anything about this route?'

'Not much. I saw it, of course, when I did the survey. But I didn't go and look at it. There was a fair amount of small traffic using it. Why?'

'If we get to Kodowa and this damned war has started, you're right in saying that we can't turn back to the coast. But I'm not happy about going on to Bir Oassa either. There's nothing up there that isn't brought in: no food supplies, no water –'

'Not even fuel,' he said with a wry smile. 'It's all crude.'

'Exactly. The desert is a godawful place to be stranded in. And if the rebels have the airfield, they won't simply let us fly out. They'll hold all personnel in what the press calls a hostage situation. So I don't think we want to go there, do you?'

He looked at me in horror. All his careful plans were being overturned, and now here I was about to suggest the whackiest scheme imaginable.

'You want me to take a three hundred ton load on a multi-artic trailer over an unsurveyed route into the depths of nowhere? What for, for God's sake?' he asked.

'Look at the road going west. It goes back towards the rainforest. There are several villages, lots of chances to find food and water. And fuel, both gas and diesel. It may not be a good road, but it exists. At the Katali it follows the water course down to Lasulu and the coast. I saw the beginning of that road beyond Lasulu and it wasn't too bad. We would meet the river here – at Lake Pirie.' It wasn't really a lake but a considerable widening of the river. 'There's even a moderately sized town there, Fort Pirie, as big as Kodowa apparently.'

'Yes, I see all that. I take your point about the food, and water, and possibly fuel. But there's something else, isn't there?'

'Yes indeed. There's Manzu.'

'The Republic of Manzu? But we can't get there by crossing

82

the river with the rig. There's no bridge. And it's another country, Neil. We don't have the necessary papers to enter. We've got no business with Manzu.'

I felt a wave of exasperation. 'Basil, use your head! If necessary we abandon the rig. Yes, abandon it. I know it's valuable, but the crew matters more. We can get them across the river, and they're safe in a neutral country. And as refugees, and whites at that, we'll get plenty of help and plenty of publicity. I bet nobody would dare touch the rig or the rest of the convoy with a bargepole; they'd be valuable assets for negotiations to either side.'

Actually I didn't believe this myself. I thought that without our expertise to handle it the rig, abandoned in the rainforest, would be so much junk and treated as such by all parties. But I had to convince Kemp to see things my way. I knew what the priorities were, and they didn't include taking a team of men into the desert to become hostages to either side in a shooting war. Or food for the vultures either.

'I'll have to think about it.'

'Naturally. There's a lot we need to know. But keep it in mind. Nothing will happen until we get to Kodowa, and we're not there yet. And by then the whole picture may have changed.'

'Right you are. Can we get back to here and now, please? Are you staying with us?'

'I sure am. I'd hate to try and drive back to the coast without knowing what's going on there. When do you plan to get started?'

'Immediately. We should get to Kodowa tomorrow morning. I won't stop too close to the town, though, not in these circumstances. Will you ride with me in the Land Rover? We can plan as we go. I'll get someone else to bring your car.'

A little later we were on the move once more. Rumbling along in the dust, the rig and its attendants were left behind as we set off to find out what was happening in Kodowa. Yesterday Kemp had expected to be buying fresh fruit and vegetables in the marketplace; today his expectations were entirely different.

83

8

As Kemp pulled ahead of the convoy I saw with approval that two of Sadiq's motorcyclists shot past us and then slowed down, holding their distance ahead, one at about a quarter of a mile, one at half a mile. Kemp drove fairly slowly, carefully scrutinizing the road surface and checking the bends. Once or twice he spoke over the car phone to the rig but otherwise we drove in silence for some time. He was deeply preoccupied.

After we had gone a dozen miles or so he said, 'I've been thinking.'

The words had an ominous ring.

'Pull over and let's talk.'

He asked me to flesh out the political situation and I added my speculations concerning the Air Force and Sadiq's attitude. I sensed his growing truculence, but when the reason for it finally surfaced I was dismayed. If I had thought of John Sutherland as lacking in imagination he shrank into insignificance beside Kemp.

'I don't think much of all this,' he said. 'There's not one solid bit of evidence that any of it is happening.'

'A while ago back up the road there was a guy who wanted to shoot up the convoy,' I said. 'What do you call that?'

'All they did was threaten, get excited. They may well have been on exercises. The jets that came over – we've seen others before. I'm not sure I believe any of this, Neil. And that army detachment is way ahead of us by now.'

'How do you know? They may have stopped round the next corner. And there are others, not all necessarily as friendly.' But I knew I wasn't getting through to him. Something had set his opinions in concrete, and I had to find out what it was and chip it out fast.

I said, 'As soon as we get to Kodowa I'm going to have a try at getting back to Port Luard. I may be able to get a plane, or at least an army escort. I want to get the gen from headquarters, and not on the air. Before I go I'll want the names of every man you've got with you.' I took out a notebook and pen. Kemp looked at me as if I were going crazy.

'Why do you want to know that?'

I noticed he didn't query my intention to return to base. Perhaps he'd be pleased to see the back of me. 'Just tell me,' I said.

'I insist on knowing why.'

I thought it wise to be brutal.

'To tell their next of kin, and the company, if they get killed. That goes for you too, of course.'

'My God! You're taking this seriously!'

'Of course I am. It is serious, and I think you know it. Let's have those names.'

He was reluctant but complied. 'There's Ben Hammond; the drivers are McGrath, Jones, Grafton and Lang. Bert Proctor, on rig maintenance with Ben. Two boys on the airlift truck, Sisley and Pitman – both Bob, by the way. Thorpe, who came with you. Burke and Wilson. In the commissary truck we've got Bishop and young Sandy Bing. Fourteen with me. I don't know their addresses.' This last was said sarcastically but I treated it as a straight fact.

'No, we can get those from head office if necessary. You might want to write a message for me to take back to Wingstead – assuming I get back.'

'You really mean to try? It could be –'

'Dangerous? But I thought you said there wasn't any danger?'

He fiddled with the car keys. 'I'm not totally stupid, Mannix. Of course I realize there could be trouble. But your plan –'

At last we were getting to the root of his problem. Something about my hastily formulated escape plan had touched a nerve, and now I could guess what it was. 'I'll leave you a written letter too, if you like. If there is danger and the rig looks like holding up any chances of your all getting clear, you're to abandon it immediately.'

I had guessed right. His face became set and stubborn. 'Hold on a minute. That's the whole thing. I'm not abandoning this job or the rig just on your say-so, or for any damned local insurrection. It's got too much of our sweat in it.'

I looked at him coldly. 'If you're the kind of man who would trade a pile of scrap metal for lives you can consider yourself fired as of now.'

His face was pale. 'Wyvern has a contract. You can't do that.'

'Can't I? Go ahead and sue the company; you'll be stripped naked in public. Christ, man, the transformer is worth ten times as much as the rig and yet I'm prepared to drop it like hot coal if it hinders getting the men out alive. I can order you to leave the rig and I'm doing it. In writing, if you like. I take full responsibility.'

He couldn't find words for a moment. He was outraged, but perhaps at himself as much as at me. He had seen the chasm under his feet: the moment when a man puts property before life is a crisis point, and as a normally ethical man he had realized it.

'Come on, Basil.' I softened. 'I do understand, but you've got to see reason. Damn it, British Electric will have to make good if you abandon your rig on my say-so. You'd have your money back in spades one day.'

'Of course the chaps' lives come first – my own too. It's just that I . . . I can't get used to the idea of –'

'Leaving it to rot? Of course not. But war does funny things to men and equipment alike, assuming there is going to be a war. And we dare not assume otherwise. Think again.'

He sat silent, pale and shaken. Then at last he said, 'All

right, if we have to do it, we will. But not unless we absolutely must, you hear me?'

'Of course not. And in any case, you don't have to throw it off a mountain top, you know. Just park it in some nice lay-by and you can come and pick it up when the shooting's over.'

He gave me a wan smile.

'I'd like to drive back to the rig,' he said. 'I want a word with Ben. And we could do with something to eat.' It was a truce offering, and I accepted.

The rig was crawling along into the growing heat of the day, moving so slowly that it disturbed relatively little dust. Strung out ahead and behind were the rest of the convoy and the military vehicles. There was a timeless, almost lulling atmosphere to the whole scene, but I wondered how much of it I could take. The rig drivers must be specially trained in patience and endurance.

Kemp signalled the chuck wagon out of line and Bishop started a brew up and a dispensing of doorstep sandwiches. My hired car had suddenly come into its own as a delivery wagon, to Kemp's pleasure freeing the Land Rover from that chore. 'We'll keep this car on,' he said. 'We should have had an extra one all along.'

'I'm sure Avis will be delighted.'

Sadiq reported that he had sent scouts ahead to find out how things were on the Kodowa road. He had stationed a similar escort well behind the convoy lest anything else should come up from the direction of the bridge. He was working hard and doing quite well in spite of the unexpected pressures.

Over tea and sandwiches Hammond and Kemp had a long conversation which seemed to be entirely technical, something to do with the rig's performance since the air bags had been removed. It wasn't a major problem but one of those small hitches which enthrall the minds of technicians everywhere. Presently Kemp said that he wanted to drive alongside the rig for a while, to watch her in action, and invited me to join him.

Just as we were starting we heard a whisper from the air and looked up to see the contrails of jets flying northwards high up. There were several of them, not an unusual sight, and nobody mentioned it. But our eyes followed them thoughtfully as they vanished from sight.

The rest of that morning moved as slowly as though the mainspring of time itself had weakened. We were entering the foothills of the escarpment which separated the scrubland from the arid regions ahead, and there were a series of transverse ridges to cross so that the road rose and dipped like a giant roller coaster. We would crawl up a rise to find a shallow valley with the next rise higher than the last. At the crest of every rise the dim, blue-grey wall of the escarpment would become just that little more distinct. Kemp now had three tractors coupled up to haul on the hills and control the speed on the down slopes. When he got to the escarpment proper he would need all four.

Curiously enough the vegetation was a little lusher here and the country seemed more populous. There was a village every mile or so and a scattering of single huts in between. The huts were made of grass thatched with palm leaves, or double walls of woven withies filled with dried mud. If one burnt down or blew over it could be replaced in a day.

The villagers grew corn, which the British called maize, and sweet potatoes, and scrawny chickens pecked among the huts. They herded little scraggy goats and cows not much bigger, and thin ribby dogs hung about looking for scraps. The people were thin too, but cleanly clothed and with a certain grave dignity. They lined the route to watch us go by, clearly awed and fascinated but not in a holiday mood. In one village a delegation took Sadiq away to talk to their headman, and the men of the village seemed a little threatening towards the troops. No women or children were to be seen which was unusual.

Sadiq came back with bad news. 'Hussein's battalion went through here very fast and a child was killed. Nobody stopped and the people are all very angry.'

'My God, that's awful.' Suddenly Kemp looked much more as though he believed in our talk of civil war. I thought of what Napoleon had said about eggs and omelettes, but people weren't eggs to be smashed. If there were much of this sort of thing going on there would be scant support from the rural populace for either side, not that the local people had any say in what went on.

Kemp asked if we could do anything to help, but was told that it would be best to keep going. 'They know it wasn't you,' Sadiq said. 'They do not want you here but they have no quarrel with you. You cannot help their grief.'

We moved out again to catch up with the rig and I asked to ride with Sadiq. I had some more questions to ask him, and this seemed like a good moment. As we pulled away I began with an innocuous question. 'How come there are so many people living here? There seem to be more than at the coast.'

'It is healthier country; less fever, less heat. And the land is good, when the rains come.'

Then the radio squawked and Sadiq snatched up the earphones and turned up the gain. He listened intently, replied and then said to me, 'Something is happening up the road. Not so good. I'm going to see. Do you want to come?'

'I'd like to.' I hadn't the slightest desire to go hurtling into trouble, but the more I could learn the better.

He eased out of the line and barrelled up the road. Behind us his sergeant crouched over the earphones though I doubt that he could have heard anything. Several miles ahead of the place where Kemp and I had previously stopped and turned back we came across one of Sadiq's troop trucks parked just below the top of a rise; the motorcyclists were there too. The corporal who headed the detachment pointed along the road, towards a haze of smoke that came from the next valley or the one beyond.

'A bush fire, perhaps?' I asked. But I didn't think so.

'Perhaps. My corporal said he heard thunder in the hills an

hour ago. He is a fool, he said he thought the rains were coming early.'

'No clouds.'

'He has never heard gunfire.'

'I have. Have you?' I asked. He nodded.

'I hope it is not Kodowa,' he said softly. 'I think it is too near for that. We shall go and see.' He didn't mention the planes we'd all seen earlier.

We went off fast with the cyclists about a mile ahead and the truck rattling along behind. There was nothing abnormal in the next valley but as we climbed the hill a cyclist came roaring back. Sadiq heard what he had to say and then stopped below the crest of the hill. He went back to the truck and the men bailed out, fanning into a line.

He signalled to me and I followed him as he angled off the road, running through the thick scrub. At the top of the ridge he bent double and then dropped flat on his belly. As I joined him I asked, 'What is it?'

'There are tanks on the other side. I want to know whose they are before I go down.'

He snaked forward and fumbled his binoculars out of their case. He did a quick scan and then stared in one direction for some time. At last he motioned me to come forward and handed me the glasses.

There were four tanks in the road. One was still burning, another was upside down, its tracks pointing to the sky. A third had run off the road and into a ditch. There didn't seem to be much the matter with the fourth, it just sat there. There were three bodies visible and the road was pitted with small, deep craters and strewn with debris.

I'd seen things like that before. I handed him back the glasses and said, 'An air strike with missiles. Hussein?'

'His tanks, yes. They have the Second Battalion insignia. I see no command car.'

He looked around to where his corporal waited, made a wide sweeping motion with one hand and then patted the top of his own head. That didn't need much interpretation: go around the flank and keep your head down.

In the event there was no need for caution; there were no living things on the road except the first inquisitive carrion birds. Sadiq had the vehicles brought up and then we examined the mess. The three bodies in the road had come out of the burning tank. They were all badly charred with their clothing burnt off, but we reckoned they had been killed by machine gunfire. The tank that seemed intact had a hole the size of an old British penny in the turret around which the paint had been scorched off until the metal showed. That damage had been done by a shaped charge in the head of a stabilized missile. I knew what they'd find in the tank and I didn't feel inclined to look for myself. Anyone still inside would be spread on the walls.

Sadiq gave orders to extinguish the fire in the burning tank, and the dead bodies were collected together under a tarpaulin. There was no sign of the rest of the men except for some bloodstains leading off into the bush. They had scarpered, wounded or not.

I said, 'Nothing is going to get past here until this lot is shifted. We need one of Kemp's tractors. Shall I go back and tell him what's happened? Someone can bring one along. He's only using three.'

'Yes, you can ride on the back of one of the motorcycles. I do not think there is any danger – now.' But we both scanned the sky as he spoke. There wasn't much that needed discussion, but it seemed evident to me that the civil war had finally erupted, and the Air Force had gone with the opposition. I felt a wave of sickness rise in my throat at the thought of what the future was likely to hold.

We returned to the convoy and the cyclist dropped me without ceremony at Kemp's car, then shot off to pass orders to the rest of the military escort. Kemp stared and I realized that for the second time in that long day he was seeing me dusty and scratched from a trip through the bush.

91

'That war you didn't like to think about is just a piece up the road,' I told him. 'We can't get through for wrecked tanks. There are four of them, stragglers from Hussein's outfit. All kaput. We need the spare tractor and a damn good driver. I'd like it to be McGrath. And a couple of other guys. And you, too; you are in the heavy haulage business, aren't you?'

I may have sounded just a touch hysterical. Kemp certainly looked at me as if I were.

'You're not kidding me?'

'Jesus, maybe I should have brought one of the bodies as evidence.'

'Bodies?'

'They happen in a war.'

I looked along the road. The rig was crawling towards us, but ahead of it was the extra tractor, driven by Mick McGrath. I waved him down and he stopped alongside, alive with curiosity. Everyone had seen the sudden activity of our military escort and knew something was up.

'Basil, get the rig stopped. Better here than too close,' I said.

Kemp looked from me to the rig, then slowly unhooked the microphone from the dashboard of the Land Rover. Stopping the rig was a serious business, not as simple as putting on a set of car brakes, more like stopping a small ship. For one thing, all three tractor drivers had to act in concert; for another the rig man, usually either Hammond or Bert Proctor, had to judge the precise moment for setting the bogie brakes, especially on a hill. Although they were all linked in a radio circuit, they were also directed by a flag waved from the control car; a primitive but entirely practical device. Now Kemp poked the flag out of the car window, and followed his action with a spate of orders over the mike. McGrath got out of his tractor and strode over. 'What's going on, Mister Mannix?'

'A war.'

'What does it look like over there?'

'Like any old war. Hussein got shot up from the air and lost

92

four tanks. One of them should be no trouble to move, but three are blocking the road. We'll need your help in clearing the way.'

By now several of the men were milling around talking. McGrath overrode the babble of conversation.

'Any shooting up there now, Mister Mannix?'

'No, and I don't think there will be. We think that both sides will leave us alone. We're precious to them.'

McGrath said, 'Any bad corners on the way there?'

'None that matter. It's pretty easy going.'

'Right you are then. I'll take Bert from the rig. Barry, you whip a team together and follow us up. Tell the fuel bowser boys to stay back, and leave the airlift team behind too. We could do with your car, Mister Mannix. OK? Sandy, go and send Bert to me, then you stay up there and tell Mister Hammond what's going on.'

He issued this stream of orders with calm decision, then strode off back to the tractor. I was impressed. He had taken the initiative in fine style and seemed to be dependable. It would be interesting seeing him in action if things got tough, as I was certain they would.

Kemp rejoined me and I briefed him and saw that he approved. 'He's a good organizer, is Mick. A bit hot-headed but then what Irish rigger isn't? Ben will stay here with the rig and the rest of the crew. A detachment of the escort can hold their hands. I'm coming with you. Get in.'

He made no apology for doubting that this might happen. The tension that had gripped him in Port Luard was returning, and I realized with something between horror and exasperation that what was bothering him wasn't the prospect of an entire country devastated by civil war, but the sheer logistic annoyances of any delays or upsets to his precious transportation plans. He was a very single-minded man, was Kemp.

As we pulled out to overtake the tractor Kemp said, 'You mentioned bodies. How many?'

93

'I saw three, but there'll be more in the tanks. The rest have scarpered.'

'God damn it, as though we didn't have enough problems of our own without getting mixed up in a bloody war,' he grumbled.

'It could be worse.'

'How the hell could it be worse?'

'The planes could have shot up your rig,' I said dryly.

He didn't answer and I let him drive in silence. I was thankful enough myself to sit quietly for a while. I felt drained and battered, and knew that I needed to recharge my batteries in a hurry, against the next crisis.

The scene of the air strike hadn't changed much except that the bodies had been moved off the road and the fire was out. Sadiq was waiting impatiently. 'How long to clear it, sir?' he asked at once.

Kemp looked dazed.

'How long, please?' Sadiq repeated.

Kemp pulled himself together. 'Once the tractor arrives, we'll have the tanks off the road in an hour or so. We don't have to be too gentle with them, I take it.'

I wasn't listening. I was looking at the ridge of hills ahead of us, and watching the thick black haze of smoke, several columns, mingling as they rose, writhing upwards in the middle distance. Sadiq followed my gaze.

'My scouts have reported back, Mister Mannix. Kodowa is burning.'

'Still reckoning on buying fresh vegetables there?' I couldn't resist asking Kemp. He shook his head heavily. The war had happened, and we were right in the middle of it.

McGrath and Proctor were experts in their field and knowledgeable about moving heavy awkward objects. They estimated angles, discussed the terrain, and then set about connecting shackles and heavy wire ropes. Presently McGrath shifted the first of the stricken tanks off the road as though it were a child's toy. The rest of us, soldiers and all, watched in fascination as

94

the tank ploughed to a halt deep in the dust at the roadside, and the team set about tackling the next one.

Sadiq went off in his command car as soon as he was satisfied that our tractor could do the job, heading towards Kodowa with a cycle escort. The work of clearing the road went on into the late afternoon, and Kemp then drove back to the convoy to report progress and to bring the rig forward. He had decided that we would stop for the night, a wise decision in the aftermath of an exhausting and disturbing day, but he wanted to cover as much ground as possible before total nightfall.

McGrath and Proctor were resting after moving the up-turned tank, which had been a tricky exercise, and gulping down the inevitable mugs of hot tea which Sandy had brought along for everyone. I went over to them and said, 'Got a spade?'

McGrath grinned. 'Ever see a workman without one? We use them for leaning on. It's a well-known fact. There's a couple on the tractor.'

Proctor, less ebullient, said quietly. 'You'll be wanting a burial party, Mister Mannix?'

We buried the bodies after giving the soldiers' identity tags to Sadiq's corporal. Afterwards everyone sat around quietly, each immersed in his own thoughts. McGrath had vanished, but presently I heard him calling.

'Hey, Mister Mannix! Bert!'

I looked around but couldn't see him. 'Where are you?'

'In here.' His voice was muffled and the direction baffling. I still couldn't see him, and then Bert pointed and McGrath's head appeared out of the turret of the tank that he hadn't needed to shift, the one that had run into the ditch. He said cheerily, 'I don't think there's anything wrong with this one.'

'You know tanks too?'

'The army taught me. There isn't anything on wheels I don't know,' he said with simple egotism. Proctor, alongside me, nodded in his grave fashion.

I said, 'Can you drive it out?'

'I'm pretty sure so. This thing never got a hit. The crew just

95

baled out and she piled herself up in the dust here. Want me to try?'

'Why not?'

His head bobbed down and after a lot of metallic noises the engine of the tank burst into noisy song. It moved, at first forward and digging itself deeper into the ditch, and then in reverse. With a clatter of tracks and to spattered applause it heaved itself out of the gulley and onto the road. There was a pause and then the turret started to move. The gun traversed around and depressed, pointing right at us.

'Stick 'em up, pal!' yelled McGrath, reappearing and howling with laughter.

'Don't point that thing at me,' I said. 'Once a day is enough. Well, it looks as though we've just added one serviceable tank to the Wyvern fleet. Captain Sadiq will be delighted.'

9

It was an uneasy night. Nothing more happened to disturb us, but very few of us got a full night's sleep; there was a great deal of coming and going to the chuck wagon, much quiet talking in the darkness, a general air of restlessness. The day had been packed with incident, a total contrast to the normal slow, tedious routine, and nobody knew what the next day would bring except they could be sure that the routine was broken.

The rig had reached the valley where the tanks had been hit, and was resting there. Kemp had no intention of moving it until we knew much more about what had happened in Kodowa, and Sadiq had taken him off at first light to look at the road. I had elected to stay behind.

Talk over breakfast was sporadic and I could sense the crew's tension. Certainly I knew they had been discussing their own safety and the chances of their coming through the conflict unscathed, with less than full confidence, and I suspected that Johnny Burke and Bob Sisley were pushing the shop floor angle rather hard. That could bear watching. I began to put some words together in my mind, against the time when I'd have to give them reasoned arguments in favour of doing things my way. They weren't like Sadiq's army lads, trained to obey without question.

Ben Hammond had gone with Kemp to look at the road. McGrath and three or four of the men were still playing with the tank, which they had cheerfully but firmly refused to turn over to the military until they had tinkered with it for a while longer. The others, including myself, were doing nothing much; everything looked remarkably peaceful and normal if one ignored the three tanks piled up in the gulley by the roadside.

When the interruption came it was heart-stopping.

There was a mighty rush of air and a pounding roar in our ears. Men sprang to their feet like jack-in-the-boxes as five air force jets screamed overhead at low altitudes, hurtling up over the ridge beyond us.

'Christ!' A pulse hammered in my throat and my coffee spilled as I jerked to my feet.

'They're attacking!' someone yelled and there was a dive for cover, mostly under the shelter of the rig itself, which would have been suicidal if an attack had followed. But no missiles or bombs fell. The formation vanished as suddenly as it had appeared. Men resurfaced, staring and chattering. Soldiers grabbed belatedly for their rifles.

'Was it an attack?' Ritchie Thorpe asked me. Having driven up with me he'd been tacitly appointed the position of spokesman.

'No. They were going much too fast. I'm not sure they were even aware of us.'

'Where do you think they're going?'

'God knows.' I felt as if we were on a desert island, with no news getting through. 'Are you sure you can't raise anything on the radios? Any local station?'

'Sorry, Mister Mannix. It's all static. Everything's off the air, I think. Mister Kemp said he'd call in on the half-hour, so I'll be listening in then. Maybe he'll have some news for us.'

There was a distant roar and our faces snapped skywards again. One of the jets was returning, but flying much higher, and as we watched it made a big sweeping circle in the sky and vanished in the direction of the rest of the formation. For a moment it seemed to leave a thin echo behind, and then I stiffened as I recognized what I was hearing.

'Bert. There's another plane. A small one. Can you see it?'

He too stared round the sky.

'No, but I can hear it.' He raised his voice to a shout. 'Any of you see a light plane?'

Everyone stared upwards, and three or four of them

98

scrambled up onto the rig for a better vantage point. It was Brad Bishop on top of the commissary truck who first shouted, 'Yes, over there!' and pointed south.

A moment later I'd seen it too, a small speck of a plane flying low and coming towards us. Longing for binoculars, I kept my eyes glued to the approaching plane and felt a jolt of recognition. I'd never been a flier myself, and though I'd logged hundreds of hours in small company planes as well as in commercial liners I had never developed an eye for the various makes, but this one I definitely knew.

'It's the BE company plane,' I called out. 'We've got visitors.'

'Where can they land?' Thorpe asked me.

'Good question. Kodowa's got a town strip somewhere but I don't know if it's going to be usable. He can't land here, that's for certain.'

But that was where I was wrong.

It wasn't an intentional landing, though. As the plane came nearer we recognized signs of trouble. It was flying in a lopsided, ungainly fashion. A thin trail of smoke came from it, and the full extent of the damage became visible. Part of the undercarriage was missing, and the tailfin was buckled out of alignment.

'She's going to crash.'

'Do you think the jets attacked her?'

I said, 'No – too high, too fast. That was a ground attack. Damn it, she's not a fighter plane, not even armed!'

We watched in alarm as it began a wobbly circle over the bush country, slowly spiralling downwards.

'Bring up the water carrier!' I shouted, and sprinted for the hire car. Three or four others flung themselves in beside me. The car was ill-equipped for bouncing off the road into the bush but with the Land Rover gone there wasn't much choice. The water tanker and some of the military stuff followed. I concentrated on charting the course of the stricken plane and on avoiding the worst of the rocks and defiles in front of me. The others clung on as they were tossed about, leaning out of

99

the car windows in spite of the choking dust clouds to help keep track of the aircraft.

Soon it dipped to the horizon, then went below it at a sharp angle. I tried to force another fraction of speed out of the labouring car. The plane reappeared briefly and I wondered if it had actually touched down and bounced. Then it was gone again and a surge of dust swirled up ahead.

My hands wrenched this way and that to keep the car from slewing sideways in the earth. I brought it joltingly through a small screen of thorn bushes and rocked to a halt, and we looked downhill towards the misshapen hulk that had been airborne only moments before.

We piled out and started running. The danger of fire was enormous. Not only would the plane erupt but the bush was likely to catch fire, and we all knew it. But there was no fire as yet, and the plane was miraculously upright.

As we got to the plane a figure was already beginning to struggle to free himself. The plane was a six-seater, but there were only two men visible inside. Our men clambered up onto the smashed wing and clawed at the pilot's door. The water tanker was lumbering towards us and Sadiq's troops were nearer still; I waved the oncoming vehicles to a halt.

'No further! Stay back! If she burns you'll all be caught. No sparks – don't turn your ignition off,' I shouted. 'Wilson, you and Burke start laying a water trail down towards her.'

As one of the big hoses was pulled free and a spray of water shot out, the door was pulled open and the two men inside were helped out. I ran back to the car and brought it closer. One of the plane's occupants seemed to be unhurt; two of our men were steadying him but he appeared to be walking quite strongly. The second was lolling in unconsciousness, carried by Grafton and Ron Jones. As they came up to my car I recognized both new arrivals.

The unconscious man was Max Otterman, our Rhodesian pilot. The other was Geoffrey Wingstead.

*

100

Max Otterman was in a bad way.

He'd done a brilliant job in bringing his plane down in one piece, upright and more or less intact, but at a terrible cost to himself. His left arm was broken, and he had contusions and cuts aplenty, especially about the face in spite of goggles and helmet. But there was something more drastic and this none of us was able to diagnose for certain. He recovered consciousness of a sort in the car as we drove him and Geoff Wingstead back to the rig site, moving as gently as possible. But he was obviously in great pain and kept blacking out. We got him bedded down in the rig's shade eventually, after letting Bishop have a good look at him. Bishop had first aid training and was pretty useful for day-to-day rig accidents, but he didn't know what was wrong with Otterman, apart from being fairly sure that neither his neck nor his back was broken.

It was the most worrying feature so far of a very worrying situation.

Wingstead was in good shape apart from one severe cut on his left shoulder and a selection of bruises, but nevertheless both Bishop and I urged him to take things very carefully. He saw Otterman bedded down, then sank into a grateful huddle in the shade with a cold beer to sustain him.

The men tended to crowd around. They all knew Geoff, naturally, and it was apparent that they thought a great deal of their boss. Their astonishment at his unorthodox arrival was swamped in their relief at his safety, and curiosity overrode all.

Presently I had to appeal to them to leave him for a while.

'Come on, you guys. He doesn't exactly want to give a press conference just this minute, you know,' I said. I didn't want to speak too sharply; it would be unwise to trample on their good will. But they took my point and most of them moved a little way off.

Wingstead said, 'I'll have to thank everybody properly. You all did a damned good job, back there.' His voice was a little shaky.

'None better than Max,' I said. 'There's plenty of time,

101

Geoff. Time for questions later too. Just rest a bit first.'

In fact I was aching to know what had brought him up to us, what he knew and what the situation was that he'd left behind him. Kemp and Sadiq should hear it too, though, and one account from Wingstead would tax him quite sufficiently. So I went a little way off, and saw Wingstead's head droop forward as he surrendered to the sleep of exhaustion. I was anxious for Kemp to rejoin us. He seemed to have been gone for ever, and I was eager to give him our latest piece of dramatic news. But it wasn't until nearly noon that we saw Sadiq's escorted car returning, and I walked down the road to intercept them.

'Neil. There's a pack of problems up ahead of us,' said Kemp.

'We haven't done too badly ourselves.'

Kemp's eyes immediately flashed to the rig. 'Problems? Have you been having trouble?'

'I wouldn't quite put it that way. Look, I'm damned keen to hear what you've got to tell, but I guess our news has priority. We've got visitors.'

'Who – the army?'

Sadiq had got out of the car and already had his glasses unslung, scanning the road. I knew he wouldn't see the plane from where we were standing, though. I'd have preferred to discuss the latest developments with Kemp alone, but Sadiq had to be told: he'd find out fast enough in any case.

'No. We were overflown by some air force planes but I don't think they were looking for us or had any business with us. But a small plane came up a while ago. It crashed – over there.' I waved my hand. 'It had been shot up, I think. There were two men on board and we got them both out, but one's badly hurt.'

'Who the hell are they?'

'You're going to like this, Basil. One's your boss. And he's in pretty fair shape.'

'Geoffrey!' As with the men, astonishment and relief played

102

over Kemp's face, and then alarm. 'Who was with him – who's hurt?'

'It's our pilot, Max Otterman. He made a damn good landing, probably saved both their necks, but he's in a bad way. The plane's a write-off.'

It was sensational stuff, all right. They were both suitably impressed, and had more questions. After a while I managed to get rid of Sadiq by suggesting that the guarding of the plane was probably not being done to his satisfaction. He went away at once, to go and see for himself. Kemp would have gone along too but I detained him.

'You can look at the wreckage later.'

'I want to see Geoff and the pilot.'

'One's sleeping and the other's damn near unconscious. You can't do a thing for either just yet awhile. I'd rather you briefed me on what you've found out down there.'

Kemp said, 'The road is in good shape right up to the environs of Kodowa. The town is in a hell of a mess. It's been strafed and it's almost completely burnt up. The people are in shock, I'd say, and they certainly won't be much use to us, and there's not enough of us to be much use to them. It's a pretty ghastly situation. You're right it is a war.'

It was as much of an apology as I'd get.

'We didn't go right in because we got a lot of opposition. They felt ugly about anyone in uniform, and Sadiq didn't have enough force with him to do much about it. But we'll have to go back in eventually. Look, did Geoff say anything to you?'

'Not yet. I didn't let him. I want to hear his story as much as you do, but I thought he should rest up and wait for you to come back. Where's Ben Hammond, by the way?'

Kemp made a despairing gesture. 'You'll never believe it, but the damned troop truck broke down on the way back. String and cardboard army! Nobody knew what to do about it except Ben, so he's still out there doing a repair job. Should be along any moment, but Sadiq said he's sent some men back to give them support if they need it. There's nobody on the road. They shouldn't have any trouble.' But I could see that he was worried at having been persuaded to leave Ben out in the middle of the bush with a broken down truck and a handful of green soldiers. I didn't think much of the idea myself.

'He'll be OK,' I said hopefully. 'You'd better get yourself something to eat – and drink.'

'By God, yes. I could do with a beer.' He thought for a moment and then said, 'On second thoughts, no. We'd better go gently on our supplies from now on. I'll settle for a mug of gunfire.'

We exchanged humourless smiles. The slang term for camp tea had suddenly become alarmingly appropriate.

Ben turned up two hours later, hot, sticky and desperate for sustenance. Kemp broke into the newly-rationed beer stores for him; we hadn't yet told the men about this particular form of hardship and Kemp was not enjoying the prospect. Wingstead had slept steadily, and we didn't want to waken him. Otterman, on the other hand, seemed worse if anything. He tossed and muttered, cried out once or twice, and had us all extremely worried.

'There must be doctors in Kodowa, but God knows how we'll find them, or whether they'll be able to help,' Kemp said fretfully. He was concerned for Max, but he was also disturbed by the increasing rate of entropy about us. The rapid breakdown from order to chaos was something he seemed ill-equipped to cope with.

'What do you plan to do?' Hammond asked Kemp.

'Go on into Kodowa this afternoon, with enough chaps of my own and of Sadiq's to make a reasonable show of solidarity. We have to locate their officialdom, if any, and find out the precise facts. And we're going to need food, and water – they ran a hell of a lot out of the tanker – and medical help. I'd like you both to come and I'll choose a few of the others.'

We were interrupted by Sandy Bing, coming up at the run.

'Brad says will you come, Mister Kemp. Mister Wingstead's awake.'

'Be right there.'

The awning had been strung up at the rig's side and under it Geoff Wingstead was sitting up and seemed a lot brighter. He reached up to pump Kemp's hand with obvious pleasure.

'You're all OK, then?' he said.

'Yes, we're fine. Problems, but no accidents,' said Kemp.

'I had to come up here and see for myself how you were doing. But I can't fly a plane and Max . . .' He broke off for a moment, then went on. 'Well, he's quite a fellow. They tell me he's in a bad way. Can we get help for him?'

Briefly, Kemp put him in the picture concerning the situation up ahead at Kodowa, or as much of it as we ourselves knew. Wingstead looked grave as we recapped the events of the past couple of days.

Finally he said, 'So we're OK for fuel, not too good for water, food or doctors. Well, you may not know it all, but you can probably guess that you're a damn sight better off here than if you had stayed in Port Luard. At least you're all alive.'

'Is it that bad?' I asked.

'Bloody bad. Riots, strife, total breakdown of authority. Shooting in the streets. Looting. Docks burning, police helpless, military running amok in every direction. All the usual jolly things we see on the nine o'clock news.'

'Oh, great. No getting out for us benighted foreigners, I suppose?'

'In theory, yes. But the airport's in rebel hands and the commercial planes aren't coming in. Kigonde's off somewhere trying to rally his army. I heard that Ousemane was dead, and that Daondo's managed to slip out of the country – which figures. He's a smart one, that lad. But none of the news is certain.'

Kemp, Hammond and I stared at him as he reeled off the grim facts.

'It's a shambles, and I don't quite know what we're going

105

to do about it. I had to get up here, though. Guessed you'd not be getting regular news bulletins and might feel a bit lonely without me.'

'Too true, Geoff. We all feel *much* better now,' I said sardonically, and he grinned at me. 'Yes, well, it didn't seem too difficult at first. I asked Max if he was game and he couldn't wait to give it a bash. And we'd have done all right, too, only . . .'

He paused for a moment.

'We'd seen the air force types streaking about here and there, taking no notice of us. And quite a lot of ground movement, tank troops, armoured columns and so on, but no actual fighting once we were clear of Port Luard.'

'How did you achieve that, by the way?'

'Oh, real *Boy's Own* stuff. It'll make a good tale one day. Anyway we figured we'd catch up with you about Kodowa. You're nicely to schedule, Kemp, by the way. My congratulations.'

Kemp snorted.

'We reckoned to land there and cadge a lift back to you. There hadn't been any sign of the insurrection, you see, so we thought it was quieter up here. And then . . . it all happened at the same moment. I saw you, saw the rig parked and we started to come in for a closer look . . . there were some military trucks quite close and I wasn't sure if it was your official escort or not. And then there was this almighty slam and jerk and Max said we'd been hit. Christ, I . . . still can't really believe it. We hadn't *seen* any planes, couldn't believe we were being attacked. Max was superb. I think he was hit by a bit of metal, because he was already bleeding when he decided he had to put us down. It was a marvellous show, wasn't it, Neil? You saw it happen, didn't you?'

'Yes. It was great.'

He lay back against the pillow. 'I can fill you in with lots of detail about what's going on back in Port Luard, but I'm afraid I've come up here without a thought in my head about getting you all out,' he said apologetically. He was looking a little faded, I thought. I decided to let him rest, but perhaps in a more optimistic frame of mind.

'We've got a plan, haven't we, Basil?'

'You have?'

'Oh, yes,' Kemp said, playing along stoutly. 'Neil's idea really, and it's a very good one. We've every reason to think it may work. Look, I think you'd better rest up a bit. We're not going anywhere for what's left of today, not with the rig anyway. And the more rest you have now the more use you'll be to us tomorrow.'

Out of Wingstead's earshot we stopped and took a simultaneous deep breath.

'Do you think what I think?' Kemp asked.

'I do,' I said grimly. 'What I'd like to know is whether half of our gallant captain's men are rebels, or whether it was all nicely official from the start. Sadiq couldn't have known that Geoff was coming, but he may have left blanket orders to stop anyone who tried to get to us. He's inclined to be over-protective. Alternatively, he's got traitors in his ranks and doesn't know it.'

'Or he's one himself.'

'I don't think so. In that case he'd have immobilized us quite easily, long before this.'

'Are you going to ask him?' Hammond asked.

'Not yet. I think we should string him along a little. I suggest that we say nothing of this to anyone, and go ahead with the plan to inspect Kodowa a little more closely. We need Sadiq for that, and as long as we keep alert, we may as well make the most use of him we can.'

When we breasted the rise and looked down, my first thought was that the problem was not that of getting beyond Kodowa but *into* it. Much of the town was still burning.

The central core of Kodowa consisted of two short streets running north and south and two intersecting streets running east and west. None of them was as wide or as well made as

107

the great road on which we'd been travelling so far. This was the modern, 'downtown' area. The biggest building was three storeys high, or had been. Now it and most of the others lay in rubble on the streets.

The rest of the town had been of the local African architecture. But palm thatch burns well, and mud walls crumble with ease, and it looked as though a little section of hell had been moved into that valley. I don't know if the local authorities ever had any fire regulations, but if so they hadn't worked. Flames, driven by a wind which funnelled up the valley, had jumped across the streets and there wasn't going to be much left when the fires finally died.

Sadiq said, 'They have killed this place.' His voice sounded bitter.

I twisted in my seat. I was driving with Sadiq because Kemp and I had planned it that way. Kemp had packed the Land Rover and the car with his own men so that there was no room for me. The idea was that I should be at hand to keep an eye on Sadiq.

Where the road narrowed as it entered the town it was blocked by a slow moving line of ramshackle traffic, beat up old cars and pick-up trucks, bullock carts and bicycles, all moving outwards, and slowed even more by one large limousine which had stalled right across the road. Sadiq drove off the road and unhooked his microphone. I got out and went towards the stalled car. The hood was up and two men were poking about under the bonnet, one a Nyalan and the other one of the Asiatic merchants who seem to monopolize so much of small retail business all over Africa. In this case he was a Syrian.

I tapped him on the shoulder. 'Get this car off the road. Push it.'

He turned a sweaty face to me and grimaced uncomprehendingly. I made gestures that they should shift the car and he shook his head irritably, spat out a short sentence I didn't understand, and turned back to the car. That was enough. I leaned over his shoulder, grabbed a handful of wiring and pulled. The only place that car could go now was off the road.

The Syrian whirled furiously and grabbed my shoulder. I let him have a fist in the gut, and he sprawled to the ground. He tried to scramble to his feet and clawed under his coat for some weapon so I kicked him in the ribs and he went down again just as Sadiq came up, unfastening the flap of his pistol holster.

'You have no right to attack citizens, Mister Mannix,' he said angrily.

I pointed to the ground. A heavy cosh had spilled out of the Syrian's jacket and lay near his inert hand.

'Some guys need a lot of persuading,' I said mildly. 'Let's get this thing out of here.' The other man had vanished.

Sadiq's pistol was a better persuader than my voice. He grabbed four able-bodied men out of the milling throng and within three minutes the road was cleared. As he reholstered his pistol he said, 'You believe in direct action, Mister Mannix?'

'When necessary – but I'm getting too old for brawling.' In fact the small display of aggression had done me the world of good. I'd really been needing to let off steam and it had been the Syrian merchant's bad luck to have been a handy target.

'I would prefer you do no more such things. For the moment please stay with your own men. Tell Mister Kemp I will meet him in the central square soon.' He was off before I had a chance to respond.

I pushed through the crowds and found our Land Rover parked at the intersection of the two main roads. Dozens of distressed, battle-shocked people milled about and smouldering debris lay everywhere. Our eyes watered with the sting of acrid smoke. Broken glass crunched under our boots as we picked our way through the rubble. The Nyalans shrank away from us, weeping women pulling their bewildered children from our path. It was incredibly disturbing.

It became obvious pretty soon that there was no one in charge; we saw no policemen, no soldiers apart from Sadiq's own troops, and no sign of a doctor, a hospital or even a Red Cross post. Attempts to get sensible answers from passers-by

109

proved useless. Presently, utterly dispirited, we decided to withdraw.

The stream of refugees thinned out as we left the town but there were still a lot of them, going God knows where. But I was interested and pleased to see that on the outskirts Sadiq had set up the rudiments of a command post, and slowly his troops were beginning to bring order out of the chaos, reuniting families and doing a little crude first aid of their own. A makeshift camp was already taking shape and people were being bedded down, and some sort of food and drink was being circulated. It made me feel more confident about Sadiq.

We left him to get on with it. Our men were ready enough to give assistance, but we were not welcome and what little we had to offer wouldn't go nearly far enough. Kemp was anxious to keep our unit together; the crew were his responsibility and he was still thinking in terms of the safety of the rig. We drove back to our camp site in the dusk feeling very depressed.

Kemp went to give Wingstead an edited version of what we'd found. I settled down for a quiet cigarette while waiting for the meal that Bishop was preparing for us, and into the silence McGrath and Ron Jones settled down alongside me. Two cigarettes and one foul pipe glowed in the dusk.

'A hell of a thing, this,' Ron Jones said presently. The Welsh lilt in his voice seemed more pronounced than in full daylight. 'Shouldn't we be back there helping?'

'We can't do much,' I said. 'And I don't think Captain Sadiq really wants us. If he needs us he knows where we are.'

'We could spare them a bit of food, though.'

McGrath snorted.

'There could be five thousand people out there, Ron, and none of us is Jesus Christ. Five French loaves and two lobster tails?' I asked.

McGrath said, 'They get wind of our food stocks and they'll mob us, as like as not. I'd be happier with a gun in my fist, myself.'

'I don't know if you're right. Nyalans are peaceable folk. A gun may not be such a good idea. People tend to get the wrong impression when armed foreigners wander about taking part in someone else's war.'

'I'd still be happier with a gun in my cab,' he said. 'One of those Russian Kalashnikovs that the black lads carry, maybe. Better still, a Uzi like Sadiq has in his car.'

I glanced at him. 'You're observant.'

'It pays. I told you I was in the army once myself.'

'What rank?'

He grinned. 'Never more than sergeant. But I made sergeant three times.'

Ron Jones laughed. 'I never had the pleasure of army life,' he said. 'This is my idea of something to watch on the telly, not be caught in the middle of.'

Wingstead had said something similar. I reflected that a lot of men of my age were comparative innocents, after all.

McGrath said, 'Not this mess, maybe. But there are worse lives.' In the twilight he seemed even bigger than he looked by day, a formidable figure. He tamped down his pipe and went on, 'I've seen sights like this before though, many times, in other countries. It's all right for the soldiers but for the civilians it's very sad indeed. But there's nothing you or I can do about it.'

I had seen it before too. I thought back to my young days, to Pusan and Inchon, to the wrecked towns and refugee-lined roads, the misery and the squalor. I didn't want to see it ever again.

McGrath suddenly dug his elbow into my ribs.

'There's someone out there – with a white face. I think it's a woman!'

He scrambled to his feet and ran into the growing darkness.

10

Her name was Sister Ursula and she was a nun, and how in hell McGrath had detected that she had a white face in the semi-darkness I'll never know because it was blackened and smudged with smoke and wood ash. Her habit was torn and scorched, and slashed down one side showing that she wore long pants to the knee. She managed it so decorously that it didn't show most of the time.

She was tired but very composed, and showed few signs of strain. I once knew a man who was an atheist; he was also a plumber and had done a week's stint in a convent fixing the water system. He'd gone in with the firm conviction that all religious types were nutters of some sort. When he finished I asked him what he now thought about the contemplative life. He said, 'Those women are the sanest lot of people I've ever met,' and seemed baffled by it.

I went to my gear and fetched out a bottle of whisky. This was no time to be following Kemp's camp rules. When I got back she was sitting on a stool surrounded by our men. They were full of curiosity but polite about it, and I was pleased to see that they weren't badgering her with questions. McGrath's eyes gleamed when he saw the whisky. 'A pity it's only Scotch,' he said. 'Irish would be better, wouldn't it, Sister?'

Her lips curved in a small, tired smile. 'Right now, whisky is whisky. Thank you, Mister – Mannix, is it?'

I'd have said that she was about thirty-five, maybe forty, but she could well have been older; it's never easy to tell with nuns. When Hollywood makes movies about them they pick the Deborah Kerrs and Julie Andrews, but Sister Ursula wasn't like that. She had a full jaw, her eyebrows were thick black bars which gave her a severe and daunting look, and her face was too thin, as though she didn't eat enough. But when she smiled she was transformed, lovely to look at. We found out that she didn't use that radiant smile very often; and with reason, just at that time.

I said, 'Someone get a glass, please.'

'From the bottle is good enough,' she said, and took it from me. She swallowed and coughed a couple of times, and handed it back to me. The men watched transfixed, though whether this was the effect of the nun or the bottle I wasn't sure.

'Ah. It tastes as good as it did last time – some six years ago.'

'Have some more.'

'No, thank you. I need no more.'

Several voices broke in with questions but I overrode them. 'Pipe down, you guys, and quit crowding.' Obediently they shuffled back a pace. I bent over Sister Ursula and spoke more quietly. 'You look pretty beat; do you want to sleep somewhere?'

'Oh no, but I would dearly like a chance to clean up.' She put her stained hands to her face and then brushed at her skirts. Although she was a nun, she was vain enough to care about her appearance.

I said, 'Sandy, see there's some hot water. Ben, can the lads rig a canvas between the trucks to make a bathroom? Perhaps you'll join us for a meal when you're ready, Sister.'

Young Bing sped off and Hammond set the men to putting up a makeshift tent for her. McGrath was helping her to her feet and hovering like a mother hen; presumably as a Catholic he regarded her in some especially proprietorial light. Eventually she thanked us all and disappeared into the tent with a bowlful of water and a spare kettle and someone's shaving mirror.

Kemp had been with Wingstead and Otterman and had arrived a little late for all this excitement. I filled him in and he regarded the tent thoughtfully.

'I wonder where the others are?' he said.

113

'Others?'

'There'll be at least one more. Nuns are like coppers – they go around in pairs. Most likely there's a whole brood of them somewhere. With any luck they're a nursing sisterhood.'

I was being pretty slow, perhaps simply tired out, but at last the penny dropped. 'You mean they'll come from a hospital or a mission? By God, perhaps you're right. That means they may have a doctor!'

She came out half an hour later, looking well-scrubbed and much tidier. We were ready to eat and I asked her if she wished to join us, or to eat on her own. Someone must have lent her a sewing kit for the rip in her habit had been neatly mended.

'I'll join you, if I might. You're very kind. And you'll all be wanting to hear what I have to say,' she said rather dryly.

I noticed that she said a short, private grace before actually coming to the table, and appreciated her courtesy: doing it publicly might well have embarrassed some of the men. She sat between Kemp and me and I quickly filled her in on our names and business, of which she said she had heard a little on the radio, in the far-off days of last week before the war broke out. We didn't bother her while she was eating but as soon as was decent I asked the first question. It was a pretty all-embracing one.

'What happened?'

'It was an air raid,' she said. 'Surely you know.'

'We weren't here. We were still further south. But we guessed.'

'It was about midday. There had been some unrest, lots of rumours, but that isn't uncommon. Then we heard that there were tanks and soldiers coming through the town, so Doctor Katabisirua suggested that someone should go and see what was happening.'

'Who is he?' Kemp asked.

'Our chief at the hospital.' There was an indrawing of breath at the table as we hung on her words. Kemp shot me a look almost of triumph.

'Sister Mary sent me. It wasn't very far, only a short drive into town. When I got there I saw a lot of tanks moving through the town, far too quickly, I thought. They were heading north, towards Ngingwe.'

Ngingwe was the first village north of Kodowa, which showed that Sadiq had probably been right when he said that Hussein's lot would go northwards to join forces with his superior.

'They got through the town but some soldiers stayed back to keep the road clear. We heard that there were more tanks still coming from the south of the town.' Those would be the tanks that we had seen shot up. 'There were still a lot of people in the town square when the planes came. They came in very fast, very low. Nobody was scared at first. We've seen them often, coming and going from the Air Force base out there.' She pointed vaguely westward.

'How many planes, Sister?' Kemp asked.

'I saw seven. There may have been more. Then things happened very quickly. There was a lot of noise – shooting and explosions. Then the sound of bombs exploding, and fires started everywhere. It was so sudden, you see. I took shelter in Mister Ithanga's shop but then it started to fall to pieces and something must have hit me on the head.'

In fact she had no head wound, and I think she was felled by the concussion blast of a missile. She couldn't have been unconscious long because when I saw the shop next day it was a fire-gutted wreck. She said that she found herself coming to in the street, but didn't know how she got there. She said very little about her own part in the affair after that, but we gathered that eventually she got back to the hospital with a load of patients, her little car having escaped major damage, to find it already besieged by wailing, bleeding victims.

But they were not able to do much to help. With a very small staff, some of whom were local and only semi-trained, and limited supplies of bedding, food and medicines they were soon out of their depth and struggling. Adding to their problems were two

115

major disasters: their water supply and their power had both failed. They got their water from a well which ran sweet and plentiful normally, but was itself connected to other local wells, and somewhere along the line pipes must have cracked, because suddenly the well ran dry except for buckets of sludgy muck. And horrifyingly, shortly after the town's own electricity failed, the hospital's little emergency generator also died. Without it they had no supply of hot water, no cooking facilities bar a small backup camping gas arrangement, and worst of all, no refrigeration or facilities for sterilizing. In short, they were thrown back upon only the most basic and primitive forms of medication, amounting to little more than practical first aid.

It was late afternoon and they were already floundering when the hospital was visited by Captain Sadiq. He spent quite a time in discussion with the doctor and Sisters Mary and Ursula, the leading nuns of the small colony, and it was finally decided that one of them should come back with him to the convoy, to speak to us and find out if our technical skills could be of any use. Sister Ursula came as the doctor couldn't be spared and Sister Mary was elderly.

Kemp asked why Captain Sadiq hadn't personally escorted her to the camp and seen her safe. He was fairly indignant and so was I at this dereliction.

'Ah, he's so busy, that man. I told him to drop me at the military camp and I walked over. There's nothing wrong with me now, and walking's no new thing to us, you know.'

'It could have been damned dangerous.'

'I didn't think so. There were a score of people wishing to speak to the Captain, and no vehicles to spare. And here I am, safe enough.'

'That you are, Sister. You'll stay here tonight? I'm sure you could do with a night's sleep. In the morning we'll take you back to the hospital, and see what we can do to help.'

Kemp had changed quite a lot in a short time. While not inhumane, I'm fairly sure that as little as three days ago he would not have been quite so ready to ditch his transportation job at the drop of a hat to go to the rescue of a local mission hospital. But the oncome of the war, the sight of the burnt out town with its hapless population, and perhaps most of all the injury to one of his own, our pilot, had altered his narrow outlook.

Now he added, 'One of our men is badly hurt, Sister. He was in a plane crash and he needs help. Would you look at him tonight?'

'Of course,' she said with ready concern.

Ben Hammond had left the table, and now came back to join us with a stack of six-packs of beer in his arms.

'We've relaxed the rationing for tonight,' he said. 'Everybody deserves it. Sister, you wouldn't take a second shot of whisky, but maybe you'll settle for this instead?' He handed her a can from the pack.

She tightened her fist around the can.

'Why, it's ice cold!'

Hammond smiled. 'It just came out of the fridge.'

'You have a refrigerator? But that's marvellous. We can preserve our drugs then, praise be to God!'

Kemp and Hammond exchanged the briefest of glances, but I could guess what they were thinking. There was no way that refrigerator could be left at the hospital, urgent though its need might be; it was run by the generator that was solidly attached to the rig, and without which nothing could function.

Things looked better the next morning, but not much. No smoke wreathed up from the distant town but I suspected that this was because there was nothing left there to burn. We were greatly cheered when Sam Wilson told us that he had located a source of clean water, a well at a nearby village which hadn't been affected by the bombing, and which seemed to have a healthy supply. He intended to fill the water tanker and top up drinking containers. When he learned about the water shortage at the hospital he said that there should be enough for them too, assuming they had some sort of tank in which to store it.

Geoff Wingstead joined us for breakfast and met Sister

117

Ursula for the first time. She had been to see Otterman but wanted him taken to the hospital for the doctor to see, and now looked professionally at Wingstead's gash and bruises and approved of what had been done for them. Wingstead insisted that he was now perfectly well and was eager to see the town and the hospital for himself. In spite of his heavy financial commitment, he seemed far less anxious about the rig and Wyvern Transport's future than Kemp did. Perhaps it was just that he was younger and more adventurous.

I drove back to the town in the Land Rover with Kemp, Wingstead, Sister Ursula, and Hammond. Sadiq came over just before we left and said that he would see us at the hospital a little later. He looked drawn and harassed. The lack of communication from his superiors and the consequent responsibility was taking its toll, but even so he was bearing up pretty well. Kemp and I still had a nagging doubt as to his loyalty, but we'd seen nothing to prove the case one way or the other, except that he was still with us, which probably counted for something. As for the shooting down of our plane, nothing whatever had been said about it and I was content to let the question lie.

The fires had burnt themselves out and the heavy pall of smoke of yesterday was replaced by a light haze fed by ash and still smouldering embers. Kodowa had nothing left worth destroying. A few isolated buildings still stood, but most of the centre was gone, and it was by no means sure that when we cleared the rubble we would find an intact road surface beneath it.

People wandered about still, but very few of them. Many had simply melted back into the bush, others had gone to cluster round the hospital or the army encampment, and we'd seen pathetic faces hovering near our own camp during the early hours of the morning. We didn't spend much time in the town, but asked Sister Ursula to direct us to the hospital which stood slightly apart and to the east. The road getting there was not in good condition.

The hospital looked exactly like the casualty station it had become. We threaded our way through the knots of Nyalans

118

who were already setting up their makeshift homes in the grounds, avoiding the little cooking fires and the livestock which wandered about underfoot, and the small naked children. People stared at us but there was none of the crowding round that usually happened in the villages in happier times. Sister Ursula, though, was accosted and hailed by name as we left the car and made our way indoors.

We met Sister Mary, who was elderly and frail, and two younger nuns, all fully occupied. I noticed that none of them seemed surprised to see Sister Ursula back with a team of British men, or even particularly relieved at her safe return from what might have been regarded as a dangerous mission; the impression I got was that they all had the most sublime faith in her ability to take care of herself, and to turn up trumps in any eventuality. I could see their point of view.

She led us into an office, asked us to wait and vanished, to return very soon with the surgeon in tow.

Kemp said, 'We're very pleased to meet you, Doctor –'

He was a tall, saturnine Nyalan with a strong Asian streak, grey-haired and authoritative. He wore tropical whites which were smudged and blood-streaked. He put out a hand and took Kemp's, and smiled a mouthful of very white teeth at all of us.

'Katabisirua. But here everyone calls me Doctor Kat. It is a pleasure to have you here, especially at this moment.'

'Doctor – Doctor Kat, I'm Basil Kemp of Wyvern Transport. You probably know what we're doing here in Nyala. This is my partner, Mister Wingstead. Mister Hammond, our chief mechanic. Mister Mannix is from our associated company, British Electric.' He ran through the introductions and there were handshakes all round, very formal. Ben hid a smile at the man's nickname.

'Gentlemen, I can offer you little hospitality. Please forgive me.'

Wingstead brushed this aside.

'Of course you can't, and we don't expect it. There's work to be done here. Let me say that I think we have got your

119

water problem sorted out, thanks to some of my lads, provided you've got tanks or somewhere to store the stuff.'

Dr Kat's eyes lit up. 'Thank God. Water is a pressing need. We have a storage tank which is almost empty; I have been trying to take nothing from it until we knew about replacement, but naturally everyone is in need of it.'

'We'll get the tanker up here as soon as we can. We expect Captain Sadiq to join us soon; he's the officer of the military detachment here. When he comes, I'll get him to send a message to our camp,' Wingstead said. He and Dr Kat were on the same wavelength almost immediately, both men of decision and determination. Basil Kemp's tendency to surrender to irritation and his stubborn inability to keep his plans flexible would be easily overridden by these two.

'Now, what about the electricity? We cannot make our generator work. We have bottled gas, but not much. What can you do to help us there?' Dr Kat asked. He had another attribute, the calm assurance that every other man was willing to put himself and his possessions completely at the service of the hospital at any time. Without that self-confidence no man would have been capable of even beginning to run such a project, for the obstacles Katabisirua must have had to overcome in his time would have been enormous.

'Hammond and I are going to have a look at your generator. We've some experience at that sort of thing. I can't make any promises but we'll do our best,' Wingstead said.

Sister Ursula interrupted. 'What about your refrigerator?' she asked.

Dr Kat's head came up alertly. 'What refrigerator?'

Wingstead hadn't known about last evening's conversation and Kemp, for whatever motives I didn't quite like to think about, hadn't referred to it. Sister Ursula said firmly, 'Doctor Kat, they have a working fridge on their transporter. We should send all the drugs that must be kept cold and as much food as possible down there immediately. We can save a lot of it.'

His face beamed. 'But that's wonderful!'

120

Sister Ursula went on inexorably, 'And also they have electricity. Lights, cooking, even a deepfreeze. I saw all this last night. Isn't that so, gentlemen?'

'Of course we have,' Wingstead concurred. 'We're going to do what we can to use our power supply to restart yours. We'll have to get the rig up here, though, and that isn't going to be at all easy.'

Kemp looked troubled. 'I've been studying the road up here. What with the refugees and the condition of the road itself, I'd say it's going to be damn near impossible, Geoff.'

The nun interrupted, her jaw set at its firmest. 'But all we want is your generator. We don't need that huge thing of yours. We could do with your deepfreeze too; and with the generator our own refrigerator will run. You gentlemen can manage without cold beer, but we need that facility of yours.'

The Wyvern team exchanged looks of despair.

'Ma'am, Doctor Kat, that just isn't possible,' Hammond said at last.

'Why not, please?' The surgeon asked.

Sister Ursula showed that she'd picked up a bit of politics during her evening at our camp. 'Mister Mannix,' she said, 'you represent a very wealthy company. Please explain to your colleagues that it is imperative that we have this facility! I am sure your board of executives will approve. It is of the highest importance.'

I was dumbfounded and showed it. 'Sister, that just isn't the problem. British Electric would give you anything you asked for, but they're not here. And the reason you can't have the generator isn't economic, it's technical. Explain, some-one.'

Hammond took up a pad of paper lying on the desk, and his pen began to fly over the paper as he sketched rapidly.

'Look here, ma'am. You too, Doctor.'

They bent over the sheet of paper and I peered over Ben's shoulder. He had produced a lightning and very competent sketch of the entire rig. He pointed to various parts as he spoke,

121

and it must have been obvious to his whole audience that he was speaking the truth.

'Here's the generator. To drive it you have to have an engine, and that's here. The actual generator is really a part of the engine, not a separate section. If you looked at it, just here, you'd see that the engine casting and the generator casting are one and the same; it's an integral unit.'

'Then we must have the engine too,' said Sister Ursula practically.

Kemp choked.

Hammond shook his head. 'Sorry. The engine has much more to do than just drive this generator. Sure, it provided the electricity to power the fridge and freezer, and light the camp at night and stuff like that, but that's just a bonus.'

He pointed to the illustration of the transformer.

'This big lump on its trailer is now resting on the ground, practically. Before we can move off we have to lift three hundred and thirty tons – that's the load plus the platform it's resting on – through a vertical distance of three feet. It's done hydraulically and it needs a whole lot of power, which comes from the engine. And when we're moving we must have power for the brakes which are also hydraulically operated. Without this engine we're immobile.'

'Then you must – '

Hammond anticipated the nun's next demand.

'We can't ditch our load. It took a couple of pretty hefty cranes to get it in place, and it'd need the same to shift it off its base. Some flat-bed trucks have the mobility to tip sideways, but this one hasn't, so we can't spill it off. And any attempt to do so will probably wreck the entire works.'

It was stalemate. Kemp tried to hide his sigh of relief.

Into the disappointed silence Wingstead spoke. 'Don't be too downhearted. We *can* refrigerate your drugs and a lot of your food too, if you think it's safe to do so, at least while we're here. And we can probably get the whole rig up here so that we can couple up with your lighting and sterilizing units.

Sister Ursula did look thoroughly downcast.

Katabisirua said gently, 'Never mind, Sister. It was a good idea, but we will have others.'

'But they're going to be moving along. Then what can we do?'

Wingstead said, 'We won't be moving anywhere for a bit, not until we know a little more about the general situation and have a decent plan of action. Let's take this one step at a time, shall we? I think we should go back to our camp now. Would you like to make a pack of all your drugs that need to go into the refrigerator, Sister? We'll take them with us. If you need any in the meantime we can arrange for the Captain to put a motorcyclist at your disposal. What do you suggest we do for our wounded pilot?'

'I will come with you. I think I should see him. They must spare me here for a little while,' the Doctor said. After a quick conference, Sister Ursula went off to supervise the packing of drugs and other items that could do with refrigeration, while Dr Kat collected the ubiquitous little black bag and said that he was ready to go.

We found a soldier standing guard over the Land Rover, and parked nearby was Sadiq's staff car. The Captain was speaking to a knot of Nyalan men, presumably the elders of Kodowa, but left them to join us.

'Good morning, sir. You are better now?' This was addressed to Wingstead, who nodded cheerfully.

'I would like to know what your plans are, sir. There is much to do here, but do you intend to continue upcountry?' Sadiq asked.

'We're not going immediately,' Wingstead said. I noticed how easily he took over command from Kemp, and how easily Kemp allowed him to do so. Kemp was entirely content to walk in his senior partner's shadow on all matters except, perhaps, for the actual handling of the rig itself. I wasn't sorry. Geoff Wingstead could make decisions and was flexible enough to see alternative possibilities as he went along. He was a man after my own heart.

Now he went on, 'I'd like to discuss plans with you, Captain, but we have to sort ourselves out first. We are going to try and help the doctor here, but first we're going back to camp. Can you join me there in a couple of hours, please?'

At this moment Sadiq's sergeant called him over to the staff car, holding out earphones. Sadiq listened and then turned dials around until a thin voice, overlaid with static, floated out to us as we crowded round the car. 'Radio Nyala is on the air,' Sadiq said.

It was a news broadcast apparently, in Nyalan, which after a while changed into English. The voice was flat and careful and the words showed signs that they had come under the heavy hand of government censorship. Apparently 'dissident elements' of the Army and Air Force had rioted in barracks but by a firm show of force the Government had checked the rebels. The ringleaders were shortly to stand trial in a military court. There was no need for civil unease. No names or places were given. There was no mention of Kodowa. And there was no other news. The voice disappeared into a mush of palm court music.

I smiled sourly as I listened to this farrago. Next week, if the Government survived, the 'dissident elements' would be plainly labelled as traitors. The news broadcasts would never refer to a state of war, nor give more than the most shadowy version of the truth. Of course, all that depended on whether the broadcast station remained in government hands. If the rebels took it there would be an entirely different version of the 'truth'.

None of us made much comment on what we'd heard, all recognizing it for the fallacy that it was. We piled into the Land Rover with Dr Kat and drove back in silence to the convoy camp.

11

Three hours later after a short discussion with Wingstead I gathered the people I wanted for a conference. But I had decided that this wasn't going to be a committee meeting; I wasn't going to put up my proposals to be voted on. This was to be an exchange of ideas and information, but the only person who was going to have the final say was me.

I had found McGrath shaving in front of his tractor. 'Mick, you've just got your old rank back.' He looked a bit blank while the lather on his chin dried in the hot sun. 'You're back to sergeant. We might be going through a tough time in the next few days, and I want someone to keep the crew whipped in line. Think you can do it?'

He gave a slow grin. 'I can do it.'

'Hurry up with your shaving. I want you to sit in on a conference.'

So we had McGrath, Hammond, Kemp, Wingstead, Captain Sadiq and me. Katabisirua had been joined at our camp by Sister Ursula and they were included as a matter of courtesy; any decisions would affect them and in any case I didn't think I had the power to keep them out. I had already realized they made a strong team: just how strong I was shortly to find out.

Firstly I outlined the geographical position, and gave them my reasons for changing our direction. Instead of going on up to the arid fastness of Bir Oassa we would turn at right angles and take the secondary road to the Manzu border at Lake Pirie on the Katali River. Here we had two options whereas at Bir Oassa we had only one, or slightly less than one; we could turn back along the coast road to Lasulu and the capital if the

125

country had by then settled its internal quarrel and things were judged safe, or we could get the men at least across the Katali into Manzu and diplomatic immunity.

Wingstead had already heard all this from me and was resigned to the possibility of losing his rig and convoy, and of not being able to fulfil the terms of his contract with the Nyalan Government. He did not contest my arguments. I had already spoken to Kemp, and Hammond had heard it all from him. Kemp was still obviously fretting but Hammond's faith in Wingstead was all-encompassing. If his boss said it was OK, he had no objections. I asked McGrath what he thought the men's reactions might be.

'We haven't got much choice, the way I see it. You're the boss. They'll see it your way.' He implied that they'd better, which suited me very well.

Sadiq was torn between a sense of duty and a sense of relief. To take the long hard road up to the desert, with all its attendant dangers, and without any knowledge of who or what he'd find waiting there, was less attractive than returning to a known base, in spite of the unknown factors waiting in that direction as well. But there was one problem he didn't have that we did; any decision concerning the moving of the rig.

We discussed, briefly, the possible state of the road back. It was all guesswork which Kemp loathed, but at least we knew the terrain, and there was a bonus of the fact that it was principally downhill work, redescending the plateau into the rainforest once more. We would not run short of water; there were far more people and therefore more chance of food and even of fuel. And we wouldn't be as exposed as we would be if we continued on through the scrublands. I hadn't discounted the likelihood of aerial attack.

Hammond and Kemp, with an escort of soldiers, were to scout ahead to check out the road while McGrath and Bert Proctor began to organize the convoy for its next stage forward, or rather backward. Wingstead asked McGrath to call a meeting of the crew, so that he could tell them the exact score before

126

we got down to the business of logistics. Everything was falling nicely into place, including my contingency plans to help the hospital as much as possible before we pulled out.

Everything didn't include the inevitable X factor. And the X factor was sitting right there with us.

The moment of change came when I turned to Dr Katabisi-rua and said to him, 'Doctor Kat, those drugs of yours that we have in refrigeration for you; how vital are they?'

He tented his fingers. 'In the deepfreeze we have serum samples and control sera; also blood clotting agents for our few haemophiliac patients. In the fridge there is whole blood, plasma, blood sugars, insulin and a few other things. Not really a great deal as we try not to be dependent on refrigeration. It has been of more use in saving some of our food, though that is being used up fast.'

I was relieved to hear this; they could manage without refrigeration if they had to. After all, most tropical mission hospitals in poor countries work in a relative degree of primitiveness.

'We'll keep your stuff on ice as long as possible,' I said. 'And we're going to have a go at repairing your generator. We'll do all we can before leaving.'

Dr Kat and Sister Ursula exchanged the briefest of glances, which I interpreted, wrongly, as one of resignation.

'Captain Sadiq,' the Doctor said, 'Do you have any idea at all as to whether there will be a measure of governmental control soon?'

Sadiq spread his hands. 'I am sorry, no,' he said. 'I do not know who is the Government. I would do my best for all civilians, but I have been told to stay with Mister Mannix and protect his convoy particularly, you see. It is very difficult to make guesses.'

They spoke in English, I think in deference to us.

'The people of Kodowa will scatter among the smaller villages soon,' Kat said. 'The area is well populated, which is why they needed a hospital. Many of them have already gone.

127

But that solution does not apply to my patients.'

'Why not?' Kemp asked.

'Because we do not have the staff to scatter around with them, to visit the sick in their homes or the homes of friends. Many are too sick to trust to local treatment. We have many more patients now because of the air raid.'

'How many?'

'About fifty bed patients, if we had the beds to put them in, and a hundred or more ambulatory patients. In this context they could be called the "walking wounded",' he added acidly.

'So it is only a matter of extra shelter you need,' said Sadiq. I knew he was partly wrong, but waited to hear the Doctor put it into words.

'It is much more than that, Captain. We need shelter, yes, but that is not the main problem. We need medical supplies but we can manage for a while on what we have. But our patients need nursing, food and water.'

'There will be dysentery here soon,' put in Sister Ursula. 'There is already sepsis, and a lack of hygiene, more than we usually suffer.'

'They also are vulnerable to the depredations of marauding bands of rebels,' said Dr Kat, a sentence I felt like cheering for its sheer pomposity. But he was right for all that.

'As are we all, including the younger nurses,' added the Sister. It began to sound like a rather well-rehearsed chorus and Wingstead and I exchanged a glance of slowly dawning comprehension.

'Am I not correct, Mister Mannix, in saying that you consider it the safest and most prudent course for your men to leave Kodowa, to try and get away to a place of safety?'

'You heard me say so, Doctor.'

'Then it follows that it must also be the correct course for my patients.'

For a long moment no-one said anything, and then I broke the silence. 'Just how do you propose doing that?'

128

Katabisirua took a deep breath. This was the moment he had been building up to. 'Let me see if I have everything right that I have learned from you. Mister Hammond, you say that the large object you carry on your great vehicle weighs over three hundred tons, yes?'

'That's about it.'

'Could you carry another seven tons?'

'No trouble at all,' said Hammond.

'Seven tons is about the weight of a hundred people,' said Katabisirua blandly.

Or one more elephant, I thought with a manic inward chuckle. The silence lengthened as we all examined this bizarre proposition. It was broken by the Doctor, speaking gently and reasonably, 'I am not suggesting that you take us all the way to the coast, of course. There is another good, if small, hospital at Kanja on the north road, just at the top of the next escarpment. It has no airfield and is not itself important, so I do not think it will have been troubled by the war. They could take care of us all.'

I doubted that and didn't for a moment think that Dr Kat believed it either, but I had to hand it to him; he was plausible and a damned good psychologist. Not only did his proposition sound well within the bounds of reason and capability, but I could tell from the rapt faces around me that the sheer glamour of what he was suggesting was beginning to put a spell on them. It was a *Pied Piper* sort of situation, stuffed with pathos and heroism, and would go far to turn the ignominious retreat into some sort of whacky triumph. The Dunkirk spirit, I thought – the great British knack of taking defeat and making it look like victory.

There was just one little problem. Kanja, it appeared, was on the very road that we had already decided to abandon, heading north into the desert and towards the oilfields at Bir Oassa. I was about to say as much when to my astonishment Wingstead cut in with a question which implied that his thinking was not going along with mine at all.

He said, 'How far to Kanja?'

'About fifty miles. The road is quite good. I have often driven there,' the Doctor said.

Hammond spoke up. 'Excuse me, Doctor. Is it level or uphill?'

'I would say it is fairly flat. There are no steep hills.'

McGrath said, 'We could rig awnings over the bogies to keep off the sun.'

Hammond asked, his mind seething with practicalities, 'Fifty odd patients, and a staff of – ?'

'Say ten,' said Sister Ursula.

'What about all the rest, then?'

'They would walk. They are very hardy and used to that, and even those who are wounded will manage. There are a few hospital cars but we have no spare petrol. I believe you do not go very fast, gentlemen.'

'We could take some up on top of the trucks. And we've got your car, Mister Mannix, and Mister Kemp's Land Rover, and perhaps the military could give up some space,' Hammond said.

'And the tractors?' the Sister asked.

'No, ma'am. They're packed inside with steel plates set in cement, and the airlift truck is full of machinery and equipment we might need. But there's room on top of all of them. Awnings would be no problem?'

McGrath said, 'There'd be room for a couple of the nippers in each cab, like as not.'

'Nippers?' the doctor asked.

'The children,' McGrath said.

I looked from face to face. On only one of them, and that predictably was Basil Kemp's, did I see a trace of doubt or irritation. Minds were taking fire as we talked. Geographical niceties were either being entirely overlooked or deliberately avoided, and somehow I couldn't bring myself to dash cold water on their blazing enthusiasm. But this was madness itself.

130

Dr Kat regarded the backs of his hands and flexed his fingers thoughtfully. 'I may have to operate while we are travelling. Would there be room for that?'

'Room, yes, but it would be too bumpy, Doctor. You'd have to work whenever we were stopped,' said Hammond. He had a notebook out and was already making sketches.

Sadiq spoke. 'I think my men can walk and the wounded will ride. They are our people and we must take care of them.' He squared his shoulders as he spoke and I saw the lifting of a great burden from his soul; he had been given a job to do, something real and necessary no matter which side was winning the mysterious war out there. It called for simple logistics, basic planning, clear orders, and he was capable of all that. And above all, it called for no change in the route once planned for him and us by his masters. It was perfect for him. It solved all his problems in one stroke.

Sister Ursula stood up.

'Have you a measuring tape, Mister Hammond?'

'Yes, ma'am. What do you want it for?' he asked.

'I want to measure your transport. I must plan for beds.'

'I'll come with you,' he said. 'Tell me what you want.'

McGrath lumbered to his feet. 'I'll go round up the lads, Mister Wingstead,' he said. 'You'll be wanting to talk to them yourself.' The Doctor too rose, dusting himself off fastidiously. He made a small half-bow to Geoff Wingstead. 'I have to thank you, sir,' he said formally. 'This is a very fine thing that you do. I will go back now, please. I have many arrangements to make.'

Sadiq said, 'I will take the Doctor and then prepare my own orders. I will come back to advise you, Mister Mannix. We should not delay, I think.'

Around us the conference melted away, each member intent on his or her own affairs. Astonishingly, nobody had waited to discuss this new turn of events or even to hear from the so-called bosses as to whether it was even going to happen. In a matter

131

of moments Kemp, Wingstead and I were left alone. For once I felt powerless.

Kemp shrugged his shoulders. 'It's all quite mad,' he said. 'We can't possibly get involved in this – this –'

'Stunt?' Wingstead asked gently. 'Basil, we *are* involved. I've never seen a piece of manipulation more skilfully done. Those two have run rings round the lot of us, and there isn't any way that we could put a stop to this business. And what's more,' he went on, overriding Kemp's protests, 'I don't think I'd want to stop it. It is crazy, but it sounds feasible and it's humanely necessary. And it's going to put a lot of heart into our lads. None of them likes what's happened, they feel frustrated, cheated and impotent.'

I finally got a word in. 'Geoff, we'd already decided that we shouldn't carry on northwards. This would be a very fine thing to do, but – '

'You too, Neil? Surely you're not going to fight me on this. I think it's damned important. Look, it's fifty miles. Two, maybe three days extra, getting there and back here to Kodowa. Then we're on our own again. And there's something else. The news that we must turn back is one they were going to take damned hard. This way they'll at least have the feeling that they've done something worthwhile.'

He stretched his arms and yawned, testing the stiffness in his side.

'And so will I. So let's get to it.'

Down near the commissariat truck McGrath had called all hands together. Wingstead and I went to meet them. On the way I stopped and called Bishop over to give him an instruction that brought first a frown and then a grin to his face. He in turn summoned Bing and they vanished. 'What did you tell him?' Wingstead asked.

'Bit of psychology. You'll see. Don't start till he's back, will you?'

Bishop and Bing returned a few moments later, lugging a

132

couple of cardboard boxes. To the assembled men I said, 'Here you go, guys. A can apiece. Send them around, cookie.'

Bishop began handing out six-packs of beer. 'Management too,' I reminded him. 'And that includes the Doctor and Sister Ursula.' There was a buzz of conversation as the packs went out, and then I held up a hand in silence.

'Everybody happy?'

Laughter rippled. Cans were already being opened, and Barry Lang paused with his halfway to his mouth. 'What are we celebrating, chief? The end of the war?'

'Not quite. We're celebrating the fact that this is the last cold beer we're all going to get for a while.' At this there was a murmur of confusion. I held up an open can. 'Some of you may know this already. We're using the fridge to store the hospital's drugs and as much food as possible for the patients, especially the kids. From now on, it'll be warm beer and canned food for the lot of us. My heart bleeds for you.'

This brought another laugh. Grafton said, 'We're staying here, then?'

This was Wingstead's moment, and he jumped lightly onto the top of the cab. He had recovered well from his shake-up in the air crash, unlike Max Otterman, who still lay unconscious in the shade of the water tanker and was a constant source of worry to all of us.

Wingstead said, 'No, we're not staying here. We're moving out, maybe today, more likely tomorrow. But we're not going much further north.'

Into an attentive silence which I judged to be not hostile he outlined the geographical picture, the political scene such as we knew it, and the reasons for abandoning the contract. The crew accepted everything without argument, though there was a lot of muted discussion, and I was impressed again by Wingstead's air of command and his control over his team. I'd had my eye on Sisley and Lang as being the two most likely hard liners, but there was no opposition even from them. The argument in favour of saving their own skins was a strong one, and

133

unlike Wyvern's management they had no direct stake in the outcome of the job.

Wingstead went on to the second half of the story, and now their astonishment was obvious. There was a burst of talking and signs of excitement and enthusiasm beginning to creep into their voices. It was almost like giving a bunch of kids a dazzling new game to play with.

'So there it is, chaps. We move out as soon as we can, and we're taking a whole lot of sick and injured people and all the hospital staff with us, and everybody who can walk will be tailing along for their daily bandage changes. We're going to pack the badly injured onto the rig and carry as many of the rest as we can on the trucks. We're going to need every ounce of your energy and good will. Are we agreed?'

There was a ready chorus of assent. Wingstead went on, 'Any bright ideas you may have, pass them along to Mick or Mister Hammond or me. Any medical questions direct to the Sister.' I smiled briefly at the division between those who were 'Mister' and those who were not, even in these fraught moments; another example of the gulf between their country and mine.

'When we've seen them safe at the hospital in Kanja, we'll turn round and set off towards the Katali. We reckon on only two extra days for the mission. Thank you, chaps.'

Mick McGrath rose and bellowed.

'Right, lads! Five minutes to finish your beer and then let's be at it. There's plenty to be done.'

As Wingstead and I walked off, well pleased with the way our bombshell of news had gone down, Sister Ursula waylaid us, having, no doubt got all she wanted from Ben Hammond.

'Mister Mannix, I want transport back to the hospital, please.'

'No you don't,' I said. 'You're wanted here. The crew is going to be pestering you with questions and ideas, and Geoff and I have got quite a few of our own.'

'I'll be needed at the hospital.'

134

'I'm sure you will. But Sister Mary is there with the others and you're the only one here. And the rate your Doctor Kat works, there'll probably be a first load of patients arriving within the hour. The lads will work under your direction, yours and Ben's that is. They've got awnings to rig up, bedding to get cut, all sorts of stuff. And you have to choose a spot for your operating theatre.'

'I've done that already.' But she wasn't stubborn when faced with plain good sense, and agreed readily enough to stay and get on with her end of the job, for which I was grateful. If it came to the crunch I didn't think I would ever win out against her.

We all worked hard and the rig was transformed. Sadiq's men rounded up some of the local women who knew how to thatch with palm leaf fronds and set them to work, silently at first and then as the strangeness and the fear began to wear off, singing in ululating chorus. As it took shape the rig began to look pretty strange wearing a selection of thatched umbrellas. I was amused to think what Kemp would have to say: he had gone off to check the road leading northwards out of town.

Awnings were being made for the tops of each of the trucks as well, and reeds from the river were beginning to pile up to make bedding for each of the patients as we found places for them. All four tractors were similarly bedecked. Even the tank McGrath had salvaged was to carry its share of patients, perched in the turret. The gun had been ditched once it was clear that there was no ammunition for it. I doubt if you could see anything in the world more incongruous than a thatched tank.

Sadiq had unearthed a couple of old trucks which Ben Hammond pronounced as serviceable and we thatched one of those. The other already had a canvas awning. There were few other vehicles in Kodowa that had escaped either the strafing or the fires.

135

There was moderately good news about fuel. Outside the town we found a full 4000-gallon tanker. It must have been abandoned by its driver at the onset of the air attack. Both it and our own tanker escaped thatching because I jibbed at carrying bedridden patients on top of potential bombs. The water tanker wasn't thatched either, being the wrong shape for carrying people.

Sister Ursula was endlessly busy. She supervised the cutting of bedding, to make sure that none was wet and that the worst of the insect life was shaken out of it, checked through our food supplies and made a complete inventory, rounded up towels and sheets from everybody, and selected a place on the rig for Dr Kat's mobile surgery, the top of the foremost tractor cab, as being the only really flat surface and the one least likely to get smothered in the dust we would stir up in our progress. It was, she pointed out, very exposed but in our supplies we had a couple of pup tents and one of these, after some tailoring, made a fairly passable enclosed space. The other formed a screen for the patients' toilet, a galvanized iron bucket.

It was all quite astonishing.

The Sister then proceeded to go through the camp like a one-woman locust swarm, sweeping up everything she thought might be of any use. Every pair of scissors she could find she confiscated; she almost denuded the commissary wagon of knives; and she kept young Bing on the run, setting him to boil water to sterilize the things she found.

Once done, they were wrapped in sheets of polythene. Everything as sterile as she could make it. And then they were stored in a corner of our freezer, to slow down bacterial activity. She confiscated packets of paperclips and went through Kemp's Land Rover, removing clips from every piece of paper in sight, garnering sticky tape, elastic bands and string. Our several first aid boxes all went into her hoard.

Military trucks began arriving from the hospital carrying, not people yet, but goods; food, medications, bandaging, implements, dishes and hardware of all sorts. Among other things

136

was a contraption on a trolley that Sister Ursula dismissed with annoyance.

'That thing doesn't work. Hasn't for a long time. It's a waste of space.'

'What is it, Sister?' It was Ben Hammond who asked, and who seemed to be in constant attendance, not in Mick McGrath's proprietorial fashion but as head gofer to a factory foreman. Her demands fascinated and challenged him.

'It is, or was, a portable anaesthetic machine.'

'If it were fixed, would it be of use?' She nodded and he fixed it. He was a damned good mechanic.

The Sister found a place for Max Otterman and he was gently lifted onto his pile of bedding; Wyvern Transport Hospital's first inmate. He'd been showing some signs of recovering consciousness in the past few hours but the portents were not good; he looked and sounded awful.

I kept busy and tried not to think about him, putting him in the same mental folder in which lurked other worries: the state of the nation, the progress of war, the possibility of aircraft bombing us as we sat helpless. Our fuel or water might run out, there could be sickness or mechanical breakdowns. There was no communication with the world apart from the unreliable and sporadic messages received on the Captain's radio. I kept going, knowing that when I stopped the problems would close in.

It was a long, complex and exhausting day. There was little talking as evening fell and we ate thoughtfully and turned in. I lay fighting off despair, and even coined a phrase for it: Mannix' Depression. But I couldn't raise a laugh at my own joke. The odds against us seemed to be stacked far too high.

12

There was another change of plan that afternoon. We were to move the rig to the hospital rather than risk moving the patients before it was necessary. At daybreak we got going, the oddly transformed convoy passing slowly through the town that wasn't a town any more, to Katabisirua's headquarters beyond. The command car bumped over rubble as we passed the remains of the shattered tanks which we had laboured to shift and crunched through cinders and debris in what had been the main street of Kodowa. The place still stank of death and burning.

We passed a truncated and blackened telegraph pole from which a body dangled. Sadiq said laconically, 'A looter, sir.'

'Have you had many?'

'A few. He was one of the first. He discourages the others, as they say.'

Every now and then Sadiq's obviously broader than average education showed through. For a locally trained lower echelon officer of a somewhat backward country he was surprisingly well-read in military matters. It seemed a pity that he had been given so little room to do his own thinking, but was still tied by the bonds of discipline.

I saw a sign on a blackened but still standing shop front and a soldier who stood in front of the door, cradling a gun. 'Will you stop a minute, Captain? May I go in there?'

'It is off limits, Mister Mannix.' Again the flash of an unexpected phrase.

'Yes, and we both know why.'

I got out of the car without waiting for any more objections

138

and gestured to the soldier to let me by. Sadiq entered the ruined premises behind me. I picked my way through a jumble of fallen stock, farm implements, clothing, magazines, household stuff, all the usual clutter of an upcountry store, to a locked glass-fronted cupboard towards the back. The glass was shattered now, and the doors buckled with heat. I took a hunting knife from a display rack, inserted the point just below the lock, and pushed smartly sideways. There was a dry snap and the doors sagged open. There wasn't much of a choice, just six shotguns; four of them double-barrelled which the British still favour, and two pump action. Four were fire-damaged.

I picked up a Mossberg Model 500, twelve-gauge with six shot capacity, and laid it on the counter. Then I started to attack the warped drawers below the gun rack, praying that I'd find what I wanted, and did so; two packs of double-o buckshot, magnum size. Each shell carried nine lead pellets, a third of an inch in diameter, and capable of dropping a 200-pound deer. And a deer is harder to kill than a man.

I dumped the shells next to the gun, added a can of gun oil, then as an afterthought searched for a scabbard for the hunting knife and put that with the rest. Sadiq watched without comment. Then I tore a piece of paper from a singed pad on the counter, scribbled a note, and dropped it into the open till. I slammed the till drawer shut and walked out of the store with my collection.

'Are you going to hang me for a looter, Captain? That was an IOU I put in the cash till. The owner can claim from British Electric.'

'If he is still alive,' said Sadiq dryly.

He watched as I ripped open a packet of shells and started to load the gun. 'Are you expecting trouble at the hospital, Mister Mannix?'

'You're a soldier. You ought to know that an unloaded gun is just a piece of junk iron. Let's say I may be expecting trouble, period. And you may not be around to get me out of it.'

'Please do not wave it about, then. I will not ask you for a

139

licence; I am not a policeman. I authorize you to hold it. I would feel the same, myself.'

He surprised me by his acquiescence. I had expected him to make it hard for me, but I was determined to go no further without any sort of personal weapon. I made sure the safety catch was on and then laid the gun down by the side of my seat. 'You have some pretty fine weapons yourself,' I said. 'One of my men was casting an envious eye on your Uzi. Keep a close check on all your guns, Captain; I don't want any of them to go missing.' It was Mick McGrath I was thinking of. Something had made me think quite a while back that I'd always be happier if he remained unarmed.

'I will take care. Take your own precautions, please,' Sadiq said, and we drove on to catch up with the rest of the convoy.

I suppose you could call the setup at Katabisirua's a field hospital. Everyone seemed to have been moved out of the buildings into a field, and nurses scurried about their business. To me it just looked like a lot of people dying in the open air. Last time I'd only seen the offices, and all this was pretty horrifying.

After a while I began to see order in the apparent chaos. Way over at one end were a lot of people, sitting or walking about, some supported by friends. Scattered cooking fires sent plumes of smoke into the air. In the field were rows of makeshift beds with friends or families in attendance. Hastily erected frond screens hid what I assumed to be the worst cases, or perhaps they were latrines. In the middle of the field were tables around which moved nurses in rumpled uniforms. A stretcher was being lifted onto a table presided over by Dr Katabisirua. At another Sister Mary, frail and leaning on a stick, was directing a nurse in a bandaging operation. I couldn't see Sister Ursula anywhere.

Away from this area were two newly filled in trenches and a third trench standing open. Slowly I walked across to look at

140

it. It had been half filled with loose earth and stones and scattered with lime. A single naked foot protruded and I choked on the acridity of the chloride of lime which did not quite hide the stench of decay.

I turned away with sweat banding my forehead, and it had nothing to do with the morning sun.

Sadiq's car had gone but a man was standing waiting for me. He was white, smallish and very weathered, wearing shorts and a torn bush jacket; his left arm was in a sling and his face was covered with abrasions.

'Mannix?' he said huskily.

'That's right.'

'You might remember me if I were cleaner. I'm Dan Atheridge. We met in the Luard Club not long ago.'

I did remember him but not as he was right now. Then he had been a brisk, chirpy little man, dapper and immaculate, with snapping blue eyes that gave a friendly gleam in a walnut face. Now the skin was pasty under the surface tan and the eyes had become old and faded. He went on, 'Perhaps I'd have been better off if I'd stayed there . . . and perhaps not. What exactly is going on here? I understand you're moving everybody out. That right?'

I said, 'I could say I was glad to see you, but they're not quite the right words under the circumstances.'

He moved his arm and winced. 'Got a broken flipper – hurts like hell. But I survived.' He nodded towards the open grave. 'Better off than those poor buggers.'

'How come you're here?'

'I run beef on the high ground up past Kanja. I brought a truck down here for servicing three days ago. I was standing on what was the hotel balcony watching the troops go by when all hell let loose. I say, are you *really* going to evacuate the hospital up to Kanja?'

'We're going to try.'

'Can I come along? My home's up that way. My wife will be worrying.'

I tried to imagine what it would be like to be a woman on a remote farm in the Nyalan uplands with a war breaking out and a husband vanished into a bombed out town, and failed. Then I had another, more practical thought. He'd know the Kanja route backwards.

'You'd be more than welcome. We can find you a meal, perhaps – and a warm beer.'

'Great!' His warm smile lit the weary eyes.

'Mister Mannix!'

I turned to see Dr Kat approaching. 'Damned good chap, that,' Atheridge muttered.

The doctor looked wearier than ever; his eyes were sunken deep into his head and his cheeks were hollow. I judged he was driving himself too hard and made a mental note to see if Sister Ursula could get him to slow down. Come to that, she probably needed slowing down herself.

'We lost fifteen in the night,' Dr Kat said. 'The worst cases, of course.'

'Triage?' Atheridge murmured.

I knew about that. Triage was a grisly business used in many armies, but perfected by the French at Dien Bien Phu. The idea was that the wounded were sorted into three categories; lightly wounded, medium but salvageable, and hopeless. The lightly wounded were the first to get treatment so they could be pushed back into action quickly. And it saved on badly needed medical supplies. But it also meant that a lot of others died who might have been saved; a coldly logical, strictly military solution to a medical problem.

'Nothing of the sort,' snapped Katabisirua. 'They had the best attention but they still died. This is not an army. Even you, Mister Atheridge, waited your turn.'

'I'm sorry. You're quite right, of course.'

Dr Kat turned to me. 'I see you have prepared the convoy for us, Mister Mannix.' We glanced over to the distant, thatch-draped rig. 'I have seen what you have done and am most grateful.'

142

'Have you seen your new operating theatre? You'd be amazed at how much Sister Ursula has achieved.'

'I would not be amazed in the least. I know her.'

I asked, 'What is your worst problem right now, Doctor?'

'All those who had extensive burns or severe wounds are already dead or will die soon – later today, I should think. Now the death rate will fall rapidly. But it will rise again in two days?'

'Why?'

'Sepsis. I would give a fortune for ten gallons of old-fashioned carbolic. We have no disinfectants left, and we are running out of sterile bandaging. Operating on a patient in these conditions is like signing his death warrant. I cannot heal with my knife in times like this.'

I felt helpless; I had absolutely no medical knowledge and sympathy seemed a pretty useless commodity. I offered the only thing I had. 'We'll get you all to Kanja as quickly as possible, Doctor. We can start in the evening, when it's cooler, and travel through the night. Mister Atheridge will be invaluable, knowing the road so well.'

The doctor nodded and went back to work.

I'd never make a doctor, not even a bad one, because I guess I'm too squeamish. Medical friends have told me it's something you get used to, but I doubt if I ever could. I'm tough enough at boardroom and even field politics, but blood and guts is another matter. What we loaded onto the rig weren't people but cocooned bundles of pain. The burn cases were the worst.

It was a long and bitter job but we did it, and when we had got everyone aboard somewhere or other, and as comfortable as possible, I went in search of Katabisirua. I found him with Sister Ursula, and as I approached she was saying in a stern voice, 'Now don't argue, Doctor Kat. I said I'll stay. It's all arranged.' She turned to me and said in no less stern a tone, 'Try and get him to have some rest, Mister Mannix. And you too. All of you.' She marched off across the field without

143

waiting for an answer, heading for one of Sadiq's trucks which stood isolated from the rest in the comparative shade of a couple of palms. Two soldiers leaned casually against it and close by three white bundles lay on the ground. A couple of Nyalans squatted over them, waving palm fronds to keep off the flies.

I said, 'What's all this about?'

'Those are the last of the bad burn cases, three of them. Two men and a woman. They can't be moved. Sister Ursula will stay with them and comfort them in their dying. When they are dead the soldiers will bury them. Then they'll bring her to join us. I cannot persuade her otherwise.'

I looked at the stiff-backed figure walking away. 'She's quite a lady.'

'Yes. Very stubborn.'

Coming from him that was ridiculous, almost enough to make me smile but not quite. I said, 'We're all set to move. I'm about to check with Basil Kemp. Are you ready to board, Doctor?'

'Yes, I suppose so.' We both glanced briefly round at the desolation, the bloodstained earth, the abandoned beds and fireplaces, the debris and impedimenta of human living strewn all about. There had been no time to tidy up, and no reason either. The vultures could have it all.

I went in search of Basil Kemp. He had been very quiet all day, looking punch-drunk like a concussed boxer after a losing fight. He did his job all right but he did it almost as though by memory. Ben Hammond was forming a perfect backup for him, covering up whatever weaknesses he sensed in his boss, though he was doubtless motivated more by his faith in Geoff Wingstead.

'Doctor Kat's coming on board,' I told him. 'That's the last of it. We're ready to roll any time you say.'

He had planned to push on well into and maybe right through the night. He had not had time to reconnoitre the road very far ahead, but he had the previous surveys to go by, and

144

there were no very sharp bends or steep gradients in the next twenty miles or so. Up as far as the next river course there were no foreseeable problems. That river lay between us and Kanja which was a pity, but all things being equal we shouldn't have too much trouble. All things weren't equal, of course; somewhere a war was probably still being fought, but in the total absence of any news on that score the only rational thing to do was to ignore it. We'd heard no further aircraft activity and the airport itself, a mile or so outside the town, was reported by Sadiq to be completely deserted.

'Right, we'll get moving. I hope to God these damn thatch roofs don't become a nuisance.' He didn't say it, but I could hear in his voice the phrase, 'Or the people either'. Not the man to depend on for kindness, but at least his concern for his precious rig would keep him attentive.

I drove the hire car. Atheridge and I were in front and between us a Nyalan nurse. She was not on the rig as she had injured a leg. In the back were four of the walking, or rather riding, wounded, three of them teenage children.

As I pulled out to drive to my allocated place, ahead of the rig and among the troop trucks, I said to the girl, 'You do speak English, don't you?'

'Oh yes.'

'Will you tell these people behind to yell out if I do anything to hurt them? I'll try to drive smoothly.'

She half-turned and spoke in Nyalan over her shoulder.

'What's your name, honey?'

'Helen Chula,' she said.

'Can you drive a car, Helen?'

'Yes, I can. But my leg – I would have to go slowly.'

I laughed briefly. 'Don't worry, slowly is what we'll all be doing. If necessary you can take over. Mister Atheridge can't do much with that arm of his, though I guess he could stand on a foot pedal if he had to.'

Sadiq's staff car passed us and I remembered something. I hooted and when he stopped I jumped out and ran over to

145

retrieve the shotgun and pack of shells from his car. Walking past us towards his tractor, Mick McGrath stopped dead and looked at the gun with interest.

'Hey, Mister Mannix. You got yourself a shooter. Now what about me?'

'Who do you want to kill, Mick?'

He shrugged. 'Oh hell, nothing like that. It's just that I feel naked being in a war and me without a gun.'

I grinned. 'Get your own fig leaves.'

He went on and I got back into my car, feeling another slight ripple of unease. Atheridge also eyed the weapon quizzically but said nothing as I stowed it with some difficulty, down alongside the driving seat. Behind us the whole convoy was breaking into the gutteral growls that signified engines churning to life, blue smoke belching from exhaust pipes. I stuck my head out of the car window and listened.

My imagination was irrational. Had there really been cries of pain from the sick and wounded people on the rig, I would never have been able to hear them over the rumbling of the transports. But my stomach clenched in sympathy as I visualized the shuddering, lurching torment of the rig's movement under their bodies. I caught Helen Chula's eyes and knew that she was thinking exactly the same thing.

It had to be done. I shrugged, put the car in gear, and moved out. Vehicle by vehicle, the entire procession pulled away from the hospital and the ruins of Kodowa.

13

The road beyond Kodowa continued to switchback but the gradients were slightly steeper and the hills longer. The average speed of the rig dropped; it was slow enough downhill but really crawled up the long reverse slopes. In general the speed was about a walking pace. Certainly the flock of Nyalans in our wake, injured though some of them were, had no difficulty in keeping up. They were a hardy people, inured to the heat, and well used to walking those dusty roads.

But we worried about these refugees. We had discussed the need to provide them with food and Sadiq had told us that it would have to be gathered on the way. But there were too many women carrying babies or helping toddlers, old men, and wounded of all ages. It wasn't really our responsibility but how else could we look upon it?

As we got going Helen Chula said, 'If I sleep will you wake me in an hour, please?' and promptly did fall asleep, her head pillowed on Atheridge's good arm. I checked on the four Nyalans behind me; two were asleep and the others stared with wary brown eyes. All were silent.

We travelled for nearly two hours, incredibly slowly, and the morning heat began to give way to the fierce sun of noonday. Atheridge and I didn't talk much because we didn't want to wake the girl. Around us dust billows clouded the little groups of Nyalans into soft focus, and here and there among them walked soldiers. I began to worry about the car engine overheating.

Suddenly I realized that I was being the biggest damn fool in creation; the heat must have fried my brains. I tapped the horn, cut out of the column and nosed through the refugees who were walking ahead of the rig to avoid the worst of the dust. I caught up with Sadiq's command car at the head of the column and waved him down. He had two Nyalan women in the back of his car, but his sergeant was still up front beside him.

I said, 'Captain, this is crazy. There's no law which says that we all have to travel at the same speed as the rig. I could get up to Kanja in under two hours, dump my lot at their hospital and come back for more. What's more, so can all the other faster transport. We could get them organized up there, alert them to what's coming.'

Sadiq shook his head. 'No, Mister Mannix, that would not be a good thing.'

'In God's name, why not?'

He looked up and for a moment I thought he was scanning the sky for aircraft. Then I realized that he had actually looked at a telegraph pole, one of the endless line that accompanied the road, and again I cursed my slow brains. 'Damn it, you've got a handset, Sadiq. We can telephone ahead from here.'

'I have tried. That is what is worrying me – there is nothing. I can understand not being able to reach back to Kodowa, but the line to Kanja is also dead.'

'There'll be a lot of people dead if we keep this pace. There seem to be a hell of a lot more than Doctor Kat reckoned on, and most of them aren't injured at all.'

'I cannot stop them, Mister Mannix. They are simply coming with us.'

I felt nonplussed. More mouths to feed? Surely we weren't obliged to lead the entire remaining population of Kodowa to safety.

'Well, how about some of us pushing on? There's my car, the two trucks we found plus your four. Even the tank can move faster than this, and there are six people on board her. The Land Rover has to stay with the rig, but even you –'

'I stay with the convoy. Also my trucks,' said Sadiq flatly.

'Mister Mannix, have you noticed that there is no traffic coming southwards? Have you thought that Kanja might be just like Kodowa?'

I had, and the thought was unnerving. 'If so, now's the time to find out,' I said.

'I am finding out. I have sent a motorcycle patrol on ahead.' He checked his watch. 'They should be back soon with news, perhaps with help too.'

I mentally apologized to Sadiq. I thought he'd been as stupid as me. He went on, 'If they are not back within the hour then I think it will mean bad trouble at Kanja. They will at least be able to warn us, though; they have one of the radio sets.'

I sighed. 'Sorry. You win on all points.'

He acknowledged my apology with a grave nod. 'It is very difficult, sir. I appreciate that you are doing all you can for my people.'

I returned to my car to find Atheridge standing beside it and Helen Chula stretching herself awake. 'Captain Sadiq's on the ball,' I said. But he wasn't listening to me. Slowly, out of the dust and the crowd, another car was pulling ahead to join us. It was a battered Suzuki. I hadn't seen it before.

'Good God, Margretta,' Atheridge breathed. The car stopped alongside us and a woman climbed out stiffly. She was tall, fiftyish and clad in workman-like khaki shirt and pants. Her grey hair was pulled back in a loose bun. She looked as though she was ready to collapse.

'Gretta, my dear girl, how did you get here?' Atheridge asked.

'You're not hard to follow, Dan.' Her voice wasn't much more than a whisper.

'Gretta, this is Neil Mannix – Mannix, I'd like you to meet Doctor Marriot,' Atheridge said formally.

There were deep wrinkles round her eyes and her skin was leathery; she had the look of a woman who'd had too much sun, too much Africa. I turned and opened the passenger door of my car.

149

'Good morning, doctor. I think you'd better sit down.'

She nodded faintly. 'Thank you. I think it will be better,' she said. Her voice sounded Scandinavian.

'Are you a doctor of medicine?' I asked.

'Medical missionaries, from outside Kodowa,' Atheridge said. He bent over her and said gently, 'Where's Brian, Gretta? We all thought you two were in Port Luard.'

Which explained why nobody had mentioned them before. She spoke to Atheridge for some time in a low voice, and then started crying softly. Helen Chula got out of the car and came round to stay with Dr Marriot while I drew Atheridge aside.

'What is it, Dan?'

'Pretty bloody, I'm afraid. They drove up from the coast to Kodowa just when the air strike hit us. Brian, her husband, was killed outright. She must have been in shock for over a day, you know. She came out to the hospital and found Sister Ursula still there, and insisted on catching up with us.'

'Christ, that's a lousy deal.' We turned back to her.

'You look as though you could do with a drink, ma'am. How about a lukewarm Scotch?' I said.

'It wouldn't be unwelcome.'

I got a bottle from the trunk and poured a measure into a dusty glass. Atheridge glanced wistfully at the bottle but made no comment as I screwed the cap firmly back on. From now on this was strictly a medical reserve.

'I have come to help Doctor Kat,' she said after downing the Scotch in strong swallows. 'The Sister says he will need all the help he can get, and we have often worked together. Where is he, please?'

'Never mind where he is. Right now you need some sleep. Helen, tell her how much better she'll feel for it.'

Helen smiled shyly. 'Indeed the gentleman is right, Doctor Marriot. Sleep for an hour, then Doctor Kat will be most happy to have you with him. I am going to help him now.' She gently lowered the doctor's head onto the back of the seat.

'How's your leg?' I asked her.

150

'I will be all right up there,' she said, pointing towards the rig. 'I will wait here until it comes.'

In the car Dr Marriot was already sagging into sleep.

'Hop in, Dan. We'll move on slowly. At least moving creates a draught,' I said. The crawling pace was more frustrating than ever but I had to content myself with the thought that Captain Sadiq was coping very efficiently, better than I had done, and that in Dr Margretta Marriot we had a very useful addition to our staff. The Wyvern Travelling Hospital ground on through the hot African day. The sooner we got to Kanja, the better.

Half an hour later the whole pattern changed again. We seemed to be living inside a kaleidoscope which was being shaken by some gigantic hand. A motorcyclist, one of Sadiq's outflankers, roared up and said that Captain Sadiq would like to see me. I pulled out of line hoping not to disturb Dr Marriot, though I doubted if anything short of an earthquake would waken her.

Kemp and Wingstead were already with Sadiq, talking to two white men, more strangers. Behind them was a big dreamboat of an American car which looked as out of place in that setting as an aircraft carrier would on Lake Geneva. Atheridge and I got out and joined them.

One of the men was tall, loose-limbed and rangy, wearing denim Levis and a sweat-stained checked shirt, and un-believably he was crowned by a ten-gallon hat pushed well back on his head. I looked at his feet; no spurs, but he did wear hand-stitched high heeled boots. He looked like Clint East-wood. I expected him to produce a pack of Marlboros or a sack of Bull Durham tobacco.

By comparison the other guy was conventional. He was shorter, broad-shouldered and paunchy, and dressed in a man-ner more suitable for Africa; khaki pants and a bush jacket. Both looked dusty and weary, the norm for all of us.

I said, 'Hello there. Where did you spring from?'

The tall man turned round. 'Oh, hi. Up the road a way. You folks got the same trouble we have.'

151

Kemp's face was more strained than usual.

'Neil, there's a bridge down further along the road.'

'Christ! The one you were worried about, way back?'

Kemp nodded. 'Yes. It's completely gone, they've just told us. It spans a ravine. And it's this side of Kanja. It would be.'

Wingstead looked more alert than worried, ready to hurl himself at the next challenge. He was a hard man to faze.

I said, 'I'm Neil Mannix, British Electric. I guess it's a pleasure to meet you, but I'm not sure yet.'

The tall man laughed. 'Likewise. I'm Russ Burns and this is Harry Zimmerman. We're both with Lat-Am Oil. There are some other guys up the road too, by the way – not our lot; a Frenchman and a couple of Russki truckers.'

'What happened? Did you see the bridge go down?'

Burns shook his head. 'We were halfway to the bridge when the planes hit Kodowa. Mind you, we didn't know for sure what the hell was happening but we could guess. We'd seen a lot of troop movement a few days before, and there were stories going round about a rebellion. We couldn't see the town itself but we heard the bombing and saw the smoke. Then we saw the planes going over.'

His hand went to his shirt pocket. 'We didn't know what to do, Harry and me. Decided to push on because we didn't fancy turning back into all that, whatever it was. Then we met up with the Russkies.'

'A convoy, like ours?' I watched with fascination as he took out a pack of cigarettes. By God, they *were* Marlboros. He even lit one the way they do in the ads, with a long, appreciative draw on the first smoke. He didn't hand them round.

'No, just one big truck. The Frenchman's driving a truck too. He had a buddy he'd dropped off in Kodowa. I guess he must have got caught in the raid. You didn't see him?'

Nobody had. Write off one French trucker, just like that.

'I was shoving my foot through the floorboards the first ten miles after that raid,' Burns said. 'Even though I knew we couldn't outrun a jet. Maybe thirty miles from here we turned

152

a corner and damn near ran into this pipe truck. The Soviets. They hadn't seen or heard anything. Then the Frog guy turned up, him and a nig . . . a Nyalan assistant.' He glanced at Sadiq as he said this.

Zimmerman spoke for the first time. 'We four camped together that night, and the next day we pushed on in our car with one of the Russians. I speak Russian a little.' He said this almost apologetically. 'Ten miles on there's this bridge.'

'*Was* this bridge. By God, it's just rubble at the bottom of that ravine now. Took a real hammering.'

'Was it bombed?' I asked.

'Yeah, I reckon so. We could see the wreckage, five hundred feet down the hillside.'

'Any chance of getting across?' I asked, even though I could already guess the answer.

'No chance. Not for a truck. Not for a one-wheel circus bicycle. There's a gap of more than two hundred feet.'

Burns inhaled deeply. 'We all just stuck around that day. Nobody wanted to make a decision. Our radios only picked up garbage. We couldn't go on, and we didn't feel like coming back into the middle of a shooting war. The Soviets had quite a store of food and the Frenchie had some too. All *we* had to put in the pool was some beer, and that didn't last long, believe me. Then this morning we decided we'd go two ways; the Frenchie was to have a try at Kodowa with the two Reds, and Harry and me said we'd have a go at getting through the gorge on foot and make for Kanja.'

'Can't say I was hankering for the experience,' put in Harry.

'Then just as we were about to get going, up comes these two guys.' Burns indicated Sadiq's riders. 'We thought at first the rebels had caught up with us. Hell of a note, and us with just a couple of popguns between us. Then they told us what was going on back here. It didn't sound real, you know that?'

I made mental note. They had weapons.

'Travelling circus,' Kemp muttered.

'Wish it was, buddy. Elephants now, they'd be some use.

153

Anyway, we changed our plans, left the truckers to wait up ahead, and Harry and me came back to see for ourselves.'

I asked, 'Is it possible to cross on foot?'

'I reckon so, if you're agile.'

I looked at Sadiq. 'So?'

Wingstead said, 'What's the use, Neil? We can't send the wounded and sick that way and even if the Kanja hospital is still in business they can't send help to us. You know what we have to do.'

I nodded. One problem out of a thousand raised its head.

'Basil,' I said, 'how do you turn your rig around?'

'We don't need to,' Kemp said. 'It'll go either way. We just recouple the tractors.' His mind was shifting up through the gears and his face looked less strained as he started calculating. There was nothing better for Basil Kemp than giving him a set of solid logistics to chew on.

Sadiq said, 'What will you do now, Mister Mannix?' He too looked as though the ground had been pulled from under his feet.

I studied our two new arrivals. 'What we're going to do first is get these two gentlemen a beer and a meal apiece. And we have a lady who joined us recently who'd also be glad of something to eat. Geoff, could you get Bishop to organize that? As long as the convoy's stopped, we may as well all stoke up. We'll have a conference afterwards. Captain Sadiq, could you pass the word around that we are no longer going towards Kanja? Everyone must rest, eat if they can, and then be ready to move.'

Wingstead said, 'Who's the lady?'

'She's a medical doctor. She was widowed in the raid on Kodowa, and right now she's asleep in my car. I'm going to have a word with Doctor Kat and I'll take her along. As a matter of fact, Dan knows her quite well . . .'

I tailed off. Behind us, standing quietly, Dan Atheridge looked pasty grey over his tan. During our briefing from the Lat-Am men Atheridge had been listening and their news

154

touched him more closely than any of us. His wife was waiting for him, somewhere beyond Kanja. He was cut off from his home.

'Dan –'

'It's OK. Susie's going to be perfectly safe, I know. You're quite right though, you can't get the patients across the gorge. But I know a way over, a few miles downstream. Perhaps you'll lend me an escort, Captain, and take me there?' He spoke in a flat, controlled voice.

'Don't worry, Dan. We'll get you across,' I said, hoping like hell I could keep my word. 'Come on, you guys, let's get you outside that beer and hear the rest of it.' We got back into my car and turned back towards the rig, Kemp following with the two newcomers. As we drove past the stream of refugees the little huddled groups were preparing for the long drowsy wait. The bush telegraph was way ahead of modern communication.

14

Dr Margretta Marriot and I stood looking up at the rig. It was an extraordinary sight, covered here and there with windblown thatching, piled with sheet-covered bodies lying on lumpy reed bedding, draped with miscellaneous bits of cloth, towels and pillowcases hung from anything handy to give shade. Figures clambered about the rig carrying bandaging and other necessities. Sister Mary had been forbidden to travel on the rig because of her own precarious health and was standing at the base of the huge wheels shouting instructions to her nurses. Several of our men were helping by supporting those of the wounded who could move about, taking them to and from the makeshift latrines. The chuck wagon was in action as Bishop and young Bing prepared a canned meal for us and our visitors.

During the day Sister Ursula had arrived. She saw me and waved, then lit up on catching sight of Dr Marriot.

'Doctor Gretta! What are you doing here?'

Mick McGrath was at her side instantly to give her a hand down. She knew at once that all was not well, and gently led the doctor away to the far side of the rig.

McGrath said, 'Why have we stopped, Mister Mannix? Rumour is there's more trouble.'

'That there is. There's a bridge down between us and Kanja, and no way we can get there. We haven't made the decision official yet, but I can tell you we're going to have to turn back.'

'Take the east-west road, then, like you planned? With all this lot?'

'Maybe. Ask Doctor Kat to come down, would you.'

'He won't come.'

'Why not?'

'He's busy,' McGrath said. 'Soon as we stopped he went into action at the operating table. Right now I think he's lifting off the top of someone's skull.'

I said, 'All right, don't bother him yet. But when you can, tell him that Doctor Marriot is here. I think it will please him. Tell him her husband was killed at Kodowa, though. And I'd like a word with him as soon as possible.'

I walked back to where the Wyvern management and the Lat-Am men were sitting in the shade of the trucks. Atheridge was not with them. As I approached, Wingstead said, 'Neil, I've put Harry and Russ in the picture geographically. They travelled the east-west road, a few months ago and say it's not too bad. The two rivers come together at a place called Makara. It's very small, not much more than a village, but it may be of some strategic importance. It's a crossroads town, the only way up from the coast used to be from Lasulu and Fort Pirie through Makara to here, before Ofanwe's government built the new road direct.'

'Is there a bridge there?'

'Yes, apparently quite good but narrower than the new bridge that you crossed when you met the army. Assuming it's still there. We'll send outriders ahead to find out; if our gallant Captain's on the ball they've already gone. And someone's gone to fetch down Lat-Am's friends to join us.'

'The army might be there. If I were commanding either side I'd like to hold Makara, if it hasn't been bombed into oblivion.'

Wingstead stood up. 'We don't have to make up our minds until we hear the report. Where's Doctor Kat?'

'Operating. He'll join us when he can, and I expect he'll have something to say about all this.'

I too stood up, and as I did so Mick McGrath came over. We knew instantly that something was wrong; he looked like thunder.

'Mister Wingstead, there's trouble,' he said. 'You're about to receive a deputation.'

157

Five other men were approaching with the dogged stomping walk you see on TV newscasts featuring strikers in action. They appeared to be having an argument with a couple of soldiers in their way, and then came on to face us. I wasn't surprised to see that the ringleader was Bob Sisley, nor that another was Johnny Burke, the man who'd been heard to speak of danger money some time past. The others were Barry Lang, Bob Pitman, and the fifth, who did surprise me, was Ron Jones. They walked into a total silence as we followed Wingstead's lead. I'd handled industrial disputes in my time but here I was an outsider, unless the Wyvern management invoked my aid directly.

Sisley, naturally, was the spokesman. He said, ignoring Wingstead for an easier target, 'Mister Kemp, these Yanks say that the bridge up north has gone, right?'

'That's right.'

I wondered how Burns liked being called a Yank, though he was free enough with derogatory nicknames himself.

'Seems we can't take the rig on, then. You planned for us to go down to Lake Pirie, before we ran into all this crap with the sickies. What's to stop us going there now? You said we could get across the border into a neutral country.'

I felt a wash of disgust at the man, and I saw my thoughts echoed on other faces. The odd thing was that one of those faces belonged to Ron Jones. Kemp still said nothing and Sisley pressed on.

'You've broken your own contract so you can't hold us to ours. We say it's getting dangerous here and we didn't sign on to get involved in any nignog's bloody political duff-ups. We're getting out of here.'

'With the rig?' Kemp asked coldly.

'To hell with the rig. We're in a jam. A war's something we didn't bargain for. All we want is out. It's your duty to see us safe, yours and the boss's here.' He indicated Wingstead with an inelegant jerk of his thumb. He may have been a good transport man, Wyvern wouldn't hire less, but he was a nasty piece of work nonetheless.

Wingstead took over smoothly.

'We're taking the rig and all transport back to Kodowa,' he said. 'Including the hospital patients. Once there, we'll reassess the situation and probably, all being well, we'll start back on the road to Port Luard. If we think that unsafe we'll take the secondary road to Fort Pirie. We are all under a strain here, and cut off from vital information, but we'll do the best we can.'

But calm, reasoned argument never did work in these affairs. Sisley made a face grotesque with contempt. 'A strain! Oh, we're under a strain all right. Playing nursemaid to a bunch of blacks who can't take care of themselves and baby-sitting a rig that's junk worthless while the food runs out and the country goes to hell in a handcart. Christ, we haven't even been paid for two weeks. You can fart-arse up and down this bloody road as much as you like, but you'll do it without us.'

'What exactly is it you want?' Wingstead asked.

'We want to get the hell back to Fort Pirie as we planned. With or without the rig – it makes no difference.'

'*You* didn't plan anything, my friend.' I knew I should stay out of this but I was livid. 'Your boss has run a hell of a risk coming up here to join you, and he's the man who does the planning around here.'

'You keep out of this, Mister Bloody Mannix.'

Wingstead said, 'Bob, this is crazy talk. How far can any of us get without the whole group for support?'

'The group! Christ, old men and babies and walking dead, mealy-mouthed nuns and God knows who else we're dragging around at our heels! Now we hear you're bringing a bunch of damned foreigners into it too. Well, we won't stand for it.'

None of the others said a word. They stood behind him in a tight wall of silent resentment, as Sisley gave full rein to his foul mouth and fouler thoughts. At his reference to the nuns McGrath's breathing deepened steadily. I suspected that an outbreak was imminent and tried to forestall it.

'You can argue shop floor principles all you want with your

159

boss, Sisley,' I said. 'But leave out the personalities, and don't foul-mouth these people like that.'

He rounded on me. 'I told you to shut up, you bigmouth Yank. Keep the hell out of this!' He cocked his arm back like a cobra about to strike. I took a step forward but McGrath grabbed my arm in a steel grip. 'Now, hold it, Mister Mannix,' he said in a cool, soft voice, and then to Sisley, 'Any more lip from you, my lad, and you'll be shitting teeth.' I think it was the matter-of-fact way he said it that made Sisley step back and drop his arm.

For a moment the whole tableau froze; the two groups facing each other, the Lat-Am men and several other Wyvern people crowding up to listen, Atheridge behind them, and myself, McGrath and Sisley in belligerent attitudes front and centre. Then from nowhere Ben Hammond's voice broke in.

'Right, you've had your say, and very well put it was, Bob. Now you'll give Mister Wingstead and Mister Kemp five minutes to talk it over, please. Just you shift along, you chaps, nothing's going to happen for a while. Sandy! Where's that grub you were getting ready? Go on, you lot, get it while it's there. Bert, we've got a spot of bother with the rear left axletree.'

It was masterly. The tableau melted like a spring thaw and I found myself alone with Kemp and Wingstead, shaking our heads with relief and admiration. Hammond's talents seemed boundless.

Wingstead said, 'Sisley and Pitman run the airlift truck. It's obvious they'd be in this together, they've always been buddies and a bit bloody-minded. Johnny Burke is what the Navy would call a sea lawyer, too smart for his own good. He's a fair rigger, though. And Lang and Jones are good drivers. But Sisley and Pitman are the specialists, and we'll need that airlift again. Who else can run it?'

Kemp shook his head but Hammond, who had rejoined us after some skilful marshalling of the men, said, 'I can. I can run any damned machine here if I have to. So could McGrath, come to that.'

160

'We'll need you both on the rig,' said Kemp.

'No you won't. You're as good on the rig as I am,' Hammond said. 'I could work with Sammy Wilson though.'

'I suppose we must assume that Sisley's had a go at everyone,' I said. 'So whoever wasn't with him is on your side?'

'I have to assume that. I'm surprised about Ron Jones, I must say,' said Wingstead. 'So we've still got Grafton and Proctor, and Ritchie Thorpe too. Thank God you brought him up here, Neil.'

'He might not thank me,' I said.

Our rueful smiles brought a momentary lightening of tension.

'I wouldn't like an inexperienced man on a tractor when it's coupled to the rig,' Kemp said. 'We can get along with three tractors at some expense to our speed. And we can ditch that damned tank. I don't suppose you can drive a tractor, Mannix?' I smiled again, but to myself, at Kemp's single-mindedness. There were times when it came in handy. Right now he was too busy juggling factors to get as fully steamed up at having a mutiny on his hands as any good executive should.

'No, but I might find someone who can.'

Wingstead and Kemp conferred for a while and I left them to it. The breakaway group had taken their food well away from the others, and a huddle of shoulders kept them from having to look at their mates while they were eating. The faithful, as I mentally dubbed them, were laughing and talking loudly to demonstrate their camaraderie and freedom from the guilt of having deserted. It was an interesting example of body language at work and would have delighted any psychologist. The Nyalans, sensing trouble, were keeping well clear, and there was no sign of any of the medical people.

Presently Wingstead called me over.

He said, 'We're going to let them go.'

'You mean *fire* them?'

'What else? If they don't want to stay I can hardly hold them all prisoner.'

161

'But how will they manage?'

Wingstead showed that he had become very tough indeed.

'That's their problem. I've got . . . how many people to take care of, would you say? I didn't ask for it, but I'm stuck with it and I won't weasel out. I can't abandon them all for a few grown men who think they know their own minds.'

Suddenly he looked much older. That often talked of phenomenon, the remoteness of authority, was taking visible hold and he wasn't the boyish, enthusiastic plunger that he'd seemed to be when we first met in the workshop garage in England. He had taken the whole burden of this weird progression on his own shoulders, and in truth there was nowhere else for it to lie. I watched him stand up under the extra load and admired him more than ever.

'Tell them to come over, Basil.'

The rebels came back still wary and full of anger. This time, at Wingstead's request, McGrath stayed a little way off and exerted his own powerful authority to keep bystanders back out of earshot. Wingstead said, 'Right, we've had our chat. Are you still sure you want out?'

'Bloody sure. We've had it, all of this.'

'Do you speak for everyone?' Wingstead looked past him to the other four, but no-one spoke. Sisley said, 'You can see that.'

'Right you are then. You can buzz off. All five of you. You're fired.'

The silence this time was almost comical.

Sisley said at last, 'All right then, just you try that. You can't just bloody well fire us! We're under contract, aren't we, Johnny?'

'That's right,' Burke said.

'You said yourself that if our contract with Nyala was broken, which it is, then so was yours. Hop it,' Wingstead said.

'Then what about our pay? We missed two weeks, plus severance. We want it now.'

I stared at him in astonishment.

162

'Go on, give them a cheque, Geoff,' I said sarcastically. 'They can cash it at the bank in Kodowa.'

'I'll write vouchers for the lot of you. You can be sure that Wyvern will honour them,' Wingstead said. 'You can collect them from Mister Kemp in one hour's time.'

'We'll do that,' said Sisley. 'But we want some security against them too. We'll take one of the trucks.'

Hammond said, 'The hell you will, Bob!'

'Or the airlift truck. There's room for all of us at a pinch, and it's worth more. Yes, that's what we'll do.'

Hammond was beginning to lose his temper. 'Over my dead body!'

Wingstead held out a hand to calm him. 'There'll be no arguments. I forbid you to touch the transports, Sisley,' he said.

'And just how are you going to stop us?'

This had gone far enough. It was time I intervened. 'You're not taking that airlift truck anywhere. Or any other vehicle. Wyvern Transport is heavily in debt to British Electric and I'm calling that debt. In lieu of payment I am sequestering all their equipment, and that includes all vehicles. Your vouchers will come from me and my company will pay you off, when you claim. If you live to claim. You've got one hour and then you can start walking.'

Sisley gaped at me. He said, 'But Fort Pirie is –'

'About two hundred and fifty miles away. You may find transport before then. Otherwise you can do what the people you call nignogs are doing – hoof it.'

He squared himself for a fight and then surveyed the odds facing him. Behind him his own men murmured uneasily but only Burke raised his voice in actual protest. Hearing it, McGrath came across, fists balled and spoiling for a fight once again, but still with the matter-of-fact air that made him all the more dangerous. The mutineers subsided and backed away.

Sisley mouthed a few more obscenities but we ignored him. Soon they moved off in a tightknit, hostile group and disappeared behind one of the trucks.

163

'Keep an eye on them, Mick, but no rough stuff,' Hammond said.

Wingstead let out a long steady breath.

'I'd give a lot for a pull from that bottle of Scotch of yours. Or even a warm beer. But I'll settle for a mug of gunfire very gladly indeed.'

'Ditto,' I said, and we grinned at one another.

'You're my boss now, do you know that?'

'Sure I am. And that's my first order: a cup of that damned hellbrew of Bishop's and a plateful of whatever mess he's calling lunch,' I said. 'You too, Basil. Save the figuring for afterwards.'

Later that afternoon I had my chance to talk to Dr Katabisirua. The defection of five of our men troubled him little; they were healthy and capable, and he felt that having taken their own course it was up to them to make it in safety. The addition to our number of two more Americans and the expected arrival of a Frenchman and two Russians also meant little to him, except in so far as he hoped they might have some medical stores in their vehicles. The arrival of Dr Marriot he saw as pure gold.

He fretted about malnutrition, about sepsis, and was more perturbed than he liked to admit about the jolting his patients were receiving. For me, his worst news concerned Max Otterman, who was sinking into unconsciousness and for whom the future looked very grave.

He'd heard about the bridge, of course.

'There is no way to get to Kanja, then? No way at all?'

'Only for fit men on their own feet, Doctor. I'm sorry.'

'Mister Atheridge said he knew a way, I am told.'

'Yes,' I said, 'but he's wounded, over fifty, and in some shock. He's driven up there with some soldiers and one of our men to have a look but they won't be back before nightfall, I reckon. I don't think for a moment that they'll find any feasible way of getting across that ravine.'

He sighed. 'Then you are going to turn back.'

'To Kodowa, yes. And then south or west. Probably west. Do you know the town of Makara? Is there a medical station there?'

But he said that Makara patients had always been brought to him at Kodowa. There wasn't even a trained nurse, only a couple of midwives. Then he brightened. 'There is the cotton factory,' he said. 'They have very large well-built barns but I have heard that they stand almost empty and the factory is idle. It would make a good place to put all my patients.'

'If it's still intact, yes.' And, I thought, if some regiment or rebel troop hasn't turned it into a barracks first.

Shortly afterwards the two Russians and the Frenchman arrived. The Russians were as alike as peas in a pod, with broad Slavic features and wide grins. They had polysyllabic unpronounceable names and neither spoke more than ten words of English. God knows how they'd managed in earlier days. Zimmerman, who had worked alongside Russians laying pipelines in Iran, was able to interpret reasonably well. Later they became known as Brezhnev and Kosygin to everybody, and didn't seem to mind. Probably the way we said the names they couldn't even recognize them. They were hauling a load of pipe casing northwards to the oilfields.

The Frenchman spoke fair English and was called Antoine Dufour. He was carrying a mixed load for Petrole Meridional. They were all glad of company and resigned to a return journey, but they were unwilling to quit their trucks, especially when they found we had a store of reserve fuel. After a lot of trilingual palaver, Wingstead's French being more than adequate, they agreed to stick with us in a policy of safety in numbers.

So did Russ Burns and Zimmerman. But they had a different problem.

'I hear you have gas,' Burns said. 'We're about dry.'

'We've got gas,' I told him. 'But not to burn up in your goddam air-conditioning, or hauling all that chrome around Africa.' I walked over to look at their car. The overhang behind the rear wheels was over five feet and the decorations in front

165

snarled in a savage grin. 'Your taste in transport is a mite old-fashioned, Texas?'

'That's a good American car. You won't find me driving one of those dinky European models. Hell, I can't get my legs under the wheel. Anyway, it's a company car. It wouldn't look good for an oilman with Lat-Am to drive an economy car; that would show lack of confidence.'

'Very interesting,' I said, 'but so far you've been on the blacktop. Suppose we have to take to the country roads. That thing will lose its exhaust in the first mile, and the sump in the next. It'll scrape its fanny every ten yards.'

'He's right, Russ,' said Zimmerman.

'Oh hell,' Burns said sadly, unwilling to give up his status symbol.

I pointed to a tractor. 'Can either of you drive one of those?'

'I can,' said Zimmerman promptly, 'I started my working life as a trucker. I might need a bit of updating tuition, though.'

'Well, you know our problem. Five guys walked out and two of them were drivers. You won't be asked to drive it coupled up, Kemp wouldn't buy that. I'm leaving the hire car here because it's never going to make the dirt roads. You'll have to do the same, because you get no gas from me. You drive the tractor uncoupled, and take care of the sick folk up on the roof.' I turned to Burns. 'And you can drive with me in the Land Rover. There's plenty of leg room there.'

He sighed and patted his car on the hood. 'So long, baby. It's been nice knowing you.'

It was dark as I'd guessed it would be before Atheridge and his party returned, quiet and dispirited. The ravine crossing which he remembered from many years before was now over-grown, the ledges crumbled and passage impossible. Thorpe told me privately that they had had quite a job persuading Atheridge to return with them; he was passionately determined to try crossing on his own, but he was quite unfit to do so.

Eventually the entire camp settled down to an uneasy night's sleep. The five mutineers, strikers, whatever one wanted to call

166

them, had vanished, their gear gone. Wingstead and I felt itchy with unease about them, both for their safety and for our own future without their expertise. I'd had a guard of soldiers put around every vehicle we possessed, just in case any of them decided to try to collar one. There wasn't much left to say, and at last we all turned in and slept, or tried to, and awaited the coming of morning.

15

The morning brought the usual crises and problems attendant on any normal start of a run, plus of course the extra ones imposed by our status as a mobile hospital. Somewhere in the middle of it, while Kemp was supervising the recoupling of the tractors to the other end of the rig it was discovered that McGrath was missing. The air was lively with curses as both Kemp and Hammond sought their chief driver. At about the same time Sadiq's sergeant came to tell us that the hire car was missing too.

And then suddenly there was McGrath, walking into our midst with one arm flung round the shoulders of a cowed and nervous Ron Jones. Tailing up behind them were Lang and Bob Pitman, looking equally hangdog, pale and exhausted.

'Mister Kemp,' McGrath called out in a cheerful, boisterous voice, 'these lads have changed their minds and want to come with us. Would you be taking them back onto the payroll? I promised I'd put in a word for them.'

Kemp wasn't sure what to do, and glanced at me for guidance. I shook my head. 'I don't hire and fire around here, Basil. Have a word with Geoff.'

But of course there wasn't any doubt about it really; the hesitation was only for form's sake. After a long private talk Geoff announced that the three delinquents were to be taken back into the fold, and a reallocation of driving jobs ensued, somewhat to Harry Zimmerman's relief.

It was impossible to find out exactly what had happened; McGrath kept busy and enquiries would have to wait until later. Wingstead did tell me that according to all of them, Bob

Sisley and Johnny Burke had refused point blank to return when McGrath caught up with them. It seemed that he had taken the car and gone off at first light. The other three were less committed to Sisley's cause and Jones in particular had been a most unwilling mutineer. The three of them would bear careful watching but there was no doubt that we were greatly relieved to have them back.

We camped that night back near Kodowa, but not at the hospital, where Dr Kat decreed that there would be too much danger of infection from the debris left behind. Instead a cleaner site was found further west on the road we were to take. It had been a day wasted. We arrived in the late afternoon and buried our dead, four more, and then began the laborious process of settling in for the night, and of planning the start for Makara in the morning.

At the end of it I had had a gutful. I was weary of talking and of listening, settling arguments, solving problems and doling out sympathy and advice. The only good news we heard all evening was from Dr Marriot, who told us that Max Otterman seemed to be making progress towards recovery.

Eventually I went off for a walk in the warm night. There were refugees everywhere and I had to go a long way to put the camp behind me. I had no fear of meeting wild animals, the noise and stench of our progress had cleared both game and predators for miles around, and as I looked back at the cooking fires glowing like fireflies I wondered where the food was coming from.

I'd been tempted to take the dwindling bottle of whisky with me but had resisted, and now I regretted my self-denial. I stopped well out of sight and earshot of the camp and sat down to soak in the solitude for a spell. Finally, feeling rested, I started back. I'd gone about ten paces when something ahead of me crunched on dry vegetation and my heart thudded. Then a voice said softly, 'Mister Mannix – can I talk to you?'

It was Ron Jones. For a moment I felt a fury of hot

169

resentment at not being left alone even out here. Then I said, 'Jones? What do you want?'

He was still downcast, a shadow of his cheery former self. 'I'm sorry to intrude, Mister Mannix. But I must talk. I have to tell *somebody* about what happened. But you must promise me not to tell anyone who told you.'

'I don't know what you're talking about.'

'I'll tell you, if you promise first.'

'Be damned to that, Jones. Tell me or not as you please. But I make no bargains.'

He paused, thinking about this, and then said, 'It's about Bob Sisley. He's dead.'

'Dead? What the hell do you mean?'

'He's dead, I tell you. Mick McGrath shot him.'

Christ, I thought. I'd been right. All along I'd had an uneasy feeling about McGrath, and this news came as less of a shock than a grim confirmation of my thoughts. 'You'd better tell me all about it. Let's sit down.'

'But you really mustn't let on who told you,' Jones said again. He sounded terrified and I could hardly blame him.

'All right, I promise. Now tell.'

'It was like this. When we left we took as much of our kit as we could carry and went off towards Kodowa. Bob wanted to nick a truck but they were all guarded. Then he said we'd be sure to find transport in Kodowa. After all, there were lots of cars left behind there.'

He said nothing about the events which had led up to the mutiny, nor about his own reasons for going along with it, and I didn't ask. All that was past history.

'We didn't get very far. Walking, it's not like being in a motor, not out here especially. It was bloody hot and hard going. Those Nyalans, they're pretty tough, I found out . . . anyway we pushed on for a while. We'd nicked some food and beer, before we left. Brad Bishop didn't know that,' he put in, suddenly anxious not to implicate the cook in their actions. It

170

was things like that which separated him from Bob Sisley, who wouldn't have cared a damn.

'Then we heard a car and up comes Mick on his own. He tried to talk us into going back, but pretty soon it turned into an argument. He and Bob Sisley got bloody worked up. Then Bob went for him but Mick put him down in the dust easy; he's the bigger man by a long chalk. None of the rest of us wanted a fight except maybe Johnny Burke. But he's no match for Mick either and he didn't even try. To be honest, Barry and Bob Pitman and me, we'd had enough anyway. I really wanted to go back.'

He hesitated and I sensed that the tight wound resolution was dying in him. 'Go on. You can't stop now. You've said too much and too little.'

'Then Mick took us off the road and –'

'How do you mean, took you? You didn't have to go anywhere.'

'Yes we did. He had a gun.'

'What kind of gun?'

'An automatic pistol. He took us off the road and down into the bush, where nobody else could see us. Then he said we had to go back or we'd die out there. He said he could beat us into agreeing, one at a time. Starting with Bob Sisley. Bob had some guts. He said Mick couldn't keep us working, couldn't hold a gun on us all the time. He got pretty abusive.'

'Did they fight?'

'Not again. Sisley said a few things he shouldn't and . . . then Mick shot him.'

'Just like that?'

'Yes, Mister Mannix. One second Bob was standing there, and the next he was on the ground. That bloody Irishman shot him through the head and didn't even change his expression!'

He was shivering and his voice wavered. I said, 'Then what happened?'

'Nobody said anything for a bit. Someone upchucked – hell, it was me. So did Barry. Then Mick said again that we were to

171

go back. He said we'd work the rig, all right. And if any of us talked about what had happened he'd get kneecapped or worse.'

'Kneecapped – that was the word he used?'

'Yes. Bob Pitman got down to look at Sisley and he was stone dead, all right. And while we were all looking. Johnny Burke he took off and ran like hell, through the bush. I thought Mick would shoot him but he didn't even try, and Johnny got clean away.'

'Do you know what happened to him?'

'Nobody does.'

'What happened next?'

'Well, we said OK, we'd go back. And we'd shut up. What else could we do? And anyway we all wanted to come back by then. Christ, I've had this bloody country.'

'What happened to Sisley's body?'

His voice shook again. 'Mick stripped it and him and Barry put it down in a gulley and covered it up a little, not buried. Mick said the wildlife would get him.'

'He was right about that,' I said grimly. 'You did the right thing, telling me about this. Keep your nose clean and there'll be no more trouble out of it for you. I'll do something about McGrath. Go back to the camp now, and get a good night's sleep. You're out of danger, or at least that sort of danger.'

He went, thankfully, and I followed more slowly. I had one more lousy job to do that night. Back at camp I strolled across to the Land Rover and got into it on the passenger side, leaving the door open. There was still some movement here and there and as one of the men walked past I called out to him to find McGrath and tell him I wanted to see him.

I switched on the interior light, took the shotgun I had liberated, emptied and reloaded it. Previously, when I'd tried to put in a fourth shell it wouldn't go, and I had wondered why, but now I had the answer; in the States pump and automatic shotguns are limited to a three-shot capacity when shooting at certain migratory birds. To help remind hunters to keep within the law the makers install a demountable plug in the magazine, and until it's removed the hunter is limited to three fast shots. I guessed the gun makers hadn't bothered to take out the plugs before exporting these weapons.

Now I began to strip the gun. When McGrath came up I was taking the plug out of the magazine. He looked at it with interest. 'That's a fine scatter-gun,' he said easily. 'Now, how many shots would a thing like that fire before reloading, Mister Mannix?'

'Right now, three. But I'm fixing it to shoot six.' I got the plug out and started to reassemble the gun.

McGrath said, 'You've done that before.'

'Many times.' The gun went together easily. I started to put shells into the magazine and loaded the full six. Then I held the gun casually, not pointing at McGrath but not very far away from him, angled downwards to the ground. 'Now you can tell me what happened to Bob Sisley,' I said.

If I'd hoped to startle him into an admission I was disappointed. His expression didn't change at all. 'So someone told you,' he said easily. 'Now I wonder who it could have been? I'd say Ronnie Jones, wouldn't you?'

'Whoever. And if anything happens to *any* of those men you'll be in even more trouble than you are now – if possible.'

'I'm in no trouble,' he said.

'You will be if Sadiq strings you up the nearest tree.'

'And who'd tell him?'

'I might.'

He shook his head. 'Not you, Mister Mannix. Mister Kemp now, he might do that, but not you.'

'What makes you say that?' I hadn't meant the interview to go this way, a chatty debate with no overtones of nervousness on his part, but the man did intrigue me. He was the coolest customer I'd ever met.

He grinned. 'Well, you're a lot tougher than Mister Kemp. I think maybe you're nearly as tough as me, with a few differences, you might say. We think the same. We do our own dirty work. You're not going to call in the black captain to do yours for you, any more than I did. We do the things that have to be done.'

'And you think Sisley had to be killed. Is that it?'

'Not at all. It could have been any one of them, to encourage the others as the saying goes, but I reckon Sisley was trouble all down the line. Why carry a burden when you can drop it?'

The echo of Sadiq, both of them using Voltaire's aphorism so glibly and in so similar a set of circumstances, fascinated me against my will. 'I don't need lessons in military philosophy from you, McGrath,' I said. 'What you did was murder.'

'Jesus Christ! You're in the middle of a war here and people are dying all around you, one way or the other. You're trying to save hundreds of lives and you worry about the death of one stinking rat. I'll tell you something. Those other bastards will work from now on. I'll see to that.'

'You won't touch them,' I said.

'I won't have to. You found out; the word will spread to everyone, you'll see. Nobody else is going to turn rat on us, I can promise you . . . and nobody is going to touch me for it.'

'Why did you really do it, McGrath? Loyalty to Wyvern Transport?'

'Be damned to that, Mannix. I want out of this and I want out alive and unhurt. And the more we've got pulling for us, the better chance each man has. You have to have unity on this. You owe it to your people, and they to you.'

There at last was the political undertone I'd been expecting. I said, 'All right, what are you, McGrath? IRA or Ulster Loyalist?'

'Do I have to be either.'

'Yes, you do. Unity in face of oppression, casual shooting, kneecapping threats – it's all there. And I'm not one of your American pseudo-Irish sympathizers. As far as I'm concerned, both of your bloody so-called movements can fall into the nearest bog and the sooner the better.'

174

As I'd hoped, this sort of talk did get some rise out of him. He shifted one hand instinctively to his right-hand coat pocket, arresting the movement almost instantly. But it was a dead giveaway.

'All right,' I said, having achieved what I wanted. 'We won't talk politics. Let's change the subject. Where did you get the gun?'

'I found it in the tank we salvaged.'

'And where is it now?'

'In my cab.'

I shook my head gently, hefting the shotgun very slightly.

He actually laughed. 'You're in no danger from me, Mister Mannix. You're one man I look to to get us all out of this mess.'

I said, 'I'll have that gun, McGrath – now.'

With no hesitation he dipped into his pocket, produced the pistol and tossed it onto my lap. 'There'll be others,' he said.

'And from now on, you can consider yourself under open arrest.'

Now he gave me a belly laugh. 'Ah, it's the military ways you're picking up, Mister Mannix. Just like old times.'

'Old times in what army, McGrath? And just by the way, I suppose that isn't your real name. No doubt you're on a good few wanted lists, aren't you?'

He looked pensive. 'They were the days, all right. Well, the name now, that's something of a convenience. I've had several, and passports to match in my time. All this –' He waved at the darkness around us, '– this was going to be a bit of a holiday for me. Things were getting a little hot at home so I thought I'd take a sabbatical. Now I find it's a working holiday.'

I wondered what to do. Keeping McGrath around would be like leading a tiger on a length of string. He was a killing machine, proficient and amoral; a most dangerous man, but extremely useful in times of war. I couldn't trust him, but I found that I couldn't quite dislike him, which troubled my conscience only a little. And I felt we could work together for

175

the moment at all events. There would be a showdown one day, but not yet.

I could hand him over to Sadiq, and he might be strung up from the next telegraph post; but quite apart from my liking the man, it would be a course of action very deleterious to our morale. The crew were civilians and nothing scares a civilian more than summary military law. I thought about McGrath's views on our relative toughness, and said abruptly, 'How old are you, McGrath?'

He was mildly surprised. 'Forty-nine.'

So was I; and only an accident of birth had prevented me from being even more like him than he realized. In spite of what I'd said about Irish politics, I could to a degree understand the motives that drove him, and saw that they might have been my own. It was only chance that my weapon had become a boardroom rather than a gun. 'Listen carefully,' I said. 'If you don't keep in line from now on you won't make your half-century. You were right, McGrath – we *do* think the same. But from now on even more so. Your thoughts and your actions will be dictated by me. You won't do one single goddamn thing without my say-so. And I'll pull the plug on you any time I feel it's better that way. Am I understood?'

He gazed at me steadily. 'I said you were a tough man. I know what you're thinking, Mannix. You're thinking that I'd be a good man to have around if things get tougher. You're thinking that you can point me like a weapon and I'll go off, aren't you? Well, I won't argue with you about that, because I feel much the same myself. And speaking of guns –'

'You're not getting it back.'

'Oh, that's all right,' he said. 'There's nothing so easy to come by in a war as a gun. All I was going to say was that I've not had a chance to clean it up yet. Careless of me, I know. You'll want to do it yourself, I imagine.'

I secured the safety catch on the shotgun and lowered it to the floor of the Land Rover. 'Just remember this, McGrath. I'm never going to stop watching you.'

'On probation, am I?'

'Not at all. You're awaiting trial. Be sure and stay around. Don't go jumping bail, will you?'

'Out there on my own? You have to be joking, Mannix. Now what did you think I went to all this trouble for, if not to prevent that very thing from happening with my lads . . . and I still wish I knew for sure which one came running to you. It wasn't really necessary now, was it?'

I waved a hand in dismissal. I felt no sense of danger from McGrath for the moment, and he must have had the same feeling about me, for he raised a hand and ambled away.

'We'll all be needing a bit of sleep, I think. See you in the morning, Mannix. Thanks for the chat,' he said and was gone.

I sat for a while longer wondering if I was doing the right thing.

16

Early next morning I did a check round the camp. There seemed to be more Nyalans than ever camped some little distance from where we were sited, and the soldiers' camp was further off still, so that we covered a pretty vast area. Lights still burned on the rig, because full daylight had not yet arrived, and there was movement as the medical staff tended their patients, the skeleton night watch making way for the full team. I found Sister Ursula tidying up in the makeshift operating theatre.

'Morning, Sister. Everything all right?'

She offered a wry smile. 'Not exactly all right, but as well as we can expect.' She bustled about just as she would in a regular hospital, and probably saw nothing incongruous in her newly acquired methods; habit skirts tucked into her belt, one hand free to grasp at holds as she swung expertly about the rig.

'No deaths last night, thanks be to God. It's a pity about Kanja, but no doubt we'll manage.'

I told her about the cotton warehouses and she nodded. 'Cool and spacious, much easier for my nurses, certainly.' We had reached the fridge and she opened it, checked the contents against a list, reshuffled the dwindling stores and closed it swiftly, to let as little cold air escape as possible. 'This has been a Godsend,' she commented.

She somehow pronounced the word with an audible upper-case G.

'From God via Wyvern Transport,' I said a little more harshly than was kind. I sometimes tired of the religious habit of thanking God for strictly man-made assistance. She took me up on it at once.

'Don't you believe in God, Mister Mannix? Or in thanking Him?'

Having spent some time the night before in a short seminar on the philosophy of terrorism from McGrath, I didn't feel in the least like getting into another on religion. 'We'll debate it some other time, Sister. We've both got enough else to do at the moment. Where are the doctors?'

'Doctor Marriot's having coffee and Doctor Kat is still asleep.' She smiled. 'He didn't know it but last night I put a sleeping draught in his tea. It knocked him out.'

She showed all the signs of being a very bossy woman. 'Don't ever try that on me, Sister,' I said, smiling back, 'or there'll be trouble. I like to make my own decisions.'

'You have enough sense to know when to stop. But the Doctor was out on his feet and wouldn't admit it.'

'But what happens if there's an emergency? He'd be no good to us doped to the eyebrows.'

She raised one at me. 'I know my dosage. He'll wake up fresh as a daisy. In the meantime there is Doctor Marriot, and me. By the way, Sister Mary is still not to be allowed up here, please. She can travel in the truck again, with the children. Don't listen to anything she says to the contrary.'

She was indeed a bossy woman. She went on, 'I've got Nurse Mulira and Nurse Chula who are both well-trained, and the others are doing well too. Sister Mary doesn't realize how frail she is.'

'Point taken, ma'am. By the way, how much sleep did you get last night?'

'Mind your own business.' Before I could object to that blunt statement she went on, 'I've just been with Mister Otterman. He's not too well again . . .' She looked down past me. 'Someone wants you. I think it's urgent.'

'It always is. Be ready to move in about an hour, Sister.'

I swung down off the rig. Sadiq's sergeant looked harassed. 'The captain wants you, please. It is very urgent.'

I followed him to the command car and found Sadiq examin-

179

ing a battered map. He had an air of mixed gloom and relief. He said, 'The radio is working. I have just had new orders. I have been reassigned.'

I leaned against the car and suddenly felt terribly tired.

'Good God, that's all we need. What orders? And where from?'

'I have heard from a senior officer, Colonel Maksa. I am to take my troops and join him at Ngingwe.' This was on the nearside of the blocked road to Kanja.

'Ngingwe! Sadiq, does this make sense to you?'

'No, sir. But I am not to query orders from a superior.'

The sergeant returned with Geoff Wingstead. I recapped what Sadiq had told me, and Wingstead looked as puzzled as I had. 'I can't see how this Colonel Maksa got to Ngingwe, or why he wants Captain Sadiq there,' he said.

The only good thing in all this was that the radio was working again. If someone had got through to us, we could perhaps get through to others. And we were desperate for news.

'Tell me what Colonel Maksa's politics are,' I asked Sadiq.

'I don't know, Mister Mannix. We never spoke of such things. I don't know him well. But – he has not always been such an admirer of the President.'

'So he could be on either side. What will you do?'

'I cannot disobey a direct order.'

'It's been done. What did you say to him?'

'We could not answer. The lines are still bad, and perhaps we do not have the range.'

'You mean he spoke to you but you couldn't reply. So he doesn't know if you heard the order. Did it refer directly to you or was it a general call for assembly at Ngingwe?'

'It was a direct order to me.'

'Who else knows about this?' I asked.

'Only my sergeant.'

Wingstead said, 'You want him to put the headphone to a deaf ear, to be a modern Nelson, is that it?' We both looked at Sadiq, who looked stubborn.

180

'Look, Captain. You could be running into big trouble. What if Colonel Maksa is a rebel?'

'I have thought of that, sir. You should not think I am so stupid as to go off without checking.'

'How can you do that?' Wingstead asked.

'I will try to speak to headquarters, to General Kigonde or someone on his staff,' he said. 'But my sergeant has tried very often to get through, without any luck. Our radio is not strong enough.'

Wingstead said abruptly, 'I think we can fix that.'

'How?' I knew that his own intervehicle radios were very limited indeed.

He said, 'I've got reason to think we're harbouring a fairly proficient amateur radio jockey.'

'For God's sake, who?' I asked.

Wingstead said, 'Sandy Bing. A few days ago we caught him in your staff car, Captain, fiddling with your radio. There was a soldier on duty but Bing told him he had your permission. We caught him at it and I read him the riot act. But I let it go at that. We're not military nor police and I had other things on my mind besides a bored youngster.'

'Did you know about this talent of his?' I asked.

'I'd caught him once myself fiddling with the set in the Land Rover. That's really too mild a word for what he'd been doing. He had the damn set in pieces. I bawled him out and watched while he put the bits back together. He knew what he was doing and it worked as well as ever afterwards. He's damned enthusiastic and wants to work with radio one day. Sam Wilson told me that he's for ever at any set he can get his hands on.'

'What do you think he can do? Amplify this set?'

'Maybe. Come along with me, Neil. I'll talk to Bing, but I want a word with Basil first. This will delay our start again, I'm afraid.'

Sadiq agreed to wait and see if Bing could get him through to his headquarters before taking any other action. My guess was that he wanted to stay with us, but right now he was torn

181

by a conflict of orders and emotions, and it was hard to guess which would triumph.

Less than an hour later we stood watching as Sandy Bing delved happily into the bowels of a transmitter. Sadiq allowed him access to his own car radio, which Bing wanted as he said it was better than anything we had, though still underpowered for what he wanted. He got his fingers into its guts and went to work, slightly cock-a-hoop but determined to prove his value. He wanted to cannibalize one of Kemp's radios too, to build an extra power stage; at first Kemp dug his heels in, but common sense finally won him round.

'We'll need a better antenna,' said Bing, in his element. 'I'll need copper wire and insulators.'

Hammond managed to find whatever was needed. The travelling repair shop was amazingly well kitted out.

Our start was delayed by over four hours, and the morning was shot before Bing started to get results. Eventually he got the beefed-up transmitter on the air which was in itself a triumph, but that was just the beginning. General Kigonde's headquarters were hard to locate and contact, and once we'd found them there was another problem; a captain doesn't simply chat to his commander-in-chief whenever he wants to. It took an hour for Sadiq to get patched through to the military radio network and another hour of battling through the chain of command.

I'll give Sadiq his due; it takes a brave and determined man to bully and threaten his way through a guard of civilian secretaries, colonels and brigadiers. He really laid his neck on the block and if Kigonde hadn't been available, or didn't back him, I wouldn't have given two cents for his later chances of promotion. When he spoke to Kigonde the sun was high in the sky and he was nearly as high with tension and triumph.

'You did OK, Sandy,' I said to Bing, who was standing by with a grin all over his face as the final connection came through. Wingstead clapped him on the shoulder and there were smiles all round.

Sadiq and Kigonde spoke only in Nyalan, and the Captain's side of the conversation became more and more curt and monosyllabic. Sadiq looked perturbed; obviously he would like to tell us what was going on, but dared not sever the precious connection, and Kigonde might run out of patience at any moment and do his own cutting off from the far end. I was sick with impatience and the need for news. At last I extended a hand for the headphones and put a whipcrack into my own voice.

'Tell him I want to speak to him.'

Before Sadiq could react I took the headphones away from him. There was a lot of static as I thumbed the speak button and said, 'General Kigonde, this is Mannix. What is happening, please?'

He might have been taken aback but didn't close me out.

'Mister Mannix, there is no time for talk. Your Captain has received orders and he must obey them. I cannot supervise the movement of every part of the army myself.'

'Has he told you the situation at Ngingwe? That it is a dead end? The road goes nowhere now. We *need* him, General. Has he told you what's happening here, with your people?'

Through the static, Kigonde said, 'Captain Sadiq has orders to obey. Mister Mannix, I know you have many people in trouble there, but there is trouble everywhere.'

That gave me an idea. I said, 'General Kigonde, do you know who gave Captain Sadiq his orders?'

'I did not get the name. Why do you ask?'

'Does the name Colonel Maksa mean anything to you?' It was taking a gamble but I didn't think the chances of Maksa or anyone on his staff overhearing this conversation were strong. It was a risk we had to take.

Static crackled at me and then Kigonde said, 'That is . . . perhaps different. He was in command of forces in the north. I have not heard from him.'

Doubt crept into Kigonde's voice.

I said urgently, 'General, I think you do have doubts about

183

Colonel Maksa. If he were against you what better could he do than draw off your troops? Captain Sadiq is completely loyal. Where would you get the best use out of him? Here with us, or cut off upcountry? If I were you I'd cancel those orders, General.'

'You may be right, Mister Mannix. I must say the Captain would be better off for my purposes further west. I will send him to Makara instead.'

'But we're going to Makara ourselves. Can he stay with us until we get there?'

I was really pushing my luck and I wasn't surprised when he demanded to speak to Sadiq again. It was a long one-sided conversation, and when he rang off we could all see that he had been told something that had shaken him badly.

He remembered his manners before anything else, turned to Bing and said, 'Thank you very much. I am grateful to you,' which pleased Bing immensely. But Sadiq didn't look grateful, only distressed.

'Let's go and sit down, Captain,' I said. 'Geoff, you, me and Basil only, I think. Move it out, you guys. Find something to do.'

Sadiq filled us in on the conversation. He was to move westwards to Makara with us, but once there he was to push on towards Fort Pirie, leaving us to cope. It was as much as we could have expected. But it occurred to me that the General must be in a bad way if he was calling such minor outfits as Sadiq's to his assistance.

'The General says that the Government is in power in Port Luard once again. The rebellion is crushed and almost all the rebels are rounded up,' Sadiq said. That was what Kigonde would say, especially on the air, and none of us put too much faith in it. But at least it meant that the Government hadn't been crushed.

'The rebellion was premature, I think,' Sadiq said. 'The opposition was not ready and has been beaten quite easily in most places.'

'But not everywhere. Does he know where this Colonel

184

Maksa is? I think we have to assume he's on the wrong side, don't you?' I said.

'Yes, the Colonel's politics are suspect. And he is known to be hereabouts. There are planes looking for him and his force.'

'Planes?' said Wingstead in alarm. 'Whose planes?'

'Ah, it is all most unfortunate, sir. We were wrong, you see. The Air Force, Air Chief Marshall Semangala is on the side of the Government.'

'Ouseman's *allies*?' My jaw dropped. 'Then why was Mister Wingstead's plane shot down, for God's sake?'

'I don't know, Mister Mannix. But perhaps the Air Force expected that any civilian planes flying in the battle area belonged to the rebels,' Sadiq said unhappily. I thought of Max Otterman, fighting for his life somewhere on the rig, and rage caught in my throat.

Geoff Wingstead was ahead of me. 'What about the bombing of Kodowa, then? The troop moving through the town at the time was Kigonde's own Second Battalion. Are you going to tell us that was a mistake, too?'

'Ah, that was very bad. Air Force Intelligence thought that the Second Battalion was already with the Seventh Brigade at Bir Oassa. When they saw troops moving north they thought it was the enemy trying to cut off the Seventh Brigade from coming south. So they attacked.' Sadiq looked anguished.

A mistake! They'd bombed their own men thinking they were the enemy. It wouldn't be the first time that had happened in a war. But they'd bombed them in the middle of a town when they could easily have waited to catch them out in the open. So would somebody eventually apologize for this colossal, tragic mistake? Apologize for the pits full of corpses, the ruined town, the wrecked and tortured people on the rig or hobbling through the wasted country? To Sister Ursula and Dr Kat, to Dr Marriot for the killing of her husband? To Antoine Dufour for the death of his partner?

Somebody ought to say they were sorry. But nobody ever would.

17

We left Kodowa again.

We went north-west this time, descending from the scrubland to the rainforest country of the lower plains, the same sort
of terrain that we'd moved through on our journey northwards.
The people in the little villages we passed through came out to
see us but they weren't laughing this time. They gazed at the
great rig and the strange load it carried and their faces were
troubled. Even the children were subdued, catching the uneasiness of their elders.

The rig's passengers varied. Some improved and were allowed to ride in one of the trucks, others collapsed and were
given a place on the bedding. Two women gave birth on the
rig, and Dr Kat removed a swollen appendix from a ten-year-old
boy. The medical supplies dwindled steadily.

At each village Sadiq sent his men out to forage. A couple
of beat-up trucks were added to the convoy as well as provisions.
Occasionally they found petrol and it was added to our store.
Our own food became more basic and the beer had long since
run out. But we managed.

In one village we found a small cache of clothing and
bartered food for it, and it did feel wonderful to be wearing
something clean for a while. The men were beginning to look
shaggy as beards sprouted.

With each few hours the make-up of the flock of Nyalans
that trailed along after us subtly altered. The convoy was
behaving much like a comet in space, picking up and losing bits
of its tail as it went along. Groups of Nyalans would arrive at
some village where they had kin or were too weary to walk

further, and would leave us there. Others would follow along. There may have been several hundred in our wake, and there was something of a ritual, almost mystic, quality in their behaviour. Often one or more would approach the rig and reach up to touch it wonderingly before dropping behind again.

It was Dan Atheridge who explained it to me. He'd lived here for many years, and spoke a little Nyalan. His arm troubled him and he had to be restrained from doing too much; but I knew that he was deliberately driving himself into exhaustion in an attempt to numb the pain and horror of leaving his wife Susie somewhere behind him in the hills beyond Kanja. He had begged to be allowed to go off and try to find her, but had finally been persuaded not to.

I asked him about the Nyalans.

'Your rig's turning into a juggernaut, Neil,' he said.

'That's an Indian thing, isn't it? A sort of God-mobile?'

That got a smile from him. 'You could put it that way. Actually it's one of the names of the god Krishna. It became applied to a huge idol that's dragged through the streets in a town in India annually in his honour. In the olden days sacrificial victims were thrown under it to be crushed to death. A rather bloodthirsty deity, I fear.'

'It isn't inappropriate,' I said. 'Except that nobody's been run down by the rig yet, which God forbid.'

'It's followed in procession by thousands of devotees, who regard it as a sacred symbol of their wellbeing. That's the similarity, Neil. This rig of yours has become a fetish to the Nyalans. You're leading them to the promised land, wherever that is. Out of danger anyway.'

'I hope that's true, Dan. Still, I guess they have to believe in something.'

I mentioned the parallel with the Pied Piper and he smiled again. 'I hope you think of them as children rather than as rats, Neil.'

I got precisely the other viewpoint from Russ Burns some

187

time later that day, when we stopped at last, more than halfway to Makara.

Several of us were waiting for whatever Brad Bishop could offer as an evening meal. Making idle conversation, I mentioned Atheridge's theory about the new role of the rig as a fetish, and Wingstead was fascinated. I could see him formulating an article for some truckers' magazine. Burns' attitude was very different and typical of him.

'More like rats,' he said when I invoked the Pied Piper image. 'Little brown bastards, eating up everything that isn't nailed down. Probably carrying disease too.' I felt a strong desire to hit him. Wingstead got up and walked away.

After a strained silence Burns spoke again. 'How come you work for a limey outfit?' He seemed to enjoy baiting me.

'Good pay,' I said briefly.

He snorted. 'For pushing this thing along?'

'Good enough,' I said. He seemed to have got the notion that I was a transport man and I didn't bother to disillusion him. It wasn't worth the trouble, and in any case right now it was nearer the truth than otherwise.

'What do you do with Lat-Am?' I asked him.

'I'm a tool pusher. Harry here's a shooter.'

'Come again? I don't know oil jargon.'

Zimmerman laughed. 'Russ is a drilling superintendent. Me, I make loud bangs in oil wells. Blasting.'

'Been in Nyala long?' I didn't take to Burns but Zimmerman was a much more likeable man. They made an odd pair.

'A while. Six months or so. We were based in Bir Oassa but we went down to the coast to take a look. The desert country's better. We should have stayed up there.'

'You can say that again,' Burns said, 'then we'd be out of this crummy mess.'

'I was up in Bir Oassa earlier this month,' I said. 'Didn't have much time to look at the oilfields, though. How you doing there?'

'We brought in three,' Zimmerman said. 'Good sweet oil,

188

low sulphur; needs no doctor at all. Lat-Am isn't doing badly on this one.'

'What about the war, though?'

Burns shrugged. 'That's no skin off Lat-Am's ass. We'll stop pumping, that's all. The oil's still in the ground and we've got the concession. Whoever wins the war will need us.'

It was a point of view, I suppose.

They talked then between themselves for a while, using oilfield jargon which I understood better than I'd let on. Burns appealed to me less and less; he was a guy for whom the word chauvinist might have been invented. Texas was Paradise and the Alamo was the navel of the earth; he might grudgingly concede that California wasn't bad, but the East Coast was full of goddamn liberals and Jews and longhaired hippies. You might as well be in Europe, where everyone was effete and decadent. Still, the easterners were at least American and he could get along with them if he had to. The rest of the world was divided between commies, niggers, Ayrabs and gooks, and fit only for plundering for oil.

The next day we arrived at Makara. It was no bigger than other villages we'd passed through, but it earned its place on the map because of the bridge which spanned the river there. Further west, near Lake Pirie where the river joined the huge Katali there was a delta, and building a bridge would not have been possible. Our first concern was to find out whether the river was passable, and Sadiq, Kemp and I went ahead of the convoy to take a look. To our relief the bridge stood firm and was fit for crossing.

We halted outside the village and sent off another scouting party to investigate the cotton warehouses. Word came back that they were intact, empty and serviceable as a hospital, and so we moved to the cotton factory and camped there. Apart from the grave faces of the local people there was no sign of trouble anywhere.

That was the last good thing that happened that day.

189

Dr Katabisirua came to look at the warehouses and arranged for some Nyalan women to give the largest a clean through before bringing in the patients, which he wouldn't do until the next day. 'My nurses are tired from the journey,' he said, 'and that is when mistakes are made.'

He was very despondent. Two more burn patients had died and he feared for one of the new born babies. Some of the wounded were not improving as he would wish. 'And now Sister Ursula tells me we have no more Ringer's lactate.'

'What's that?'

'A replacement for lost plasma. We have no substitute.' There was no hospital closer than Lasulu, and that was as far away as the moon. He also fretted about Sister Mary who was sinking into frail senility under the stress.

By the end of our talk I was even more depressed than he was. There wasn't a thing I could do for him or his patients, and I was profoundly frustrated by my helplessness. Never before in my adult life had I been unable to cope with a situation, and it galled me.

Burns, passing by, said casually, 'Hey, Mannix, the coon captain wants you,' and walked on.

'Burns!'

He looked back over his shoulder. 'Yes?'

'Come here.'

He swung back. 'You got a beef?'

I said, 'This morning Captain Sadiq persuaded his superior officer to let him stay with this convoy. He put his career on the line for us. What's more, over the past few days he's worked harder than you could in a month, and a damned sight more willingly. Around here you'll speak respectfully of and to him. Got the idea?'

'Touchy, aren't you?' he said.

'Yes I am. Don't push me, Burns.'

'What the hell do you want from me?' he asked.

I sighed, letting my neck muscles relax. 'You will not refer to the Captain as a coon or a nigger. Nor his soldiers, nor any other Nyalans, come to that. We're fed up with it.'

'Why should I take orders from you?' he asked.

I said, 'Because right now I'm top man around here. As long as you're with us you do what I say, and if you don't toe the line you'll be out on your can. And you won't hold a job with Lat-Am or any other oil company after this is over. If you don't think I can swing that then you just ask Mister Kemp.'

I turned my back and walked away, seething. If I'd been near him much longer I couldn't have kept my hands off him, which wouldn't have solved any problems. I passed a couple of staring men and then McGrath was beside me, speaking softly.

'Need any help, Mannix?'

'No,' I said curtly. McGrath stuck in my craw too.

'I'll be around if you do.' He returned to his job.

I recalled that the reason for this outburst had been that Captain Sadiq wanted a word, and I set about finding him. It was a routine matter he wanted settled. After our business was over I pointed to the milling flock of Nyalans around the camp.

'Captain, how many of them are there?' I asked.

'Perhaps two hundred, Mister Mannix. But they do not stay with us for long. It is only that there are always more of them.'

'Yes, I've noticed that. I understand they've attached themselves to the rig, made some sort of mascot of it. Do you know anything about it?'

'I am of Islam,' he said. 'These people have different ideas from you and me. But they are not savages, Mister Mannix. Perhaps it is no more than the thing Mister Lang hangs in the cab of his tractor. It is a lucky charm.'

'That's a rabbit's foot. I see what you mean,' I said, impressed by his logic. 'Just a bigger talisman than usual. But I'm worried about them. Are they getting enough food and water? What if a real sickness strikes among them? What can we do to stop them, make them return to their homes?'

'I do not think anything will stop them, sir. They manage

191

for food, and none will walk further than he can achieve. For each of them, that is enough.'

One thing it ensured was a redistribution of the local population, a reshuffle of families, genes and customs; perhaps not altogether a bad thing. But it was a hell of a way to go about it. And suppose ill fortune should fall on these people while they were tailing us. Would they see their erstwhile lucky talisman becoming a force of evil instead, and if so what might they take it into their collective heads to do about it, and about us?

I reflected on the crusades. Not all of them were made by armed and mailed men; there was the Peasants' Crusade led by Peter the Hermit, and the Children's Crusade. If I remembered my history, terrible things happened to those kids. And come to think of it, Hamelin's rats and children didn't do too well either.

I didn't much relish the role of a twentieth century Peter leading a mad crusade into nowhere. A whole lot of people could die that way. The thought of an armoured column ploughing through this mob chilled my blood.

The run-in with Burns later that day was inevitable, a curtain-raiser to the real drama that followed. The men who work the oil rigs are a tough bunch and you don't get to boss a drilling crew by backing down from a fight. Maybe I should have handled Burns more tactfully, maybe I was losing my touch, but there it was. I had threatened him and I might have known he wouldn't stand still for it.

But that was yet to come. First we had to set up the cotton warehouse for Dr Kat to move in to the next day, and we parked the rig close by in order to run a cable from its generator. Ben Hammond, as usual, provided ideas and the equipment to put them into action, and his goody box included a sizeable reel of cable and several powerful lamps.

While this was being done I had a look around the warehouse. It was just a huge barn about a quarter full of cotton stacked at the far end. The bottom stacks were compressed but the upper layers were soft and would provide comfort for everybody soon, including myself. I intended to sleep there that night. The biggest mattress in the world, but better not smoke in bed.

Late in the afternoon I saw Harry Zimmerman sitting on an upturned box near the Land Rover, smoking and drinking a mug of tea. I sensed that he was waiting for me, though his opening remark was casual enough.

'Been a busy day,' he said.

'Sure has. And it'll be a busy night. I've got another job for you, anytime you're ready.' I dropped down beside him. 'Trade you for a mouthful of that gunfire, Harry.'

'What have you got to trade?' he asked as he handed over the mug. I took a swig and passed it back.

'Good soft bed for tonight.'

'Now you're talking. Anyone in it?'

'Sorry, only me – and probably all the rest of the crew. We may as well doss down in comfort for one night before handing the warehouse over to the medics.'

He was silent for a spell and then said, 'Seen Russ about?'

'No. Why?'

'Just thought I'd mention it. He's spoiling for a fight. Can be nasty, once he's off and flying.'

It was a fair warning and I wasn't particularly surprised. I nodded my thanks and crossed to the Land Rover. Zimmerman seemed to be waiting for something to happen. It did. As I opened the door an object rolled off the seat and smashed at my feet. It was my bottle of Scotch, and it was quite empty.

'Russ did this, Harry?'

'I'm afraid so.'

He'd left the bottle where I'd find it; it was a direct challenge. There would have been just enough in it to put an edge on his appetite for supper, or for a brawl.

'Where is he?'

'Neil, Russ is one tough guy to tangle with. Be careful.'

I said, 'He's not going to hurt me. I'm going to straighten your buddy out.'

'Hell, he's not my buddy,' Zimmerman said, and there was an edge to his normally placid voice. 'We just work together. I've seen this before and I don't have a taste for it. He's having a game of poker with some of your guys.'

I picked up the pieces of glass and ditched all but the largest which had the label still attached, and closed the car door. Zimmerman added, 'Watch his left. He has a sneaky curve punch there.'

'Thanks.'

I knew where to find Burns. One of the lamps leading from the generator cable had been looped over a tree so that the light shone on the ground below. Five men were sitting playing cards, using a suitcase as a table. I didn't notice who they were; I had eyes only for Burns. He played a hand casually but I knew he'd seen me arrive and his back had stiffened.

I stopped just outside the circle of light and said, 'Burns, come here. I want you.'

He looked up and shaded his eyes. 'Why, it's our top man,' he said. 'What can I do for you, Mannix?'

Cards went down all round the circle. I said, 'Come over here.'

'Sure. Why not?' He uncoiled his lean length from the ground.

I watched him come. He was younger, taller, heavier and probably faster than I was, so I'd have to get in first. It's a stupid man who starts a fight without reckoning the odds. Burns knew that too; he was spoiling for a fight, as Zimmerman had warned me, and he had set up the time and place. It was years since I'd done much fighting except with words, while he was probably well in practice.

I was aware of figures forming the inevitable spectators' ring, but I couldn't afford to take my eyes off Burns. Witnesses were in any case going to be more on my side than on his, so long as I could hold my own.

194

I held up the bottle shard. 'Did you drink my whisky?'

'Sure I drank it. What's wrong with borrowing a little booze? It was good stuff while it lasted.'

I controlled my anger, and was so intent that when the interruption came I couldn't quite credit it. A hand came over my shoulder and took the broken glass from me. 'Do you mind if I have a look at that?' a voice said.

McGrath stepped out beside me and peered at the label. Everyone else stood motionless.

'I've seen this before. Isn't it the bottle you were keeping for medical emergencies, now?'

Then without warning the hand not holding the shard connected with Burns just at the angle of his jaw and the Texan grunted, staggered and dropped as though poleaxed. Only afterwards did I see the cosh.

I grabbed McGrath by the arm. 'God damn it, McGrath, I told you not to go off half-cocked!'

He said so that only I could hear, 'You couldn't have whipped this bucko and we both know it. He'd take you to pieces. I've had my eye on him; he's dangerous.' Coming from McGrath that was a ludicrous statement. 'Now if I don't defuse him he'll come looking for both of us and he might have a gun by then. He has to be made harmless. That OK with you?'

'Christ, no! I don't want him killed,' I said.

'I wouldn't kill him. I said made harmless. Now, have I your leave?'

I didn't have much choice. 'Don't hurt him,' I said.

'Not really hurt, no,' McGrath said. He pushed his way through the knot of men who had gathered round Burns. They made way instantly, though none faster than Jones and Bob Pitman. Neither Wingstead nor Kemp were present.

McGrath took Burns by his shirtfront, hauled him to his feet and shook him. 'Are you all right, Texas?' he asked.

Burns' eyes looked fogged. He put a hand up to his jaw and mumbled, 'You son of a bitch – you busted it!'

'Not at all,' said McGrath, 'Or you couldn't be saying so. I

195

didn't hit you all that hard, did I now? And I don't think that's the language for someone in your position to be using.'

The hand that had held the cosh came up again and this time there was a knife in it. McGrath was a walking armoury. He pressed the sharp edge against Burns' throat and a ribbon of blood trickled down. He pushed Burns until the Texan's back was against a truck.

'Now listen,' McGrath said in a matter-of-fact voice, 'You can have your throat cut fast, slow or not at all. Take your pick.'

Burns choked. 'Not – not at all.'

'Well, then, you can answer a couple of questions, and if you give the right answers you get a prize, your life. Here comes the first question. Are you ready?'

'Yes,' whispered Burns.

McGrath said, 'Right, this is it. Name one boss in this camp.'

'Y-you.'

'Wrong,' said McGrath pleasantly. 'You're losing points, sonny. But I'll give you another go. Guess again.'

Burns hesitated and the knife shifted. More blood soaked into his shirt. 'Mannix?'

'Mister Mannix, yes. But a little more respect with it, please. Now here comes the next question. Are you ready for it?'

'Christ, yes.' Burns face was running with sweat.

'Then here goes. Name another boss.'

'Wing . . . Mister Wingstead.'

'Oh, very good. See how well you can do when you try. So from now on when Mister Mannix or Mister Wingstead says for you to jump, you jump. Got that?'

'Yes.'

'And if you give either of them any trouble, guess what? Third question.'

'You bastard –'

McGrath's hand moved once more. Burns gasped, 'I won't give them any trouble. Let go of me, damn you!'

196

McGrath did just that and Burns sagged against the truck. His hand went to his throat and came away covered with blood. He stared at McGrath and then appealed to me. 'He's crazy! You keep him away from me.'

'He'll never touch you again. Not if you do what he's just told you,' I said. Then I pressed the lesson home. 'You said you'd borrowed that Scotch. I want it returned.'

He gaped at me. 'You're as crazy as he is! You know I can't do that.'

'In my book a man who takes what he can't return is a thief.'

He said nothing and I let it go at that. I turned to the others. 'All right, the show is over. There's no –'

I was interrupted by a distant commotion of voices.

'Mannix! Ben Hammond, you there?'

It was Kemp calling. Hammond shouted back, 'We're both here. What is it?'

Kemp came out of the dark at a jog trot, looking strained. Burns was forgotten in the face of a new crisis.

'Come up to the rig. Geoff wants you.'

'What the hell is it?'

'It's Max. He's gone into convulsions. We think he's dying.'

There was a murmur around us. To most of the crew Otterman was not well-known but he was the man who'd saved Wingstead's life at risk to his own. They were taking a close interest in his progress, and at that moment were no more free of superstition than the Nyalans who followed their talisman through the countryside: Otterman's sudden turn for the worse was a bad omen. As for me, I'd flown with him, liked him, and felt a stab of sorrow at Kemp's news.

And then the quiet of the night was shattered again. To the east there was thunder. There followed noises like Fourth of July rockets, and the earth shook underfoot. It was the sound of heavy gunfire and small arms. The war was catching up with us at last.

197

18

Things began to happen fast.

From the military camp soldiers came running towards the warehouse. People milled about in the darkness and shouted questions. The men around me were galvanized into agitation which could become panic.

I shouted for attention. 'That was gunfire. Keep together and stay quiet. Let the soldiers do their job. Hammond, you there?'

'Yes, I'm here.'

'Set guards round all the transports, especially the trucks and cars. The rig can't be shifted so it's reasonably safe. Basil, go tell the doctors and staff to stay put whatever happens. I'm sorry about Max, but tell Geoff I need him here fast.'

He ran off and I went on, 'Zimmerman – if Russ Burns isn't fit get him to the medics. I'm going to find the Captain.'

I heard Burns mumble, 'I'll be OK, Harry,' and turned away. I wondered what had become of McGrath; at the very first sound of battle he had disappeared, cat-like, into the night. I headed off towards the military area, stumbling over camp litter. I heard guns firing again before I found Captain Sadiq.

He was at his staff car, and inevitably on the radio. He spoke for some time, looking alarmed, and then ripped off the headphones.

'What's happening?' I asked.

'Army units coming from the east, from Kodowa. They ran into a patrol of men and started shooting.'

'We heard a big gun.'

'I think they shelled a truck.'

198

'They must be the rebels,' I said.

'Maybe, Mister Mannix. Men become nervous in the dark.'

'How many?'

'I don't know yet. My corporal reported many vehicles coming this way. Not in battalion strength but not far short. Then the transmission stopped.'

So a whole platoon of Sadiq's men was possibly wiped out. I asked if he knew how far off they were.

'Six miles, maybe. They could be here in half an hour or less.'

This could be a nasty mess. With the Nyalan civilians strung out all the way to the bridge, with our sick and wounded, and with a small bunch of virtually unarmed white rig-pushers, there could be a massacre. And to prevent it a handful of soldiers armed with rifles and one or two light mounted guns.

Sadiq said, 'If we stand and fight it will be useless. We couldn't combat a company, let alone this strength. Sergeant! Get the men ready to pull out. There must be no shooting under any circumstances. We'll be moving that way.' He pointed away from Makara. This had been in English and was clearly for my benefit, but he carried on in Nyalan. The sergeant went off at a run.

I said, 'So you're pulling out – leaving us? What the hell are we supposed to do on our own?'

He raised a hand to silence me. Danger had increased his authority and he knew it. 'No, Mister Mannix. There are tracks beyond the warehouses which lead into the bush. I'm going to hide my men there. If I am to be of any use it can only be from a position of surprise. I suggest that you make your camp look as peaceful as possible. And that means hiding all weapons, including your shotgun. And anything that Mister McGrath may have.'

'You know about him?'

'I am *not* a fool, Mister Mannix. You took a pistol from him, but he may have some other weapon. When the soldiers

199

come act peacefully. As soon as possible give me a signal. If they are loyal troops you fire this.'

He handed me a Very pistol and a couple of cartridges.

'The white star will signal no danger. If there is trouble, fire the red. Try not to provoke them.'

Sadiq could simply vanish into the bush and desert us but I felt that he would do no such thing. I said, 'Thank you, Captain. And good luck.'

He saluted me, jumped into his car, and was gone into the night.

'Remarkable,' said a voice behind me. Wingstead had been listening. I nodded briefly, then called Bing. 'Get back to the rig, Sandy. Tell the men to gather round quietly and wait for us. And take the guards off the trucks. Tell Mister Hammond I said so.' I debated giving instructions to immobilize the transports but reflected that it might do us as much harm as our enemy.

Zimmerman was beside me. I said to him, 'Please go fetch Mister Kemp. He'll be at the rig. And get Doctor Kat as well. Tell him he must leave his patients for a few minutes.'

Wingstead said, 'I gather we aren't sure if it's the goodies or the baddies who are coming along, right?'

'Exactly right. So we play it as cool as we can. What's happened with Otterman?'

'He was having some sort of convulsion. God knows what it is; the medics have nothing left to sedate him with. I feel responsible but I can't do him one bit of good. I've never had a man working for me die before.'

'Well, he's not dead yet. They'll pull him through if they can,' I said, but it was hollow comfort. We hurried back to the rig, and I noticed that the Nyalan refugees had vanished; like the soldiers, they had dissolved back into the land. It had needed no bush telegraph to pass the word. They had heard and recognized the gunfire.

Back at the rig Hammond had got my message and gathered the men together. 'The army's pulling out,' someone said.

'Who's doing the shooting?'

'Hold it! Just shut up and listen. Harry, you translate for our Russian friends, please. This is the position as far as we know. There's a force coming down from Kodowa. They ran into one of Sadiq's patrols and we think they shot them up, so it's likely that they're rebels. But we can't be sure yet. Mistakes happen in the dark.'

And in broad daylight too, I thought, remembering the bombing raid on Kodowa.

'If they are rebels they'll be too much for Sadiq to handle, so he's done a little disappearing act with his men. We'll signal to let him know if the new arrivals are friendly or otherwise. If they want to know where Sadiq is, he's gone off with his men. It's important that everybody tells the same story. He left us as soon as we got here. Right?'

Kemp asked, 'Why this flimflam? He's supposed to stay and guard the rig, isn't he?'

Not for the first time I despaired of Kemp's single-mindedness. I said, 'I'll explain later,' and turned back to the men.

'When they get here I want the camp to look normal. Remember, we know nothing about their politics and care less. We're paid to push the rig, that's all. We're a crowd of foreigners in the middle of a shooting war, trying to keep our noses clean, and we're scared.'

'None of us will have to be Laurence Olivier to act that part,' someone said.

'Let Mister Wingstead or me answer any questions. And no rough stuff, no opposition, no matter what.' This wouldn't be easy. Men like this wouldn't willingly allow themselves to be pushed around. But it was essential. Opposition could only bring reprisal.

A voice said, 'Why stay here? Why don't we scarper and hide out in the bush till they've gone, same as the army?'

Dr Kat said sharply, 'I am not leaving my patients.'

'I don't think it'd wash, or I'd be the first to go,' Wingstead put in. 'If there's no-one here they'll get suspicious and come looking for us.'

His calm decisiveness was what was needed. There wasn't a man amongst them who didn't respect him.

I said, 'Right, let's get this camp looking peaceful.'

I left Wingstead to organize things and went to the Land Rover to get the shotgun and its shells. I took them into the warehouse and hid them deep inside a bale of cotton, hoping that nobody had seen me do it. Then I went back to rejoin Wingstead at the rig.

He had persuaded the doctors and Sister Ursula to accept our need for deception, and to brief the nurses. I had a quick look at Otterman and was not reassured. He looked desperately ill.

Geoff and I made a quick tour of the camp, checking to make sure that everything looked reasonably normal. Of the Nyalans there was no sign whatsoever, and Sadiq had taken off his platoon complete with all their transport. Camp fires had been extinguished and there was nothing to show that his departure had been anything other than orderly.

We settled down around the rig, tense and nervous, to wait for our visitors. They took about an hour to reach us, and it was probably the longest wait of our lives.

19

We heard them before we saw them.

Bert Proctor cocked his head at the distant rumble, then settled at the table and picked up his cards. 'Just go on with the game,' he said quietly.

Ron Jones got up. 'Count me out, Bert. I'm too nervous,' he said.

I took his place. 'Deal me in. Just take it easy, Ron. No sweat.'

As Proctor dealt I noticed that Russ Burns was one of my fellow players. To my surprise he spoke to me directly.

'You play goddamn rough, Mannix,' he said. The 'Mister' had disappeared. 'Where did you get that goon you set on me?'

'I didn't get him. I inherited him. He's one of Wyvern's best rig hands,' I said. I didn't expect friendship from Burns but he sounded easy enough.

'I really thought he was going to cut my throat. He's pretty dangerous,' Burns said.

'I'll try to keep him on a leash,' I said casually. 'By the way, anyone seen Mick lately?'

There were headshakes all round.

Burns looked at his cards and cursed them. 'We've got a few things to sort out, you and me, after this is over,' he said, 'but if there's trouble in the meantime, I'm with you. What say?'

'Suits me.' We played a round or two with less than full attention. The engine noises were louder and there were voices shouting. Soon we put our cards down to watch the arrival of the army.

A few motorcyclists came first. They roared to a halt just over the crest of the hill that led down to Makara and the camp, and there was a glow in the sky behind them as the rest followed. Soldiers came through the bush on each side of the road. I hoped they wouldn't fan out far enough to find Sadiq's team.

The minutes ticked by and there were rustling sounds in the undergrowth. They were being cautious, not knowing what they were getting into, and nervous men could do stupid things. We stood fully illuminated while they closed in around us, and felt terrifyingly vulnerable.

Wingstead said loudly, 'I'm going to bed. We've got a busy day ahead. Goodnight, everyone.'

I followed his lead. 'Me too. That's enough poker for one night.'

Hammond, in a flash of inspiration, said equally loudly, 'What about all the activity out there, Mister Wingstead? Anything we should know about?'

'No, I don't think so,' he replied. 'Just manoeuvres, I should guess. They won't bother us.'

Truck after truck was coming over the crest towards us. I couldn't see any tanks but the trucks' headlights began to light up the whole camp in a glaring display. A ring of armed soldiers was gathered on the fringes of the camp, and we knew we were surrounded.

I shouted to carry over the engine roar, 'We've got company. Let's hope they can spare us some food and medical stuff.'

Into the light came a command car. In the back was a captain, his uniform identical to Sadiq's except that he wore a red brassard on his right arm. He was unlike Sadiq in looks too; where Sadiq had a distinctly Arabic cast and a light skin this was the blackest man I had ever seen. He was huge and burly and most unnervingly wearing enormous dark glasses; in combination with his dark skin and the night the effect was weird.

He stood up in the back of the car and looked from us to the rig and then back. He said in English, 'Who are you?'

I answered. 'The rig team of Wyvern Transport. Who are you?' But my counterattack didn't work; I hadn't thought it would.

'Are you in charge of – of this?' He indicated the rig.

'No,' I said, 'that's Mister Wingstead here. I am his associate. We were taking a transformer up to the oilfields. But now we have to head back westward.'

'Where is Captain Sadiq?' he asked abruptly.

I'd been expecting that question.

'He should be well on the road to Fort Pirie by now. He left at first light with his men.'

'You're lying,' the captain said. 'Where is he?'

One of his men hitched his rifle. We were in the hands of a military power, and an unfriendly one at that. I hadn't been accustomed to shutting up at anyone else's say-so for a long time and it was an unpleasant sensation. I put an edge on my voice. 'Now wait a minute, captain. You're not dealing with soldiers now. You'd better consult your superior officer before you start dictating to civilians. I told you that Captain Sadiq left this morning and pushed on. He had orders reassigning him. I don't know where he is now and I can't say I care. He left us flat.'

All this rolled off his back without touching. 'I do not believe you,' he said. 'There is much that is strange here. Who are all the people we found on the road as we came up?'

'Women and children? They're local folk, following us for food, and they're in a bad way. I think you should be doing something to help them.'

He regarded the rig again. 'What is that stuff up there?' He'd recognized the incongruity of the thatching.

'That's a long story,' I said. 'You've been in Kodowa lately? Then you'll know what it was like there. The hospital wasn't usable so we turned the rig into a travelling hospital. We're trying to get the patients to Fort Pirie. Perhaps you can help us, Captain.'

He looked at me unbelievingly. 'Why didn't you take them to Kanja? There's a hospital there and it's closer.'

'We tried. But there's a bridge down in between.'

Apparently he hadn't known that, because he fired questions at me about it and then called a couple of messengers and rattled off orders to them. Then he turned to me and said curtly, 'I am leaving soldiers on guard here. You will stay until I return or until the Colonel arrives.'

'We're going no place, Captain,' I said. 'Not until morning, at any rate. Then perhaps you can help us get the rig across the bridge.'

He gave another order and the car swung round and drove off. A circle of soldiers, rifles at the ready, stood around us. The guns they held were Kalashnikovs.

I sighed and sat down.

'Well done. You're quite a con man,' Wingstead said.

'Cool it, Geoff. God knows how many of them understand English.'

Then we realized that the soldiers had orders to do more than just stand around watching us. A sergeant was doing what sergeants do, and corporals were doing what corporals do; passing orders from top to bottom. They began to swarm over our camp and vehicles and I heard the sound of breaking glass.

'Hold on! What are you doing there?' Kemp asked angrily.

'We follow orders. You go back,' a sullen voice answered.

I turned to a sergeant. 'What's the name of your colonel?'

He considered the question and decided to answer it. 'Colonel Maksa,' he said. 'He will be here soon. Now you go back.'

Reluctantly we retreated away from the vehicles. I hoped to God the soldiers wouldn't try clambering over the rig too, and that they'd respect the doctors and nurses.

We stood around helplessly.

'What the hell do they want?' Kemp asked.

'You could try asking Colonel Maksa when he arrives, but I don't recommend it. I bet he's another man who asks questions and doesn't answer them. I'm pretty sure these are rebel troops; the regulars would be more respectful. But I remembered Hussein and doubted my own words.'

'Are you going to send that signal to Sadiq?'

'Not yet. Let's keep that ace in the hole for when we really need it.'

Kemp said, 'Bloody terrorists. Don't they know they can't win?'

'I wouldn't be too sure of that,' Wingstead said. 'And I wouldn't use that word too freely. One man's terrorist is another man's freedom fighter. No doubt they see themselves as glorious liberators.'

The doors of the warehouse opened and light streamed out. Soldiers were manhandling two men into the open; they were Dan Atheridge and Antoine Dufour, who had retired to sleep on the cotton bales. Atheridge was writhing as someone wrenched his broken arm clear of its sling.

'Good God, what are they doing to them?' Kemp asked in horror.

'I'd like to know,' I said grimly. 'Those two are about the most pacifist of the lot of us.' I wondered if it had anything to do with the shotgun I'd hidden.

Into this scene drove two staff cars; in one was our black-goggled Captain and in the other a large, impressive man who must have been Colonel Maksa. He had the Arabic features of many of his countrymen, marred by a disfiguring scar across his face. His uniform looked as though it had just been delivered from the tailors, in marked contrast to the bedraggled appearance of his Captain and men. He stood up as his car stopped and looked at us coldly.

I tried to take the initiative.

'I must make a formal protest, Colonel Maksa,' I said.

'Must you?' This was a more sophisticated man than the Captain, and just those two words warned me that he could be very dangerous.

'We are a civilian engineering team. Your soldiers have

207

been interfering with our camp and assaulting our men. I protest most strongly!'

'Have they?' he asked indifferently. He alighted from his car and walked past me to look at the rig, then returned to confer with his Captain.

At last he turned back to us.

'Line up your men,' he ordered. Wingstead gestured to the crew and they came to stand with him in a ragged line. The soldiers brought Dufour and Atheridge and dumped them among us. Both looked dazed. I glanced down the line. The two Lat-Am men were there, Burns at his most belligerent and being restrained by a nervous Zimmerman. So were both the Russians, and I hoped that Zimmerman would remember that if they were slow in obeying orders because they couldn't understand them there might be trouble. It would be ironic if they were killed by Moscow-made weapons.

All our own men were there save Mick McGrath, and on him I had begun to pin absurd hopes. None of the medical people were present. There were soldiers in front and behind us, and paradoxically the very fact they were behind us made me feel a little better, because otherwise this would look too much like an execution.

Maksa spoke to his Captain, who barked an order.

'Go into the warehouse.'

'Now wait a goddamn –' began Wingstead.

The Captain thrust his black-visored face alarmingly close. 'I would not argue. Do what the Colonel wishes,' he said. 'He doesn't like arguments.'

I didn't know if this was a warning or a threat. We walked forward between a line of guards and entered the warehouse.

We crowded towards the rear where the cotton was piled. Atheridge collapsed to the floor. Dufour looked dazed still but was on his feet. The doors were closed and a line of Maksa's troops stood just inside them, holding sub-machine-guns.

I had to know about the shotgun. I said to Hammond, keeping my voice low, 'Drift over to the corner behind you, to the left. Get some of the others to do the same. I need a diversion at the door. I want their attention away from that corner for a few seconds.'

Russ Burns said softly, 'I'll do it.'

'Right. Just keep them talking for a few moments.'

He nodded curtly and edged away. I passed Bishop as I moved slowly towards the corner and said to him, 'Brad, keep Sandy out of this if you can.'

He moved in the opposite direction, taking Bing by the arm as he did so. Zimmerman followed Burns and the two Russians went with him as though connected by magnets. We were spread about, and the five soldiers couldn't watch all of us.

Burns went up to the soldiers and started talking. They converged on him threateningly and their voices rose. As all eyes were on them I slipped away into the corner, shielded by the little knot of men around Ben Hammond.

I scrabbled at the cotton searching for the exact spot, and my fingers encountered nothing. The sweat on my forehead was an icy film. The shotgun was gone. I rejoined the others as the warehouse doors opened again.

We were being joined by the whole of the medical staff. They were upset and angry, both Sister Ursula and Dr Kat boiling with rage.

'What's happening out there?' Wingstead asked.

'They made us leave our patients,' Dr Kat said hoarsely. 'They turned guns on us. *Guns*! We are medical people, not soldiers! We must go back.'

The black bars of Sister Ursula's eyebrows were drawn down and she looked furious. 'They are barbarians. They must let us go back, Mister Mannix. There's a baby out there that needs help, and Mister Otterman is dangerously ill.'

'Where's Sister Mary?' someone asked, and Sister Ursula looked more angry still. 'She's ill herself. We *must* make their leader see reason!'

Until the Colonel came there was nothing to do but wait. I considered the two missing factors: McGrath and the shotgun.

It was inevitable that I should put them together. When I hid the shotgun, I had thought I wasn't seen but there was no knowing how much McGrath knew. He was used to acting independently, and sometimes dangerously so, and I knew him to be a killer. I hoped that he wasn't going to do anything bull-headed: one wrong move and we could all be dead.

I was still brooding when the warehouse doors opened and Maksa walked in. When I saw the shotgun in his hands I felt as though I'd been kicked in the teeth.

He stared at us then said, 'I want to talk to you. Get into a line.' A jerk of the shotgun barrel reinforced the order. He gave a curt command and the soldiers filed out except for one sergeant and the doors closed behind them. We shuffled into a line to face our captor.

He said, 'I am Colonel Maksa, commander of the fifteenth Infantry Battalion of the Nyalan Peoples' Liberation Army. I am here in pursuit of an unfriendly military force under the command of Captain Sadiq. I have reason to think you are shielding them in an act of aggression against the Nyalan Peoples' Republic and I intend to have this information from you.'

'Colonel, we really don't –' Wingstead began.

'Be silent! I will ask you in due course. I will begin by knowing all your names and your business, starting with you.' He thrust the shotgun in the direction of Ritchie Thorpe, who was at the far end of the line.

'Uh . . . Mister Wingstead?'

Wingstead nodded gently. 'As the Colonel says, Ritch. Just tell him your name.'

'I'm Richard Thorpe. I work for Mister Wingstead there. For Wyvern Transport.'

The gun's muzzle travelled to the next man. 'You?'

'Bert Proctor. I drive a rig for Wyvern. I'm English.'

'Me too. Derek Grafton, Wyvern Transport.'

'Sam Wilson. Driver . . .'

The roll call continued. Some were sullen, one or two clearly terrified, a couple displayed bravado, but no-one refused to answer. The nurses, clustered together, answered in Nyalan but Dr Kat refused to do so, speaking only English and trying to get in a word about his patients. Maksa brushed him aside and went on down the line. Once the flow of voices stopped Maksa said icily, 'Well? Do you refuse to name yourself?'

Zimmerman raised his voice.

'Colonel, they don't understand you. They don't speak English.'

'Who are they?'

'They're Russians: truck drivers. Their names are -' and he supplied the two names which the rest of us could never remember. Maksa's brows converged and he said, 'Russians? I find that most interesting. You speak Russian, then?'

'Yes, a little.'

'Who are you?'

'Harry Zimmerman. I'm a blaster for Lat-Am Oil, and I'm an American. And I don't have anything to do with your war or this captain you're after.'

Maksa looked at him coldly. 'Enough! Next?'

As he looked along the line his sergeant whispered to him. The next man was Russ Burns.

'Russell Burns, Lat-Am Oil, a good Texan, and one who doesn't like being shoved around. What are you going to do about it?'

Burns was looking for trouble once again.

'My sergeant tells me he has already had trouble with you. You insulted my soldiers. Is this true?'

'You're damn right I did! I don't like being pushed around by a bunch of bastards like you.'

He stepped out of the line-up.

'Burns, cut it out!' I said.

Zimmerman added, 'For God's sake, Russ, take it easy.'

The shotgun rose in the Colonel's hand to point straight at the Texan. Burns gave way but was already too late. The Colonel stepped forward and put the muzzle of the shotgun under Burns' chin and tilted his head back.

211

'You are not very respectful,' Maksa said. 'What is this – has someone tried to kill you already?'

The shotgun rubbed against the bandage round Burns' throat, and he swallowed convulsively. But some mad bravado made him say, 'That's none of your damn business. I cut myself shaving.'

Maksa smiled genially. 'A man with a sense of humour,' he said, and pulled the trigger.

The top of Burns' head blew off. His body splayed out over the floor, pooled with blood. The line scattered with shock. Maksa backed up near the door and his sergeant flanked him with his own gun at the ready. Someone was puking his guts out, and one of the nurses was down on the warehouse floor in a dead faint. The bloody horror of war had caught up with us.

20

Horror gave way to anger. The men started to voice their outrage. I looked down at Burns' body. Nine one third inch lead slugs, together weighing over an ounce, driven with explosive force from close range had pretty well demolished him. It was the quickest of deaths and quite painless for him; but we felt it, the bowel-loosening pain of fear that sudden death brings.

Maksa's voice rose over the babble.

'Be silent!' he said. He hefted the shotgun and his eyes raked us. 'Who owns this?'

Nobody spoke.

'Who owns this shotgun?' he demanded again.

I was debating what to do when Maksa forced my hand. He stepped forward, scanning us, and then pointed. 'You – come here.' The person he had indicated was Helen Chula. After a moment's hesitation she walked slowly towards him, and he grabbed her by the arm, swung her round to face us and jammed the shotgun against her back. 'I ask for the third time, and there will not be a fourth. Who owns this gun?'

I had never found violence of much use in solving my problems, but it seemed to work for Maksa. He could give McGrath pointers in terrorism. I said, 'It's mine,' and stepped forward.

Maksa thrust Helen away. I heard her sobbing but could see nothing but the muzzle of the shotgun as it pointed at my belly. It loomed as large as a fifteen inch navy gun.

'So,' said Maksa. 'We have an American civilian, wandering around with a weapon during an armed conflict. A dangerous thing to do, would you not agree?'

213

'It's a sporting gun,' I said with a dry mouth.

'Can you produce your licence?'

I swallowed. 'No.'

'And I suppose you will also tell me that you do not work for your CIA.'

'I don't. I work for a British firm, and no-one else.'

'Backing the corruption of our so-called Government?'

'Not at all.'

'A man can have two masters,' he said thoughtfully. 'You Americans and the British have always worked in double harness. You imperialists stick together, don't you? You give up your colonies and tell the United Nations that now Nyala is self-governing. But you don't leave my country alone after that.'

I kept silent.

He went on, 'You say we are independent, but you keep the money strings tight. You choke us with loans and reap the profits yourselves; you corrupt our politicians; you plunder us of raw material and sell us the so-called benefits of Western civilization in return, to take back the money you gave us. And now you have been joined by the dogs of Moscow: the old Czarist imperialists ally themselves with you to loot our oil and ruin our country.'

He drew a long breath, controlling himself, and then changed tack.

'Now, about Captain Sadiq. Where is he and what are his plans?'

I said, 'Colonel Maksa, the Captain pulled his men out early today and went away. We know no more than that.'

He said, 'I have talked enough to you. You weary me. I can get more from the others.'

I stood frozen. The Colonel slid his hand down the gun barrel, and then a new voice cut in from high up and behind me. It wasn't very loud but it was very firm.

'If you lift that shotgun I'll cut you in half, colonel.'

Maksa glared over my shoulder. I spun round to see a big black-faced man aiming a sub-machine gun at the Colonel: I turned swiftly and took Maksa's gun away from him.

214

The man on the cotton stack swung the machine gun in a slow arc to point it at the Nyalan sergeant. Without a word the soldier put his gun down and backed away. Hammond picked it up and we held both men under guard. The man with the black face and McGrath's voice swung himself down to the floor. Voices murmured in recognition and relief, and then fell silent again. The atmosphere had changed dramatically, despite Russ Burns' body sprawling at our feet.

I said, 'Maksa, you've seen what this gun can do. One twitch from you and I'll blow your backbone out.'

'If you shoot me you'll bring the soldiers in. They'll kill you all.'

'No they won't,' Hammond said. 'They didn't come in when you shot Russ there.'

McGrath, his face and arms covered with blacking, slung the gun over his shoulder. 'Raise your hands and turn round, Maksa,' he said. Trembling with anger, the Colonel turned as McGrath's hand came out of his pocket holding the cosh. He hit Maksa behind the ear and the Colonel dropped solidly.

McGrath turned to the sergeant. 'Now you, son. Turn round.'

He obeyed unwillingly. Again there was a surge of movement and McGrath said, 'Keep it down, you flaming fools. We'll have the guards in if they hear that going on. Just you keep quiet now.'

Relief made my tone edgy. 'Where the hell have you been, McGrath?'

'Out and about.' He began to strip off the colonel's uniform jacket with its red brassard on one sleeve. 'Give me a hand. Tie him up and dump him back there in the cotton. Same with his sergeant.'

'Goddamnit, we're taking one hell of a risk, McGrath. We might have been able to talk our way out of that jam, but there's no chance now.'

'You weren't going to be given much more time to talk, Mr

215

Mannix,' he said mildly. He was right but I hated to admit it; to be that close to death was hard to accept.

McGrath went on, tugging on a pair of trousers. 'Do you know what they're doing out there? They're piling up petrol drums. They were going to burn down the warehouse.'

'With us in it?' Kemp asked in horror.

Someone said, 'For God's sake, we've got to get out of here.'

'Take it easy,' said McGrath. 'They won't strike a match before the Colonel's out.' He was dressing in the Colonel's uniform. 'Who's for the other outfit? Who fits?'

As we considered this he went on, 'I'm sorry, but I've got a bit more bad news for you.'

'What now?'

'Max Otterman's dead.'

Dr Kat said, 'I should have been with him.'

McGrath said gently, 'He was murdered.'

We stood rigid with shock.

'I saw the soldiers going over the rig after they brought you in here. They were pretty rough on everybody, even their own sick people. Then Max started convulsing and calling out, the way he's been doing, and they . . . Well, they booted him off the rig. I think his neck's broken.'

'Oh my God!' Wingstead whispered.

'I think the fall may have killed him. But one of the troops put a bullet in him as well. I'm sorry to have to tell you.'

The change in everyone's attitude was almost tangible. Neither the war, the bombing in Kodowa, our own capture, nor the death of Russ Burns had had this effect. It had come closer with the news of the intended burning of our prison. But the callous murder of our pilot had done the trick; it had roused them to fighting pitch.

Wingstead said, 'You've got a plan, McGrath, haven't you?'

'Carry on as though the Colonel were still here.' McGrath adjusted his uniform. Sam Wilson was getting into the other. Dr Kat bent over Burn's body.

216

McGrath said, 'Leave Russ where he is. He's evidence if anyone comes in. They know there was a shooting.' He picked up the sergeant's Uzi. 'Anyone know how to use this?'

'I do,' Wilson and Zimmerman both said. McGrath tossed it to Wilson. 'That's fine. It fits your image. Here, add this.' He tossed Wilson a small pot of blacking. 'It stinks but it'll do.' Wilson started to smear the stuff on his face and hands.

I held on to the shotgun, and Wingstead took the Colonel's pistol. That made four guns plus McGrath's cosh and God knows what else he had in the way of knives or other lethal instruments. It wasn't much to start a war with.

Wingstead said, 'Mick, how did you get in here?'

He pointed upwards. 'Easy. Through the roof. It's corrugated iron but some of it's so old it's soft as butter. But we're not going out that way. There's a door at the back of this shed. I couldn't open it from the outside, it's bolted. And from the inside it's hidden behind the cotton. But we can leave that way.'

Hammond said eagerly, 'Then let's go.'

'Not yet, Ben. We can reduce the odds out there a bit first. Now listen. When I saw what was likely to happen I ducked out; didn't like the idea of waiting to be rounded up. I went into the bush to look for Sadiq. I damn near got shot by his lads. They're trigger-happy.'

'How far away is he?' Wingstead asked.

'Not far. He's been scouting and these are his conclusions. This Fifteenth Battalion has been in action, probably against the loyalist Seventh Brigade, and came off worst. There are about two hundred men, a quarter of the battalion.'

'It's a hell of a lot more than we can handle,' Zimmerman said.

'Will you wait a minute, now,' McGrath said irritably. 'Maksa has sent most of them across the bridge, leaving about fifty men and a few vehicles on this side. Many of them are wounded. There are only two officers outside. Sadiq's ready to attack. His mortars can drop bombs on them like confetti at a wedding when he gets the signal.'

'Let's hear your plan,' I said.

'It goes like this. We take out the officers first. That way the men have nobody to direct them, and they'll run or surrender.'

'Just how do we do that?' Hammond asked.

'Well, as you see, I borrowed a dab or two of boot polish from the Captain, and here I am like a bloody nigger minstrel in the Colonel's uniform. If I put his cap on I reckon I can get away with it for as long as it takes to call them in here, one by one.'

'It won't work,' said Zimmerman. 'You haven't the voice for it.'

Lang said, 'We've got Doctor Kat though.'

McGrath took a piece of paper from his old jacket. 'Most of the officers are on the other side of the water. The ones here are Captain Mosira, that's the laddie in the dark glasses, and Lieutenant Chawa. We get them in here and deal with them. Then we go out the back way, smuggle the nurses back onto the rig, it's got a light guard but they'll be no problem, and then signal to Sadiq to start his action.'

Wingstead had a tough time of it with Katabisirua. The Doctor was concerned about violating his noncombatant status as a medical man.

'For Christ's sake, Doctor, we're not asking you to kill anyone. Just talk to them,' McGrath said. Eventually Dr Kat agreed to do what we wanted.

I said to McGrath, 'What happens after we knock off the officers?'

McGrath took out a knife and squatted on the floor. 'When Sadiq makes his attack he doesn't want any interference from across the bridge. So our job is to hold the bridge.' He scratched lines in the dirt floor. 'Here's the river and here's the bridge. On it near the other side they've stationed a Saracen armoured troop carrier. We have to stop it coming across and at the same time block the bridge somehow.'

'What's it armed with?'

'A heavy machine gun in a turret, and twin light machine guns on a Scarfe ring.'

218

Hammond blew out his cheeks. 'How in hell do we stop a thing like that? Bullets will bounce off. It'll be moving as soon as Sadiq attacks.'

'I stop it,' said McGrath. 'With Barry Lang's help.'

Lang stared at him.

'Look, here's the rig. All our tractors bar one have been coupled, ready to take it across the river. The free tractor is here, near the bridge. We take it onto the bridge and ram that bloody Saracen with it.'

Wingstead said sharply, 'You won't have a chance, Mick. The heavy machine gun will shoot hell out of you.'

'Not if we go backwards,' said McGrath simply.

Lang's face lit up.

'Behind that cab are twenty tons of steel plate set in cement. The thing's armoured like a tank. Nothing they've got will penetrate it and it outweighs the Saracen by a long chalk. What we need is covering fire. The cab windows aren't armoured and we'll have to lean out to see our way backwards. The rebels on this side will be busy but there may be some shooting and it'll be up to the rest of you to give us protection.'

Kemp said, 'With what?'

I said, 'We've already got three guns and a pistol and we'll get more from each officer. And there are four or five guards out there with sub-machine-guns that we can pick up too. I think the time for talking is over.'

'I agree,' McGrath said briskly, standing up. 'I want everybody lined up again, except for a couple of you behind the doors.'

'What about me?' I asked.

'When an officer walks through that door he'll expect to see Maksa, you and Mister Wingstead, because you're the boss men. So you'll be right there in line, under the guns.' He gave his knife to Lang and the cosh to Bert Proctor. 'You two take anyone coming through that door but only after the doors are closed. Harry, you take the other machine-gun and go stand up there where I was. If the guards do come in you can fire

219

over our heads, and if that happens everyone ducks fast. Doctor Kat, you're in line too. Think your voice can carry outside?'

The doctor nodded reluctantly.

'I'll take the shotgun, Mister Mannix, if you don't mind,' McGrath said. I handed it over to him with some hesitation, but he was right, he had to look the part. It left me feeling vulnerable again.

We stood like actors waiting for a curtain to rise. Facing me was McGrath looking surprisingly like Maksa even from where I stood. Just as I had taken over from Kemp and Wingstead in one crisis, so now McGrath had as easily taken over from me. He was a natural leader and afterwards he would be damned hard to control. If there was an afterwards.

21

McGrath went and opened one of the doors. He put his arm through the narrow opening, holding the shotgun at the ready. Dr Kat stood immediately behind him out of sight, so that the voice should seem to come from the bogus colonel. McGrath's head was averted as though he were keeping an eye on his prisoners, but light fell on his shoulder tabs and brassarded arm. When Dr Kat spoke it didn't sound much like Maksa but we could only hope that the soldiers would accept it. McGrath closed the door and breathed a sigh of relief.

'Right,' he said. 'Two officers are coming in. You ready, you three?'

The attack team nodded silently, and at the rear of the warehouse Zimmerman waved his machine-gun and dropped out of sight behind the topmost stack of cotton. McGrath strode across to Burns' body and stood beside it with his back to the doors. His legs were apart and he held the shotgun so that it pointed down towards the shattered skull. It was a nice piece of stage setting; anyone entering would see his back and then their eyes would be drawn to Burns, a particularly nasty sight.

McGrath judged it was too quiet.

'Say something, Mister Mannix,' he said. 'Carry on your conversation with the Colonel.'

'I don't want your bloody oil,' I improvised. 'I'm not in the oil business. I work for a firm of electrical engineers.' Behind McGrath Proctor had his ear to the door and the cosh raised. I carried on, 'We're certainly not responsible for how you run your country . . .'

The door opened and two officers walked in, Mosira still

221

wearing his dark glasses and a much younger officer following him. I went on speaking. 'Colonel Maksa, I demand that you allow our medical people to see their . . .'

Proctor hit the lieutenant hard with the cosh and he went straight down. Captain Mosira was putting up a struggle, groping for his pistol. Lang had an arm round the Captain's neck but his knife waved wildly in the air. Mosira couldn't shout because of the stranglehold but it was not until McGrath turned and drove the butt of the shotgun against his head that he collapsed.

Outside all was quiet, and in the warehouse nobody spoke either. McGrath turned to Barry Lang and held out his hand for the knife. 'I said, don't be squeamish,' he said coldly.

Lang gave him the knife. 'I'm sorry, Mick, I just –'

'Who can use this?'

'I can,' said Hammond.

McGrath instantly tossed him the knife. 'Right, lads, let's pick up our loot and get this lot out of the way.'

Both officers had worn pistols and the lieutenant had a grenade at his belt. In the distribution I got one of the pistols. We looked to McGrath for guidance.

'Let's get those guards, lads. There are only six or seven of them. It'll be easy.'

It was entirely McGrath who made it work, his drive and coolness that kept the exercise moving. But paradoxically Maksa's own personality also helped us. He was clearly a martinet and no enlisted man was going to question his orders. The guards entered on demand and were easy to deal with.

We looked round the warehouse. The soldiers were laid in a row behind the cotton bales, together with the body of Russ Burns. The door in the rear was opened with ease and we were ready to leave.

McGrath said, 'As soon as possible we get that signal off. You know the drill, Mister Mannix?'

I nodded. The back of the warehouse faced away from our camp so we'd have to go around it and might run into enemy soldiers at any moment. One group was to get the medical team and Dan Atheridge to the rig and then rejoin the rest of us, who'd be in cover as close to the bridge as we could get. We'd leapfrog one another to get in place, ready to protect McGrath and his tractor team-mate. There had been some doubt as to who that would be.

McGrath looked at Barry Lang speculatively. He had jibbed at knifing Mosira and this made McGrath uncertain of his mettle. But they usually teamed up, and it was safer to work with a man one knew, so McGrath said to him, 'Right then, Barry, you're with me in the cab. Just stick close, you hear me?'

'What's the signal for Sadiq to attack? The Very pistol?' I asked.

'Yes, a red flare the way you planned.'

'The Very pistol's still in a suitcase by the rig, unless they found it.'

He grinned, swarmed up on top of the cotton and came down again with the Very pistol in his hand. 'Full of surprises, aren't I?' he said.

I didn't ask him how he knew where it was. He'd obviously been hiding nearby when I hid the thing. He might have seen me go off with the shotgun too, and I wondered again how Maksa had come by it.

'You take it,' McGrath said, handing me the signal pistol. 'You'll be in charge of this exercise, Mister Mannix.'

I said, 'Just what are you going to do?'

He grinned. 'I'm going to march Barry out of here at gunpoint. I still look like the Colonel, and I've got Sam as my sergeant. We're going to take Lang down to the bridge and when we're near enough we'll make a break for the tractor. Sam will get into cover and wait for you to come up, if you're not there already.'

It was audacious but it could work. Wingstead said, 'You'll have every eye on you.'

'Well, it's a chance, I'll grant you. But it should get us to

223

the cab. You get off the signal the instant we make our break, so that Sadiq can keep those laddies too busy to think for a bit.'

As quietly as possible we barricaded the front doors with cotton bales, and were ready to go. I opened the rear door a crack and looked out. There was some moonlight, which would help McGrath in the tractor later on, and the night was fairly quiet. We left cautiously.

As we rounded the warehouse we could see the fires from the rebels' camp, and brighter lights around our rig. I could see soldiers in the light near the rig but there weren't many of them. There was plenty of cover all the way to the bridge, just as we had visualized.

'OK, Mick, start walking,' I whispered.

We moved away from the warehouse according to plan. McGrath and his party stepped out, Lang first with a sub-machine-gun jammed into his spine. Next was Wilson, his sergeant's cap pulled well down over his face. McGrath followed with the shotgun. It looked pretty good to me. I paced myself so that I was not too far ahead of McGrath, and the rest passed me to fan out ahead.

The marchers were almost opposite the rig when a soldier called out. I heard an indistinguishable answer from McGrath and a sharp retort, and then the soldier raised his gun. He didn't fire but was clearly puzzled.

Then there came the rip fire of an Uzi from beyond the rig. Someone had been spotted. The soldier turned uncertainly and McGrath cut him down with the shotgun. Then he and Lang bolted for their tractor. Wilson disappeared into the roadside cover. The shotgun blasted again and then gunfire crackled all around us, lighting up the night with flashes. I pointed the Very pistol skywards and the cartridge blossomed as I ran for cover, Bert Proctor at my side.

Soldiers tumbled out everywhere and guns were popping off all over the place. Then there was an ear-splitting roar as engines churned and a confusion of lights as headlamps came

224

on. The night was split by the explosions of mortar bombs landing in the rebels' camp.

We left the cover of the bushes and charged towards our convoy. The nearest vehicle was Kemp's Land Rover and we flung ourselves down beside it. An engine rumbled as a vehicle came towards us and when I saw what it was I groaned aloud. It was a Saracen. Maksa's men must have already got it off the bridge. It moved slowly and the gun turret swung uncertainly from side to side, seeking a target.

'It's coming this way!' Proctor gasped.

Behind us the deeper voice of our tractor roared as McGrath fired its engine. The Saracen was bearing down on it. We had to do something to stop its progress. The Uzi wouldn't be much good against armour but perhaps a Very cartridge slamming against the turret would at least startle and confuse the driver. As the Saracen passed us, already opening fire on the tractor, I took aim and let fly. The missile grazed the spinning turret and hit the armoured casing behind it, igniting as it landed. I must have done something right; there was a flash and a vast explosion which threw us sideways and rocked the Land Rover. When we staggered up the Saracen was on fire and inside someone was screaming.

I groped for my pistol but couldn't find it, and watched the burning Saracen run off the road into the bushes as our tractor passed it. McGrath leaned out and yelled at me.

'Lang's bought it. Get him out of here!'

I ran to the passenger side of the cab. The Saracen had set bushes burning and in the flaring light I saw blood on Lang's chest as I hauled him out of his seat. Proctor took him from me as we ran alongside the tractor.

McGrath yelled at me, 'Stay with me. Get in!' I clung onto the swinging cab door, hooked a foot over the seat and threw myself inside.

'Welcome aboard,' McGrath grunted. 'Watch our rear. Say if anything gets in our way.' He looked rearwards out of his own window. I followed suit.

Driving backwards can be tricky on a quiet Sunday morning in the suburbs. In these conditions it was terrifying. The tractor swayed from side to side, weaving down the road and onto the bridge. In the rear mirror I could see the second Saracen at the far end. There were heavy thumps on the tractor casing; we were being fired on by the Saracen as it retreated ahead of us. The driver had decided that he'd have more room to manoeuvre and fight off the bridge. We wanted to ram him before he could leave. We made it by a hair.

The Saracen's driver misjudged and reversed into the parapet; his correction cost him the race. The tractor bucked and slammed with an almighty wrench into the front of the Saracen, and there was a shower of sparks in the air. Our engine nearly stalled but McGrath poured on power and ground the tractor into the Saracen.

'Go, you bastard, go!' McGrath's face was savage with joy as he wrestled with wheel and accelerator.

There wasn't much doubt that we'd won. The armoured car was a solid lump of metal but it didn't weigh much over ten tons to the tractor's forty. The impact must have knocked the Saracen's crew out because the shooting stopped at once. The turret was buckled and useless.

McGrath kept up a steady pressure and the tractor moved remorselessly backwards, pushing the armoured car. He judged his angle carefully and there was a grinding crunch as the Saracen was forced against the coping wall of the bridge. But we didn't want the bridge itself damaged and McGrath stopped short of sending it into the river, which would have shattered the wall.

The Saracen's engine was ground into scrap and wasn't going anywhere under its own power. The bridge was effectively blocked to the enemy, and Sadiq was free to get on with the job.

McGrath put the tractor gently into forward gear. There was no opposition as we travelled back across the bridge and stopped to form a secondary blockade. We tumbled out of the cab to an enthusiastic welcome.

'Where's Barry?' I asked.

'We've got him back to the rig. He's with the medics,' Proctor said.

McGrath stirred and stretched hugely. I said, 'That was damn good driving, Mick.'

'You didn't do too badly yourself. What the hell did you use on that first Saracen – a flame-thrower?'

'I fired the Very gun at it. It shouldn't have worked but it did.'

Looking around, we could see figures heading off towards the river downstream from the bridge. There was some scattered shooting. The remains of Maksa's force were intent only on escaping back to their own side. More mortars fired and the shooting stopped.

We tensed up at this renewal of hostilities but it was happening a long way off from us, to our relief.

Geoff Wingstead was beside me. 'I've had it. This is Sadiq's war. Let him fight it from now on. I'm all for going back to being a truck driver.'

'Me too – only I'll be happy just to ride that desk of mine.'

McGrath said, 'I'll be happier when we've got a detachment down here; they still might try to rush that bridge and Sadiq isn't nearby. We might still be wanted.'

'I hope to God not. We've had one casualty and we don't want any more.'

Wingstead said, 'I'm afraid we've had more than one.'

I said, 'Who else, then?'

He pointed to a group of men at the foot of the water tanker, consisting of Harry Zimmerman, a Russian, and Brad Bishop.

'One of the Russians bought it,' Wingstead told me. Together we walked over to Zimmerman, who was looking sadly at the huddled body. 'I'm sorry about this, my friend,' I said to his fellow countryman, standing impassively by, then to

227

Zimmerman, 'Who was he – Brezhnev or Kosygin?' I never could tell them apart.

Zimmerman sighed. 'His name was Andrei Djavakhishkili and he came from Tbilisi in Georgia. He was a nice guy when you got to know him.'

The remaining two hours to dawn were quiet. Sadiq had joined us, and we sat in the cover of our vehicles, waiting for the morning light. We didn't expect the enemy to try anything; their only passage was blocked off and the decisiveness of Sadiq's action, and our own, must have rocked their morale.

With the rising of the sun we could see no sign of movement from across the river. The scene was one of destruction; burnt out vegetation still smouldered, the camp site littered with debris, and the wreckage of the first Saracen huddled in a ditch. We found the bodies of three men near it, one shot and two who had died of burns. There were more bodies up the hill at the soldiers' camp but Sadiq's men were taking care of them and we didn't want to see the site of that battle.

Our tractor blocked the nearside of the bridge and at the far end the second Saracen lay canted over diagonally across the road and forced up hard against the coping. There was no sign of men or vehicles beyond.

I said to Sadiq, 'What now, Captain?'

He studied the opposite bank carefully through binoculars, holding them one-handed as his left arm was in a sling. He was no longer the immaculate officer whose pants were creased to a knife edge and whose shoes gleamed. He'd lost his boot polish to McGrath. His uniform was scorched and rumpled.

There were lines of strain about his eyes and mouth. Presently he said, 'We watch and wait for one, two hours maybe. If everything is still quiet I will send scouts across the river.'

'Risky.'

'Would you expect anything else in war, Mister Mannix?'

'You did well last night, Captain. It was a fine operation.'

228

He nodded gravely. 'Yes, we did well. But you all did well, especially Mister McGrath. He is very efficient. Without him it might not have come about.'

I knew that and didn't want to dwell on it. I would have liked to admire McGrath whole-heartedly but found it impossible. I was pleased to hear that Sadiq had sustained no losses among his men, and only a couple were wounded.

Our losses were worse.

The Russian was dead. Lang was in a bad way and lay on Dr Kat's operating table. Proctor had a bullet graze on the leg and Kemp on the shoulder, and others had an assortment of bruises and abrasions. But a roll call proved one man missing. After a search we found the body of Ron Jones, shot through the head and stomach by machine-gun bullets.

22

It was ten o'clock before Sadiq took his chance on the bridge. First he wanted the tractor shifted so that if necessary he could get troops across fast, and we were wary of sending anyone out of cover to do that until we felt fairly sure it was safe. Sadiq would not send scouts across, as being too dangerous. He was going to cross first himself in the Scorpion tank, which was a brave thing to do because even a lone infantryman might have a tank-killing weapon. He was taking three men with him, a driver, a gunner and a radio operator, and he left instructions that nobody was to move until he came back or sent a coded all clear signal.

Before that we'd cleaned up the camp, repairing what was possible and listing what needed repair when we could spare the time. Luckily Maksa's men had not destroyed much of importance, though there were two car windows shattered and sundry minor damage done here and there. Bishop and Bing, with help from the others, got a food supply moving, and on the rig the medical people were kept very busy.

Max Otterman's body had been found at the foot of the rig with a bullet in his back and two ribs broken, presumably by the fall though the damage could have been done by a boot. It was an appalling death. We organized a digging party off the road and held a mass funeral service. Otterman, Burns, Ron Jones and Andrei Djavakhishkili, a Rhodesian, an American, a Welshman and a Russian, shared one grave, though we gave them each separate headboards. In another grave were two of Sadiq's men and with them four rebels, all with the common bond of being Nyalans.

Both the ailing infant and the hospital's other serious patient, Sister Mary, had survived the night. But the two doctors and the nursing staff were under great strain and an urgent discussion on ways and means was long overdue.

Astonishingly, during the early hours of the morning we had visitors.

Sandy Bing, carrying a bucket of hot water towards the rig, stopped and said, 'I'll be damned, Mister Wingstead! Just look at them.'

In the distance, quietly and almost shyly, little clumps of Nyalans were reappearing, still mostly women and children, to stand in respectful yet wary homage to their travelling talisman. Some of them spoke to the soldiers, and Dr Kat and two of the Nyalan nurses went down among them, to return with news that the vast majority had melted away just far enough to be within earshot of the fight, and close enough to come back if they felt all was safe again. It was truly extraordinary.

'I think it may mean that the other soldiers have all gone,' Dr Kat told us. 'They speak of them as evil, and they would not come back if they were still close by.'

'But they'd be across the river, Doctor Kat. How could these people know?'

'I think you call it the bush telegraph,' the surgeon said with his first smile for a long time. 'It really does work quite well. You will see, the Captain will return to give us an all clear. In the meantime, they have brought me a woman who broke her leg last night. I must go back and see to her.'

I went to have a look at the Saracen that had caught fire. I was curious to see why it had happened; an armoured car isn't a paper bag to be burned up by a Very flare.

It was simple enough when we reconstructed what had occurred. At the time that the shooting started someone must have been filling the gas tank and in the hurry to get things moving the fuel tank cap hadn't been screwed back on properly. When the Very ignited, a spark must have gone straight into the tank, blowing up the vehicle in fine style. We found the cap

231

still on its hinge, military fashion, but hanging loose.

I had another job to do that I didn't relish, and that was to speak to McGrath alone. I started by telling him about the Saracen and he grinned approval.

'Dead lucky. We have to have some of it,' he commented.

I said, 'McGrath, there's something bothering me.'

'Why then, let's have it,' he said calmly.

'In the warehouse you told us that Maksa was getting ready to burn it down with us inside. But I found no petrol drums anywhere near the warehouse, and there's no fuel of theirs this side of the river. Our tanker is still locked and nobody took the keys.'

'Well, maybe they were going to do it another way,' he said easily.

'Don't mess with me, McGrath. Did you actually hear them say anything like that?'

'Oh for Christ's sake,' he said, driven out of his normal calm, 'I had to say *something* to get you lot moving! You were just going to stand there and take it. Or try talking your way out, I suppose.'

'You were safe enough, free and armed. Why the hell did you bother to come back for us?'

'If I thought I could have got away through this benighted country on my own, Mannix, I'd have done so. I need you, that's why.' He crowned this casually selfish statement with one more shocking. 'I must say Otterman's death came in handy. That really did the trick.'

I felt disgusted, and then had another appalling idea.

'McGrath, did you kill Ron Jones?'

He looked amused rather than alarmed. 'Why should I do that?'

'You know why. And you had time to do it. In God's name, how can I believe you even if you say you didn't?'

'Well now, you can't, Mannix, so if I were you I'd stop worrying about it. I didn't as a matter of fact, though he's no great loss for all that. In fact he was more dangerous to you than I've ever been.'

232

I couldn't help rising to the bait. 'What do you mean?'

'Well, he was a bit of a sniveller, wasn't he? You know that, the way he came babbling things to you that he shouldn't. He saw you take the shotgun into the warehouse, Mannix, and it was he who told the Colonel about it. I heard him myself.'

Quite suddenly I knew that this was the truth. I recalled Jones's fear in the warehouse, the way he hung back from Maksa as he'd always hung back from McGrath, perhaps fearing lest he be unmasked before us all for Maksa's pleasure. Any regret I had for his death ebbed away, and despite myself I felt a nagging touch of understanding of McGrath and his ruthlessness. He'd manoeuvred us into doing the one thing he knew best; fighting and killing. He'd done it all for the most selfish of reasons, and without compunction. And yet he was brave, efficient and vital to our cause; and perhaps justified as well.

I walked away from him in silence. I would never know if he had killed Ron Jones, but the worst of it, and the thing that filled me with contempt for myself as well as for him, was that I didn't care. I prayed that I wouldn't become any more like him.

McGrath was a maverick, intelligent, sound in military thinking and utterly without fear. I felt that he might be a useful man to have about in a war, but perhaps on the first day of peace he ought to be shot without mercy, and that was one hell of an assessment.

Sadiq had decided that it was time to go.

'Mister Mannix, if I do not return I have told my sergeant to take command of the soldiers,' he said. 'And they are to stay with you unless given alternative orders in person by a superior.'

'Thank you. I wish you good luck.'

He saluted and climbed up into the Scorpion, dropping down through the command hatch and dogging it shut. He was taking no chances. The tank trundled slowly across the bridge. Sadiq had reckoned he could pass the wrecked Saracen but

233

might have to nudge it aside and he proved right. Once past it he picked up speed and the driver did not bother to avoid the scattered bodies. I remembered being told back in Korea that if one wanted to sham dead on a battlefield better not to do it with tanks around.

Not a shot was fired as the tank left the bridge. It began to climb the hill beyond, then swerved and entered the bush and was lost to view. We settled down to wait in the hopeful expectation of hearing nothing. It was a long hour before the Scorpion rumbled back up the hill towards us. Sadiq got out and said, 'There is nothing. They have pulled out and gone.'

There was a ragged cheer from soldiers and civilians alike.

'Which way, do you think?' Wingstead asked.

'Their vehicles must have gone on up the road.' This wasn't good news because it was to be our route too. He went on, 'We found two of them damaged and off the road, and there are many uniform jackets lying there. I think the Fifteenth Battalion has disbanded. They were nearly finished anyway, and the fight with us has destroyed them.'

'Now that I am certain the bridge is clear I will send scouts further ahead. I will place men to form a holding force while we decide what must be done next.'

And so the next item on the agenda was a council of war.

Sadiq's active force was down to twenty-two. There were sixteen of us and a medical staff of nine including three semi-trained nurses. On the rig were fifteen Nyalans, including the mother and her sick baby. So we totalled some seventy odd people, many of whom could not take care of themselves. We couldn't stay where we were nor could we turn back, which left us with an obvious conclusion. We had to carry on towards Lake Pirie and possible freedom in Manzu if we couldn't travel on to Port Luard.

Food and medical supplies were in shorter supply than ever, and our stock of petrol was dwindling fast. The only thing we had in plenty was water. The soldiers had run short of ammunition and had no mortar bombs left. We were ragged, weary and uncomfortable. But morale was high.

We reckoned that we could make Fort Pirie in three days or less, and it would be downhill all the way, with villages scattered along the route. We debated yet again leaving the rig but there were still too many sick people to accommodate in the other vehicles, and by now the contraption was beginning to take on a talisman-like quality to us as well as to the Nyalans. We'd got it this far: surely we could get it the rest of the way.

Kemp and Hammond went to inspect the bridge. Though well constructed it had taken a battering and they were concerned for its integrity. They decided that it was sound enough to get the rig across but with nobody on board except for the drivers. That meant that the invalids must be carried across, and Dr Kat set Sister Ursula to organize this with her usual barnstorming efficiency. We had little rest for the remainder of that day. At last we settled down for a final night in the Makara camp, a guard of soldiers on watch, ready to move out at first light.

Kemp and Hammond drove the rig, McGrath had charge of the towing tractor, and Thorpe joined Bob Pitman in running the airlift truck to give the rig its necessary boost. There was a large audience as Nyalans emerged to stare as the rig inched its way across; the Saracen had been towed clear and someone had had the mangled bodies removed. After an hour of tension it was across, and the job of transferring the sick on improvised stretchers began.

It was mid-morning before we really got going. We had quite a selection of vehicles to choose from, our inheritance from the Fifteenth Battalion. In spite of possible fuel problems Sadiq insisted on taking the remaining Saracen, but we ditched some of the trucks. We left the Russian pipe truck but took Dufour's vehicle with us, at the Frenchman's insistence. Brad Bishop said that he had so little cooking to do that the chuck wagon might as well be ditched too, but he didn't mean it.

235

Kemp, who had been a passenger on the rig because of his shoulder wound, had joined Wingstead and me in the Land Rover. Atheridge drove with Dufour. Their common ordeal at the hands of Maksa's men had forged a bond between them, just as one now existed between Harry Zimmerman and the Russian, Vashily Kirilenko; with his partner's death the nicknames had disappeared.

Wingstead said, 'Ben Hammond can move the convoy out. Let's drive on. We have to talk about McGrath.'

'I think he's psychopathic,' Wingstead went on. 'He's been with you more than with anyone else lately, Neil. What do you think?'

Kemp intervened, 'He's an unscrupulous bastard, and it was me who hired him. If you think I've made a mistake for God's sake say so.'

'Don't take this personally,' Wingstead said. 'If you want my candid opinion, he's the best bloody truck man you've ever hired. He's a damned marvel with that tractor.'

'Amen to that,' I said.

Kemp was still on the defensive. 'Well, I knew that. I couldn't afford to turn him down, Geoff. I knew we'd need the top men for this job. But his papers weren't in order. I advertised for heavy haulage drivers and he applied. He could do the job and had the necessary certificates, but I found discrepancies. I think he's travelling on a false passport.'

Kemp had come a long way on his own.

I told them what I knew, both fact and speculation. At the end there was silence before either spoke.

Then Kemp said, 'He *killed* Sisley? But why should he?'

'He has only one answer to every problem – violence. I think he's a hard line gunman on the run from Ireland. He's dangerous. To look at he's a big amiable Mick straight from the bog. He works at that image.'

Wingstead asked, 'Do you think he could have killed Burke too?'

'Not the way Jones told it.'

'And you're not sure about Ron Jones' death.'

'No, that's only a gut feeling. But four men saw McGrath gun Sisley down. Burke ran off and is very likely dead by now. Jones is dead. Lang is gravely wounded, though thank God I know that one isn't at McGrath's door. That leaves Bob Pitman and if I were he I'd be walking carefully right now. Whatever we know or suspect about McGrath I suggest we keep it buttoned up, or we could find ourselves in deep trouble.'

We turned our attention to the future.

'There's a biggish town, Batanda, not far across the Manzu border,' Wingstead said. 'I haven't found anyone who's been there, but the country itself is known to be relatively stable. There must be a road from Batanda to the ferry on Lake Pirie, because a lot of trade goes on between the two countries at that point. If we can take the ferry to Manzu and drive to Batanda we should be safe.'

'What's Fort Pirie like?' Kemp asked.

'Another Makara, not much there at all. And there may have been military activity there, so God knows what we'll find.'

Kemp asked, 'What are Sadiq's plans?'

'He'll stay with us as far as Fort Pirie, and help us cross the ferry if the road to Lasulu isn't clear. He won't cross himself, of course. He'll keep his men inside his own border. But I think he'll welcome our departure.'

'Not half as much as I will,' Kemp said fervently.

The bush country was left behind and the rainforest began to close in, green and oppressive. The exuberant plant life had eroded the road surface, roots bursting through the tarmac. The trees that bordered the road were very tall, their boughs arched so that it was like driving through a tunnel. There was more bird life but the game, which had been sparse before, was now nonexistent.

In the days before Maro Ofanwe improved matters this road had been not much more than a track, only one car wide for miles at a stretch. Traffic was one way on Mondays, Wednesdays

237

and Fridays, and the other way on Tuesdays, Thursdays and Saturdays. Sundays you stayed home or took your chances and prayed to God. A lot of other roads in Nyala were still like that.

Occasionally there was a hard won clearing, usually with a scattering of grass huts clustered about a warehouse. These were the collection points for the cotton, coffee and cacao beans from the plantations hewed out of the forest. There were people in all these villages but little in the way of food or goods, and hardly anyone spoke English. We asked for news but it was scanty and the people ill-informed.

One or two villages were larger and we were able to drain storage tanks and pumps of available petrol. It was a good sign that there was some, as it meant that there'd been little traffic that way. Somehow enough food was found to keep us going, though it was pretty unpalatable. Behind and around us, our escort of Nyalans swelled and diminished as people joined in for a few miles, dropped out and were replaced by others. The train was growing, though; Sadiq told us there were several hundred people now, coming as remorselessly as a horde of locusts, and with consequences for the countryside nearly as disastrous. There was nothing we could do about it.

Two days passed without incident. On the rig, Lang's condition worsened and one of the soldiers died of his wounds. Sister Ursula nursed with devotion, coming among us to do spot checks on our continuing health and bully us into keeping clean, inside as well as out. If she could she'd have dispensed compulsory laxatives all round.

Margretta Marriot did the rounds too, changing bandages and keeping a watch for infection. There was little for her to do on the rig now except basic nursing, and sometimes she rode with one or other of us. A dour woman at best, I thought, and now she had retreated into a pit of misery that only work could alleviate. Sister Ursula, for all her hectoring, was more of a tonic.

On the morning of the third day Sadiq's scouts returned with news that they'd reached the Katali river and seen Lake Pirie shining in the sun. From where we were camped it was only a couple of hours' drive in a car, and spirits lifted; whatever was going to happen there, we'd reached another of our goals with the convoy still intact.

I'd travelled for most of the previous day in the cab of the water tanker with Sam Wilson (we each gave one another a turn in the comparative comfort of the Land Rover) and now I was with Thorpe in the travelling workshop when a messenger came asking me to join Captain Sadiq.

'I am going ahead, Mister Mannix,' he told me. 'I wish to see for myself what the situation is. There is a village ahead with petrol pumps. Would you and Mister Kemp drive there with us to look at it, please?'

I said, 'Harry Zimmerman told me there was a fuel depot hereabouts, one of his own company's places. We'll take him with us.'

Zimmerman, Kemp and I pushed on behind the soldiers, glad of the release. Soon enough we saw a welcome bottle-green expanse spreading out between the trees, and the road ran down through them to emerge on the shore of a large body of water, a sight quite astonishing after the endless days of bush and forest, and incredibly refreshing to the eye. It stretched away, placid in the blazing sun.

For a while we just sat and stared at it. Then we drove along the lakeside road for another mile or two.

Eventually we arrived at what might have passed for civilization. The place consisted of a roadside filling station with a big, faded Lat-Am fascia board; it was obviously a gas and oil distribution centre. Behind it was an extensive compound fenced in by cyclone netting, which contained stacks of drums. I supposed the gas and oil would be hauled along the road by tankers, transferred to ground tanks here and then rebottled in the drums for distribution to planters and farmers.

If anyone spoke English we were likely to find him here,

239

though I did curse my lack of foresight in not bringing an interpreter with us. It proved not to be necessary.

At first there was nobody to be seen and few sounds; a water pump chugging somewhere, scrawny chickens pecking about, the monotonous tink of some wild bird. I eyed the chickens speculatively, then blew a blast on the horn which scattered them, though not very far. They were used to traffic. A hornbill rose lazily from a tree and settled in another, cocked its head and looked down with beady eyes, as unconcerned as the chickens. At the sixth blast the door of the cabin behind the pumps opened, and a brown face peered warily at us through the crack.

We'd had this sort of nervous reaction before and could hardly blame the locals for being cautious, but at least our non-military car and clothing should prove reassuring. I called out cheerfully, 'Good morning. Are you open for business?'

The door opened wider and a Nyalan stepped out into the sun. He wore a tired overall on which the logo of Lat-Am was printed, a travesty of the livery which they inflicted on their gas station attendants in more affluent places.

'I am not open,' he said. 'I got no custom.'

I got out of the car into the scorching morning air. 'You have now,' I told him. Through the open door I saw a familiar red pattern painted on an ice box. 'You got cold Coca-Cola in there?'

'How many?' he asked cautiously.

'I could drink two. Two each – six of them. I'll pay.' I pulled out a handful of coins, wondering as I did so how he managed to keep them cold. He thought about it, then went in and returned with the Cokes, blissfully chilling to the touch in the narrow-waisted bottles that were still used in this part of the world. I sank half of my first in one swallow. 'Quiet around here, is it?'

He shrugged. 'There is trouble. Trouble come and the people they stop coming.'

'Trouble meaning the war?'

He shook his head. 'I don't know about no war. But there are many soldiers.'

Kemp asked, 'Soldiers where – here?' It certainly didn't look like it. Our untapped mine of information doled out another nugget. 'Not here. In Fort Pirie they are come.'

I swallowed air this time. Soldiers in Fort Pirie could be bad news if they were rebels, and I wondered how Sadiq was getting on.

'Has there been any fighting here at all?' Kemp asked.

A headshake. 'Not here.'

'Where then?'

This time we got the shrug again. 'Somewhere else. I do not know.'

This was like drawing teeth the hard way. I downed some more Coke in silence and tried to keep my impatience under control. Then, surprisingly, the attendant carried on unasked. 'Two tanks come two days ago from Fort Pirie. Then they go back again. They not buy nothing.'

'Did they threaten you? I mean, were they bad people?'

'I think not so bad. Gov'ment people.'

They might or might not be, but it sounded a little better. At least they weren't hellbent on destruction like the last lot we'd met up with.

The attendant suddenly went into his cabin and returned with another opened Coke, which he began to drink himself. I recognized a social gesture; he must have decided that we were acceptable, and was letting his guard down a little by drinking with us. I wondered with amusement how much of his stock vanished in this way, and how he fiddled his books to account for it. I didn't yet know him very well.

'Soldiers come by now, one half-hour ago. Not many. They go that way. Also they go that way this morning, then come back. They not stop here.'

He indicated the direction of the river and I realized that he was talking about Sadiq, but we weren't in a hurry to enlighten him about our association with any military force.

241

We exchanged a few more generalities and then, noticing the wires leading down to the cabin from a pole across the road, I said, 'Do you mind if we use your telephone?'

'No use. It dead.'

That would have been too easy. 'It's the trouble that caused it, I suppose. What about your radio?'

'It play dance music, long time only music. Sometimes nothing at all.' He decided that it was his turn to ask questions. 'You people. Where you from?'

'We've come from Kodowa.'

'A man said that Kodowa is not there no more. Is bombed, burnt. Is that true?'

'Yes, it's true. But Makara is all right. Was Fort Pirie bombed?'

Now we were trading information. 'No bombs there. No fighting, just many soldiers, the man he say. Where you go?'

'We are going to Fort Pirie, if it's safe there. We have more people waiting back there for us, men and women. We are not soldiers.'

'White women? Very bad for them here. They should stay in city, here is dangerous.' He seemed genuinely anxious.

'Believe me, my friend, they'd like nothing better. We are going to go back and get them, tell them it's safe here. When we come back we would like to buy gas, OK?'

'I not sell gas.'

'Sorry, I mean petrol. Petrol and other things if you have them to sell. Meantime, how many Cokes have you got in that ice box in there?'

'Many. Maybe twenty, twenty-four.'

'I'll buy the lot. Find a box and if you've got any more, put them in the cold right away. We'll buy them when we come back.'

He seemed bemused by this but was quite ready to deal with me, especially as I produced the cash at once. Kemp said, 'Do you have many people living here? Could we get food for our people, perhaps?'

242

The attendant thought about this. He was careful with his answers. 'Not so many people. Many of them go away when trouble comes, but I think maybe you can get food.'

Kemp had noticed the chickens, and caught a glimpse of a small field of corn out behind the cabin. Even his mind, running mainly to thoughts of fuel, road conditions and other such technicalities, could spare a moment to dwell on the emptiness of our stomachs. The station hand was back with us now with some twenty icy bottles in a cardboard box, for which he gravely accepted and counted my money and rung it into his little till. Zimmerman, who'd said nothing, watched with interest as he filled our tank with gas and rung up that sale as well. After we drove off he said, 'He runs a pretty tight ship. That's good to see. We're both on the same payroll, him and me. We've got to give him a square deal when we bring the convoy in.'

Zimmerman was a Lat-Am man and he regarded the station in a rather proprietorial manner.

'Don't worry, Harry,' I said to him, feeling unwarranted optimism rising inside me. 'We won't rip him off, I promise you.' I patted the box of Cokes. 'This is going to make them sit up, isn't it? Something tells me that it's going to be easy all the way from now on.'

It wasn't quite like that.

23

There was some restrained rejoicing when we got back to camp with the news and the Cokes, which hadn't yet lost all their chill. Geoff Wingstead decided that unless we heard anything to the contrary from Sadiq within an hour, he'd move the rig on as far as the filling station, thus saving some valuable time. I suggested that he leave Kemp in charge of this phase of the operation and come on ahead again with me. I'd had a couple of ideas that I wanted to check out.

He agreed and we left taking Zimmerman with us and adding Ben Hammond to the Land Rover complement. Proctor was quite able to take Hammond's place for this easy run. This time I bypassed the gas station and we carried on for a little way, with the forest, which was still quite dense at the station, now thinning away until there was only a narrow screen between the road and the gleam of sunlight on water. When we had a clear view I pulled off and stopped. At this point Lake Pirie was about five miles wide, broadening out to our right. We were told that where the ferry crossed it was a couple of miles across, with the far bank visible, but I wasn't sure how far downwater that would be from where the road came out; local maps were not entirely accurate, as we had often discovered.

Wingstead said, 'It doesn't look like a river.'

It wouldn't, to an Englishman to whom the Thames was the Father of Waters, but I recalled the Mississippi and smiled. 'It's all part of the Katali,' I said. 'It would have been better if they hadn't put the word Lake into it at all. Think of it as the Pirie Stretch and you'll have a better mental picture.' It was a long stretch, being in fact about thirty miles from where it broadened out to where it abruptly narrowed again, a pond by African standards but still a sizeable body of water.

'It's a pity it isn't navigable, like most of the European rivers,' Kemp said, his mind as ever on transport of one sort or another.

'It's the same with most African rivers,' I said. 'What with waterfalls, rapids, shoals, rocks and crocodiles they just aren't very cooperative.' Zimmerman laughed aloud. We sat for a while and then heard the rumble of traffic and a moment later a Saracen came into view, moving towards us from the river. There wasn't much we could do except hope that it was ours, and it was; a couple of Sadiq's men waved and the armoured car stopped alongside us.

'We came back to look for you, sir. To stop you going any further,' one of them said.

'What's wrong?'

It was bad news. The ferry crossing was about six miles downstream, and the Nyalan ferrypoint and the road to it were occupied by a rebel force, not a large one but probably a guard detachment. There was no ferry movement at all. All this Sadiq had seen from far off, which was bad enough, but what was worse was that he had picked up radio conversations, thanks to Bing's expertise; and it was apparent that Kigonde had not told him the whole truth. The opposition was stronger than we'd been led to believe. A large part of the army had defected and the countryside through to Fort Pirie and perhaps as far down as Lasulu was in rebel hands.

From what the soldiers told us, there was even some doubt as to whether they should be called rebels or military representatives of a new ruling Government; all news from Port Luard had ceased. There was no indication as to which way the Air Force had gone, but no doubt that whichever side they started on they'd find a way of ending up on the side of the victors.

'Thank you for the news,' I said, though I didn't feel at all thankful. 'Tell Captain Sadiq that we will bring the convoy no further than the filling station along the road there. We'll wait there until we hear from him.'

245

Sadiq would probably regard even this as dangerously close to the enemy. The Saracen turned back and so did we, bearing a cargo of gloom to the gas station. Wingstead said, 'Christ, can't anything go right?' It wasn't like him to be dejected and I hoped it was caused by nothing more than exhaustion.

'Why couldn't they have been government troops?' Zimmerman asked plaintively.

'You think that would make much difference? In a civil war the best bet for a foreigner is to stay clear of all troops whichever side they're on. There'll be bastards like Maksa on both sides.'

We arrived at the station and I took the Land Rover round the back of the cabin out of sight of the road. The Nyalan attendant popped out with a disapproving face, then relaxed when he saw who we were. 'I got more Cokes getting cold, like you said,' he announced proudly.

'You know the trouble we talked about? Well, it's not far away, my friend. There are soldiers down at the ferry and they are not friends of your Government.'

The others got out of the car and joined me. I said, 'We would like to look around here. I think there is going to be more trouble, and it may come this way. If I were you I'd go tell your people in the village to go away until it's over, and that means you too.'

He said, 'Other people, they already go. But not me.'

'Why not?'

'I leave and Mister Obukwe, he kill me,' he said very positively.

'Who's he?'

'My boss in Fort Pirie.'

I thought that Mr Obukwe must be quite a terrifying guy to instil such company loyalty, and exchanged a grin with Harry Zimmerman. He came forward and said, 'What's your name?'

The attendant thought about answering him. 'Sam Kironji,' he said at last. Zimmerman stuck out his hand.

'Pleased to meet you, Sam. My name is Harry Zimmerman. Call me Harry. And I work for Lat-Am same as you. Look

246

here.' He opened a wallet and produced a plastic identification badge, to which Kironji reacted with delight.

'Very good you come. You tell Mister Obukwe I got no trade except I sell Coca-Cola.'

'Sure, I'll tell him. But if you want to leave, Sam, it'll be OK. Neil here is right, there could be trouble coming this way.'

Kironji thought about it and then gave him a great smile.

'I stay. This is my place, I take care of it. Also I not afraid of the soldiers like them.' He waved a contemptuous hand at his departed fellow inhabitants. 'You want Cokes, other things, I got them maybe.'

I said, 'Sure, we want Cokes and food and all sorts of things. Soon our trucks will come here and we'll want lots of petrol too.' Probably more than you've ever seen sold in a year, I thought. I pointed to a hard-surfaced track which led away from the road. 'Tell me, Sam, where does that track go to?'

'The river.'

'But you're already at the river.'

'It go compound, back there,' he said, waving a vague hand.

'How far is it?'

'Not far. Half an hour walking maybe.'

I said, 'We're going to take our car down there and have a look. If any white men come by here, tell them to wait for us.'

'Hey, man,' he said, 'that company property. You can't drive there.'

I looked at him in amusement and wondered if Lat-Am knew how lucky they were. 'Harry?'

Zimmerman persuaded him that we were going on company business and Kironji finally gave way to our demands.

The track was better surfaced than I had expected and showed signs of considerable use. Wherever it was rutted the ruts had been filled in with clinker and the repair work was extensive and well done. Presumably Mr Obukwe of Lat-Am Oil had need of this track and we wondered why.

It wasn't all that wide, just enough to take a big truck through the trees. On the right they pressed in thickly but on

247

the left they barely screened the water. The trees showed signs of continual cutting back, the slash marks ranging from old scars to new-cut wood still oozing sap.

The track ran parallel to the main road to the lake shore. We emerged into a clearing to see the sun striking hard diamond reflections from the water and to find yet another fenced compound full of drums. There was also a landing stage, a rough structure consisting of a wooden platform on top of empty oil drums making a floating jetty about ten feet wide and eighty feet long.

There was even a boat, though it was nothing much; just a fifteen-foot runabout driven by an outboard. I walked out onto the landing stage which swayed gently and looked closely at the boat. It was aged and a bit leaky, but the outboard looked to be well maintained. I turned my attention to the lake itself.

The distance to the far side was about four miles and through binoculars I thought I could see the shore and a ribbon of track leading up from it. That was Manzu, a country blessedly free of civil war and as desirable as Paradise. But as far as we were concerned it might as well have been the far side of the moon. It was ironic to think that if we had no-one to worry about but ourselves we four could have crossed this stretch of water to safety in no time.

'Pretty sight, isn't it,' Wingstead murmured as he took his turn with the binoculars. He was thinking my thoughts.

I turned back to the clearing. It was easy now to see the reason for the good road. Delivery to and from this petrol dump was made by water, probably from Fort Pirie to this and other drop points along the shore. It would be easier than road transport especially if the fuel came prepacked in drums.

There was a locked wooden shed standing nearby. By peering through the boards we could see that it was a workshop and toolroom. There was every sign that it was used regularly for maintenance work, though everything was tidy. I walked back along the pontoon and prowled around the perimeter of the compound. I found a gate which was also locked and there was a palm-thatched hut just inside it. It crossed my mind that the clearing, which was very long, would be a good place to put the rig and the rest of the convoy off the road and out of sight. The road down was rough but I had learned enough from Kemp to judge it would stand the traffic, and Wingstead confirmed this.

'It's not a bad idea. And it brings us at least within sight of our goal,' he said when I put the proposition to him.

On the far shore we could make out a cluster of buildings where there was possibly another landing stage. On the water itself there were no boats moving. Traffic on Lake Pirie might simply be infrequent or it may have been brought to a halt by the advent of war.

When we got back to the station we arranged for Kironji to load the balance of his Cokes and a few other items into the car. The cabin wasn't exactly a shop but there was some tinned foodstuff for sale and a few bits of hardware that might be useful. He also had a little first aid kit but it wasn't worth ransacking. As Kironji closed the cooler lid on the last load of Cokes I saw something else down there.

'Are those beer cans, Sam?'

'Mine.' He closed the lid defiantly.

'OK, no sweat.' A ridiculous statement in this scorching weather. This train of thought made me wipe my forehead. Kironji watched me, hesitated, and then said, 'You want a beer?'

'You'd be a hero, Sam.'

He grinned and handed me a cold can. 'I got a few. Only for you and your friends. I not sell them.'

It tasted wonderful. Our warm beer had long been finished.

I looked around as I drank. The interior of the cabin was neat and tidy. It was a combination of office and store, with a few tyres in racks and spare parts on shelves. I thought that Hammond could make something of all this, and in fact he had already been browsing through the stock. At the back was a door which led to Kironji's living quarters; he was a bachelor and preferred to live where he worked, presumably to protect

249

his precious Lat-Am property. There was a supply of tools here too, and a small workbench.

'Do you do all your own repair work, Sam?'

'I got plenty tools, sir, and much training. But mostly I work by the lake.' The shed we had seen housed a fair amount of stuff, a well-equipped workshop for boats as well as vehicles.

'Who does the boat belong to?' I asked.

'To me. I go fishing sometime.'

'I'd like to hire it from you. I want to have a look at the lake.'

He shook his head at my folly but we agreed on a hire fee, and he jotted it down on what was becoming a pretty healthy tab. He wasn't going to be done out of a penny, either by way of business or personally.

Wingstead came in and to his great delight Kironji handed out another beer. He disposed of it in two swallows.

Kironji asked, 'You say you have other people coming. What you doing here, man?'

'We were going to Bir Oassa with parts for the oilfields,' Wingstead said. 'We met the war and had to turn back. Now we must try to get back to Lasulu.' He said nothing of the Manzu border. Kironji pondered and then said, 'You know this hospital?'

'Which hospital?' I asked, thinking he meant that there was one in the vicinity. But his reply only proved the efficiency of the bush telegraph once again.

'I hear it go travel on a big truck, lots of sick people. The other they follow where it go, all through the country.'

'By God,' Wingstead exclaimed. 'The juggernaut's famous! If Sam here has heard about it it'll be all over the damn country by now. I don't know if that's good news or bad.'

I said, 'Yes, Sam, we are travelling with that hospital. The sick people are on a big trailer, all the way from Doctor Katabisirua's hospital in Kodowa.'

He brightened. 'Doctor Kat! I know him. He very good doctor. One day he fix my brother when he break a leg.' That

250

was good news; if our doctor was well thought of his name was a reference for the rest of us.

'He'll be here later today, Sam,' Wingstead said.

Kironji looked only mildly incredulous.

Hammond came to the doorway. 'The Captain's here, Mister Mannix. He's asking for you.'

I tossed him two beers. 'One for you and one for Harry,' I said, 'but don't go back and boast about it. There isn't any more.'

'You said no soldiers,' said Kironji reproachfully as I passed him.

'Not many, and they are friends. Doctor Kat knows about them.'

Sadiq was waiting outside. I thanked him for his message, and went on, 'I've suggested to Mister Wingstead that we stop here, and he's agreed. There's a good road down to the lake and it's well hidden. We can put the whole convoy there, including the rig, and your men too if you think fit.'

Sadiq liked the idea and went to see for himself. Kironji watched him go from the cabin doorway.

'Sam,' I said, 'have you ever used the ferry?'

'Me, no. What for? I not go Manzu, I work here.'

'Who does use the ferry?'

He considered. 'Many truck from Manzu go to oilfields. Farmers, Government people. Many different people go on ferry.'

In happier times the international border here was obviously open and much-used. It was the only route to the Bir Oassa fields from countries north of Nyala. Kironji's information that trucks crossed on it suggested that it was larger than I would have expected, which was encouraging news.

Geoff Wingstead beckoned to me.

'When the rig gets here we will get it off the road. We're a little too close to Fort Pirie for comfort, and there's no point in buying trouble. There's plenty of room at the lakeside and it can't be seen from up here. But we'll have to widen the turn-off.'

251

For the next hour he and I together with Zimmerman and Hammond laboured. Widening the turn for the rig involved only a few modifications. We heaved rocks and equipment to one side, uprooted vegetation and chopped down a small spinney of thorn bushes, and generally made a mess of Sam Kironji's carefully preserved little kingdom. If it hadn't been for the fact that Zimmerman was from Lat-Am Kironji would never have allowed us to do it. As it was he could barely bring himself to help.

Four hours later the rig was bedded down in the clearing by the lake, its load resting on the ground and the weight taken off the bogies. The clearing held most of the vehicles and those that couldn't be fitted in were scattered off the road where they could leave in a hurry, or be used to block the way to the rig. We might have been bypassed and remain invisible if it wasn't for the Nyalans who were still doggedly following us. They camped in the trees all about us, chattering, cooking, coming and going endlessly. According to Sam Kironji many lived nearby but preferred our company to their homes.

Sadiq set his men to try and persuade them to leave us but this was a wasted effort. The rig was a magnet more powerful than any of us could have imagined, and politely but obstinately its strange escort insisted on staying. The countryside was steadily pillaged for whatever food could be found, and Sam Kironji's chickens disappeared before we could bargain for them.

I found Sister Ursula tearing a little pile of bedding she'd found in Kironji's cabin into bandaging strips and said to her, 'Let me do that. You've got more important things to do.'

'Thank you.' She had discarded her coif and her hair, cut close to the scalp, was sheened with sweat.

'How are things, Sister?'

'Not too bad,' she said briskly. 'We've lost no more patients and I really think the infant is going to make it, thanks be to God. We worry about Mister Lang, though.' He had taken Max Otterman's place as their most serious case. 'Doctor

252

Marriot says that Sister Mary is a little better. But she shouldn't exert herself in the slightest. We do need to get to a hospital soon though. What are our chances?' she asked.

I put her in the picture. 'Do you know of any hospitals in Manzu?' I then asked.

She didn't, and hadn't heard that we intended to try and reach the neighbouring country. Few people had as yet, for the sake of security, but now I told her.

'It's a fine idea, and just what we need. All these poor people who are following us, they do need a place to settle down in peace once more.'

'But they're Nyalans. They'd be in a foreign country without papers.'

She laughed. 'You're naïve, Mister Mannix. These people think of it simply as land, Africa. They haven't much nationalistic fervour, you know. They cross borders with little fear of officialdom, and officialdom has better things to do than worry about them. They just go where the grazing and hunting is good.'

I wished it was as simple for us, but we had a lot to do first. I left the Sister to her bandages and went to find Hammond, McGrath and Sam Wilson.

We walked down to stand at the pontoon, looking out over the water. Hammond said, 'I don't see many possibilities. If there was a bridge we could at least fight for it.'

'The ferry point is swarming with rebels,' I said. 'I don't think we've got the force we'd need.'

'You know, I was getting really worried about fuel,' Hammond said. 'It's ironic that now, when we can't go anywhere, we've got all we want and more.'

'I've been thinking about that,' said McGrath. 'We could float petrol down to the ferry and set it alight, construct a fire ship.'

Wilson said, 'Pleasant ideas you have, Mick,' and I caught an undertone I recognized; here was someone else who mistrusted the Irishman.

253

Hammond said, 'We can get people across Manzu in threes and fours, with this little boat . . . or perhaps not,' he added as he crossed the pontoon to look down into it. He hopped up and down, making the pontoon bobble on the water, then came back ashore looking thoughtful.

'I wonder why they have a pontoon instead of a fixed jetty,' he said.

'Does it matter?' I was no sailor and the question wouldn't have occurred to me, but Wilson took up Hammond's point. 'A fixed jetty's easier to build, unless you need a landing stage that'll rise and fall with the tide,' he said. 'Only there's no tide here.'

'You can see the water level varies a little,' Hammond said. He pointed out signs that meant nothing to me, but Wilson agreed with them. 'So where does the extra water come from?' I asked. 'It's the dry season now. When the rains come the river must swell a lot. Is that it?'

'It looks like more than that. I'd say there was a dam at the foot of the lake,' Hammond hazarded. McGrath followed this carefully and I could guess the trend of his thoughts; if there was a dam he'd be all for blowing it up. But I didn't recall seeing a dam on the maps, faulty though they were, and hadn't heard one mentioned.

But this wasn't Hammond's line of thinking at all.

'They have level control because the lake rises and falls at times. That's why they need a floating jetty,' he said.

'So?'

'The point is that the jetty is a tethered raft.' He pointed to the dinghy. 'That isn't very seaworthy but if we cut the pontoon loose it could be towed across the lake with people on it.'

Now he was giving me ideas. 'Only a few at a time,' I said.

'But we could build a bigger one. We might find other outboards,' Hammond went on, growing interested in his own hypothesis.

'Supposing you could do it. What does everyone do at the other side without transport? It's a long way to Batanda.'

'I hadn't got that far,' he admitted glumly.

I looked around. One boat, one pontoon, one outboard motor, plenty of fuel, a workshop . . . a work force . . . raw materials . . . my mind raced and I felt excitement rising. I said, 'All of you go on thinking about this. But don't share your ideas with anyone else for the time being.'

I got into the Land Rover and shot off up the road to the filling station and went up to Sam Kironji's cabin, which was latched. He let me in with some reluctance.

He said bitterly, 'You come, now they all come. Stealers! You didn't tell me this big crowd come. They steal everything I got. They steal things I don't got.' He was hurt and angry.

'Relax, Sam. We didn't bring them, they followed us. You said yourself you heard the travelling hospital was big magic.'

'That not magic. That *theft*. How I relax? How I explain to Mister Obukwe?'

'You won't have to. Mister Zimmerman will explain and Lat-Am Oil will be very pleased with you. You'll probably get a bonus. Got another beer?'

He stared at the desk top as I opened the cooler, which was empty, and then looked along his shelves which were as bare as Mother Hubbard's cupboard. Kironji looked up sardonically. 'Stealers! I tell you. Here.' He reached under the desk and came up with a beer can which he thrust out at me as if ashamed of his own generosity. I took it thankfully and said, 'There's still lots of stuff here, Sam.'

'Who eat tyres? Who eat batteries? You tell me that.'

I sat down on the edge of his desk. 'Sam. You know all those petrol drums you've got outside and down by the lake?'

'Why? You want to steal them?'

'No, of course not. How big are they?'

He addressed the desk top again. 'Forty-two gallon.'

'Imperial?'

'What you mean? Gallons, man – that what they are.'

Forty-two imperial gallons, which is what they probably

255

were, equalled about fifty American. I had tried to decipher the marks on one but they were pretty rusty.

'Sam,' I said, 'please do me a big favour. Give me some paper and a pen or a pencil, let me borrow your office, and go away for a bit. I have to do some calculating, some planning. I'll be really grateful.'

He reluctantly produced a pad of paper with Lat-Am's logo on it and a ballpoint pen. 'I want my pen back,' he said firmly and began to retreat.

'Wait a moment. What's the weight of an empty drum?'

He shrugged. 'I dunno. Plenty heavy.'

It didn't matter too much at this stage. 'How many empty drums have you got here?'

Again his shoulders hunched. 'Too many. No supplies come, I use 'em up. Many empty now.'

'For Christ's sake, Sam, I don't want a long story! How many?'

'Maybe a thousand, maybe more. I never count.'

I jotted down figures. 'Thanks. Sam, that cooler. Where do you get your power from?'

'Questions. You ask too much questions.' He jerked his thumb. 'You not hear it? The generator, man!'

I had got so accustomed to hearing the steady throb of a generator on the rig that it hadn't penetrated that this one was making a slightly different sound. 'Ah, so you do have one.'

'Why? You want to steal it?' He flapped his hand dejectedly. 'You take it. Mister Obukwe, he already mad at me.'

'Don't worry,' I told him. 'Nobody will steal it, or anything else. But buying would be different, wouldn't it? My company is British Electric. Perhaps we can buy your generator from you.'

'You pay cash?'

I laughed aloud. 'Not exactly, but you'll get it in the end. Now let me alone for a while, Sam, would you?'

Before he left he went and wrote down one can of beer on my tab.

256

24

I had a bit of figuring to do. For one thing, while we Americans think our way of doing things is always best, the European metric system is actually far better than our own multi-unit way, even the conservative British are adopting it, and oddly enough an imperial gallon is a better measure than our American gallon because one imperial gallon weighs exactly ten pounds of fresh water. It didn't take much figuring to see that a drum would hold four hundred and twenty pounds of water.

There was some other reckoning to be done and I persevered, even to cutting shapes out of paper with a rusty pair of scissors. At last I stretched, put Kironji's pen safely back in a drawer, took a hopeful but useless look in the cooler and set off down to the lakeside on foot. It was only a short distance and I used the walk to do some more thinking. I went straight down to look at the pontoon once again.

It was a rickety enough contraption, just a few empty oil drums for flotation with a rough log platform bolted on top. It was very weathered and had obviously stood the test of time, but it was as stable as a spinning top just about to lose speed and I wouldn't have cared to cross Central Park Lake on it.

I yelled for anybody and Bob Pitman responded.

'Bob,' I said, 'go round up a couple of people for me, will you? I want Kemp, Hammond, and Geoff Wingstead. Oh, and Mick McGrath. Ask them to meet me here.'

'Will do,' he said and ambled off. When they had all arrived I found that Zimmerman had got wind of the conference and had made himself part of it, though without his Russian mate. I looked around at them and drew a deep breath.

'I have a nutty idea,' I started.

This drew a couple of ribald comments and I waited until they died down before I carried on. 'It's crazy and dangerous, but it just might work. We have to do something to get ourselves out of this fix. You gave me the idea, Ben. You and Mick.'

'We did?' Hammond asked.

'Yes. I want us to build a raft.'

'I know I mentioned that but you shot that idea down in flames. You had a point too.'

'I've developed your idea. We don't use this thing as a basis, we build our own. I've done some figuring on paper and I think it will work. The trouble is that the lake isn't made of paper.' I filled in for the benefit of the others. 'Ben suggested that if we towed the landing stage it could form a raft on which we could get people over to Manzu. The pontoon isn't big or stable enough and we'd need transport on the far shore. But I think I've worked something out.'

'Build a bigger raft?' asked Wingstead.

'How could you power it?'

'What do we make it of?'

'What do you think this is, a navy shipyard?'

I held up my hand. 'Hold it. Give me a chance and I'll explain.' There were two phases to my scheme and I thought it wiser to introduce them one at a time, so I concentrated on the concept of the raft first. 'To start with, every one of these drums in the compound, when empty, has a flotation value of four hundred pounds, and there are hundreds of them. We won't need more than say one hundred for my plan to work.'

'Sounds idiotic to me,' said Kemp. 'A hundred of these drums won't make a raft big enough to take anything anywhere.' I knew he was trying to visualize the rig floating across the lake on a bed of oil drums and failing, and had indeed done that myself.

'Building a raft is the first part of my plan. And it'll do to

258

go on with, unless someone has a better one. We can't stay here indefinitely.'

'It sounds like you have a pretty big job lined up,' Wingstead said. He didn't sound encouraging. 'Let's hear it.'

'Think about the raft. To make it we need material and muscle. And brains, I guess. We've got the brains between us and there's a hell of a lot of suitable raw material lying about. As for the muscle, that's how the pyramids were built, and the Great Wall of China. God knows we've got enough of that.'

'The Nyalans?' Hammond asked. He was beginning to kindle with excitement. I wanted them all to feel that way.

'We'll need a work force. The women to plait lianas to make a lot of cordage, and some of the men to cart stuff about. I've got the basic blueprints right here.' I held up the pad of paper.

Zimmerman and Hammond looked ready for any challenge. Kemp had a stubborn set to his jaw and I knew that he was thinking about the rig to the usual exclusion of everything else, and ready to oppose any plan that didn't involve saving it.

Geoff Wingstead was oddly lacklustre, which disappointed me. I'd hoped to enrol his enthusiasm first of all, and wondered why he was hanging fire. McGrath had said nothing and was listening intently in the background. With the odd, unwanted rapport that I sometimes felt between us I knew he was aware that I had something tougher yet to propose, and he was waiting for it.

Hammond said, 'How do we persuade the Nyalans to co-operate? We can't pay them.'

'Sister Ursula gave me the answer to that. We can take as many of them across to Manzu as want to go. When the war's over they'll probably drift back again, but right now they're as threatened as we are. I think they'll help us.'

Kemp had been drawing in the sand, and now he said, 'Look, Neil, this is ridiculous. To build a raft big enough to take maybe a couple of hundred people is crazy enough, but to take vehicles across on them is beyond belief. Good God,

259

each tractor weighs forty tons. And how do we embark and disembark them?'

I said, 'You're thinking the wrong way. I agree with you, and I've already rejected that idea. We don't build a raft to get people to Manzu.' It was time to drop the bombshell.

'What? Then what's all this about?'

I said, 'We're going to use it to capture the ferry.'

They stared at me in total silence. McGrath's face warmed into a broad grin of appreciation.

Wingstead said at last, 'You're out of your mind, Neil.'

'OK, what the hell do we do? Sit here and eat ants until the war goes away? We have to do something. Any immunity as foreigners and civilians we might have had was shattered when we met up with Maksa's force. We played soldiers then. And I have a bad feeling about this war; if the Government forces were going to win they'd have done so by now. The rebels are gaining strength and if they take over they aren't going to be exactly lenient.'

Wingstead said, 'You're right. It just seems so far-fetched.'

'Not at all,' said McGrath. 'It's a lovely idea, Mannix. Lovely. How did I give you the idea, if I might ask?'

'You mentioned fire ships,' I said shortly. I needed him desperately but I was damned if I could make myself at ease with him. 'We're going to attack the ferry from the water, the one thing they won't expect.'

I had him with me, naturally. I thought I had Hammond too. He was fully aware of the danger but absorbed by the technical challenge. Kemp might disapprove but couldn't resist putting his mind to the problem.

Hammond said, 'I think at this stage you want to keep this rather quiet, don't you, Mister Mannix?'

'Yes. Why?'

'I'd like Bert Proctor in on it from the start. He's got a good head, and I've worked with him on projects so often –'

I said, 'Yes, of course. Go get him.'

He went off at the double and Wingstead smiled. 'They

260

really are quite a team, you know.' I was still worried about his lack of enthusiasm. He was the kingpin of the team and they looked to him for direction.

Proctor, grave and attentive as always, listened as I recapped. He calmly accepted the idea of Wyvern Transport men turning into privateers, and I understood why Hammond wanted him.

I showed them my idea for building the raft. I hadn't yet calculated the load but I reckoned on as many men as we could muster, at least one or maybe two trucks and whatever we could develop in the way of weapons – a formidable prospect. They were dubious but fascinated and the engineers among them could see the theoretical possibilities. We had to build a raft before considering the rest of the plan.

To Kemp I said, 'Basil, I've got an idea about the rig too. I know how important it is. We'll talk about that later.' This was a sop; I had no ideas about the rig but I couldn't afford to let him know it.

McGrath asked, 'How many men do you think we'll have?'

I said, 'All of Sadiq's men, that's twenty-three. We can't conscript our crew but I don't think anybody will want to be left out. I make that sixteen. Thirty-nine in all.'

'Say thirty-five, allowing for accidents,' said McGrath.

'Fair enough.'

'What did Sadiq have to say about the ferry?'

'They have a guard detachment there. Exactly how many we don't know, but it doesn't sound formidable. If we come out of the dark yelling at them they'll probably scatter like autumn leaves.'

Faces brightened. It didn't sound quite so bad put that way.

McGrath said, 'We'd need much more accurate information than that, Mannix.'

'Oh, I agree. By the way, I haven't spoken to Sadiq yet, but we will soon. I want to propose an expedition, using Sam Kironji's boat. You, McGrath, Geoff, Sadiq and myself. It won't take any more. Down river by night.'

261

Wingstead said, 'Oh my God, Neil, I don't think we should do that.'

I was dumbfounded. 'What the hell's the matter with you, Geoff? I'm depending most of all on you. For God's sake stop being such a damned pessimist.'

I'd never let fly at an executive in front of his men before. But it was vital to keep morale high and a waverer at the top of the command line could ruin all our plans. He made a strangely listless gesture and said, 'I'm sorry, Neil. Of course I'm with you. Just tired, I guess.'

Zimmerman broke into the embarrassed silence. "I don't think Geoff should go anyway, Neil. He's got enough on his plate already. Let me come instead.'

I was relieved. Damn it, I wanted Wingstead with me, and yet in his present mood he might be a liability. I wished I knew what was eating him.

'Suppose we succeeded, took the ferry. What then?' Hammond asked. 'Wouldn't their main force get to know about it?'

'Very likely, but they're at Fort Pirie and we'd silence radios and prevent getaways,' I said. 'The only thing we have to pray for is that the ferry is operative, and from what Kironji told me it's been in regular use recently so it ought to be.'

'Then what?' Wingstead asked.

'We bring up the rig and get all the invalids on board the ferry, cram it full of people and shoot it across to Manzu. When it comes back we pile on as many vehicles as it can take, trucks for preference, and the last of the people. Once in Manzu it's a doddle. Get to Batanda, alert the authorities and send back transport for the stragglers. I bet they've got cold beer there.'

They chewed on this for a while. I had painted a rosy picture and I knew they wouldn't entirely fall for it, but it was important to see potential success.

Hammond stood up and rubbed out the sketch marks in the sand with his foot. 'Right – how do we start?' he asked practically.

Wingstead looked up, absurdly startled. His face was

262

pale under its tan and I wondered fleetingly if he was simply afraid. But he hadn't been afraid back in the warehouse at Makara.

'I don't know,' he said uncertainly. 'I'd like to think about it a bit, before we start anything. It's just too –'

The hesitation, the slack face, were totally unfamiliar. Doubt began to wipe away the tentative enthusiasm I had roused in the others. Wingstead had cut his teeth on engineering problems such as this and he was deeply concerned for the safety of his men. I had expected him to back me all the way.

The problem solved itself. He stood up suddenly, shaking his head almost in bewilderment, took a dozen paces away from us and collapsed in the dust.

We leapt up to race over to him.

'Go and get a doctor!' Kemp barked and Proctor ran to obey. Gently Kemp cradled Wingstead whose face had gone as grey as putty, sweat-soaked and lolling. We stood around in shocked silence until Dr Kat and Dr Marriot arrived.

After a few minutes the surgeon stood up and to my amazement he looked quite relieved. 'Please send for a stretcher,' he said courteously, but there was one already waiting, and willing hands to carry Wingstead to the mobile hospital. Dr Marriot went with him, but Dr Kat stayed behind.

'I should have seen this coming,' he said. 'But you may set your minds at rest, gentlemen. Mister Wingstead will be perfectly all right. He is not dangerously ill.'

'What the hell is it then?' I asked.

'Overstrain, overwork, on top of the injuries he suffered in the plane crash. He should have been made to take things more easily. Tell me, did you notice anything wrong yourselves?'

I said, feeling sick with anger at myself, 'Yes, I did. I've seen him losing his drive, his energy. And I damned well kept pushing at him, like a fool. I'm sorry –'

Kemp cut me off abruptly.

'Don't say that. I saw it too and I know him better than

263

anyone else here. We must have been crazy to let him go on like that. Will he really be all right?'

'All he needs is sleep, rest, good nourishment. We can't do too much about the last but I assure you I won't let him get up too soon this time. I might tell you that I'm very relieved in one respect. I have been afraid of fever – cholera, typhoid – any number of scourges that might strike. When I heard that Mister Wingstead had collapsed I thought it was the first such manifestation. That it is not is a matter of considerable relief.'

The Doctor's report on Wingstead was circulated, and the concern that had run through the convoy camp like a brush fire died down.

I found Hammond. 'I want to talk to all the crew later this evening. The medical staff too. We'll tell them the whole plan. It's risky, but we can't ask people to work in ignorance.'

Then I went to find Sam Kironji.

'Sam, what's in that little hut inside the compound?' I asked him.

He looked at me suspiciously. He'd already found the compound gate unlocked and Harry Zimmerman and two others counting empty drums, much to his disgust. 'Why you want to know?'

I clung to my patience. 'Sam, just tell me.'

There was nothing much in it. The hut held a miscellany of broken tools, cordage, a few other stores that might be useful, and junk of all sorts. It was where Sam put the things he tidied away from everywhere else.

I made a space in the middle of it, had Kironji's desk brought in, and established it as my headquarters. The roadside cabin was too far from the camp and too exposed. Some wag removed a Pirelli calendar from the cabin wall and hung it in the hut, and when Kironji saw this I think it hurt him most of all.

'Stealers! Now you take my women,' he said tragically.

'Only to look at, same as you. You'll get them back, I promise. Thank you for the desk and the chair, Sam.'

264

He flapped his hand at me. 'Take everything. I not care no more. Mister Obukwe, he fire me.'

Hammond was listening with amusement. 'Never mind, Sam. If he does I'll hire you instead,' I said and hustled him outside. I sat down and Hammond perched on the end of the desk. We each had a pad of paper in front of us.

'Right, Ben. This is what I've got in mind.'

I began to sketch on the pad. I still have those sketches; they're no masterpieces of the draughtsman's art, but they're worth the whole Tate Gallery to me.

Take an empty drum and stand it up. Place around it, in close contact, six more drums, making damn sure their caps are all screwed home firmly. Build an eight-sided wooden framework for them, top, bottom and six sides, thus making a hexagon. No need to fill the sides solidly, just enough to hold the drums together like putting them in a cage. This I called the 'A' hexagon, which was to be the basic component of the raft. It had the virtue of needing no holes drilled into the drums, which would waste time and effort and risk leaks.

How much weight would an 'A' hexagon support?

We got our answer soon enough. While we were talking Sandy Bing reported breathlessly to the office. 'Mister Mannix? I got forty-three and a half gallons into a drum.' He was soaking wet and seemed to have enjoyed the exercise.

'Thanks, Sandy. Go and see how many empties Harry Zimmerman has found, please.' Zimmerman and his team were getting very greasy out in the compound.

The drums were forty-two gallons nominal but they were never filled to brimming and that extra space came in handy now. We figured that the natural buoyancy of the wooden cage would go some way to compensate for the weight of the steel drums, and Bing had just handed me another few pounds of flotation to play about with. We decided that my 'A' hexagon should support a weight of 3,000 pounds: one and a half tons.

But there wouldn't be much standing room. And a floating platform about six by five feet would be distinctly unstable. So my next lot of figures concerned the natural development upwards.

All this would take a little time to produce but it shouldn't be too difficult. Testing the finished product as a floating proposition would be interesting, and finding a way to push it along would stretch a few minds, but I didn't really doubt that it could be done. And the final result, weird of shape and design, was going to win no prizes for elegance. I jiggled with a list of required materials; some of them were going to be hard to find if not impossible. All in all, I couldn't see why on earth I was so confident that the plan would work.

'We have to go up a stage, Ben,' I said, still sketching. 'Look at this.'

The hexagon is a very useful shape, ask any honey bee, but I doubt if it has been used much in naval architecture.

'Start off assuming we've built an 'A'-gon,' I told Ben. That was how new words came into a language, I guess, though I didn't think this one would last long enough to qualify for *Webster's Dictionary*. Ben caught on and grinned in appreciation. 'Here's what comes next.'

Take an 'A'-gon and float it in shallow water so that a man could stand on the bottom and still handle equipment. Float another six 'A'-gons round it and fasten together the hexagons of the outer ring. There is no need to fasten the inner one because, like the first drum, it is totally surrounded and pressed in from all sides.

The result is a 'B' hexagon, a 'B'-gon in our new nomenclature, with a positive buoyancy of ten and a half tons, enough to carry over a hundred people or a medium sized truck. We decided to make two of them, which is why we needed a hundred drums.

Hammond was impressed and fascinated. 'How do we make the cages?' he asked.

'We'll have to find timber and cut pieces to the exact size,' I said. 'That won't be too difficult. I'm more concerned about finding planking to deck it, otherwise it'll be unsafe to walk on.

Nyalan women make good cordage, and we can lash the 'A'-gon frames together, which will save nails. But I'm worried about the fastening of the larger 'B'-gons. Rope and fibre won't help us there. We need steel cable.'

'I've got some,' he offered, a shade reluctantly.

'I don't want to have to use that yet. We'll figure out something else.'

I stood up. 'It's only four o'clock and I need some exercise. There's two hours of daylight yet. Let's go build us an 'A'-gon.'

We were just leaving the office when Bing arrived back.

'Mister Zimmerman says they've only found sixty-seven drums.' he said.

At the compound we found Zimmerman, Kirilenko and Derek Grafton looking mucky with old oil and somewhat bad-tempered. It appeared that there were not many empty drums. Kironji seldom got them back, and these had not been placed neatly away from the full drums but stood all over the place. Here Kironji's normal tidiness had deserted him, to our detriment. It didn't help that neither Grafton nor Kirilenko knew why they had to find empty drums, and of the two only the Russian was equable about taking unexplained orders.

I commiserated with them and sent them off for a breather, after we'd rolled eight or nine drums down to the lake shore. Zimmerman stayed with us. Hammond left in search of Kironji, to get the workshop unlocked; he would cut some timber frameworks and we decided to use rope, which we knew was available, for the prototype 'A'-gon.

'I don't see how we're going to find enough empties,' Zimmerman grumbled.

'Ever hear about the guy who went into a store to buy some eggs? There was a sign up saying "Cracked Eggs Half Price", so he asked them to crack him a dozen eggs.'

Zimmerman smiled weakly.

'You mean empty out full drums?'

'Why not? To start with we'll fill every fuel tank we can with either gas or diesel, and all our spare jerrycans too. If there are still not enough drums we'll dig a big pit somewhere well away from the camp and ditch the stuff. And put up a "No Smoking" notice.'

He realized I wasn't joking and his jaw dropped. I suppose that as an oil man he was more used to getting the stuff out of the earth than to putting it back in. Then we were interrupted by Sam Kironji in his usual state of high indignation.

'You cut trees! You use my saw. You never stop make trouble.'

I looked enquiringly at Sandy Bing who had raced in behind him. 'Yes, Mister Mannix. Mister Hammond found a chain saw in the workshop. But it won't be good for long. The teeth are nearly worn out and there's no replacement.'

Kironji shook his head sadly. 'You use my saw, you welcome. But you cut tree, you get in big trouble with Mister Nyama.'

'Who's he, Sam?'

'Everybody know Mister Nyama. Big Government tree man. He cut many tree here, with big machine.'

I said, 'Are you telling us that there's a government logging camp near here?'

'Sure.'

'Well where, for God's sake?'

Sam pointed along the lake. 'One, two mile. They use our road.'

I recalled that the road led on past the compound, but I hadn't given any thought as to where it went. A bad oversight on my part.

'Chain saws,' Zimmerman was saying, his voice rising to a chant of ecstasy, 'Axes, felling axes, trimming axes, scrub cutters.'

'Fantastic. Get off there right away. We've got enough drums to be going on with. Take some men, some of Sadiq's if you have to. I'll clear it with him. And Harry, plunder away; we'll make everything good some time. Break in if you have to. My bet is that there'll be nobody there anyhow.'

Zimmerman went off at a run and Kironji said dolefully, 'You steal from Government, you steal from *anybody*.'

Hammond rejoiced at the good news and had some himself. 'Found an oxyacetylene welding kit in there with a few bottles. And a three-and-a-half inch Myford lathe that'll come in handy.'

'Bit small, isn't it?'

'I'll find a use for it. There's another outboard engine, too, and some other useful bits and pieces.'

'Take them,' said Kironji hysterically. 'No need you steal. I give.'

I chuckled. When he saw us pouring his precious gasolene into a hole in the ground he'd be a broken man. 'Come on, let's build our 'A'-gon.'

It took six of us nearly two hours to build the prototype 'A'-gon but then we were inventing as we went along. From the middle distance the Nyalans watched us and wondered. Our people came to watch and make comments. At last we wrestled it down to the water and to our relief it floated, if a trifle lopsidedly. We dragged it ashore again as the light was fading and Bing arrived to say that a meal was ready. I felt tired but surprisingly contented. This had been a fruitful day. I was careful not to dwell on the possible outcome of my plans.

After an unsatisfying meal everybody gathered round, and between us as Hammond and I explained the basics of the scheme. We said little about the military side of the operation and discouraged questions. We concentrated on the more immediate goal, the building of the 'B'-gons.

Grafton was sceptical, possibly because he'd had first-hand experience of the labour involved.

'It took you two hours to make that thing. How many do you need?'

'Fourteen for two 'B'-gons. Possibly more.'

He looked appalled. 'It'll take days at that rate.'

'Ever hear about Henry Ford's biggest invention?'

'The Model T?'

269

'No, bigger than that. The assembly line.'

Hammond said at once. 'Ford didn't invent that. The Royal Navy had one going in Chatham in seventeen ninety-five for making ships' blocks.'

'I think the Egyptian wall paintings show something like an assembly line,' put in Atheridge.

'We won't be chauvinistic about it,' I said. 'But that's what we're going to do. We build simple jigs, stakes driven into the sand will do, one at each corner to give the shape. Then the teams move along the rows. That's the difference between this line and those in Cowley or Chicago. Each man goes along doing just one job. They lay down the bottom planking, put the drums on top, drop the side members between the stakes and make them fast. Then they put on a top and do likewise.'

They listened intently, and then Antoine Dufour spoke up. His English was good but heavily accented.

'I have worked in such a place. I think it is better you take the Japanese model, piecework is no good here. You will have too many people moving about, getting confused perhaps. You want teams each in one place.'

It took very little rethinking to see that he was right, and I said so.

'Great going, Antoine. It will be better that way. Each team builds one 'A'-gon from the bottom up, complete. Another team to go along doling out material. Another one rolling the drums to them. And a couple of really strong teams to shift the finished 'A'-gons to the water, probably towing them on mats. We've got rubber matting in the trucks.'

I looked at Dufour. 'You say you've had some experience at this. How would you like to be in charge of the work teams, you and Dan?'

He considered and then nodded. 'Yes. I will do it.'

His matter-of-fact acceptance of the feasibility of the programme did a lot to encourage the others. Questions and ideas flew about, with me taking notes. At last I held up a hand for silence.

270

'Enough to go on with. Now let's hear from Doctor Kat.'

The Doctor gave us a brief report on Lang and on Wingstead, who was sleeping soundly and would be none the worse as long as he was restrained for a few days. 'Sister Mary is much better, and taking care of Mister Wingstead is the perfect job for her. She will keep him quiet.'

I hadn't seen much of the senior nun but if she was anything like Sister Ursula there was no doubt that Geoff Wingstead would shut up and obey orders.

Of the other invalids, he said that as fast as they got one person on their feet so another would go down with exhaustion, sickness or accident. The rickety thatched wards were as busy as ever.

I turned to Harry Zimmerman.

'Harry's got some good news he's been saving,' I said.

'We found a logging camp,' he reported cheerfully. 'We brought back two loads of equipment, in their trucks. Chain saws, axes, hammers, nails and screws, a whole lot of stuff like that. The big power saws are still there but they work.'

'But you did even better than that, didn't you?' I prompted.

'Yeah. Planks,' he breathed happily.

'We'll be bringing in a load in the morning. That means our decking is sorted out, and that's a big problem solved. And we can get all the struts for the cages cut to exact measurements in no time.' The assembly responded with more enthusiasm than one might have thought possible, given how weary they all were.

'It's amazing,' said Dr Marriot. 'I saw your 'A'-gon. Such a flimsy contraption.'

'So is an eggshell flimsy, but they've taken one tied in a bag outside a submarine four hundred feet deep and it didn't break. The 'A'-gon's strength lies in its stress factors.'

She said, 'It's your stress factors we have to think about,' and got a laugh. Morale was improving.

The meeting over, we dispersed without any discussion about the proposed attack on the ferry for which all this was

271

merely the prologue, and I was grateful. Those who were to be my fellow travellers in the boat stayed on to talk. We decided to move out by first light and return upriver in time to get cracking on the coming day's work. Sadiq had been briefed and while not exactly enthusiastic he had agreed to come with us, to see the enemy for himself.

Later I lay back looking at the dark shape of the rig looming over us, a grotesque shape lit with the barest minimum of light. I wondered what the hell we were going to do with it. I had enough thinking to keep me awake all night long.

But when I hit the sack I didn't know a thing until I felt Hammond gently awakening me, three hours before dawn.

25

In the raw small hours we assembled at the pontoon, keeping our torches hooded and trying to keep quiet as we crossed the scrubby clearing. We couldn't leave totally unobserved but this was a practice run for later on, when keeping quiet would be vital.

Overnight Hammond had had the boat baled out and the outboard tested and found to run as sweetly as any outboard does, which is to say fitfully and with the occasional lurch and stutter to give you a nervous leap of the pulse. There was ample fuel, a small fluke anchor and a rond anchor for digging into an earth bank if necessary, some water canteens and a couple of long coils of line.

We had found oars for the dinghy but only one rowlock so someone had cobbled up another out of a piece of scrap iron bent to shape in the lathe; this and its more shapely companion were wrapped in cloth to minimize noise. The best we could do for balers were old beer cans with the tops cut out.

The five of us made a pretty tight fit. Hammond and McGrath took the centre thwart to row us out, we'd only start the engine well away from shore, I as the lightest sat forward, and Zimmerman and Sadiq crowded onto the after thwart. It was going to be no pleasure jaunt.

'What about crocodiles?' Hammond asked.

Zimmerman, who'd had years in Africa, snorted. 'Not a chance, Ben. They like shoaling water and they'll be sluggish before dawn anyway. Lazy brutes. Why bother with a boat when the bank's swarming with breakfast?'

Sadiq said gravely, 'Mister Hammond, we need not fear the crocodiles. They seldom attack boats with an engine.'

273

McGrath said, grinning, 'No, it's the hippos we have to think about,' giving Hammond another direction in which to cast his fears. I told him to lay off. What I didn't say was that, being no sailor even of the Sunday-in-the-park variety, I had a strong conviction that this frail craft was likely to tip us out and drown us at any moment. When we pushed off and the chill water lapped at the gunwales I was certain of it.

We didn't sink, of course, but we did get pretty wet about the feet and the face. After some time Hammond suggested that we start the outboard. This was achieved with only a few curses and false alarms. The little boat rocked wildly before the motor settled down to a welcome steady purr and we began to pick up some pace. We hugged the shoreline though not too close for fear of reed beds, and the light was beginning to allow us to distinguish details.

We were travelling with the current and so moved along swiftly. Hammond had calculated that we should arrive within sight of the ferry at about five o'clock, an hour before dawn. We would shut off the engine and slip along under oars until we could see the ferry point, then pull back upriver to find a concealed landing place. From there we'd reconnoitre on land.

'What happens if the ferry's on the far shore?' Zimmerman asked.

'We can cross in this thing and collect it. No sweat,' Hammond said. 'Come right a little, Mick.'

'What about the ferry people?' I said. 'They aren't simply going to lend us their craft, are they?'

'No, more likely they'll run it for us themselves, at a price.'

I'd been wondering who was going to handle the ferry. There would be a lot of local knowledge involved apart from familiarity with the craft itself. I said, 'Good thinking. Once we've taken the ferry point here we send a delegation and get the ferry back in business – just for us.'

'Well, it might work,' said McGrath dubiously. His form of payment would probably be a gun at the pilot's belly.

'First let's take the ferry,' I said. Perhaps it would be held

274

by about five men whom we could capture or rout with a minimum of fuss, but I doubted that it would be that easy.

There was no further talk as we cruised steadily on until we saw the shapes of man-made buildings along the bank. We had arrived, and it still lacked half an hour to dawn.

'There it is,' I whispered, pointing. Instantly Zimmerman cut the engine and we used the oars to hold us stemming the tide. Shapes were emerging but confusingly, all detail obscured. There was a huge dark shape in the water a hundred yards offshore that we couldn't identify as yet. An island, perhaps? Hammond and McGrath back watered to keep us upstream while we scanned the shore anxiously for movement.

As all dawns do in central Africa, this one came in minutes. The air became grey and hazy, a shaft of early sunlight sprang out across the water and it was as if a veil had been lifted. Several voices whispered together.

'It's the ferry!'

She was anchored offshore, bobbing gently, a marvellous and welcome sight. She was big. Visions of a hand-poled pontoon, one-car sized and driven by chanting ferrymen, not at all an uncommon sight in Africa, receded thankfully from my mind. Kironji had said it took trucks, and trucks he meant. This thing would take several vehicles at one crossing. And there was something else about her profile in the watery light which nagged at me: a long low silhouette, bow doors slanted inwards to the waterline and a lumpy deck structure aft. She was a far cry from the sleek and sophisticated modern ferries of Europe.

We slid out from under the shadow of her bow and made rapidly for shore. Hammond rowed us out of sight of the ferry point and tucked into the bank in as secretive a spot as we could find, setting both anchors. We disembarked into the fringe of vegetation.

I looked to McGrath. He and Sadiq were the experts now, and I wasn't sure which of the two was going to take command. But there wasn't any doubt really; with assurance Sadiq started

275

giving instructions, and McGrath took it with equanimity. I think he'd approved of Sadiq as a fighting man and was prepared to take his orders.

'Mister Mannix, you and Mister Zimmerman come with me, please,' Sadiq said. 'Mister McGrath will take Mister Hammond. We are going towards the buildings. We three will take the further side, Mister McGrath the nearer. Nobody is to make any disturbance or touch anything. Observe closely. We must know how many men and officers are here, and what weapons they have. Where they keep the radio and telephone. What transport they have. The layout of the terrain. Whether there are people on the ferry, and what other boats there are.'

I whistled silently. It was a tall order. All he wanted to know was absolutely everything.

'If you are caught,' he went on, 'make as much outcry as you can, to alarm the others. But try not to reveal that they exist. If the opportunity arises for you to steal weapons do so, but do not use them.'

He looked intently at McGrath who showed no reaction but that of careful attention. Sadiq said, 'I think that is all. Good luck, gentlemen.'

The astounding thing was that it worked exactly as he planned it. In my imagination I had seen a hundred things going drastically wrong: ourselves captured, tortured, shot, the site overrun with soldiers armed to the teeth, the ferry incapacitated or nonexistent . . . every obstacle under the sun placed between us and success. In fact it was all extremely easy and may well have been the most fruitful reconnaissance mission in the annals of warfare.

This was because there were so few men there. Our team made a count of fifteen, McGrath said seventeen, and the highest-ranking soldier we could spot was a corporal. They had rifles and one light machine-gun but no other weapons that we could see. There was a radio equipped with headphones and another in one of the cars, but it was defunct; Hammond reported having seen its guts strewn about the passenger seat.

276

There were two trucks, one with a shattered windscreen, a Suzuki four-wheel drive workhorse and a beat-up elderly Volvo.

This was a token detachment, set there to guard something that nobody thought to be of the least importance. After all, nobody from Manzu was going to come willingly into a neighbouring battle zone, especially when the craft to bring them was on the wrong side of the water.

The two teams met an hour and a half later back at the dinghy and compared notes. We were extremely pleased with ourselves, having covered all Sadiq's requirements, and heady with relief at having got away with it. Perhaps only McGrath was a little deflated at the ease of the mission.

I would have liked another look at that ferry but anchored as she was out in midstream there was no way we could approach her unseen. Whatever it was about her that bothered me would have to wait.

We did some energetic baling with the beer cans and set off upriver, again keeping close to the bank and using oars until we were out of earshot of the ferry point. It was harder work rowing upstream, but once the outboard was persuaded to run we made good time. It was midday when we got back.

We reported briefly on our findings which cheered everyone enormously. We had discovered that the landing point was called Kanjali, although the joke of trying to call it the Fort Pirie Ferry, a genuine tongue twister, had not yet palled. But we didn't know if the ferry itself was in good running order. It might have been sabotaged or put out of action officially as a safeguard. And the problem of who was to run it was crucial.

After a light meal we went to see the raft builders at work.

Dufour had a dry, authoritative manner which compensated for his lack of Nyalan, which was supplemented by Atheridge. With Sadiq's men as interpreters they had rounded up a number of Nyalans who were willing to help in return for a ride to Manzu, and some who didn't want even that form of payment. These people were free in a sense we could hardly understand,

277

free to melt back into the bush country they knew, to go back to their villages where they were left to get along unassisted by government programmes, but also untrammelled by red tape and regulations. But the rig had come to mean something extra to them, and because of it they chose to help us. It was as simple as that.

One of our problems was how to fasten the outer ring of 'B'-gons together. We'd not got anywhere with this until Hammond gave us the solution.

'You'd think we could come up with something,' he said, 'with all the friends we've got here pulling for us.'

'Friends,' I murmured. 'Polonius.'

'What?'

'I was just thinking about a quote from Hamlet. Polonius was giving Laertes advice about friendship.' I felt rather pleased with myself; it wasn't only the British who could play literary games. 'He said, "Grapple them to thy soul with hoops of steel." I could do with some hoops of steel right now.'

Hammond said, 'Would mild steel do?'

'You mean you've got some?' I asked incredulously.

He pointed to an empty drum. 'Cut as many hoops as you like from one of these things.'

'By God, so we can! Well done, Ben. Is there a cutting nozzle with the oxyacetylene outfit?'

'Hold on, Neil,' he said. 'Those drums will be full of petrol vapour. You put a flame near one and it'll explode. We have to do it another way.'

'Then we need a can opener.'

'You'll have one,' he promised.

Hammond's idea of a can opener was interesting. If you can't invent the necessary technology then you fall back on muscle. Within an hour he had twenty Nyalan men hammering hell out of the empty drums, using whatever they could find in the way of tools, old chisels, hacksaw blades, sharp-edged stones. They made the devil of a row but they flayed the drums open, cutting them literally into ribbons.

278

At the 'A'-gon construction site Dufour had assembled four teams and it took each team about one hour to make one 'A'-gon. In a factory it would have been quicker, but here the work force chatted and sang its way through the allotted tasks at a pace not exactly leisurely but certainly undemanding. Dufour knew better than to turn martinet and try to hurry them.

In some of the old school textbooks there were problems such as this; if it takes one man six hours to dig a pit seven feet long by six feet deep by two feet wide, then how long will it take three men to perform the same task? The textbook answer is two hours, which is dead wrong. Those who have done the dismal job know that it's a one-man operation because two men get in each other's way and three men can hardly work at all.

Dufour, knowing this, had seen to it that nobody could get in each other's way and not one motion was wasted. For an inexperienced work force it was miraculous, any efficiency expert would have been proud of it. Altogether it was a remarkable operation.

It started at the sawmill where a team cut timber into precise measurements, and the wood was hauled down to the shore. Sufficient pieces were doled out to the construction groups, each one a fair way from the next along the shore. Each team consisted of one Wyvern man, three Nyalan men and a few women, including even those with babies on their backs or toddlers at their sides.

The four men would each lay a beam on the ground, setting them between pegs driven into the sand so that they would be in exactly the right place. Meantime another force was rolling empty, tight-bunged drums along the shore from the compound and stacking them at each site, seven at a time. The four men would stand the drums on the crossbeams inside the circle of vertical stakes which formed the primitive jig. Little pegs were being whittled by some of the elderly folk, and these went into holes drilled in the ends of each crossbeam. The sidebeams would then be dropped to stand at right angles to the bases, the pegs slotting into holes drilled close to the bottom. Another set of pegs at the top of each side beam held the top cross-members in position, and halfway up yet another set of horizontal struts completed the cage.

At this stage the 'A'-gon was held together only by the pegs and the jig in which it rested. Now the women bound it all together with cordage. This was the longest part of the operation so the men would move to a second jig.

Once the 'A'-gon was finished a strong-arm team would heave it out of the jig. It was here that the binding sometimes failed and had to be redone. They would dump it on a rubber car mat and drag it the short distance to the water to be floated off. Then the whole process started again. The guy called Taylor who pioneered the science of time and motion study would have approved.

In the water a bunch of teenagers, treating the whole thing as a glorious water carnival, floated the 'A'-gons to the 'B'-gon construction site. Four teams took about an hour to make enough basic components for one 'B'-gon. I reckoned that we'd have both 'B'-gons, plus a few spare 'A'-gons, finished before nightfall.

I went to visit Wingstead on the rig during the early afternoon. I filled him in on progress. He was wan but cheerful, and that description also precisely suited his nurse, Sister Mary, of whom he seemed in some awe. I also looked in on Lang and was saddened by his deterioration. All the nursing in the world couldn't make up for the lack of medical necessities. I found Grafton on the rig as well. He had broken his ankle slipping between two 'A'-gon drums, and this accentuated the need for decking our extraordinary craft.

This was solved by a trip to the logging mill. There were tall young trees which had been cut and trimmed for use as telegraph poles, and it was a fairly easy job to run them through the cutters so that the half-sections would form perfect decking. Getting them back proved simple, with so many hands available. This operation was in the hands of Zimmerman and Vashily, who had emptied enough empty drums for both 'A'-gons and the steel lashings. Zimmerman said that he never wanted to have anything more to do with oil for the rest of his life.

The day wore on. The Nyalan foragers had found some food for everybody. Teams of swimmers were lifting floating planks onto the deck of the first completed 'B'-gon. It was an ungainly structure, with odd scalloped edges and splintery sides, but it floated high and lay fairly steadily in the water. On measuring we found that we could get one truck of not more than an eight foot beam on to it. Provided it could be driven on board.

Zimmerman, still scrounging about the camp for useful materials, came to me for a word in private.

'Neil, you'd better know about this,' he said. 'I checked all the trucks including the Frog's.' Dufour had been careful with his truck, always driving it himself and parking it away from the others at camp stops.

'He's carrying a mixed cargo of basic supplies. Ben will be happy to know that there is some oxygen and acetylene and some welding rods. But that's not all. The guy is breaking the law. He's carrying six cases of forty per cent blasting gelignite and they aren't on his manifest. That's illegal, explosives should never be carried with a mixed cargo.'

'We ought to stop him carrying it, but what the hell can we do with it? Dump it?'

'Must we?' he asked wistfully. Explosives were his profession.

'OK, not yet. But don't let Dufour know you're on to him. Just make sure nobody smokes around his truck. No wonder he parks it way off.' It was a possible weapon with Zimmerman's expertise to make the best use of it.

Progress on the second 'B'-gon was going well, but I called a halt. We were getting tired and this was when accidents were most likely to occur.

It was time for a council of war.

281

After the evening meal the crew gathered round and I counted and assessed them. There were fifteen men but I discounted two at once.

'Geoff, you're not coming.' Wingstead had been allowed to eat with us and afterwards he must have given his watchdog nurse the slip. He was very drawn but his eyes were brighter and he looked more like the man I'd first met.

He said ruefully, 'I'm not quite the idiot I was a couple of days ago. But I can sit on your council, Neil. I have to know what you plan to do, and I might be able to contribute.'

'Fair enough,' I said. Just having Wingstead there was a boost.

'And Derek's also out of it. He can't walk, ankle's swollen like a balloon,' Wingstead said. 'He's pretty mad.'

'Tell him I'll trade places,' offered Thorpe.

I said, 'Not a chance, Ritchie – you're stuck with this. You should never have been around in Port Luard when I needed a co-driver.'

'Wouldn't have missed it for the world,' he said bravely.

I turned to the next lame duck.

'Dan,' I said gently, 'it's not on, you know.'

He glanced down at his still splinted arm and heaved a sigh. 'I know. But you take bloody good care of Antoine here, you hear me?' He and the Frenchman exchanged smiles.

'Bert, how's your leg?'

Proctor said, 'Good as new, Mister Mannix. No problem, I promise you,' for which I was grateful. He was one of the stalwarts and we needed him. Kemp's shoulder would not hamper him, and there were no other injuries among us.

I said, 'Sadiq has got twenty-one men. There's one down with dysentery. With twelve of us that makes thirty-four to their seventeen: two to one. With those odds, I don't see how we can fail.'

A figure slid into the circle and I made room for him to sit beside me. It was Captain Sadiq.

I said, 'Basically what we have to do is this. We're going downriver on the 'B'-gon. We get there before first light. We

282

try to overpower them without much fighting. We've got a few weapons and we'll be able to get theirs if our surprise is complete. Ideally we don't want any shooting at all.'

'Squeamish, Mannix?' asked McGrath.

'Not at all,' I said coldly. 'But we don't know how near any reinforcements might be. We keep this as quiet as possible.'

There was a slight stir around the circle at our exchange.

'We have to get their radio under control, don't we?' Bing asked.

I had refrained, against my first instincts, from forbidding him to join the expedition. He was nineteen and by medieval standards a grown man ripe for blooding, and this was as near to medieval warfare as you could get. He was fit, intelligent and fully aware of the danger.

'Yes, that's going to be your baby,' I said. 'Your group's first priority will be to keep it undamaged and prevent their using it. The one in the car looks out of action but you'll make sure of that too. Brad, you run the interference for Sandy, OK?' He may not know American football terms, but the inference was obvious and he nodded fervently. Bing was his responsibility.

'Captain?' I turned to Sadiq.

'My men will make the first sortie,' he said. 'We have weapons and training which you do not have. We should be able to take the whole detachment without much trouble.'

Zimmerman whispered hasty translations to Kirilenko.

'Bert, you and Ben and Antoine immobilize all the transport you can find,' I said. 'Something temporary, a little more refined than a crowbar through the transmission.'

'Not a problem,' Bert said, his usual phlegmatic response.

'Mick, you cover Bing in the radio room and then check their weapon store; pile up everything you can. Use . . .' I was about to assign Bob Pitman to him, but remembered that Pitman had no reason to trust McGrath. 'Use Harry and Kirilenko.' They would make a good team.

283

I waited to see if McGrath was going to make any suggestions of his own but he remained silent. He didn't make me feel easy but then nothing about McGrath ever did.

I turned to Pitman.

'Bob, you stick with me and help me secure the raft. Then we cover the ramp where they load the ferry, you, me and Kemp. We'll want you to look at it from a transportation point of view, Basil.' If he thought for one second that he could get his rig on board the ferry he'd be crazy but he needed to be given at least some faint reason for hope in that direction. I looked round.

'Ritchie, I need a gofer and you're the lucky man. You liaise between me, Captain Sadiq and the other teams. I hope you're good at broken field running.'

'Me? Run? I used to come last at *everything*, Mister Mannix,' he said earnestly. 'But I'll run away any time you tell me to!'

Again laughter eased the tension a little. I was dead tired and my mind had gone a total blank. Anything we hadn't covered would have to wait for the next day. The conference broke up leaving me and Sadiq facing one another in the firelight.

'Do you think we can do it, Captain?' I asked.

'I think it is not very likely, sir,' he said politely. 'But on the other hand I do not know what else we can do. Feeding women and pushing oil drums and caring for the sick – that is not a soldier's work. It will be good to have a chance to fight again.'

He rose, excused himself and vanished into the darkness, leaving me to stare into the firelight and wonder at the way different minds worked. What I was dreading he anticipated with some pleasure. I remembered wryly a saying from one of the world's lesser literary figures, Bugs Bunny: Humans are the craziest people.

26

By late afternoon the next day the lakeside was in a state of barely controlled turmoil. Tethered to the shore as close as possible without grounding lay the first 'B'-gon. It was held by makeshift anchors, large rocks on the end of some rusty chains. A gangplank of half-sectioned logs formed a causeway along which a truck could be driven on to the raft. Beyond it lay the second raft, just finished.

Nyalans clustered around full of pride and excitement at seeing their home-made contraptions being put to use. A few had volunteered to come with us but Sadiq had wisely vetoed this idea. I don't think he was any happier about us either but here he had no choice.

From the rig patients and nurses watched with interest. Our intention was to have the truck ready on board rather than manoeuvre it in the dark of the following morning.

'Why a truck at all?' Wingstead had asked. 'If you take Kanjali there'll be transport in plenty there for you. And there'll be no means to unload this one.'

'Think of it as a Trojan Horse, Geoff,' I'd said. 'For one thing it'll have some men in it and the others concealed behind it. If the rebels see us drifting towards them then all they'll see is a truck on a raft and a couple of men waving and looking helpless. For another, it'll take quite a bit of equipment, weapons and so on. They'll be safer covered up. It's not a truck for the time being, it's a ship's bridge.'

Hammond approved. He was the nearest thing to a naval man we had, having served in a merchant ship for a short time. I had appointed him skipper of the 'B'-gon. 'Inside the cab I've a much better view than from deck.'

There was a fourth reason, but even Hammond didn't know it.

The gangplank was ready. Kemp as load master beckoned the truck forward. The driver was Mick McGrath. It was going to be a ticklish operation to get the thing safely on board and he was the best we had, apart from Hammond himself. Zimmerman disappeared behind the truck as McGrath started to drive down the shore.

There was a sudden high grinding scream from the truck's engine and the vehicle lurched, bucked and came to a standstill. McGrath's face, looking puzzled and annoyed, appeared at the cab window. Voices shouted simultaneously.

'Christ, watch out! The rear wheel's adrift!'

McGrath jumped down and glared at the damage. One tyre was right off its axle and the truck was canted over into the dust, literally stranded.

'Fetch the jacks!' he called.

I said, 'No time – get another truck. Zimmerman, go drive one down here! You men get cracking and unload the gear.' I gave them no time to think and Kemp, always at his best in a transport crisis, was at my elbow. Considering that I'd anticipated the accident and he hadn't, he coped very well. Swiftly he cleared a path through the littered beach so that a second truck could get around the stranded one and still be able to mount the causeway. An engine roared as Zimmerman returned with the replacement.

Antoine Dufour sprang forward, his face suddenly white.

'No! Not that one – that's *my* truck!' he yelled.

His vehemence startled the men around him.

'Come on, Frenchie, any damn truck'll do,' someone said.

'Not that one!'

'Sorry, Dufour; it must have been the nearest to hand,' I said crisply. Dufour was furious but impotent to stop the truck as it passed us and lined up precisely at the causeway. Zimmerman leapt out of the cab for McGrath to take his place, but Dufour was on top of him.

286

'You not take my truck, by God!' He lapsed into a spate of French as he struggled to pass Zimmerman who held him back.

'Pack it in!' Kemp's voice rose. 'Dufour, ease off. This truck's part of the convoy now and we'll damn well use it if we have to.'

I said urgently, 'McGrath – get in there and drive it on fast.'

He looked at me antagonistically.

'There are other trucks, Mannix. Let the Frenchy alone.'

'Will you for God's sake obey an order!' I hadn't expected opposition from anyone but Dufour himself. McGrath's eyes locked with mine for a moment and then he pushed his way past Dufour and Zimmerman, swung himself aboard and gunned the motor. He slammed the truck into gear and jerked it onto the causeway. Then common sense made him calm down to inch the truck steadily onto the oddly-shaped 'B'-gon raft. The thing tipped under the weight but to our relief did not founder, and although water lapped about the truck's wheels it was apparent that we had a going proposition on our hands. The cheer that went up was muted. The onlookers were still puzzled by Dufour's outburst.

Kemp got men to put chocks under the truck's wheels and make lashings fast. The gear was loaded. Then the raft was hauled further out to lie well clear of the bank.

I turned my attention to Dufour.

He had subsided but was pale and shaken. As I passed Zimmerman I gave him a small nod of approval, then took Dufour's arm.

'Antoine,' I said, 'come with me. I want a word.'

As we walked away he stared over his shoulder at his truck where it rode on our ridiculous raft offshore and out of his reach.

We stopped out of earshot of the others.

'Antoine, I apologize. It was a dirty trick to play.'

'Monsieur Mannix, you do not know what you have done,' he said.

287

'Oh yes I do. You are thinking of your secret cargo, aren't you?'

His jaw dropped. 'You *know*?'

'Of course I know. Zimmerman found it and told me. It's his trade, don't forget. He could probably sniff out gelignite at a mile.'

Dufour stared at me appalled. I had to reassure him on one point at once.

'Now, listen. I don't care a damn why you have the stuff. Or where you got it. It's no bloody business of mine. But right now that stuff you've got is the best weapon in our whole arsenal, and to get ourselves and everyone else out of this mess we need it.'

'Oh, my God.' As he looked at me and I saw a bitter smile on his face. 'Gelignite. You want to use my truck to blow up the enemy, yes?'

'I hope not. But it's a damn good threat. Harry Zimmerman will pass the word around, and the assault team will know that we've got a bomb out there. It'll be like pointing a cannon. The rebels have no weapon that can reach us, and we've got one that can devastate them. That's why we have the second 'B'-gon along; if we need to we evacuate the first, aim it at the landing point and let her rip. Now do you understand?'

'Suppose I told you the gelignite was worthless.'

'Don't try. We need it.'

He sat down as if his knees had given way. After a couple of minutes he raised his face and said, 'Yes, I understand. You are a clever man, Monsieur Mannix. Also a bastard. I wish us all luck.'

Back at the camp I put my affairs in order. I wrote a personal letter to leave with the Doctor, and gave Sam Kironji an impressive-looking letter on British Electric notepaper, promising that my company would reimburse him for all expenses and recommending him for a bonus. This I implemented with a cash bonus of my own which impressed him even more.

Wingstead and I discussed the rig. If we took the ferry the

288

convoy would move to Kanjali so that the patients could be transferred. And there the rig would have to be abandoned.

'We have to be careful of Kemp, though,' Wingstead said. 'The rig means a lot more to him than to me. It's extraordinary; personally I think he's been bitten by the juggernaut bug as hard as any of the Nyalans.'

'I wonder what they'll do when it grinds to a halt and we abandon it,' I said idly.

'Go home again. It'll probably end up in their mythology.'

'And the rig itself?'

'Whoever gets into power will engage someone to drive it up to Bir Oassa, I suppose. It'll be an interesting exercise in international finance, sorting out the costs and legalities involved. But I'll tell you one thing, Neil, whoever takes it it won't be me. I've had it here. I'll sell it to the best offer.'

'And what then?'

'Go back home with Kemp and Hammond and build a better one. We've learned a hell of a lot out here.'

'Stick to hydroelectric schemes in Scotland, will you?'

He laughed. 'That's the way I feel now. As for later, who knows?'

For the second day running we embarked in the chill small hours to sail down the Katali River to Kanjali. I felt very apprehensive. Yesterday had been an unnerving experience for anyone untrained in guerrilla warfare. Today was terrifying.

The two 'B'-gons were barely visible. We used the runabout as a tender, poling it over the dark water to lie alongside the 'B'-gon on which stood the darker bulk of the truck. We scrambled aboard, passing our weapons up to be stowed in the truck.

Hammond and his work team had lashed the two 'B'-gons together, slotting hexagon shapes into one another, adding a couple of 'A'-gons here and there and assembling the thing like a child's toy.

The truck barely fitted on the after section, a foot of space

289

to spare around it. With its high rear section and flat forward deck it was a travesty of the ferry at Kanjali. Aft on a crossbeamed structure Hammond had mounted Sam Kironji's outboard motors; one was a seven horsepower job and one six, which meant they were close enough in motive power not to send us in a circle. He had a man on each throttle and would control their speed and direction from the cab of the truck.

We were all very quiet as we set off.

We'd made our farewells, temporary ones I hoped. Dr Kat said that Lang might not live to see Manzu. I wondered how many of us would.

I had one curious experience on the journey. I hadn't forgotten McGrath's belligerence on the beach, and twice since he'd jibbed at instructions in a way that I could only think of as petulant. He wasn't just important to the success of our mission, he was vital. I had to find out what was bothering him.

'McGrath, I want to talk to you.'

He turned away.

'Now!'

I moved crouching away from the others and felt some relief that he followed me. We made our way forward, where small waves broke coldly over our faces.

'Mick, what the hell is eating you?' I asked.

He looked sullen. 'Nothing. I don't know what you mean,' he said. He didn't look at me.

'If you've got a gripe for God's sake say so.'

'We're not in the army, Mannix. You're not my officer and I'm not your bloody sergeant.'

'Oh Jesus!' I said. 'A goddamn prima donna. What's your beef?'

'Stop bloody ordering me about. I'm fed up with it.'

I took a deep breath. This was crazy.

I said, 'Mick, you're the best driver we've got. You're also the nearest thing we've got to a soldier, and we're going to need your know-how more than anyone else's, even Sadiq.'

'Now don't think I'll jump when you say so, Mannix, just

290

for a bit of flattery,' he said. To my disbelief his tone was one of pique.

'OK, McGrath, no flattery. But what's really eating you?'

He shrugged. 'Nothing.'

'Then why go temperamental on me? You've never been afraid to speak your mind before.'

He made a fist with one hand and banged it into the other. 'Well, you and me were friendly, like. We think the same way. But ever since Makara and that bit of a fight at the bridge, you've hardly said a word to me.'

I regarded him with profound astonishment. This tough and amoral man was behaving like a schoolboy who'd been jilted in his first calf love.

'I've been goddamn busy lately.'

'There's more to it than that. I'd say you've taken a scunner to me. Know what that means, Yank?'

'I don't know what the hell you're talking about. If you don't take orders I can't trust you and I won't let this whole operation fall apart because of your injured feelings. When we arrive at Kanjali you stay back on the raft. Damned if I'll entrust Bing or anyone else to your moods!'

I rose abruptly to go back to the shelter of the truck. He called after me, 'Mannix! Wait!'

I crouched down again, a ludicrous position in which to quarrel, and waited.

'You're right. I'm sorry. I'll take your orders. You'll not leave me behind, will you?'

For a moment I was totally lost for words.

'All right,' I said at last, wearily. 'You come as planned. And you toe the line, McGrath. Now get back into shelter or we'll both freeze.'

Later I thought about that curious episode.

During his stint in the army and presumably in Ireland too he had never risen in rank; a man to take orders, not quite the loner he seemed. But the man whose orders he obeyed had to be one he respected, and this respect had nothing to do with

291

rank or social standing. He had no respect for Kemp and not much for Wingstead. But for me, perhaps because I'd had the nerve to tackle him directly about Sisley's murder, certainly because he'd sensed the common thread that sometimes linked our thoughts and actions, it seemed that he had developed that particular kind of respect.

But lately I had rejected him. I had in fact avoided him ever since we'd found the body of Ron Jones. And he was sensitive enough to feel that rejection. *By God, Mannix,* I thought. *You're a life-sized father figure to a psychopath!*

Once again as we neared Kanjali dawn was just breaking. The sky was pinkish and the air raw with the rise of the morning wind. Hammond instructed the engine handlers to throttle back so that we were moving barely faster than the run of the current. Before long the two bulky outlines, the ferry and the buildings on the bank, came steadily into view. Sadiq gave quiet orders and his men began handing down their rifles from the truck.

Hammond brought us close to the bank some way upstream from where he intended to stop, and the raft nuzzled into the fringing reeds which helped slow its progress. A dozen men flung themselves overboard and splashed ashore carrying mooring lines, running alongside the raft until Hammond decided to go no further. I thought of his fear of crocodiles and smiled wryly. The noise we were making was enough to scare off any living thing and I could only pray that it wouldn't carry down to the men sleeping at Kanjali.

We tied up securely and the weapons were handed ashore. Hammond set his team to separating the two parts of the raft into their original 'B'-gon shapes and transferring the two outboards to a crossbeam on the section without the truck. This was to be either our escape craft or our means of crossing to Manzu to seek help in handling the ferry.

Once on shore I had my first chance to tell Hammond privately about Dufour's truck. 'Harry saw six cases of the stuff, and checked one to be sure. If we have to we're going to

292

threaten to use it like a fire ship. Harry's got a firing mechanism worked out. He'll come back here, set it and cut the raft free.'

'It might float clear before it goes off, Neil,' Hammond said. His horror at this amateurish plan made me glad I hadn't told him about it sooner. 'Or run aground too soon. The firing mechanism might fail. Or blow itself to smithereens and never touch Kanjali at all!'

'You know that and I know that, but will they? We'll make the threat so strong that they won't dare disbelieve it.'

It was a pretty desperate plan but it was all we had. And it didn't help that at this point Antoine Dufour approached us and said, 'Please, Monsieur Mannix, do not put too much faith in my cargo, I beg of you.' He looked deeply troubled.

'What's the matter with it? If it's old and unstable we'll have to take our chances,' I said brusquely.

'Aah, no matter.' His shrug was eloquent of distress. I sensed that he wanted to say more but my recent brush with McGrath had made me impatient with other men's problems. I had enough on my plate.

Sadiq and his men moved out. The rest of us followed, nervous and tense. We moved quietly, well down in the cover of the trees and staying far back enough from Sadiq's squad to keep them in sight until the moment they rushed the buildings. We stopped where the vegetation was cut back to make way for the landing point. I had a second opportunity to look at the moored ferry where it was caught in the sun's first rays as though in a searchlight beam.

This time I recognized what had eluded me before.

This was no modern ferry. It was scarred and battered, repainted many times but losing a battle to constant rust, a valiant old warhorse now many years from its inception and many miles from its home waters. It was an LCM, Landing Craft Mechanized, a logistics craft created during the war years that led up to the Normandy landings in 1944. Developed from the broad-beamed, shallow-draughted barges of an earlier day, these ships had carried a couple of tanks, an assortment of

293

smaller vehicles or a large number of men into action on the sloping European beaches. Many of them were still in use all over the world. It was about fifty feet long.

What this one was doing here on an inland lake up an unnavigable river was anybody's guess.

I turned my attention to Kanjali, lying below us. There were five buildings grouped around the loading quay. A spur from the road to Fort Pirie dropped steeply to the yards. Running into the water was a concrete ramp, where the bow of the ferry would drop for traffic to go aboard. A couple of winches and sturdy bollards stood one to either side. Just beyond was a garage.

The largest building was probably the customs post, not much bigger than a moderate-sized barn. Beyond it there was a larger garage, a small shop and filling station, and a second barn-like building which was probably a warehouse.

Sadiq's men fanned out to cover the customs post front and rear, the store and warehouse. Our team followed more hesitantly as we decided where to go. Kemp, Pitman and I ran to our post, the landing stage, and into cover behind the garage. Thorpe was at my heels but I told him to go with McGrath and he veered away.

We waited tensely for any sounds. Kemp was already casting a careful professional eye on the roadway to the landing stage and the concrete wharf beside it on the shore. It was old and cracked, with unused bollards along it, and must have been used to ship and unship goods from smaller craft in the days before the crossing had a ferry. But it made a good long piece of hard ground standing well off the road, and Kemp was measuring it as another staging post for the rig. The steep spur road might be a problem.

We heard nothing.

'Shall I go and look?' Pitman asked after several interminable minutes. I shook my head.

'Not yet, Bob.'

As I spoke a voice shouted and another answered it. There

were running footsteps and a sudden burst of rifle fire. I flattened myself to peer round the corner of the garage. As I did so an unmistakably male European voice called from inside it, 'Hey! What's happening out there?'

We stared at one another. Near us was a boarded-up window. I reached up and pounded on it.

'Who's in there?'

'For God's sake, let us out!'

I heaved a brick at the window, shattering glass but not breaching the boards that covered it. The doors would be easier. We ran round to the front to see a new padlock across the ancient bolt. Then the yard suddenly swarmed with figures running in every direction. There were more rifle shots.

I struggled vainly with the padlock.

Kemp said, 'They're on the run, by God!'

He was right. A few soldiers stood with their arms raised. Some slumped on the ground. Others were streaking for the road. Someone started the Volvo but it slewed violently and crashed into the side of the warehouse. Sadiq's men surrounded it as the driver, a Nyalan in civilian clothing, staggered out and fell to the ground. The door to the main building was open and two of our soldiers covered as men ran across the clearing and vanished inside, Bishop, Bing, McGrath and I thought Kirilenko, en route I hoped for the radio.

Sadiq's men were hotfoot after stragglers.

Neither Kemp, Pitman nor I were directly involved and within five minutes from the first shout it was all over. It was unnerving; the one thing my imagination had never dared to consider was a perfect takeover.

Hammond came away from one of the trucks grinning broadly and waving a distributor cap. Sadiq was everywhere, counting men, posting sentries, doing a textbook mopping up operation. We went to join the others, leaving whoever was in the locked garage to wait.

'Christ, that was fantastic. Well done, Captain! How many were there?'

295

Hammond said, 'We reckon not more than fourteen, less than we expected.'

'Any casualties?'

McGrath was beside me, grinning with scorn. 'Not to us and hardly to them. A few sore heads, mostly. Those laddies were half asleep and didn't know what hit them. A few ran off, but I don't think they'll be telling tales. They thought we were demons, I reckon.'

I looked around. Several faces were missing.

'Bing?' I asked.

'He's fine, already playing with that dinky radio set of theirs. Brad and Ritchie are with him,' McGrath said.

'The Volvo's had it,' said Hammond, 'but the other vehicles are fine. We can use them any time we want to. They didn't even have a sentry posted.'

It wasn't too surprising. They had no reason to expect trouble, no officer to keep them up to the mark, and probably little military training in the first place. I said, 'We've found something interesting. There's someone locked in the garage by the landing. There's a padlock but we can shoot it off.'

We gathered round the garage door and I yelled, 'Can you hear us in there?'

A muffled voice shouted back, 'Sure can. Get us out of here!'

'We're going to shoot the lock off. Stand clear.'

One of Sadiq's men put his gun to the padlock and blew it and a chunk of the door apart. The doors sagged open.

I suppose we looked as haggard and dirty to the two men who emerged as they looked to us. Both were white, one very large and somewhat overweight, the other lean and sallow-skinned. Their clothing was torn and filthy, and both were wounded. The big man had a dirtily bandaged left arm, the other a ragged and untreated scabby gash down the side of his face. The lean man took a couple of steps, wavered and slid gently to his knees.

We jumped to support him.

'Get him into the shade,' Kemp said. 'Fetch some water. You OK?'

The big man nodded and walked unaided. I thought that if he fell it would take four of us to carry him.

I left Kemp to supervise for a moment, and took Sadiq aside.

'Are you really in full command here?' I asked. 'What about the men who ran off?'

'They will probably run away and not report to anyone. But if they do I hope it will be a long time before others get here.'

'Do you think it's safe to bring the convoy here? If we can work the ferry we won't have any time to waste.' Already hope was burgeoning inside me. Sadiq thought in his usual careful way before replying.

'I think it is worth the chance.'

I called to Kemp. 'Basil, take your team and get back to Kironji's place. Start shifting the convoy. Leave the fuel tanker and the chuck wagon. Bring the rig and tractors, and cram the rest into a truck or two, no more.'

The two newcomers were being given some rough and ready first aid. Bishop had found the food stores and was preparing a meal for us, which was welcome news indeed.

I went back to squat down beside the recent prisoners.

'I'm Neil Mannix of British Electric, and this mob works for Wyvern Transport. We're taking stuff to the oilfields . . . or were when the war started. The soldiers with us are loyal to Ousemane's government. We're all in a bit of a fix, it seems.'

The big man gave me a smile as large as his face.

'A fix it certainly is. Bloody idiots! After all I've done for them too. You're American, aren't you? I'm pleased to meet you – all of you. You've done us a good turn, pitching up like this. My name's Pete Bailey, and it's a far cry from Southampton where I got my start in life.' He extended a vast hand to engulf mine. Good humour radiated from him.

His hand bore down on the shoulder of his companion. 'And this here is my pal Luigi Sperrini. He talks good English but he doesn't think so. Say hello, Luigi, there's a good lad.'

Sperrini was in pain and had little of his friend's apparently boundless stamina but he nodded courteously.

'I am Sperrini. I am grateful you come,' he said and then shut his eyes. He looked exhausted.

'Tell the lads to hurry with that food,' I said to Bishop, and then to Bailey, 'How long were you two guys locked in there?'

'Four days we made it. Could have been a little out, mark you, not being able to tell night from day. Ran out of water too. Silly idiots, they look after their bloody cattle better than that.' But there didn't seem to be much real animosity in him, in spite of the fact that he and his companion seemed to be a fair way to being callously starved to death.

I braced myself for the question I most wanted to ask.

'Who are you guys anyway? What do you do?'

And I got the answer I craved.

'What do you think, old son? We run the bloody ferry.'

27

'Will she run?'

Bailey came close to being indignant at the question.

'Of course she'll run,' he said. 'Luigi and I don't spend a dozen hours a day working on her just for her looks. *Katie Lou* is as sweet a little goer as the girl I named her for, and a damn sight longer lasting.'

The time we spent between taking Kanjali and waiting for the convoy to arrive was well spent. We found a decent store of food and set about preparing for the incoming convoy. We found and filled water canteens, tore sheets into bandaging, and checked on weapons and other stores. We seemed to have stumbled on a treasure house.

The radio was a dead loss; even with parts cannibalized from the other Bing couldn't make it function, which left us more frustrated for news than ever. Bailey and Sperrini could tell us little; we were more up to date than they were. We were fascinated to learn, however, that the juggernaut had already been heard of.

'The hospital that goes walkabout,' said Bailey. 'It's true then. We thought it just another yarn. They said it had hundreds of sick people miraculously cured, magic doctors and the like. I don't suppose it was quite like that.'

'Not quite,' I said dryly, and enlightened them. Bailey was glad that there were real doctors on the way, not for himself but for Sperrini, whose face looked puffy and inflamed, the wound obviously infected.

'One of their laddies did that with his revolver,' Bailey said. 'First they shot me in the arm, silly buggers. If they'd been a little more polite we might have been quite cooperative. As if

I could run away with *Katie Lou* – I ask you! She can't exactly go anywhere now, can she?'

'Except to Manzu,' I said, and told him what we wanted. 'I'm surprised you didn't think of it yourselves.'

'Of course we could have taken her across,' he said tolerantly, 'but I didn't know we were supposed to be running away from anything until it was too late. The war didn't seem to be bothering us much. One minute we're unloading a shipment and the next the place is swarming with laddies playing soldiers. The head man demanded that we surrender the ferry. Surrender! I didn't know what he was talking about. Thought he'd got his English muddled; they do that often enough. Next thing they're damn well shooting me and beating up poor old Luigi here. Then they locked us both in.'

His breezy style belied the nastiness of what had happened.

'We tried to break out, of course. But I built that garage myself, you see, and made it good and burglar-proof, more fool me. They didn't touch *Auntie Bess* but the keys weren't there and I couldn't shift her. Tried to crosswire her but it wouldn't work. Must say I felt a bit of an idiot about that.'

'Who, or more likely what, is *Auntie Bess*?' I asked. We hadn't been to look in his erstwhile prison yet.

'I'll show you but I'll have to find her keys. And to be honest I'd really rather get *Katie Lou* back into service first.'

Getting the ferry into service proved quite simple. There was a small runabout which Bailey used to get out to it, and in lieu of his trusty Sperrini he accepted the aid of Dufour, Zimmerman and Kirilenko. 'Parkinson's Law, you see,' he said with easy amusement. 'Three of you for one of him. She only needs a crew of two really, but it's nice to have a bit of extra muscle.'

He took his crew out to *Katie Lou* and with assured competence got her anchors up, judged her position nicely and ran her gently up onto the loading ramp, dropping the bay door on the concrete with a hollow clang. He directed the tying up procedure and spent some time inspecting her for any damage. He found none.

Sperrini waited with resignation.

'He very good sailor,' he said. 'He never make mistake I ever see. For me, first rate partnership.'

Bailey was like Wingstead, engendering respect and liking without effort. I never had the knack; I could drive men and direct them, but not inspire them, except maybe McGrath, which didn't please me. I'd never noticed it before. The difficult journey we'd shared had opened my eyes to some human attributes which hadn't figured very strongly in my philosophy before now. On the whole I found it an uncomfortable experience.

I complimented Bailey on *Katie Lou's* performance and he beamed.

'She's a bit rusty but by God she can do the job,' he said. 'I knew we were on to a good thing from the start.'

'How the hell did she come to be here anyway?' I asked.

'Luigi and I used to run the old ferry. We've been in this trade for donkey's years, the two of us. The old ferry was a cow to handle and very limiting; only deck cargo and passengers and not too many of them. I saw that cars and trucks would want to cross as trade improved and the oilfields opened up. Manzu hasn't got any oil itself but it's got a damn sight better port for off-loading heavy gear.'

I made a mental note to remember this for later, assuming there would be a later.

'The two countries negotiated a traffic agreement. At a price, of course. We started to look for something better, and I'd always had these old bow loaders in mind. Saw them in action on D-Day and never forgot them. Remember, I've been in this trade all my life. Started in Southampton docks as a nipper.'

'Me too, I sail with my father from a boy,' Sperrini put in.

'Don't ask us how we got her down to Nyala, laddie. It's a long tale and I'll tell it one day over a cold beer. But the long and short of it is that I got wind of this old LCM lying beached up on the North African coast and bought her for a song. Well, a whole damn opera really. Then we sailed her down the coast to Manzu and arranged to bring her overland to Lake Pirie.'

I whistled. With the first-hand knowledge of large rig transport that I'd gained lately I knew this to be possible, but a hell of a job all the same. I said as much and he swelled with pride.

'A lovely operation, I tell you. Not a scratch on her – well, not too many. And has she ever paid off! Luigi and me, we're doing just fine.' He became pensive. 'Or we were. But when things get back to normal we might go looking for something bigger.'

Sandy Bing was prowling back and forth from the ferry yards up to the main road. His failure to get the radio going had niggled him and he was restless and anxious. Suddenly he ran towards us, interrupting Bailey's story with news of his own. The convoy was on the way.

I said to Bailey, 'We'll start to load invalids onto the ferry at once, plus any other Nyalans who want to go. I'd like one vehicle on board. The Land Rover, say.'

'No problem there.'

'How long will it take to unload and return? On the second run we'll want a couple of trucks. The more transport we have the better. Would there be time for a third trip?'

He said, 'I usually cross twice a day but that's not pushing it. With luck I can be back in two hours. I doubt if there'll be anybody to help at the other side, it'll take time to get your sick folk unloaded. But we'll be back as soon as we can make it.'

Sperrini pushed himself up.

'Me, I come too,' he announced firmly. 'I maybe not work so good, but I watch out for you.'

Bailey said, 'Of course you'll come, mate. Couldn't do it without you. We'll need some of your lads, Neil.'

'You'll have them.'

He said, 'If there's trouble before I get back, what will you do?'

'We've got the transport we came here with. And by God, Pete, that's something you'd have to see to believe!' But I had

302

my doubts about the 'B'-gon. It was moored too far away to be of use in a crisis. Bailey gave me one of his great smiles.

'Well, I've got the very thing if you need it. In fact I'd appreciate it if you'd bring it across anyway. You can use *Auntie Bess.*'

'Just what is *Auntie Bess*?'

'A duck,' he said, and laughed at my expression.

'A *duck*?' I had a sudden vision of Lohengrin's swan boat. 'We're going to float across the lake on a giant mutant muscovy, is that it?'

'Come and see,' he said. 'You'll love this.'

Zimmerman, Kirilenko and I followed him to the garage. We pulled the double doors wide and stared into the gloom. A long low shape sat there, puzzling for a moment and then marvellously, excitingly explicit.

'A DUKW!'

Bailey patted its hood lovingly.

'Meet *Auntie Bess*. Named for the most adaptable lady I've ever known. Nothing ever stopped her. I've found the keys and she's ready to go.'

We gathered round the thing, fascinated and intrigued. It was a low-profiled, topless vehicle some thirty feet in length, one set of tyres in front and two more pairs not quite at the rear, where dropping curved metal plates protected a propeller. It had a protruding, faintly boat-shaped front and was hung about with tyres lashed around what in a boat would be called the gunwale. The body was made of tough, reinforced metal, flanged down the sides, and the headlamps were set behind heavy mesh grilles. An old-fashioned windscreen provided all the cover the driver would get on land or water, though there were points along the sides where a framework could be inserted to carry a canvas awning.

Odds and ends of equipment for both elements on which it could travel were strapped about it; an anchor and line, a life belt, a couple of fuel cans, a tyre jack, shovel and spare tyres. Like the *Katie Lou* it was rusty but seemed in good repair.

Bailey swung himself in and the engine came to life with a healthy rattle as it slid into the sunlight. He slapped its side with heavy-handed self-approval.

'I did think of calling her *Molly Brown*,' he said, 'but after all she might sink one of these days. She's got a tendency to ship a little water. But she's crossed this pond often enough and she'll do it once more for you, I promise.'

It could carry so many men that to bring off a dozen or so would be no problem. 'How hard is she to drive?' I asked.

Zimmerman said, 'I handled one on land once. Nothing to it. Don't know about the performance on water, though.'

Bailey said, 'Come on, let's go for a swim. I'll show you.'

Zimmerman swung himself on board and in front of an admiring audience the DUKW pounded down the causeway into the water. Pete Bailey was careful with *Katie Lou* but with his DUKW he was a bit of a cowboy. It chugged away throwing up an erratic bow wave to make a big circle on the lake.

The rig was arriving as we walked up the curving spur road from the ferry yard. Kemp and Hammond brought it to a stop on the main road that overlooked Kanjali. We got busy transferring the invalids into trucks to take them on board the ferry. Bailey and Sperrini came to see the rig and get medical attention.

The rig was as impressive as ever, its massive cargo still hulking down between the two trailers. The tractors coupled up fore and aft added power to its bulk. The modifications we had imposed made it look quite outlandish. By now the thatching had been blown away and renovated so often that it appeared piebald as the palm fronds weathered. A workmanlike canvas wall framed the operating theatre but the canvas itself was mildewed so that it looked like the camouflaging used during war to disguise gun emplacements. Sturdy rope ladders hung from every level and the faces of the patients peered out from their straw beds.

'Well, I'll be damned,' Bailey marvelled. 'Worth going a mile to see, that is – good as a circus any day. Hello, who's this?'

'This' was the Nyalan escort still following their fetish, overflowing the road and looked down at the ferry yard with curiosity. Sperrini put into words what we had been feeling about this strange parade for so long.

'It is a *processione sacra*,' he said solemnly. 'As is done to honour a saint.'

I told Kemp and Hammond about *Auntie Bess*. Hammond was delighted and regretted that he would probably have no time to play with the DUKW himself.

'We may have to use it as a getaway craft,' I said.

'What about the raft and Dufour's truck?'

'We might need it yet, if there's trouble,' I said. 'Ben, you and Harry and Kirilenko could slope off and bring the raft downriver closer to Kanjali. Still out of sight but where we can fetch it up bloody fast if we have to. This is strictly a volunteer assignment, though – what do you think?'

Hammond said, 'I'll do it. It would be a shame not to have a weapon like that handy should we need it.'

Zimmerman spoke rapidly to Kirilenko, then said, 'We're both on.'

'Off you go then. I'll cover for you. Try and make it quick.'

'Very funny, Neil,' Zimmerman said. I grinned and left them.

Unloading had begun. Wingstead and the rest had heard of the taking of Kanjali from Kemp; but none were ready for the sight of the ferry resting majestically on the causeway, the ramp down to form a welcome mat. Bishop and Bing were on board handing out food and water. The invalids were laid on straw mattresses.

Dr Kat was strict about rations. 'They can feed for a month on the other side,' he said. 'But too much too soon is dangerous. Nurse, tell them that the crossing will be less bumpy than the rig and not dangerous; some of them have never been on water before. And say there will be proper food and beds for them in Manzu. Sister Mary! What are you doing carrying that child! Put her down at once. Helen, take over there, please.' His eyes were everywhere, considering a hundred details. The excitement in the air and the prospect of salvation so close made him more cheerful than I'd ever seen him.

'How do you feel, leaving Nyala?' I asked during a lull. He regarded me with astonishment.

'How do you think I feel? Only relief, Mister Mannix. At last I see a hope of saving these poor people. I am tired, sad at our losses, infuriated by this senseless wasteful war and what is happening to my country. But I will come back soon enough. I intend to rebuild the hospital at Kodowa.'

He was a man dedicated and inspired. I said, 'You'll get all the help I can muster, and that's not peanuts.'

He hesitated, then said, 'Mister Lang is not going to live, I fear.'

'But we're so close to safety.'

He shook his head.

Impulsively I took his hand. 'We're all deeply in your debt, Doctor Katabisirua. I hope that will be recognized officially one day.'

He seemed pleased by my words as he went off to supervise the rest of the changeover with vigour.

Sister Ursula upbraided me for allowing Bing to go into battle, and for letting Bert Proctor so neglect his bullet-grazed leg as to risk a major infection. There was no pleasing that woman. She was efficient over Sperrini's face but couldn't get near enough to Bailey to administer to his arm. He was jovial but dismissive and I wondered why she let him get away with it.

By now all the invalids and the Land Rover were on board. The last of the Nyalans who wanted to cross were hurrying on, full of excitement. Those who were familiar with the ferry were explaining it to others.

Hammond, Thorpe and Kemp remained, as well as McGrath, Zimmerman, Kirilenko and Dufour. Bishop and Bing went with the first shipment. So did Pitman and Athebridge and Proctor, to act as crew and help unload at the far end. Only two need have stayed, to drive on the trucks, but there was some reluctance to leave the rig until necessary.

The bow ramp of the *Katie Lou* lifted, and we watched as she backed off the causeway, her temporary crewmen warping her out to her stern anchor, aided by a gentle reverse thrust of engines. As the anchor came up the current swung her round and the engines carried on the momentum. She pirouetted lazily to face away from us. Bailey waved from the bridge and the *Katie Lou* moved steadily into midstream, bearing its cargo of refugees away from us and the danger zone to freedom, we hoped, on the other side.

A burden lifted from us. Whatever happened to us now we were responsible for nobody but ourselves. We gave vent to our feelings with cheers of relief.

And then the air exploded. There was a whistling roar and a missile plummeted into the water well astern of the *Katie Lou*. A fountain of water jetted high into the air, followed by a second which was no closer. A dull thump followed as another missile slammed into the earth just behind the causeway, flinging debris and dust into the air. There was the staccato rattle of machine-gun fire from behind us, and a scream from the roadway.

'Oh Christ, the ferry!' Thorpe gasped.

'She's clear – she's out of range,' I said sharply.

Soldiers boiled out from behind the rig and ran down the spur road. Others erupted from the bush beyond the buildings much as we ourselves had done earlier. Sadiq's men were fighting against huge odds.

Zimmerman said, 'The raft. It's our only chance.'

He and Kirilenko hurtled down the causeway. They plunged into the water and vanished under the churned-up wake from the ferry. Hammond dropped into the fringing bushes along the lakeside. McGrath, using the dust cloud from the third explosion to mask his disappearance, slipped behind the garage in which *Auntie Bess* was parked. Dufour, Kemp, Ritchie Thorpe and I stood our ground. The rebels came running towards us and it took a lot of discipline to stand and face them. In a moment we were surrounded.

307

28

They were everywhere, poking into the warehouses and garages, examining the rig and the other vehicles of the convoy, beating the bushes for fugitives. On one side of the yard those of Sadiq's men whom they'd rounded up stood under guard. There were more guards around the four of us. We'd seated ourselves on crates to appear as innocuous as possible. I was grateful that they didn't bring *Auntie Bess* out of her garage, though there was some interest shown by those who went in to look at it. I guessed that Zimmerman had the keys.

It was satisfying that the ferry had got clean away. Whatever weapons they had didn't reach far over the water, and by now the *Katie Lou* was out of sight and very likely already at her destination. I hoped Bailey would not bring her back; we had discussed this eventuality and he had reluctantly agreed that if he got wind of trouble he was to stay away.

I felt angry with myself. If I hadn't insisted on a second cargo of trucks going across we'd all be safe by now.

There was no sign of the raft team, nor of McGrath. His disappearance was entirely typical, and I could only wish him luck in whatever he might be planning. That he had deserted us I felt was unlikely, as long as we had the DUKW as a means of escape.

After a nerve-racking wait we had more company. The inevitable staff car came down the spur road with two others trailing it, a motorcycle escort and a truckload of soldiers with a 76 mm gun mounted. We stood up slowly as the leading car stopped short of the causeway.

The man who got out of it was a tall, well-turned out officer with the colonel's insignia that I had come to recognize. Like

308

Sadiq, he had an Arabic cast of feature but in his case it reminded me of the nomadic Tuareg I had seen in North Africa, fine-boned, carrying no spare flesh and insufferably haughty of expression. He wore a side arm and carried a swagger stick in gloved hands. He recalled irresistibly to mind my first senior officer in my army days; I'd hated that bastard too.

'Who are you?' he barked.

I glanced at Kemp and then took the role of spokesman. 'I'm Neil Mannix of British Electric,' I said. I was relieved that he seemed not to have heard of us by name, even if the bush telegraph had passed the word about the rig.

'The others?' he snapped impatiently.

'This is Mister Basil Kemp and this is Mister Thorpe, both of Wyvern Transport. And this is Monsieur Antoine Dufour, a friend. Who are you?'

'What?'

'Now you tell us who *you* are.'

He glowered at me but I was through with servility. I was going to stand by our rights as civilians, foreigners and employees of his country.

He nodded thoughtfully. 'You are angry. Well, Mister . . . Mannix, in your place so perhaps would I be. But I have no quarrel with you personally. You have been ill-advised and manipulated by the corrupt forces of the recent government and its military tyranny, but being ignorant of the destiny of Nyala and of your moral responsibilities towards it, your folly will have to be overlooked. I will redirect you in a more useful and productive fashion. It will be in your best interests to cooperate with good will.'

I suppose I looked as thunderstruck as I felt, and I could see from the faces of the others that they shared my amazement. This was less like Colonel Maksa's approach than anything we could have imagined.

I said, 'That all sounds most interesting, Colonel. What does it mean?'

'For you, very little. We wish you to undertake some work

for us which is not beyond your scope or ability. Though I am afraid something more drastic may be called for in this case.' He indicated one of the cars behind his own. I saw with dismay that it was Sadiq's staff car, and that Sadiq was sitting in it. He was in the back seat between two guards, and he was handcuffed.

'You can't treat a prisoner of war like that. What the hell do you think you're doing?' I asked harshly. Sadiq was a good soldier and had stood by us; we had to stand up for him now.

The officer ignored this and said, 'I am Colonel Wadzi, of the army of the Peoples' Liberated Republic of Nyala. I have certain instructions for you. Are these all of your men?'

'Let Captain Sadiq go and then we'll talk about us.'

He spoke briefly, and the car in which Sadiq was being held pulled out of line and drove up the spur road and stopped at the top.

'Captain Sadiq is not the issue here. He will be tried for his offences,' Wadzi said. 'Now – which of you is in charge of this transporter?'

Kemp stepped forward, his face white.

'Don't you do anything to damage that rig,' he said with the courage of his deepest belief.

Wadzi smiled tautly. 'I would not dream of harming it. My superiors are well aware of its value, I promise you. In fact we wish to offer you an equitable financial return for bringing it safely back to the capital, Mister Kemp, in order to renegotiate with your company for its hire in the immediate future. We intend to carry on with the project at Bir Oassa, and naturally you and your company's expertise are vital.'

As he said all this Kemp's face changed. Incredibly enough he believed all this cant. The rig was to be miraculously saved, driven in triumph to Port Luard, refitted and taken once again upcountry to the oilfields, all in perfect safety and with the blessing of financial security, under the benevolent protection of whoever claimed to be the rightful government of Nyala. And he, Basil Kemp, was the man chosen for the task. It was

310

a daydream coming true, and nothing would free him from his delusion.

Goddamn, Wingstead ought to have been here! He was the only man who could have made Kemp see reason. Me he would ignore; the others he would override; and my disadvantage was that it was only a shadow of suspicion that made me distrust all this fine talk, these promises and inducements. What Wadzi said might be true. He too was only a pawn in a political game. But I believed that there wasn't a word of validity in anything he said. We'd seen too much, been too involved. We were doomed men.

Kemp was afire with anticipation.

'Yes, I'm in charge of the rig,' he said.

'Can you drive it back to Port Luard for us?'

Kemp looked round for Hammond and McGrath. I held my breath lest in his one-track minded folly he should betray them.

'Yes, of course we can. We'll have to get fuel. We need diesel and petrol, and water. I'd have to go ahead to check the road conditions. The starter engine needs servicing, perhaps a complete overhaul. I think we need –'

His brain went into overdrive as he reviewed the most important of the many priorities facing him. Thorpe opened his mouth but caught my eye and subsided. As long as Kemp was in full spate he wouldn't mention the vital fact of the missing drivers.

Wadzi interrupted. 'It can all be arranged. I am pleased that you are willing to help us. What about you, Mister Mannix? Not so well-disposed?' The silky menace was overt and I felt a pulse thud in my neck.

'I'm damned if I'm well-disposed. Do you know who was in that ferry, Wadzi?'

He said, 'I believe you liberated the ferryman and have been so misguided as to send a number of Nyalans, including medical people of the utmost value to the country, across to Manzu. We must take steps to extradite them; that will be a nuisance. I am not pleased about it.'

'Then you know it was a hospital ship. You damned

311

well fired on a boatload of invalids, women and kids. In my book that makes you a war criminal. You're not fit to walk the earth, Wadzi. You'd disgrace any damned uniform you put on.'

My companions stared at me in horror at this reckless baiting of our captor, but it seemed to be the only way to keep his attention. The 'B'-gon team had to have a chance to get here with our only weapon, though I wasn't clear what we could do with it. Wadzi was a vain man and rose readily to my lure to justify his cause. Under the same circumstances Colonel Maksa would simply have blown my head off.

'You forget yourself! You are in no position to make such accusations, Mannix, nor question my authority. You do yourself a grave injury in this obstruction and you will pay for it!'

'I've no doubt,' I said grimly.

'I would be within my rights if I were to exercise summary justice in your case, Mannix,' Wadzi said. I wondered sickly if he was so very different to Maksa after all.

Ritchie Thorpe protested bravely.

'You can't just shoot him, Colonel, for God's sake!'

Two soldiers stepped forward, their rifles raised to enforce the threat, and I thought numbly that I'd finally gone too far. But he held them back with a cut of his stick in the air, glowered at Thorpe and said to Kemp, 'This man Mannix – is he necessary to your transport arrangements? Mister Kemp! I am speaking to you.'

Kemp was miles away, planning the rig's forthcoming journey. He was recalled with a start at hearing his own name, and looked with puzzlement from Wadzi to me. I wasn't breathing too well.

'What's that? Oh, Neil? Yes, of course I need him,' he said abstractedly. 'Turned out to be very useful on this trip. Need everyone we've got,' he went on, gazing around the yard, 'Thorpe, where's Ben Hammond? I need him right now.'

In reprieving me he had raised another bogey.

'Hammond? Who is this?' Wadzi demanded, instantly on the alert.

312

'Mister Kemp sent him on an errand,' Thorpe said the first thing that came into his head.

And at the same moment a babble of voices rose and we all turned to look at the lake. Coming downriver towards the ferry slip, moving extremely slowly, half awash with water and canted over at an acute angle, were the recoupled 'B'-gons. On the front section Dufour's truck stood uneasily, its lashings removed but the chocks still in place under the wheels. Zimmerman and Kirilenko were each handling an outboard on the after section, with Hammond giving steering instructions.

The soldiers' voices died down. Wadzi stared silently.

Handled with great delicacy and precision the raft nuzzled its way onto the ferry slip and the two outboards pushed it inexorably forward until it could go no further. With a grating sound it grounded itself with the forward section half out of the lake, resting firmly on the causeway. Our floating bomb had arrived.

Kemp looked as astonished as the Colonel.

'Neil, what the devil is this?' he asked testily. 'You know we don't need the raft any more –'

'Ah, Hammond!' I shouted to the new arrivals, drowning Kemp's voice with my own. 'Well done! That's the last truck, is it? You'll see that we have company. This is Colonel Wadzi, who's going to take the rig back to Port Luard with our help. He's asked Mister Kemp to take charge of the operation and Mister Kemp is very keen to do so.'

I was trying to give Hammond as much information as possible while at the same time preventing Kemp from saying anything to further rouse Wadzi's suspicions. The Colonel stepped forward and rapped me sharply on the arm. 'Just what is all this about?' he demanded.

'Stores for the convoy, or some of them,' I said rapidly. 'The last of our transport vehicles. We've been waiting for it to arrive.'

'Arrive? Like that?'

313

'Well, yes, we bought some of them down by water . . .'

Hammond had come ashore and was tying up the raft calmly as if the presence of armed soldiers were commonplace. Now he chipped in and said easily, 'To save fuel, Colonel. Two seven horsepower outboard engines use a lot less than one truck over long distances, so we've ferried them down this way. I suppose you'll want it added to the rest of the convoy, Mister Mannix?'

The implication appalled me. He was prepared to drive the gelignite-filled truck up among the troops and, presumably, explode it where it would cause maximum alarm and destruction. Whether it would save our lives was doubtful, but it would certainly end his.

And he was waiting for me to give him the go-ahead.

'Not just for the moment, Ben,' I said. 'Have a word with Mister Kemp first about moving the rig. He . . . needs your advice.'

Hammond looked at Kemp and at once took in his tense, barely controlled anxiety. He gave a reassuring nod.

'We'll want to plot the mileage charts afresh, Mister Kemp, won't we?' he asked calmly.

Kemp said curtly, 'I've been looking for you. Where are the maps?'

They started talking, ignoring the armed men around them. I hoped that Hammond could keep Kemp occupied. He was in a state of dangerous hypertension, and if not controlled he could be as great a threat as the enemy.

Zimmerman and Kirilenko came ashore cautiously, saying nothing. Zimmerman's hands at his side made a curious twisting gesture reminiscent of turning a key, and then he brushed his wristwatch casually. I realized what this implied: he had set a timing mechanism on the lethal truck.

'How long? Harry, how long did the trip take?' I asked loudly.

'Only fifteen minutes, Neil.'

Christ. A quarter of an hour to get us all out of range before Dufour's truck went sky-high; call it ten minutes because no hastily home-made timer could be all that accurate. Or it might

314

never go off at all. Frantically I juggled possibilities while at the same time continuing to face up to Wadzi.

He was disconcerted by my change in attitude. Before I had defied him; now I was cooperating. He said, 'Mister Mannix, are these all your men now?'

'Yes, that's it.' I mentally subtracted McGrath.

'You will all accompany us with your transporter to Fort Pirie. There we will make further arrangements,' he said briskly. 'I understand that you are not one of the drivers. Is that correct?'

I wondered just how much else he knew about us.

'That's right, Colonel. But of course I can drive a truck.'

I glanced round for inspiration. The ferry yard was full of troops and transport. Soldiers surrounded the rig up on the main road and Wadzi had placed guards on our other vehicles. Sadiq still sat in the rear of his own car at the top of the spur road. *Auntie Bess* crouched hidden in the garage. Of the ferry there was no sign.

Hammond had led Kemp to the far side of the causeway, well clear of the grounded raft, produced a map from his pocket and spread it on the ground so Kemp would have to squat down to study it. It kept his eyes off us, though it meant we would have to manage without Hammond.

Zimmerman stood near the raft-borne truck, hands in his pockets. Kirilenko was behind him, impassive as always. Next to me Thorpe stood rigid and beyond him Dufour, stiff and haggard; his eyes flickered from me to his truck and back, signalling some incomprehensible message.

This is easy, I told myself. You get into the truck, drive it among the soldiers, stall it and fiddle about until the whole damn thing goes sky-high. In the mêlée, during which with any luck quite a few of the enemy get killed including their gallant leader, your men make a dash for the DUKW and drive it off into the sunset. Nothing to it. The only small problem was that our own gallant leader was most certainly not going to survive the experience either, and I was rooted by something I franti-

315

cally hoped wasn't cowardice. Surely it was only sensible to await the play of the card we still had up our sleeve?

Surely McGrath would come up trumps once again?

He had ten minutes at the outside to do so. I swallowed, sucked in my gut and took two steps towards Dufour's truck.

'I'll take it up to join the others, shall I?' I asked Wadzi.

There was a stir among our men. Dufour's gasp was clearly heard and Wadzi reacted instantly. His revolver was out of its holster and held at arm's length pointing straight at me.

'Don't move!' Wadzi snapped.

I didn't.

'Where are the keys to that truck?' he demanded. Zimmerman clenched his fist instinctively and Wadzi saw the movement; his eyes were lynx-sharp. 'I'll have them,' he said, extending a hand with a snap of his fingers.

'Do it,' I said.

Zimmerman put the truck keys into the Colonel's hand and without taking his eyes off me Wadzi flipped them to one of his men. 'Bring that truck ashore,' he said. The words were in Nyalan but the meaning all too clear. The soldier ran down the causeway and swung himself into the cab. I closed my eyes; bad driving might be fatal.

Two soldiers removed the chocks and the truck inched its way onto the causeway, leaving the raft rocking, all but submerged and even closer to disintegration. It was certainly beyond use as an escape device. It was the DUKW or nothing now.

The truck drove slowly up the spur road. Wadzi rammed his revolver back into its holster.

'I advise you to be very careful, Mister Mannix,' he was saying. 'Do nothing without my permission . . . what is it?'

But none of us were listening to him. He whipped round to see what was holding our enthralled attention.

'Christ, it's Mick!' Thorpe shouted.

From behind one of the buildings a man came running, weaving through the troops. The sub-machine-gun in his hands spouted fire in all directions. McGrath closed rapidly in on the slowly travelling truck, hurtling past men too stunned to react.

There was a crack of gunfire. High up on the spur road Sadiq rose in the back seat of the open staff car, his manacled hands clutching a rifle. One of his guards toppled backwards out of the car. He fired again among the soldiers who were closing in on McGrath and they fell back in disarray. One man fell to the ground.

Zimmerman yelled, 'No, Mick – don't take it!' He straight-armed a soldier and at the same moment Kirilenko whirled on another and floored him with a massive kick to the groin. In horror I stared at Dufour's truck. McGrath stumbled just as he reached it and lost his grip on the sub-machine-gun.

'He's hit!'

McGrath heaved himself up and into the cab and hurled the driver out with a violent effort. The truck picked up speed and raced up the spur road towards the rig.

Beside me Wadzi opened his mouth to shout an order.

I threw myself at him and we went down in a tangle of arms and legs. I clawed for the revolver at his belt as Thorpe threw himself down to pin Wadzi's legs. As I scrambled to my feet with the gun I saw Sadiq arch out of the staff car, the rifle flying from his hands. He crashed in a sprawling mass onto the roadway. Kirilenko used his boot again on Colonel Wadzi's breastbone and the officer subsided, coughing and writhing. His men scattered.

I gasped, 'Harry, does Mick know?'

'Yes. I told him! Oh my God – it'll go any second!'

And then Dufour had hold of my arm, gripping it like a vice and shaking me violently. 'Mannix – I tried to tell you, I *tried*! It will not explode!'

'Of course it will. I've wired it!' Zimmerman snapped.

Dufour stammered, 'Only four bottles of gelignite . . . right in front . . .'

'What?'

317

As we spoke the truck rocketed up the slope, fired on from all sides. If the timing mechanism failed the bullets would do the job for us. But what in God's name was Dufour trying to say?

'Not . . . gelignite! Mother of God, Mannix, it's *gin!*'

A blinding light of understanding hit me. Spirits were illegal and therefore precious in Bir Oassa, a predominantly Arab community. The gelignite was a double bluff, to prevent officials from probing further into Dufour's illicit cargo. Few would tamper with such a load. He had been smuggling alcohol to the oilfields.

And now, instead of the shattering explosion that we'd hoped for there would be at most a small thump, a brief shock. The damage would be to the truck itself. McGrath's heroic, insane act would be all for nothing.

'Oh dear God.'

We stood frozen. Wadzi was hurt but alive and he'd be on his feet again any moment. We were still surrounded by armed men, and there was no path to freedom; nowhere to go. The revolver hung loosely in my hand and I felt sick and stunned. We had gambled and lost.

The truck veered off course, clawing its way across the dirt shoulder of the upper road. It was alongside the rig by now. Its erratic steering could only mean that McGrath was badly wounded or perhaps even already dead. It rocked and shuddered to a halt, dwarfed by the enormous structure of the rig. It half tilted off the shoulder and hung over the edge of the sheer drop to the ferry yard. My heart hammered as I saw a figure inside the cab – my last sight of Mick McGrath.

The truck exploded.

It was not, indeed, a very great event. The truck blew apart in a sheet of flame. The men and other vehicles nearby were sheltered from damage by the rig itself, an object too massive to be affected.

But under the truck was the roadway. Years old, carelessly maintained, potholed and crumbling; at this spot it clung to the hillside over a drought-dry, friable crust of earth knitted together with shallow-rooted vegetation. The road had no more stability than a child's sandpit.

The exploding truck tore this fragile structure like a cobweb.

A cracking fissure ran along the ancient tarmac just where the full weight of the rig already bore down too heavily for safety. There was a gigantic roar, a rolling billow of dust, and the entire hillside gave way under the terrible pressure of the rig.

With its load of the three hundred ton transformer and the coupled tractors the rig began to roll and tumble down the slope towards the ferry yard, dreadful in its power. With it came huge chunks of tarmac, earth, boulders and debris. It thundered downwards, gaining momentum, the air split with the tortured scream of metal and the roar of the landslide that came with it.

Men scattered like ants and fled in horror from the monstrous death racing down towards them. Engines screamed into life, rifles clattered to the ground as the soldiers dashed frantically for safety. The rig crashed with appalling, ponderous strength into the first of the outbuildings, crushing them to matchwood. The paving of the yard crumbled under the onslaught.

We stood in shock and terror as the animal we had led about so tamely turned into a raging brute trumpeting destruction. And then there was a scream wilder than any I'd yet heard.

'No! No! Stop it – don't let it happen – '

Kemp burst between us, his face contorted, his eyes bulging in horror, and ran straight towards the rig. We took a couple of steps after him and stopped, helpless to prevent the awful thing Kemp was about to do.

While all other men fled from the oncoming monster, Kemp held his hands out in front of him in a futile, terrible gesture and ran straight into its path. The juggernaut claimed many bloody sacrifices but one went willingly.

Losing momentum on the flat, the rig halted abruptly. From among crushed and unrecognizable fragments the bulk of the transformer rose twisted but identifiable. Billowing dust merci-

319

fully hid details of the trail of carnage. Remnants of one of the ferry buildings leaned drunkenly, ripped open and eviscerated.

My knees were as weak as grass stems and the skin of my face was drawn taut and painful. Hammond was sobbing in a hard, dry fashion that wrenched the breath from his body. Kirilenko was on his knees, gripping a rifle in both hands; the barrel was buckled under the strength he had exerted.

Zimmerman had his hands to his face and blood trickled down where some flying debris had cut him. Dufour and Thorpe stood in total silence; Dufour's arms were wrapped around Ritchie Thorpe's shoulders in a grip of iron. Everyone was white and shattered.

The noise of screams and moaning, voices crying for help, buckling metal and splintering wood were all around us, but we stood in a small oasis of silence. There were no soldiers anywhere near us except Colonel Wadzi himself, who was rocking slightly on his feet, his uniform ripped and dirty, his face haggard with shock.

I took a deep gasp of air.

'Let's get the hell out of here.'

Wadzi raised his face to mine, his eyes bewildered.

'My men . . .' he said uncertainly, and then more firmly, 'I have much to do. You people, you must go. We do not want you here.'

His voice was drained of every emotion. We were bad news. He had done with us for ever.

Hammond said, 'My God, that poor bloody man.'

I knew he meant Kemp, but it was McGrath I thought of.

Thorpe said softly, 'There's nothing to keep us here now.'

I nodded in complete understanding. Safe from the path of destruction the DUKW was unscathed in its waterside garage.

'*Auntie Bess* is waiting,' I said. 'Let's go and join the others.'